Almost  Like Being in Love

ALSO BY STEVE KLUGER

Fiction

Changing Pitches
Last Days of Summer

Nonfiction

Lawyers Say the Darndest Things
Yank

Stage Plays

After Dark
Bullpen
Cafe 50's
Pilots of the Purple Twilight

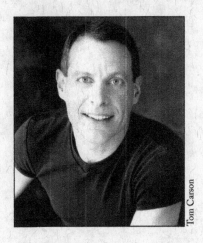

About the Author

STEVE KLUGER shook hands with Lucille Ball when he was twelve. He's since lived an additional thirty-nine years, but nothing much registered after that.

A baby boomer whose entire existence was shaped by the lyrics to *Abbey Road, Workingman's Dead,* and *Annie Get Your Gun,* Kluger has forged a somewhat singular path as a civil rights advocate, campaigning for a "Save Fenway Park" initiative (which qualifies as a civil right if you're a Red Sox fan), counseling gay teenagers, donating his free time to Lambda Legal Defense, and—on behalf of Japanese American internment redress—lobbying the Department of the Interior to restore the baseball diamond at the Manzanar National Historic Site. He plans to run for public office himself, provided he can be persuaded not to propose Carol Channing's birthday as a federal holiday.

Almost ♡
Like Being
in Love

A Novel

STEVE KLUGER

WILLIAM MORROW
An Imprint of HarperCollinsPublishers

HarperCollins books may be purchased for educational, business, or sales promotional use. For information, please e-mail the Special Markets Department at SPsales@harpercollins.com.

FIRST EDITION

Designed by Nancy Singer Olaguera

Library of Congress Cataloging-in-Publication Data

Kluger, Steve.
    Almost like being in love : a novel / by Steve Kluger.—1st ed.
    p. cm.
   ISBN 0-06-059583-3 (pbk. : alk. paper)
    1. Middle-aged men—Fiction. 2. First loves—Fiction. I. Title.

PS3561.L82A78 2004
813'.54—dc22

                                  2003065649

17 18 ❖/RRD 14 13 12 11 10 9

For my mother,

who taught me "Gypsy"—

and who's still waiting for me to marry a Jewish boy

What a day this has been,

What a rare mood I'm in . . .

1978

1978

1

Travis AND Craig

The Beckley Bugle

Vol. LXII, No. 34   BECKLEY SCHOOL • TARRYTOWN, NEW YORK   May 1, 1978

McKENNA EARNS VICTORY CUP

All-star quarterback and shortstop Craig McKenna has been awarded Beckley's Victory Cup as the year's most outstanding athlete, in the first unanimous vote since the Cup was instituted in 1943. Leading the Black-and-Grey to a 10–0 gridiron record in the fall, and with an unassailable eleven-game hitting streak in the spring, McKenna will be presented with the Cup at commencement exercises next month—a fitting farewell as he departs for Harvard and law school in September. Way to go, Craigo!

FIRST SENIOR PROJECTS TURNED IN

Three weeks ahead of the curve, Travis Puckett is the first to submit his completed Senior Project to Mr. Naylor and the English Department. Puckett—this year's Sheet Monitor in the dorm's laundry room—has titled his thesis, "Put the Blame on

Mame." In it, he examines the purported ties between Patrick Dennis' fictional aunt and the Marxist-Leninist dogma of the late 1940s. "Auntie Mame was a despot," he insists. "The House Un-American Activities Committee would have had her shot on sight." If you say so, Trav.

STAGEHANDS NEEDED FOR *BRIGADOON*

This year's spring play, produced by Beckley's boys and Mary Immaculate's girls, will be Lerner & Loewe's timeless and ever-popular classic, *Brigadoon.* Under the capable direction of art teacher Pauline Hawkins, the musical will run for three performances during the weekend before commencement. Though the leads have already been cast (sorry, guys), Mrs. Hawkins advises this reporter that "we still need a stage crew." Those willing to volunteer should do so immediately. All others will be drafted.

Craig McKenna   BECKLEY SCHOOL
Room 311   TARRYTOWN, NEW YORK

5/5/78

English Assignment
<u>**My Obituary**</u>
by Craig McKenna

(Note to Mr. Naylor: I'm pretending it's being written for the Village Voice, *so there may be some profane words in it. But not alot.)*

A legend has left us—buried beneath the epitaph he long ago chose for himself: CRAIG McKENNA, LAID AT 15. And who among us can forget the many things he was?

A world-famous Jets quarterback who threw a 98-yard pass during sudden death in Super Bowl XVI. Namath shit a brick.

A world-famous Red Sox slugger who single-handedly brought the World Series title back to Boston for the first time since 1918.

A world-famous rock and roller who packed the Garden with his bass guitar, his T-shirt off, his jeans way tight, and sweat pouring off the body that made them all horny. They called it McKennaMania.

A world-famous attorney who wasn't afraid to go after pain-in-the-ass defendants like U.S. Steel, the Mafia, and France.

And finally a world-famous gigolo who left a string of broken-hearted heiresses strewn across four continents.

He will be missed.

Yeah, right. The one time I accidentally said "hell" in front of Naylor, he threw up on *Othello*.

The way I've got it figured, there's three ways I can pull this off—and one's only a maybe.

1. Bite the bullet, see if it flies, and hope that Harvard's not allowed to take back an admissions certificate even if I flunk English at zero hour.
2. Sweet-talk Kerry Fusaro, Tom Lee, or Mike Scherago into making changes, but don't hold your breath. Everybody knows that jocks can't handle words with more than one syllable in them. Except me.
3. (This one's the maybe.) Ask Travis Puckett, the Hello Dolly guy. Even with the blue Van Heusen shirts he's smart, teachers like him, and he was the only one of us who volunteered for *Brigadoon* without getting threat-

ened first. Come to think of it, he also hasn't said Word One to me in four years, even when we pass each other in the hall. Maybe I called him something slimy in ninth grade back in the days when I was still an asshole. Or maybe he just doesn't like me. (How is that possible?)

Stick with Number 2. You're better off with a buddy who can't spell than an enemy who can.

Things to Do

___ Call St. Louis and tell Dad about the Victory Cup. Then ask him for a new car.

Travis Puckett   BECKLEY SCHOOL
Room 214   TARRYTOWN, NEW YORK

May 6, 1978

English Assignment
<u>My Obituary</u>
by Travis Puckett

WHO'S WHO IN AMERICA

TRAVIS PUCKETT *(Broadway Star)* first rose to national prominence in 1981 while attending a revival of *My Fair Lady* at the Mark Hellinger Theatre, where the legendary musical had premiered twenty-five years earlier and run for 2,717 performances. During the first act, Rex Harrison suffered a heart attack and was rushed to Roosevelt Hospital (where he survived), nearly causing the cancellation of the entire performance as the understudy had been killed earlier that morning in a fatal car accident. However, Puckett—who was seated in the third row and who'd had the entire show committed to memory since his sixth birthday—volunteered his services and was rushed into costume backstage. What resulted was a performance that brought a stunned audience to its feet and earned him a special Tony Award the following spring as the youngest Henry Higgins in the history of musical comedy.

Born in Baltimore in 1960, Puckett went on to star on Broadway with some of the Great White Way's most glamorous leading ladies: Julie Andrews, Eydie Gormé, Barbra Streisand, and Bernadette Peters (who bore him his only child).

At the time of his death, he owned the world's largest collection of original cast recordings, including Ethel Merman in *Happy Hunting*.

What I don't understand is how come I got seven thousand chromosomes that make me smart and not a single one that makes me cool. Who would it have hurt? Even at the entry level. It's not like I would have expected to be one of the gods.

Beginner Cool
Billy Joel—with the red jacket and the mike.

Intermediate Cool
Rosa Parks telling the bus driver to kiss her ass.

Top-of-the-Line Cool
Bobby Di Cicco as Tony Smerko in
I Wanna Hold Your Hand.
("Hey, Smerko!")

But no. I get stuck with the Lucille-Ball-in-*Wildcat* gene.
Craig McKenna spoke to me. Golden Boy. Mr. Jockstrap.

I'm not even sure how it happened. One minute there was this ladder and I was changing a gel on the MacConnachy Square set, and the next thing I knew I was falling backward through the air just in time for Craig to say "Whoa, there" before he caught me. Then he asked me to help him with his English essay. (Actually, there were twenty-three more words in between, but they were mostly adverbs.) I tried to pretend that I know how to talk to these goalpost people—but when I said yes, my voice squeaked. Again. I really hate when that happens. Puberty isn't supposed to last for two presidential terms. Especially when one of them is Carter's.

Oh, yeah. He called me "Travis" instead of "Puckett." Not that it makes me Bobby Di Cicco—but even Smerko had to start *some*where.

Craig McKenna   BECKLEY SCHOOL
Room 311   TARRYTOWN, NEW YORK

I was right. He knows *everything*. Like metaphors and nuclear reactors and Luke Skywalker's middle name and the ingredients of Cheerios. All in the same sentence!

So here's the deal: there's this town called Brigadoon in either Scotland or Ireland or one of those other bog places in England, where men wear skirts but don't have any balls and girls have balls but not any tits. Somehow they figured out a way to come to life only one day out of every hundred years, and the guys who wrote it weren't even on mescaline. That's the good news. On the down side, Mrs. Hawkins somehow talked Kerry Fusaro into playing the lead, which ought to give us a rough idea of what we're in for. When he sings the heather-on-the-hill song, he sounds like a pit bull got ahold of his nuts and won't let go. They're even teaching Tom Lee to dance. He must be trying to win a dare.

Things to Do

____ Ask Travis what a brigadoon is. But make it sound intelligent.

Travis Puckett   BECKLEY SCHOOL
Room 214   TARRYTOWN, NEW YORK

Brigadoon. Opened March 13, 1947, at the Ziegfeld Theatre, starring David Brooks and Marion Bell. Ran for 581 performances. Lerner & Loewe's first hit, even though it attacks organized religion, freedom of choice, and the rights of women.

I accidentally bumped into Craig in the Tuck Shop, and I only had to wait forty-three minutes to do it. Between us we had 71¢ and a button, so we split a chocolate chip cookie and sort of forgot about French class.

~~A legend has left us—buried beneath the epitaph he long ago chose for himself: CRAIG McKENNA, LAID AT 15. And who among us can forget the many things he was?~~

Pertinent facts: He's five months older than me (but right-handed), he doesn't have any brothers or sisters, his mother was an actress before she went to med school, and his father—a Harvard grad with pull—argued his first case all the way to the Supreme Court.

~~A world-famous Jets quarterback who threw a 98-yard pass during sudden death in Super Bowl XVI. Namath shit a brick.~~

When he was seven, his parents got divorced and somehow he thought it was his fault. So he tried out for Pony League even though he was too young and too short, figuring that if he could pull it off, his father would come back. It didn't work.

~~A world-famous Red Sox slugger who single-handedly brought the World Series title back to Boston for the first time since 1918.~~

His life changed forever three years ago when somebody named Carlton Fisk hit a home run.

~~A world-famous rock and roller who packed the Garden with his bass guitar, his T-shirt off, his jeans way tight, and sweat pouring off the body that made them all horny. They called it McKennaMania.~~

He taught himself to play acoustic guitar in ninth grade, but he still hasn't admitted it to anybody yet because of the "jocks don't sing" rule (which is somehow related to the "always scratch your balls" rule and the "drink until you vomit" rule, both of which he's managed to avoid so far).

~~A world-famous attorney who wasn't afraid to go after pain-in-the-ass defendants like U.S. Steel, the Mafia, and France.~~

He decided to become a lawyer instead of a rock star because he says he believes in justice. This is probably bullshit. He still wants his dad to be proud of him.

~~And finally a world-famous gigolo who left a string of broken-hearted heiresses strewn across four continents.~~

His first sexual experience was with a vacuum cleaner. But he wouldn't elaborate.

~~He will be missed.~~

This essay's going to take a lot of work. He left out all the good stuff.

Craig McKenna   BECKLEY SCHOOL
Room 311   TARRYTOWN, NEW YORK

Things He Said

When he found out I live in St. Louis he lit up like the Tappan
Zee Bridge during a fog alert and wanted to know if our house
is anywhere near 5135 Kensington Avenue, which has something to do with Judy Garland but I couldn't figure out what.

After his parents got divorced, he stayed with his father for
two years until his stepmother popped the only two screws that
weren't already loose by deciding he was going to stick open
safety pins in her pillows and throw acid in her face. So they
sent him here and told him not to come back.

When he was 15 he snuck backstage at the Tony Awards
by telling the doorman he was Carol Channing's son. He also
gets letters from people like Mary Martin and Bernadette
Peters and the mother on *The Brady Bunch* and Lotte Lenya
(who was the old bag in the James Bond movie with the knife
in her boot). This isn't bullshit. I saw them with my actual eyes.

The only thing missing from his life is an out-of-print
record of some musical called *Greenwillow* that has the guy
from *Psycho* in it. Norman Bates singing?? I think he's putting
me on, but I don't know him well enough to be sure. (Yet.)

He knows what "Hey, Smerko" means. And how old
Bobby Di Cicco is and what his favorite colors are.

Things He *Didn't* Say

When he gets nervous his voice squeaks. It isn't funny but it
makes me grin just the same.

He has three different laughs that I've almost got a lock on.
Number 1 and Number 2 were no-brainers, but I struck out on
Number 3. This is going to be a challenge.

You can tell when he's ready to pop his top because the tips of his ears get red and his forehead frowns, which I found out twice by accident when I bad-mouthed Eleanor Roosevelt and Wilma Flintstone (long story, but it has something to do with the Equal Rights Amendment and both of them getting stuck with sexist douchebags like FDR and Fred).

He picked USC for college not because of the Trojans but because L.A. is the farthest he can get from his parents.

The only reason he never said anything to me in the hallway is because he was afraid.

He needs to be talked out of wearing the blue Van Heusens.

There's nobody else like him in the whole world. And he thinks that's a handicap!

QUESTION: How come he wants to hang out with *me?*

Travis Puckett   BECKLEY SCHOOL
Room 214   TARRYTOWN, NEW YORK

Bulletin: He has a dimple in his chin that you can only see when he (a) smiles, and (b) smiles at *me*. May I be struck dumb if I'm making this up.

We passed each other in the hall after dinner. Craig said "How's it going?" and I squeaked four times. (Four times!) THEN I DID TWENTY MINUTES ON ANGELA LANSBURY, FOR CHRIST'S SAKE! What was I *thinking?* That's no way to talk to a jock. It's a whole other language. "Johnny Unitas." "Notre Dame." "Third down." "Gridlock."

My life is over. The only way he'll even *grunt* at me again is if he's hanging off a cliff by his fingers and I come to his rescue. And what are the chances of *that?!*

Craig McKenna   BECKLEY SCHOOL
Room 311   TARRYTOWN, NEW YORK

Somewhere along the line, I got it into my head that "Review
Week" meant we were only going over notes of things we were
supposed to know already, so in case you needed to catch up on
some z's during class you wouldn't be missing anything. That
lasted until third-period English when Naylor started a whole
new rap on *Wuthering Heights* that we never had before. Terrific. It *had* to be *Wuthering Heights*, didn't it? The only book
the whole year where I couldn't find the Cliff's Notes *or* the
Classic Comics version. So I hunched down in my chair by the
window and tried to turn myself invisible—which only makes
you stand out like one of your organs just fell on the floor.

"Mr. McKenna." See?

"Sir," I swallowed, sitting up straight.

"Would you care to comment on the complexities of the
relationship between Heathcliff and Catherine?" Yeah, about as
much as I'd care to have a Fleet enema, sir. Instead, I came up
with the only answer I could think of that might terminate this
conversation early, seeing as I wouldn't know Heathcliff or
Catherine if they were both peeing on my shoes.

"What relationship?" I asked, daring him to challenge me.
"Personally, I don't think he liked her all that much." Now, you
have to understand Mr. Naylor, who—while I like to give him
a hard time—may be the most dedicated teacher I ever knew in
my life. *Too* dedicated. When he asked me what Hamlet's
tragic flaw was and I answered "serious drugs," he acted like
he'd just caught me fucking his mother. This was no different.
His eyebrows nearly shot off his face.

"How can you say that?" he fired back. "My God, it's one of
the great romances of all time!" I shrugged and pretended I was
dropping the whole issue.

"Not to *me*," I retorted. Dead silence. Was he going to fall
for the bluff?

"Mr. McKenna," he said finally, "did you even *read* this book?" No. He wasn't. McKenna fumbles on the ten. Then all of a sudden there was a voice from the other side of the room. Travis.

"He's right, sir." Of course everybody looked at him. Travis says maybe four words a year, and they're almost always comparison examples that have Ethel Merman or Pearl Bailey in them. So Naylor wasn't prepared for an attack from the left.

"Mr. Puckett," he grunted, with snakes coming out his eyes, "have you something to say?" Boy, did he ever.

"According to *Peabody's Contemporary Criticism*," said Travis, "Brontë intended a level of psychosexual ambiguity in order to leave the reader wondering."

"Wondering *what?*"

"Whether Heathcliff was in fact attracted to Catherine or whether he was merely searching for a homoerotic substitute." While Naylor was picking himself up from the mat, me and Travis made eye contact for about $\frac{1}{100}$ of a second, which was just long enough for him to ESP three things to me: (1) I'm pulling this out of my ass as I go along, (2) I'll get you off the hook, and (3) we're in this together. And for a minute I even felt sorry for Naylor.

"Mr. Puckett," he glared, going for the kill. "I'm not familiar with *Peabody's Contemporary Criticism*."

"Neither was I, sir," admitted Travis, "until I found it in the reference room at Donnell Library. Third floor." And he didn't even blink while he was saying it!

I need to find out what makes Travis tick. Then maybe he can teach it to me.

Travis Puckett   BECKLEY SCHOOL
Room 214   TARRYTOWN, NEW YORK

Craig:

I finished your essay, but I sort of rewrote some of it. No
offense. I had to cut the part about the Mafia and the Jets
and the Red Sox and being half-naked at Madison
Square Garden and getting laid when you were 15. The
only thing left was half a line—where you died. So I put
in stuff about coming from Missouri and your mom
being a doctor and your dad's law practice and your Little League trophy and the way you scored three touch-
downs in one game last year and how nobody in our class
got into Harvard but you. And how come you didn't say
anything about the Citizenship Award? You were the
only tenth-grader who ever won it.

I was two hours late getting it to him, but that was only
because (a) I'd been chasing down a used copy of *Greenwillow*
from an out-of-print record store in Colorado that turned out
to be a bum lead, and (b) I had to redo all four pages when
Gordo dropped a chili cheese dog on them.

Gordon Duboise is the roommate from hell. The unsani-
tary part. At five feet ten inches, he weighs 158 pounds. Two-
thirds of that is muscle and the rest is bacteria. You can tell
where his side of the room starts and mine ends, because there's
an invisible Berlin Wall right down the middle—it kind of
looks like what would happen if an intensive care unit collided
with a city dump: randomly scattered biology notes, partly
empty Coke cans, and three pairs of toxic underpants (all left
over from junior year) in one sector, versus hospital corners,
symmetrical dustballs, and carefully labeled history books that
all smell like Windex in the other. (His half of the closet is no
better—one time I found a radial tire, a bag of peat moss, and a
1911 *New York Times*.) Far from being ashamed, Gordo claims

that he can identify any article of unwashed clothing by its aroma—even with his eyes closed.

"What stinks?"

"Sweatshirt," he says, sniffing. "Georgia Tech." And he's always *right!*

It's also impossible to keep secrets from him. Even the ones I don't know about yet.

"What's an option play?" I yawned casually, closing a physiology text and switching off my desk lamp. Gordo was sprawled out on a reprehensible mattress covered only by a World War I army blanket that hadn't been dry cleaned since the battle of Argonne, engrossed in the most recent issue of *Hustler*.

"Who's been asking you about option plays?" he replied, looking up from an improbable pair of breasts that couldn't possibly have existed prior to the silicone patent. "You got a boyfriend or something?"

I hate it when he figures me out before I have a chance to do it myself. Especially when I've been counting on at least seven more years of denial.

Craig McKenna

Room 311

BECKLEY SCHOOL

TARRYTOWN, NEW YORK

English Assignment

My Obituary

Mr. McKenna: In the unlikely event that you achieved this of your own accord without any outside assistance, you're to be commended. Otherwise, disregard the accolade.

Grade: **A+**

Shea Stadium was packed and so was the subway. We had to stand pressed together all the way from Grand Central to Willets Point and Travis squeaked six times while we were doing it.

He didn't want me to pop for his Mets ticket, but considering that I deserve an A+ in English about as much as Pete Rose does, he really didn't have a choice. So we wore our caps backwards and we used my phony ID to buy beer and we got mustard all over ourselves and by the bottom of the 9th, the Mets were trailing the Dodgers 4–3 with two out and two men on. Then Mazzilli came to the plate with "Don't fuck with me" written all over his face and you knew he was thinking "first pitch outta here." But instead it turned out to be a weak pop-up to first and I was already reaching for my jacket, when all of a sudden Steve (Your Highness) Garvey—who had the ball in his actual hands—dropped it on his Dodger Blue feet. YES! Travis and I were already jumping up and down on each other even before Foli and Flynn scored, and when Otis slugged Maz for sliding into home and the brawl started, we yelled ourselves into at least three days of laryngitis. I haven't popped my cork like that since Fisk belted the homer in '75.

Travis says that Roosevelt called us "The Arsenal of Democracy" the same week he locked up 120,000 Japanese Americans in concentration camps. Also that Black soldiers had to ride in boxcars while German POWs got to eat in the dining car. And by the way, next month is the 215th anniversary of the battle at Bunker Hill.

I have six varsity letters. How come *I* don't know these things? And where did Travis learn so much about baseball?

Travis Puckett   BECKLEY SCHOOL
Room 214   TARRYTOWN, NEW YORK

Somebody hit a ground rule double and somebody else stole a base and then a fight started, presumably for pro forma reasons. Then it was over. The blue-and-orange uniforms won.

What was I supposed to talk to him about?! Chugging brews? Naked girls? Crotch rot? If he hadn't already said something about Carlton Fisk, I'd have been up shit creek. Thank God the library had a copy of *The Baseball Almanac*. "Carlton Ernest Fisk, born December 26, 1948, in Bellows Falls, Vermont. Has played with the Boston Red Sox since 1969 and is best known for a twelfth-inning haymaker in the 1975 Series off of Reds hurler Pat Darcy." So I looked up Reds hurler Pat Darcy, who was only a short hop to Alvin Dark and the New York Giants. But that was the end of the line. When Craig asked me about Thurman Munson (sp?), I had to drag in Hitler just to throw him off the scent. I don't know how long I can keep this up.

Craig McKenna   BECKLEY SCHOOL
Room 311   TARRYTOWN, NEW YORK

Tonight me and Travis stuffed our beds with pillows and snuck into Tarrytown to see the 10:00 P.M. *I Wanna Hold Your Hand*. While we were waiting in line to buy our tickets, Travis said we still needed to resolve Critical Issue Number 1—which one of us gets to be called Smerko in this relationship? So we flipped for it and he won. (Actually he didn't, but it's not like you needed much of a brain to figure out that he wanted it a lot more than I did.)

Anybody who's never been to a movie with Travis needs to try it at least once, just for the entertainment value. First of all, he goes to take a piss exactly three minutes before showtime, even if he doesn't have to. It's a preventative measure just in case. The reason is because metabolism sometimes sneaks up on you faster than usual, and what if it suddenly happens smack in the middle of a good part?

Second of all, he won't touch any of his popcorn until the movie starts, but previews don't count and neither do the credits—you have to wait until after the director's name rolls off the screen. ("Not even one piece?" "No. That would invalidate the whole box.") Meanwhile he sits there with his hand over the top like maybe a tornado's going zip through the theater and blow some of it away or a popcorn thief is going to hit him up while he's not looking. Finally, when he *does* get to eat some, it happens in three-piece installments. No more. No less. And he spaces it out so it lasts for an hour and ten minutes.

Third of all, where we sit is another big deal. It has to be exactly three-fifths of the way back (which means counting the rows first), on the right-hand aisle. How come? The perspective is better there. Scientists didn't need to figure this out—Travis did it for them.

By the time the movie started, I was worn out. How does he do it? If *I* had to keep track of all those things, I'd wind up in a nuthouse. So I watched him for the first twenty minutes—thinking about metabolism and peeing, and eating three pieces of popcorn every seventy-five seconds, and counting the rows again to make sure we weren't one off—and suddenly it all made sense. That was the scary part.

Oh, yeah. It took a lot of work, but I finally talked him into losing the Van Heusens by giving him one of my Grateful Dead tops instead. Definitely an improvement. He wears T-shirts well. The guys at *Brigadoon* won't even recognize him anymore.

Travis Puckett   BECKLEY SCHOOL
Room 214   TARRYTOWN, NEW YORK

I don't know why I did it. It wasn't even premeditated. Kerry Fusaro was singing "Almost Like Being in Love" and all I had to do was wait for a cue from Craig and push a flat onto the stage. Period. We've done it a hundred thousand times before. But one of the baby-blue spots picked *that* moment to spill over into the wings and light him up—all 5-foot-8 of him, holding his clipboard and wearing his white T-shirt and winking at me with the one-dimple smile that nobody but yours truly ever gets, with the little crinkles around the corners of his eyes. DEFCON 3! DEFCON 3! The next thing I knew, I was wrapping my foot around the brace so that the damned flat wouldn't move, just before I heard myself whispering (in a terrific impersonation of panic), "Craig, it's stuck!" *What's the matter with me?!* Naturally I got the one-dimple thing again while he moved behind my marks and slid his arms around my chest to help me push. With his chin in my neck. And his nose in my ear. As he began humming "Almost Like Being in Love" right along with Kerry. It would have served me right if I'd had a cerebral aneurysm on the spot. Instead, I forgot all about my foot—until we shoved the flat onto the stage. I think we broke my ankle.

This is bullshit. I have finals to worry about.

Henry IV, Part I
Notes

Themes: It doesn't matter what people think of you as long as you know that your head and heart are in the right place. Everybody figured Prince Hal for a wastrel like Falstaff, but that's the way he wanted it. He was only marking time until he could prove that he was brave and honorable and righteous and loyal.

And strong.

And funny.

And gallant.

And

Craig *Craig* Craig Craig craig Craig Craig Craig Craig *Craig* Craig Craig craig Craig Craig Craig Craig *Craig* Craig Craig craig Craig Craig Craig Craig *Craig* Craig Craig craig Craig Craig Craig Craig *Craig* Craig Craig craig Craig Craig Craig Craig Craig *Craig* Craig Craig craig Craig Craig Craig

Craig Craig **Craig** Craig Craig *craig* Craig *Craig* Craig Craig
Craig Craig Craig *craig* Craig *Craig* Craig Craig **Craig** Craig Craig
craig Craig *Craig* Craig Craig **Craig** Craig Craig *craig* Craig Craig
Craig Craig **Craig** Craig Craig *craig* Craig *Craig* Craig Craig
Craig Craig Craig *craig* Craig *Craig* Craig Craig **Craig** Craig Craig
craig Craig *Craig* Craig Craig **Craig** Craig Craig *craig* Craig Craig
Craig Craig **Craig** Craig Craig *craig* Craig *Craig* Craig

Craig McKenna   BECKLEY SCHOOL
Room 311   TARRYTOWN, NEW YORK

If he ever scares me like that again, I'm going to break his neck.

How it started was when I had this really weird dream that he came barreling into my room at 7:00 in the morning, out of breath and with red ears—which usually means that (a) somebody's civil rights got violated, (b) he figured out who killed Kennedy, or (c) Ethel Merman farted. But this time he was talking so fast I could hardly understand anything he was saying. Even more than usual.

"Oh my God Craig I just opened a letter from House of Records in Scranton and they have one used copy of Greenwillow *but they can only hold it for me until 5:00 tomorrow so I've got to hitchhike to Pennsylvania can you cover for me in case anybody asks?"* Then he turned into a cat.

I didn't think much about it while I was brushing my teeth—I mean, it wasn't half as creepy as the one about Idi Amin chowing down on the Partridge family—but when I hit the dining room for breakfast and he wasn't there, I started getting worried. (It was creamed-chipped-beef-on-toast day and Smerko wouldn't have missed that even for open-heart surgery.) So I lied to Mr. Drew and said that Travis was somewhere puking—a crock of shit he'd *definitely* believe on creamed-chipped-beef-and-toast day—and then I tore up two flights of stairs to his room. But he wasn't there either, and his oversleeping roommate wasn't a hell of a lot of help.

"Gordo, listen to me carefully," I said, shaking him partly awake. "He wouldn't really hitchhike to Pennsylvania just for a *record*, would he?" Gordo stuck his head under a gray pillow that used to be white and groaned.

"At least. G'night, Craig."

For the next three hours I felt like a short traffic cop. First I told Mr. Naylor that Travis got called in to Mr. Dexter's office. Then I told Mr. Dexter that Travis was taking a makeup French quiz for Mr. Mitton. After that I told Mr. Mitton that Travis was covering study hall for Mr. Denning who had diarrhea, and finally I told Mr. Denning that Travis was still arguing with Mr. Naylor about that idiot Desdemona. Then the loop started all over again.

WHO THE FUCK HITCHHIKES TO SCRANTON?

What if some creep picks him up? Do you know what kind of people are out there? Read Helter Skelter *if you don't believe me. And how easy would it be to get run over on a freeway? Does he have enough money on him? Suppose he can't find a ride? What if he gets stranded in the rain and the only joint around is the Bates Motel?*

By dinnertime I was such a mess my stomach couldn't even handle a cupcake. Travis may be a lot of things, but a bruiser isn't one of them. And without me around to protect him, who *knew* what could happen? At least that's what I kept telling myself while I was sitting in front of the school at 9:30 tonight, waiting for him to come back.

He hitched three hundred miles for a record album. And half the time I can't even motivate my own ass across a room.

Travis Puckett   BECKLEY SCHOOL
Room 214   TARRYTOWN, NEW YORK

ANTHONY PERKINS
in
GREENWILLOW
music and lyrics by FRANK LOESSER
book by LESSER SAMUELS
Opened March 8, 1960; Alvin Theatre
95 performances

I was already playing Side Two on Craig's stereo when he finally came upstairs. (He should have known I was going to sneak in through the Common Room window. Don't I always?)

Except for a gold and white label pasted on the inside sleeve that says "Property of Leon," it was definitely worth spending three hours in the back of a Pennsylvania-bound cheese truck for. Craig doesn't think so.

"Who's that singing?" he demanded as he flopped down on the bed next to me.

"Anthony Perkins," I told him, handing over the album cover to prove it.

"Yeah? Well, I liked him a lot better when he was stabbing people in the shower."

I'm guessing that he had a bad day. He should have come to Scranton with me.

Craig McKenna   BECKLEY SCHOOL
Room 311   TARRYTOWN, NEW YORK

Moral: It's a lot easier to patch things up with somebody when he doesn't even know you were pissed off at him in the first place. And I was halfway right. Norman Bates singing sounds like what happens when you accidentally step on a dog.

While we were in the middle of our 11:00 P.M. cookie fight, one of my Chips Ahoys flew into the closet—and even though I told him he didn't have to, Travis went to get it anyway. ("Craigy, how can you go on with your life knowing it's still *lying* there?") Since it landed between a pair of sneakers and two jockstraps, I didn't think he was going to find my guitar. But duh—he found *Scranton,* didn't he? So I wasn't too surprised when I wound up cross-legged on my bed in my Jockeys singing "Leaving on a Jet Plane" to the only person in the world who wouldn't laugh at me or spill the beans to anybody else.

Actually, I thought it was cooking pretty well, but when I got to the "one more time, let me kiss you" part, Travis headed for the door and said he had to go study. (Without *me?*)

Okay—maybe Peter, Paul, and Mary I'm not.

Travis Puckett   BECKLEY SCHOOL
Room 214   TARRYTOWN, NEW YORK

If I'd stayed in that room for another nine seconds, I wouldn't have been responsible for my actions.

So on top of everything else, he sings like an angel in underpants. And he doesn't even suspect it. All he needs now is a little confidence (at last—a flaw!) and a Henry Higgins who's figured out how to pick his material. Something that fits his dimple. Something that lights up the razzle-dazzle he still doesn't know he has. And definitely something that would piss off Richard Nixon (if he still mattered).

Back to the library.

> Bob Dylan
> Joan Baez
> Laura Nyro
> Pete Seeger

Woody Guthrie
Jim Morrison*

(*This one is pure masochism. The whole point is to get him up
there onstage in skintights, twitching his ass and inflaming the
crowd with "Light My Fire." But I'd better be at least five thousand miles away when he does it—or else in a restraining harness.)

All right, maybe this is a little extreme, even for me. I
mean, what I *don't* know about Bob Dylan would have provided enough ballast to keep the *Titanic* floating for another six
hours. (FACT: His last name is really Zimmerman and so was
Ethel Merman's before she dropped the Zim. Period.) But if I
play my cards right, Craig is going to be singing "I Want You"
directly to me. What did JFK used to say? "The journey of a
million miles begins with a single step."

Come to think of it, "Light My Fire" is a really lousy idea.
It can only get me into trouble. So drop it.

Craig McKenna   BECKLEY SCHOOL
Room 311   TARRYTOWN, NEW YORK

Travis says that if I ever get a handle on "Light My Fire," I'll
own humanity for the rest of my life. Sometimes talking to him
is like reading my fortune. In Chinese.

So it turns out I had *Brigadoon* pegged all wrong. It's really
about making miracles happen with your heart. When Tommy
falls in love with Fiona and the whole village comes back to life
even after it's disappeared for a hundred years, it's the same as
me pushing Fenway Park a block and a half with my little
pinky. But Tommy had Fiona, and I don't. Sigh.

Tonight Smerko and I sat next to each other in the wings
listening to Kerry sing "Almost Like Being in Love," and for
the first time I felt the kind of high I usually only get from (a)
Clapton, (b) grass, (c) baseball, and (d) people who hitchhike

to Scranton. Either we've been hanging out with the chorus boys too long, or else Kerry's actually figured out how to put a song across. I guess I shouldn't be surprised. It only took him fifteen minutes to learn a slider.

But that was just the warm-up act. The same buzz kicked into fifth gear during the middle of the night when Smerk and I were cramming for our English finals.

Vocabulary Review
(with a little help from Travis)

incandescent

Radiant, glowing; think of a football diamond during a night game when the lights are all on and everybody's looking at you.

redoubtable

Formidable, fearsome; Carlton Fisk in 1975; you in a couple of years, after you've won your first hundred cases.

cavalier

Chivalrous, noble; remember when the guy in the Pacer called you an asshole? That wasn't cavalier. Remember when you pretended to lose the coin toss so I could be Smerko? That was.

empathetical

Sympatico, compassionate, knowing somebody inside and out; romance isn't just about roses or killing dragons or sailing a kayak around the world. It's also about chocolate chip cookies and sharing the Grateful Dead and James Taylor with me in the middle of the night, and believing me when I say that you could be bigger than both of them put together, and not making fun of me for straightening out my french fries or pointing my shoelaces in the same direction, and letting me pout when I don't get my own way, and pretending that if I play *Flower Drum Song* one more time you won't throw me *and* the record out the window.

anomaly
Paradox, enigma; imagine two disparate people who turn into best friends.

disparate
Us.

ubiquitous
Craig.

I looked up from my notes and glanced over at Travis, who was scrunched behind my desk reading *King Lear* for the third time—like he didn't know it by heart already. But his forehead was frowning again, so I knew if I asked him what "ubiquitous" really meant, he'd only throw a raisin at me. That's how—at 2:18 in the morning—I wound up opening a dictionary for the first time since Lyndon Johnson was president.

ubiquitous
Omnipresent, all-pervasive, spiritually sustaining; *see* Siddhartha.

"Smerko?"
"What?"
"Siddhartha was ubiquitous too."
"So?"
"So shouldn't you be praying to me?"
We got into a raisin fight anyway.

~

Before he went back to his room we took a shower together. Partly because we smelled and partly because it's the only place I can talk him into singing the "Miles and Miles and Miles of Heart" song for me.

"No."

"Pleeeeeeeeeeeeeeease?" I whined, soaping up his back. Usually that's enough to change his mind, but now he had another card to play. Without even turning around, he rinsed the shampoo out of his hair and glanced over his shoulder in an out-and-out challenge.

"Only if you sing 'Mr. Tambourine Man' first," he demanded (with his make-believe redoubtable face). So I put on my best Dylan and pretended I'd lost the round—even though we both knew he'd have caved in anyway. How could he not? Nobody argues with ubiquitous.

He called it a football diamond. (Grin.) Maybe I *could* move Fenway Park with my pinky.

Things to Do

____ Your groundwork. Never let him know that you always figured "If I Had a Hammer" was about construction workers. (What the hell were you *thinking?*)

____ Teach Travis how to play baseball. He definitely has the body for it.

Travis Puckett   BECKLEY SCHOOL
Room 214   TARRYTOWN, NEW YORK

THE PUCKETT/DUBOISE DEBATES

GORDO: Stop sneezing on my half of the room. You're contaminating the mold.

TRAVIS: I think I have a fever.

GORDO: So who told you to stand under a freezing
          cold shower at three o'clock in the morning?
          Didn't he notice your lips were turning blue?

TRAVIS: You just don't understand.

GORDO: Don't I? Travis, if you'd taken Trig with me
          like I asked you to, you'd know by now that
          it doesn't matter if you like boys instead of
          girls because the formulas are all the same.

TRAVIS: I never said I like boys!

GORDO: Ever beat off to *Penthouse*?

TRAVIS: No.

GORDO: Ever collect baseball cards?

TRAVIS: No.

GORDO: How old is Barbra Streisand?

TRAVIS: 36. Three weeks ago.

GORDO: What do you need—a fucking blueprint?

Craig McKenna   BECKLEY SCHOOL
Room 311   TARRYTOWN, NEW YORK

According to Travis, I'm not allowed to eat lettuce or grapes
(exploited migrant workers on the West Coast), canned salmon
(lousy living conditions for Filipino packers in Alaska), or
those little peas that look like green BBs (forced labor in central California—in 1930!). So far, no problem. I mean, he hasn't
come down on Junior Mints yet, so I'm okay.

But the shit really hit the fan at 7:26 this morning when he
caught me drinking orange juice.

Aryan Nation

MEMBERSHIP APPLICATION

NAME: Anita Bryant

ADDRESS: c/o Florida Citrus Commission, Florida State Capitol

CITY: Tallahassee   **STATE:** Florida   **ZIP:** 32399

REFERENCES: James Earl Ray, George Wallace, Strom Thurmond, Adolf Eichmann (deceased), Lester Maddox

QUALIFICATIONS: Former Miss America, popular crooner, and spokeswoman for Florida oranges. When I sing "God Bless America," people listen.

STATE BRIEFLY WHY YOU WISH TO BECOME A MEMBER OF ARYAN NATION: I got rid of all the homosexual teachers in Miami, didn't I? Wait till you see what I have on deck for the blacks, the Jews, and the handicapped.

_____
Signature

"Why do I have to do this?" I whispered in the middle of a jam-packed study hall, three days late with a biology paper that really needed me to give at least a flying fuck. "This is *forgery!*"

"Penance," he whispered back, with two curls of smoke still trailing out of his ears. "Besides, I already signed her up for the Symbionese Liberation Army. Somebody might recognize my handwriting."

"I'm going to flunk biology!"

"But at least you'll have a political conscience." Right around then, Mr. Denning glanced up from the proctor's table at the front of the room and glowered a little in our direction.

Since he only wears black suits and nobody's ever seen him smile, there's a rumor going around that he sleeps in a crypt underneath the chapel. So me and Travis shut up and began passing notes back and forth instead. Who needs a pair of fangs in their neck?

Smerko, if you had to make a list of all ten thousand important things in your life, would I be on it?

Yes. Right between Rosa Parks and *Annie Get Your Gun.*

So I signed "Anita Bryant" (whoever the fuck *she* is). I know when an inning's over.

Travis Puckett BECKLEY SCHOOL
Room 214 TARRYTOWN, NEW YORK

Beckley was trailing Stony Brook 4–2 at the bottom of the ninth, with two men on, two out, and Craig at the plate with an 0–1 count. Sound familiar? It should. Same setup as the one Bobby Thomson faced on October 3, 1951. Same results, too. Craig swung on a high and inside fastball, there was a crack and a gasp, and then I was on my feet screaming, "The Giants win the pennant! The Giants win the pennant! The Giants win the pennant!"—just like Russ Hodges did on the radio twenty-seven years ago. Craig heard me as he was rounding third and hesitated long enough to grin in surprise. It hadn't even occurred to him.

"*October 3, 1951.*"

"*Twelve days before* I Love Lucy *premiered and thirteen days before Judy Garland opened at the Palace.*"

"*Not in* this *universe. Try again.*"

"Mazeroski hit the home run?"

"Smerko, you're not paying attention. Come on."

"Wait! Bobby Thomson. Dodgers and Giants. The Shot Heard 'Round the World."

"Now we're getting somewhere."

The only other time I'd been down to Beckley's baseball diamond was the night I snuck across it on my way in to New York to see *Pacific Overtures* ($11 I could have put to a lot better use if only *Mack and Mabel* hadn't closed). Except for the prospect of Craig in form-fitting pants with the black stripe running northward from his feet to the Promised Land, I never would have gone near it again—especially considering the risks that I already know so well.

During my first two years in this joint, I was tripped, kicked, slugged, arm-locked, pummeled, egged, pissed on, spray-painted, and thumbtacked. I was also called "faggot," "queer," "cocksucker," "cornholer," "schmuckface," and "douchebag" so regularly, I no longer answered to my own name when spoken by anyone other than Gordo. Worst of all, I routinely found myself serenaded in the hall at least three times a week by a smirking quintet of singing assholes who'd mock me with the second chorus of "Hello, Dolly"—so badly executed, they still owe Carol Channing an apology.

But two months into my junior year (and after a lot of hard work hiding out in libraries and Broadway mezzanines), I finally achieved what I'd been gunning for since I was 14: absolute invisibility. And I wasn't about to rock the boat by getting anywhere near an athletic field—the one place where these people generally prefer to nest.

"Hey, faggot!" *Here we go . . .*

I was sitting nervously in the front row of bleachers on a blazingly blue Tarrytown afternoon, ready to bolt at a moment's notice if I had to, when most of the sun was suddenly blocked out by all 200 pounds of smug, orange-haired Vincent Sutter—the one who came up with the thumbtacking idea two years ago, and who's apparently still as gracious and hospitable as a yeast infection.

"Hey, Vinnie," I mumbled, staring at my feet and turning beet-red in the process.

"What's with the 'Vinnie'?" he leered, grabbing me by the back of my shirt. "You wanna blow me or something?"

Throughout most of this incandescent exchange, my best friend and his pants were warming up at shortstop, neither of them aware that I was about to be exterminated—but in reaching for a pop-up, Craig turned just in time to catch Goldfinger pouring a 16-ounce Coke over my head. Without wasting a move (and in true Bobby Thomson style), he pivoted to the right and aimed directly for Sutter's shoulder. And accuracy is one of the reasons Craig McKenna won the Victory Cup.

"Sorry, Vince," he called out sheepishly to a doubled-over Sutter, now groaning in pain by the foul line. "Guess it got away from me, huh?" As Sutter stumbled off the field looking for a Darvon, Craig threw me a covert wink—and I knew I was finally out of the woods for good. All I had to do was dry myself off and wait for the inevitable. It didn't take long.

"Outta my way, you little queer. OW!"

"Hey, cocksucker. How's about a—SHIT!"

"*Hello, Dolly, well, Hello, Dolly, it's*—FUCK, THAT HURT!"

They got the hint. By the ninth inning, Vinnie Sutter was calling me Travis.

"*October 16, 1969.*"

"*Miracle Mets.*"

"*October 1, 1961.*"

"*Maris hits his sixty-first.*"

"*Off of who?*"

"*Tracy Stallard.*"

"*Who was Eddie Cicotte?*"

"*Black Sox pitcher. I've got one for* you. *What happens on August 16, 2010?*"

"*I give up.*"

"*Craig McKenna's inducted into the Hall of Fame.*"

"*You really think so?*"

"*Yeah, but only if I get to go with you.*"

"*I already bought your plane ticket. It was supposed to be a surprise.*"

Tom Seaver once said, "There's only two places in this league: first place and no place." He must have learned that from Craig.

Craig McKenna   BECKLEY SCHOOL
Room 311   TARRYTOWN, NEW YORK

The Day That Changed Our Lives started out completely normal. We overslept, we missed breakfast, and the Tuck Shop was out of everything except onion chips and chocolate sprinkles. Which was a good excuse to cut French.

So we climbed into the gym through an open window, stripped down to our toes, dunked each other in the pool, and cut Ancient History.

Then we went to the library and read the first part of *Catcher in the Rye* out loud in whispers. That took almost an hour and we were running late—so we cut English, grabbed my guitar, and headed for the woods where nobody could hear us. This is where Capitol's next A&R megastar gave his only public performance—underneath an oak tree—to his best friend and two squirrels. Travis didn't know I'd been practicing for three days just so I could surprise him with "Subterranean Homesick Blues," "Blowin' in the Wind," and "Sweet Blindness"—and at first I couldn't tell if he liked it or not. It was only after I'd finished "Light My Fire" that he sort of yelped and wrestled me to the ground (translation: he liked it). But I pinned him first. (Grin.)

After lunch—Ring Dings and Pepsi—we had Biology staring us in the face, so we decided to let Mr. King and his bryophytes wilt without us. Instead, we changed into our jocks and socks and hit the batting cage. Travis has a good eye and a pretty decent swing, but his stance sucks. I spent two hours positioning him and he *still* couldn't get it right. What the hell. One athlete in the family is plenty. (Double grin.)

Then we took a quick shower, and while we were sitting around in our towels we calculated that by this time we'd broken roughly 61 percent of Beckley's half a million rules. So we figured it was time to go for the gold. That meant getting dressed up in our blazers and ties, sneaking off campus by the service road, and catching the 5:24 into Manhattan. (Smerko's done this so many times by himself whenever he's gone AWOL to see Liza Minnelli or somebody else in a play, the conductors all know him by heart.)

At 6:18 on the nose, we hit Grand Central. We were 131 minutes away from the biggest thing that would ever happen to either one of us, but we didn't know that yet. So we played tag on West 43rd Street and we snuck into a dirty bookstore on Eighth Avenue and then we got ticketed for jumping a subway turnstile at Lincoln Center by a cop with lousy handwriting whose name was either Victor or Viloy. After that we started getting hungry for just about anything that didn't have chocolate in it, so Travis picked Beefsteak Charlie's because it was right across the street from the Winter Garden Theater (*The*

Unsinkable Molly Brown in 1960, *Funny Girl* in 1964, and *Mame* in '66 for anybody not in the know). We had to muscle our way through a couple hundred tourists who all remembered at 7:55 that curtain time was 8:00, but we still managed to find ourselves a table in the corner where we could shut out the rest of the world. Who needed anybody else?

"I'll tell you something, Viloy," said Travis, halfway between the buffalo wings and the prime rib. "Carlton Fisk is overrated. I mean, if you put him up against Johnny Bench, he wouldn't know what hit him." Already my blood was heating up in 10-degree installments, and even though I wasn't sure if anybody'd ever gotten slugged in Beefsteak Charlie's before, Travis was bucking to be the first in line. Of course it was my own fault for giving him the *Baseball Encyclopedia*—but who expected him to memorize it? Then I noticed he was wearing his Heathcliff-and-Catherine face, where he's trying to look serious but the corners of his mouth won't stay all the way down.

"Are you saying this just to yank my chain or because you mean it?" I demanded. "And think carefully before you answer, because the ass you save may be your own." Travis hesitated, then tossed in the towel and grinned.

"You're *so* easy," he said. Then all of a sudden, the fork with the baked potato on it stopped halfway to his teeth and his skin turned snow white.

"Oh my God," he breathed, pointing over my shoulder across the emptied-out restaurant. "Viloy, look!" Not knowing whether he was putting me on again but falling for it anyway, I turned around and looked.

And there he was.

In the flesh.

Bobby Di Cicco.

At the next table.

Okay, you're the brains—what do we do now? Maybe we should just let him eat. Are you crazy? We'll never have this chance again.

Don't call me crazy. Then get the ketchup off your chin—he'll think you're brain dead. I want to talk to him first. Smerko, I want to talk to him first—pleeeeease? Fine! Talk to him first! I hate it when you whine. What do we say to him? Should we tell him we've seen the movie twenty-three times? No! He'll think we're stalking him. What if he has us thrown out for assault? Would you settle down!

After about nineteen seconds, Travis put his hand over my mouth and said, "Stop talking. I'll handle this." Then he got up, grabbed my arm, and dragged me behind him—even though I'd suddenly lost the use of both my legs. Me the quarterback. Me the shortstop. Shaking like a fucking leaf just because I was about to meet the most important human being in the universe.

"Bobby?" said Travis. Di Cicco looked up from his New York sirloin with question marks in his eyeballs and replied, "Hey, man." Holy shit. He even *sounded* like Bobby Di Cicco!

"Sorry to bother you—" Travis began. But by then Bobby had noticed me swaying and probably figured I was going to have a heart attack on his chives if he didn't do something fast—so the next thing we knew he was up on his feet shaking our hands and thanking us for stopping by. *(This isn't happening.)* Then Travis started asking him questions about movies and directors and other people I never heard of before, and pretty soon you'd have thought they were army buddies who were catching up on old times. ("Where do you get the balls?" I asked him later. "That was nothing," he said, shrugging it off. "Now, Lauren Bacall—*she* was a tough room to play.") We wrapped it up by doing our Tony Smerko imitations for him—and he even pretended we weren't assholes. Oh, yeah. I squeaked three times. Travis didn't squeak at all.

Once he'd autographed two packs of sugar for us with his actual hands, we paid the bill (who could *eat?*), then tumbled out of there like a couple of 4-year-olds with a new yo-yo and spent the next twenty-five minutes standing on the corner of 51st and Broadway, rehashing it from start to finish so we'd never forget a single word as long as we lived. And suddenly I was so fucking grateful for *Brigadoon,* I could have hugged the world. It was almost like being in love.

Neither one of us remembers much about the cab ride back to Grand Central. Times Square was all lit up, summer was around the corner, and we were just beginning the rest of our lives. But we didn't care about *any* of it. We'd met Bobby Di Cicco. Eating steak. With mortals.

What do you do when you've peaked at 18?

Travis Puckett	BECKLEY SCHOOL
Room 214	TARRYTOWN, NEW YORK

THE PUCKETT/DUBOISE DEBATES

TRAVIS: It was only dinner!

GORDO: It was a date. Trust me in this arena. Whose idea was it?

TRAVIS: His. We were down at the batting cage working on my stance again when—

GORDO: Were his hands on your ass?

TRAVIS: Well, yeah, but—

GORDO: It was a date. Travis, I hate being the one to break this to you, but you've only got about twenty-four hours of sanity left. Use them well.

TRAVIS: What was *that* supposed to mean?

Craig McKenna   BECKLEY SCHOOL
Room 311   TARRYTOWN, NEW YORK

I kissed him. I fucking kissed him. First our noses touched and then I *kissed* him.

I shouldn't have smoked the joint. I *knew* that was a mistake! But what else can you do when you're playing catch by a lake and it starts to pour? If there hadn't been one of those metal arch things with the benches underneath, it never would have happened—we'd have jogged back to school, wet and unkissed. *This was a conspiracy!*

Say no to drugs. They'll only ruin you. And I'm the proof: one toke and his eyes got bluer, two tokes and I'd have killed for his smile, three tokes and I couldn't remember a time we didn't know each other, four tokes and I would have woken up Brigadoon for him. My life is over.

Okay. Slow down. There's probably a good explanation for this.

1. *It was an accident.*
How? You tripped over a rock and your mouth fell on his?

2. *It's only a phase.*
Yeah. Like taking naked showers with him and tickling him every chance you get and telling him he needs work on his swing when all you really want to do is touch him.

3. *You were stoned.*
For the first fifteen minutes. What about the other three hours? At least he had the balls to kiss you back cold turkey.

4. *He's just a buddy.*
Which is how come every third word out of your mouth is "Travis." If they got rid of his name from the

alphabet, you wouldn't have a vocabulary left. Except for "ubiquitous."

5. *Maybe you're just searching for a homoerotic substitute.*
Maybe you just found one.

6. *You were only curious.*
Curious enough to do it again?

What's the use? I *kissed* him! It's like the atom bomb—it can't be undone.

My father would kill me.

Travis Puckett	BECKLEY SCHOOL
Room 214	TARRYTOWN, NEW YORK

It was right out of *The Sound of Music*. Rolf and Liesl in the rain. We even had a gazebo.

These are the facts: (1) I haven't eaten in fourteen hours but I'm not hungry; (2) I can't sleep because my bed's turned into the loneliest place in the world; (3) I have bruises all over my body from bumping into three doors and a carpet-cleaner; and (4) I can't remember what "fluctuate" means. Do people really survive this?

He didn't just kiss me. He ran his fingers through my hair and he made little circles on my nose with his pinky and he tickled me under my arms, and when the sun came out we walked in the woods where nobody could see us and held hands. Then we found a tree—and for the next two hours we stretched out on some wet leaves with my head on his stomach, while I tried not to remember that in three weeks he's going back to St. Louis. Not to mention September, when I'll be at USC and he'll be at Harvard. That's 2,988.2 miles, zip code to zip code.

But I can handle this. A month ago I was just Travis Puck-ett without the "Smerko." Now I've got Bobby Di Cicco's auto-graph and Craig. And no matter what else happens, I'm keep-ing them both for the rest of my life.

My father would kill me.

1998

1998

2

Travis

UNIVERSITY OF SOUTHERN CALIFORNIA

UNIVERSITY PARK • LOS ANGELES, CALIFORNIA 90007

SEMESTER: <u>Spring 1998</u>   FROM: <u>Travis Puckett</u>

CLASS: <u>American History 206</u> BUILDING/ROOM: <u>VKC/223</u>

BOOK PROPOSAL
"Alexander Hamilton and the Designated Hitter"

Issue: Once we'd won our independence from the Crown, how were we going to set up house?

Objective: Proving that baseball and the United States Constitution were founded on the same set of rules, as outlined in *The Federalist Papers* by Alexander Hamilton.

Argument: For some indefensible reason, George Washington had latched onto the witless notion of a British monarchy—a gentleman's system of government that favored the elite and screwed the poor—leaving the unspoken question, "Then what the hell did we fight a revolution for?" The way he saw it, the elected president would serve as absolute ruler, with the legislative bodies beneath him hired, ostensibly, to straighten out paper clips and put people on hold. Naturally, it was to be a one-party system (after all, there was no point in defeating a self-defeating purpose), replete with patricians in wigs, belted earls, and wards in chancery. Left to his own devices, Washington was entirely capable of turning the entire United States judiciary into a Gilbert and Sullivan operetta.

On a seemingly unrelated front, cricket was a gentleman's game played in Great Britain by the aristocracy—until the working classes got their hands on it and made the contest more democratic. Calling their version "rounders," "feeder," and "base," they brought it with them on the Mayflower in 1620 as evidence of their new moxie. Over the next century and a half, it was developed and refined across the colonies, so that by the time of the Constitutional Convention in 1787—while the royalty in Philadelphia were going through the attic to find a workable Bill of Rights—the people had already figured one out on their own.

If it hadn't been for the fact that conservative rich guy Thomas Jefferson (National League) and free-wheeling loud-mouth Alexander Hamilton (American League) detested one another on sight, the Founding Fathers might never have stumbled upon the same secret the populace had discovered years earlier on a rounders field: the dynamic upon which to build a true democracy and, incidentally, a Boston Red Sox legacy as well.*

HAMILTON

Among the most formidable of the obstacles which the new Constitution will have to encounter is the obvious interest of a certain class of men to resist all changes. . . . Candor will oblige us to admit that even such men may be actuated by upright intentions—but they are the honest errors of minds led astray by preconceived jealousies and fears. *(Translation: Why don't you go knit something, you old fart?)*

JEFFERSON
Every political measure will forever have an intimate connection with the laws of the land, and he who knows nothing of these will always be perplexed. *(Translation: Kiss my ass.)*

See, Carlton Fisk's home run off of Pat Darcy on October 21, 1975. ("We hold these truths to be self-evident that all men are created equal.")

UNIVERSITY OF SOUTHERN CALIFORNIA
UNIVERSITY PARK • LOS ANGELES, CALIFORNIA 90007

TO: Andrea Fox, History Department
FROM: William Koutrelakos, Dean
DATE: April 6, 1998
RE: Prof. Travis Puckett

Andrea:

This man is a crackpot. Make sure he doesn't carry any weapons and keep him away from the bell tower. Do you want us to be laughed out of the Pac 10?

UNIVERSITY OF SOUTHERN CALIFORNIA

UNIVERSITY PARK • LOS ANGELES, CALIFORNIA 90007

TO: William Koutrelakos, Dean
FROM: Andrea Fox, History Department
DATE: April 6, 1998
RE: Prof. Travis Puckett

Dammit, Bill! We have a football team with the IQ of corn flakes flunking everything but American History. Doesn't that tell you something?

I've already gotten a provisional "maybe" from Simon & Schuster and a "probably not, but who knows?" from Harper-Collins. And that's just based on the first hundred pages!

He only needs a $30,000 grant to finish the book by next spring. Who can it hurt?

UNIVERSITY OF SOUTHERN CALIFORNIA

UNIVERSITY PARK • LOS ANGELES, CALIFORNIA 90007

TO: Andrea Fox, History Department
FROM: William Koutrelakos, Dean
DATE: April 7, 1998
RE: Prof. Travis Puckett

That's what they said about uranium. And look how *that* turned out.

I'll consider it. But no promises.

The kids actually take him *seriously?*

UNIVERSITY OF SOUTHERN CALIFORNIA
UNIVERSITY PARK • LOS ANGELES, CALIFORNIA 90007

TO: William Koutrelakos, Dean
FROM: Andrea Fox, History Department
DATE: April 8, 1998
RE: Prof. Travis Puckett

Like he was a favorite frat brother. A weird one, granted—but that's probably why they look out for him.

And stop calling him a crackpot. He's as sane as you are.

FROM THE JOURNAL OF
Travis Puckett

How Not to Fall in Love with Your Dentist

Assume hypothetically that Dr. Goldberg retires and turns his practice over to Zack Nishimura, D.D.S.

Assume that Zack is 28—with a killer grin and twinkly brown eyes and Gap slim-fits with the seam that goes right up the crack in his ass.

Assume that you remember your name when he asks you what it is.

Assume that while he's checking your teeth and winking at you, you don't moan.

Assume that his last words to you are, "See you in six months. Looking forward to it."

1. Don't brood. He probably says that to *everyone*.
2. Don't speculate. Even straight men wear Gap slim-fits with the seam up their cracks. Sometimes.

3. Don't drive your friends crazy with this. (Except Gordo.)

4. Don't invent a pain in your upper left molar just so you can go back to see him again.

5. When you go back to see him again for the pain in your upper left molar, don't overdo the groaning unless you want him to think you need a root canal.

6. After you've survived the root canal, don't make things worse by paying for an entirely unnecessary staged reading of a lousy play you wrote in college just so you can invite him to it.

7. When he shows up at the staged reading, don't be surprised if he introduces you to his fiancée. *What the hell did you expect?!*

8. Consider telling him the truth. But not while he's holding a drill.

Then disregard rules 1–8. Carpe diem.

The only practical reason for living by the beach in Santa Monica is the view from the balcony when your heart's been shattered. As you watch the angry surf pounding the foamy sand in the orange-and-pink glow of sunset, it's a lot easier to think about drowning yourself.

Oh, Zack.

I suppose there were subtle hints right from the start: the engagement ring, the wedding invitation, and the thirty-eight pictures of the same woman plastered across his office. But Ryan was misleading too—and look how *that* turned out.

TRAVIS PUCKETT'S BOYFRIEND CHECKLIST

Name: Ryan   **Duration:** 7 weeks

Occupation: Bartender   **Where we met:** West Hollywood

BEGINNER LEVEL

- ✓ Can say "I love you"
- ✓ Isn't hiding another boyfriend
- ✓ Thinks kissing is sexy
- ✓ Has a glowy smile
- ✓ Is at least marginally sensitive
- ✓ Will probably remember my name the next morning

INTERMEDIATE LEVEL

- ✓ Can say "I love you" without my saying it first
- ___ Likes me enough to tell me I'm special
- ✓ Trusts me enough to tell me I'm wrong
- ___ Always lets me pick the first fortune cookie
- ___ Teases me when I need it but knows when to stop
- ___ Pursues making me laugh as a hobby
- ___ Pretends to like the same things I do even when he doesn't
- ___ Misses me when we're apart
- ✓ Isn't afraid to fight with me
- ___ Allows me to drive him crazy
- ___ Would rather do nothing with me than something by himself
- ___ Can fall asleep in my lap while I work—and still call it a date

TOP-OF-THE-LINE LEVEL

- ___ Can say "I love you" with his eyes
- ___ Never lies (except to spare my feelings)
- ___ Doesn't worry about losing me because he knows he can't
- ___ Forgets there was a time when we didn't know each other
- ___ Kisses me for no good reason
- ___ Celebrates my faults
- ___ Sighs when I hold him
- ___ Knows all the lyrics to *Flora, The Red Menace* (optional)

Strong Points: I could definitely spend the rest of my life with him.

Shortcomings: He killed his last boyfriend (acquitted: involuntary manslaughter).

Comments: The knockout blonde he kept having lunch with wasn't his lover—she was his attorney. Serves me right for spying on him.

I should have known it was going to be an uphill battle right from Gate 3: Adolescence. First there was a Craig, then there was a kiss, then there was a goodbye, then there were the letters, then he stopped writing to me, and then there was Cardinal Rule Number 1: Never Fall in Love When You're 17. Not unless you want to spend your entire freshman year at USC learning how to sleep by yourself again. If it hadn't been for Adam-Down-the-Hall-with-the-Sky-Blue-Eyes, I might have been playing Camille until I was a junior. As it was, I managed to hit the dirt running: before I'd even hung up my *Camelot* and *Fade Out, Fade In* posters, I'd inadvertently discovered (through some carefully orchestrated eavesdropping at the Coliseum urinal) that he was a wannabe actor from Chicago. So I wrote my one and only play—a shamefully melodramatic character study about seven ballplayers stuck in the Cubs dugout at Wrigley Field during a rain delay—solely as an excuse to (a) cast him, and (b) meet him. He didn't get the part (much to his boyfriend's disappointment), but at least I had half a dozen other men in jockstraps to choose from. That was my preliminary encounter with Puckett's Curse: I wound up with the only all-heterosexual all-male cast in the history of World Theatre. And from there, it *really* turned ugly.

1. *Gregory.* We met at my Harvey Milk vigil in November. I was 18, he was 33—an ex-Marine who still wore a high-and-tight, with a chiseled body that didn't know when to quit. How did I get so lucky? Especially when he confessed that he was God's disciple of truth, sent down to earth to find twelve apostles who'd be willing to follow him. (Into what? Sharon Tate's living room?)
2. *Robbie.* We were both 26. It was "Some Enchanted Evening" all over again. On our eight-month anniversary, he bought me the original cast recording of *Kwamina* and took me to a gang bang—without

telling me that I was the one getting banged. Men are such assholes.

3. *Michael.* Five years ago. He was a tenor. We spent our first date listening to *Götterdämmerung* on the radio while we read along from the score (for six hours!). He was obsessed with *Grove's Dictionary of Music and Musicians,* so I—with only $247, a T-bill, and a heart made out of oatmeal—promised it to him for Christmas. How was *I* supposed to know it came in eighteen volumes?! Three months later, he was sitting on a bench in Ocean Park reading "O" when a tall brunet with Armani teeth and a Calvin Klein body sat down next to him. Turned out he was an oboe player. Nobody ever heard from either one of them again.

And as long as I'm being brutally candid, I only wound up teaching American History because I followed a cute ass into the country-and-western section at Barnes & Noble and found out it was attached to an adorably self-conscious Poli-Sci professor who, in retrospect, was probably more anxious to stick a needle in his eye than have coffee with me. Three cappuccinos later, I could already envision myself stretched out on an Eames couch with my head in his lap while we both graded papers— so I applied for a job in the history department at USC. And by the time he'd introduced me to his boy toy—a gym bunny with a Ph.D. (natch)—I already had five classes and a parking space with my name on it. (Not that I ever blamed him for robbing Broadway of its brightest light. My musical comedy ambitions had been short-circuited three years earlier at the still-woundable age of 20, when I auditioned for a campus production of *On a Clear Day* at the Stop Gap Theatre and discovered quite by accident that my singing voice causes cancer.) Once again I'd chosen to sleep through Obvious Clues 101: the formal handshake instead of a kiss (he's bashful), his unflagging use of the plural possessive ("our" dog clearly meant the one his parents had bought him when he was six—Spot or Shucks or Barnacle Bill), and the three hickeys barely hidden by his Versace collar (toner cartridge fell on his neck). Also overlooked was the fact that nothing makes my skin crawl like country-and-western music—unless it's *Götterdämmerung*.

Okay. One more root canal. But that's it. Otherwise, people might start thinking I'm a little screwy.

American History 206
Professor Puckett
April 14, 1998

Impressions of the Revolution
by Chuck Navarro

Let's face it—up until 1750, we were a pain in the ass. But we still asked England to let us colonize a New Land, get some government, and borrow their ships. For *what?* In the 130 years since Plymouth Rock, we only had three specialties. (a) learning how to eat maize without dropping it all over the floor, (b) setting weird bonfires in Salem, and (c) dying of exposure. Sorry, but I'd have taxated us too.

Example: The '62 Mets, who didn't even deserve their uniforms until they got a life and a pennant in '69. Also Tom Sawyer and Huck Finn playing pirates, the same way we were playing around with being a country when we weren't one yet.

> *Travis, what the fuck does Tom Sawyer have to do with the Bill of Rights? If I wanted to take English, I would of.*
>
> —*Chuck*

Impressions of the Revolution
by Gary Petrie

King George knew he had his hands full. Dicking around about taxation and representation and stamps and embargoes is what you do when you're looking for a reason to paste somebody in the mouth, and it was probably his way of getting the fucking thing over with quick so he could go back to polishing his jewelry. Chances are he was a reasonable person. On the other hand, he never figured he was going to lose either, which maybe makes him a prick after all.

Example: The 1927 Yankees (especially Tony Lazzeri) did the same thing to the American League that the Saratoga boys did to Burgoyne. And for almost all of the same reasons, like the Red Sox and the Redcoats not taking either one of them seriously until it was too late.

Travis:

Dude. Thanks for the B+. Before I took this class I thought that George Washington was a load of crap like Santa Claus and the Seven Dwarfs and other people they make you believe in when you're too young to know any better. Even with the green picture on the dollar.

But you should lighten up a little. I mean, who really gives a shit about whose ass John Hancock had to kiss to get his name in the middle? You need a boyfriend. If you want me to keep my eyes open for somebody, just say the word.

—Gary

Impressions of the Revolution
by Corey Gambel

The Revolution solved one big problem. Up until then there wasn't exactly a boom market on social studies books because we hadn't *done* anything yet. I mean, if you were a kid who hated school, all you had to do was take American History and you'd be out of there in three days. But all of a sudden there were monuments and things like Concord and Valley Forge and Independence Hall and Old Ironsides. (And by the way. How come Paul Revere was a hero when all he did was run away and cry for help?)

Example: Ebbets Field, which probably had more important landmarks in it than all of the Bunker Hills put together. And they built it practically overnight. Sort of like the thirteen colonies who woke up one morning and there was the Bill of Rights. Baseball got instant history quicker than anybody else ever did—I mean, one box score and suddenly we had stats!

TP:

Not that I thought you were nuts, but this actually makes sense. It's also the only class I stay awake through.

—*CG*

Impressions of the Revolution
by Doug Hatten

So we get our independence and then we can't figure out what to do with it. Know what it reminds me of? Being a teenager and practically breaking apart at the seams to get out of the house for good. Until it happens. Then you spend all of your time in your old bedroom, staring at your football trophies and waiting for Mom to finish doing your laundry. Nothing's scarier than being on your own for the first time. *That's* why it took us more than a year to find a Constitution. We hadn't grown up after all, and we needed to do it fast.

Example: The 1908 Cubbies. Without a doubt. They were just these confused kids who won the World Series, and they didn't even know how the hell they got there. And once they thought they'd figured it out, they never got there again.

> *Trav, do I really have to take History 304 to find out about Carlton Fisk and the Cuban Missile Crisis? Couldn't you just give us a hint and save me four units?*
>
> —*Doug*

Impressions of the Revolution
by Tony Norris

Know what England's problem was? They were kicking the wrong country, that's what. Suppose you were somebody's asshole father who drank all night and spent the rest of the day beating the shit out of your kid. Then all of a sudden they make the little brat Chief of Police. Guess what? You're screwed. And what *really* poked England in the nuts was figuring out too late that if they'd stopped us earlier, we never would have learned how to say no.

Example: John McGraw's New York Giants. Any year'll do. The Yankees may have been a better team, but nobody knew how to say "fuck you" to the people in charge better than Mr. McGraw. Even Alexander Hamilton didn't.

> *Hey Trav,*
>
> *When I first got in this course, I didn't want a pervert teaching me. Now I don't mind.*
>
> —*Tony*

Impressions of the Revolution
by Ray Sorren

What Revolution? We got our independence the day we set sail for Massachusetts. Everybody knew that except the King. What did he think all the shouting was about?! Duh. Okay, maybe we were a little over the top, but so what? We got to dress up like Indians and dump a thousand crates of tea into the harbor, and when that was over we put on uniforms and loaded up muskets and saluted a lot and if anybody's thinking "batter up," no wonder.

Example: Rookie Tom Seaver, who looked like he was 12. Until he threw his first fastball. Suddenly the rest of the league figured out in a hurry that they'd just stepped into a bucket of shit. The same thing King George must have thought when he heard about John Paul Jones.

Travis—

If you straighten out the erasers one more time, I'm going to break your fucking fingers. Get laid, man.

—Ray

UNIVERSITY OF SOUTHERN CALIFORNIA
UNIVERSITY PARK • LOS ANGELES, CALIFORNIA 90007

Doheny Library
Faculty Research Request

DATE: <u>April 16, 1998</u>   FROM: <u>Travis Puckett</u>
DEPARTMENT: <u>History</u>   BUILDING/ROOM: <u>VKC/223</u>

MATERIALS NEEDED

All periodicals referencing shortstop Dickey Pearce around 1860. And could you find out if he came from the South?

SPECIAL INSTRUCTIONS
Julian: Try to wear the blue shirt tomorrow. The one that makes your eyes twinkle.

Here's the stuff you wanted on Dickey Pearce. From what I can make out, he had a so-so swing and a hot ass. And how should I know if he came from the South? What do I look like—his lover?

Come on, Sexy. Want to help me prove the link between the Brooklyn Atlantics and Reconstruction?

Travis, I'm 28. I go to circuit parties. I judge people by only two criteria: hot and buff. My life revolves around the pec deck and my mirror. I once spent an entire paycheck on a pair of underpants from Italy. Can you spell "shallow"?

FROM THE JOURNAL OF
Travis Puckett

THE PUCKETT/DUBOISE DEBATES

TRAVIS: I can't believe I called him Sexy.

GORDO: That's *it?* You should have written "Take off your clothes." What's this guy's name?

TRAVIS: It's Julian. He always grins at me when he gives me microfiche.

GORDO: Major event. T, wake up. Next month you're going to be 38 and you *still* don't have anybody to kick your butt or buy you a pizza or get naked with.

TRAVIS: What about Rick?

GORDO: Rick who?

TRAVIS: Rick from the Internet. We talk on the phone and he sends me e-mail.

GORDO: Ever boink him?

TRAVIS: No. He lives in Vegas.

GORDO: Nice town. You can fuck a whore but you can't make a U-turn.

There are only two reasons I let Gordo move in with me: (1) I know I can trust him to keep his hands off my original cast recording of *Illya Darling;* and (2) over the last two decades, I've gotten used to the smell.

When he first decided to gamble on California twelve years ago, he was one of ten million waiters-with-screenplays residing tentatively in the City of Angels—albeit, with one foot out the door. But he got lucky on both fronts: Jerry's Deli hired him to manage the takeout counter, which meant that we were able to live the high life for eighteen months on smoked salmon, Kosher brisket, and noodle kugel; and somebody at Universal actually bought *Cellarful of Blood* from him, seeing it as a vehicle for Bruce Willis and Mel Gibson. Instead, after four years in development, it premiered as an offbeat love story called *One Special Summer,* starring Gwyneth Paltrow and Emma Thompson, set in turn-of-the-century Kensington. Gordo's name was nowhere to be found on the credits, but the $750,000 in underhanded option extensions had long before cleared the Bank of America. ("At least when they fuck you, it doesn't hurt.") Since then, he's found something of a home at Universal: his grisly but historically accurate *Murder at Toma-hawk Ridge*—after it had been "polished" by the director—was retitled *He Loves, She Loves* with Sandra Bullock and Ben Affleck, and set domestic box office records for a romantic comedy; while the dopey but genuinely funny *Honolulu Honey-moon* (released as *Stalked at Midnight*) established new industry standards for the slasher film—despite the fact that the script was attributed to thirty-four different screenwriters, none of whom was Gordo.

So we bought a townhouse in Santa Monica with two bedrooms, an eat-in kitchen, and a clear-cut set of rules: I get the top floor, he gets the bottom, and a verbal visa is required to cross the border. That way he's not threatened by my Lysol and I'm not confronted with the all-female "I'm Auditioning for the Future Ex-Mrs. Gordo" parties he can afford to throw twice a month—particularly when he's in one of his fetish moods (e.g., pierced navels and green pubic hair). But that's never held him back from stepping in as my voice of reason:

TRAVIS: Which sounds better—"Travis and Julian" or "Julian and Travis"?

GORDO: Did I ever tell you about Kyle?

Which is where he usually fixes me up with any number of studio deadbeats presently harassing him for free rewrites, free options, or coke money. It's a relatively easy procedure—when he can't get them off the phone, he has them call me instead. Know what's worse? I go out with them! (Gordo never considers compatibility an issue. The way he figures it, as long as we both have dicks it ought to work.) I once did dinner with a development creature who refused to sleep with me because I didn't have enough of an edge. Apparently, he thought I was a pitch meeting. Then he picked up somebody in the men's room and left me with the check. But I got even. I don't go to movies any more. Especially his.

"Kyle and Travis." Actually, that sounds kind of cute.

TRAVIS PUCKETT'S BOYFRIEND CHECKLIST

Name: Kyle

Occupation: Film Agent

Duration: 55 minutes

Where we met: Gordo's half of the living room

BEGINNER LEVEL

_____ ~~Can say "I love you"~~

_____ ~~Isn't hiding another boyfriend~~

_____ ~~Thinks kissing is sexy~~

_____ ~~Has a glowy smile~~

_____ ~~Is at least marginally sensitive~~

_____ ~~Will probably remember my name the next morning~~

INTERMEDIATE LEVEL

_____ ~~Can say "I love you" without my saying it first~~

_____ ~~Likes me enough to tell me I'm special~~

_____ ~~Trusts me enough to tell me I'm wrong~~

_____ ~~Always lets me pick the first fortune cookie~~

_____ ~~Teases me when I need it but knows when to stop~~

_____ ~~Pursues making me laugh as a hobby~~

_____ ~~Pretends to like the same things I do even when he doesn't~~

_____ ~~Misses me when we're apart~~

_____ ~~Isn't afraid to fight with me~~

_____ ~~Allows me to drive him crazy~~

_____ ~~Would rather do nothing with me than something by himself~~

_____ ~~Can fall asleep in my lap while I work—and still call it a date~~

TOP-OF-THE-LINE LEVEL

_____ ~~Can say "I love you" with his eyes~~

_____ ~~Never lies (except to spare my feelings)~~

_____ ~~Doesn't worry about losing me because he knows he can't~~

_____ ~~Forgets there was a time when we didn't know each other~~

_____ ~~Kisses me for no good reason~~

_____ ~~Celebrates my faults~~

_____ ~~Sighs when I hold him~~

_____ ~~Knows all the lyrics to *Flora, The Red Menace* (optional)~~

Strong Points: Not applicable

Shortcomings: He's alive.

Comments: Kill Gordo.

ARGOSY ENTERTAINMENT
Literary Representatives

LOS ANGELES   TORONTO
NEW YORK   LONDON

Mr. Gordon Duboise
100 Bay Street
Santa Monica, California 90405

Re: Representation Agreement

Dear Gordon:

As you are aware, Universal is still waiting for your draft, which is now two months overdue. I attempted to placate them with *The Potato People*, but they already have an Irish famine picture in development.

Then this morning I received from you the first nineteen pages of *Hell in Harlem*. You're joking, right? Perhaps you didn't understand me. They're looking for a love story. A whole one.

Gordon, it might be a good idea for you to seek more appropriate representation elsewhere.

You have three weeks to change my mind. Govern yourself accordingly.

Very truly yours,
Henry A. Duboise

FROM THE DESK OF
Gordon Duboise

Pop:

This *is* a love story. It's about an interracial marriage. And since when did Universal start reading scripts? You should have slapped a new title page on *Code Name Shapiro* and sold it to them again.

ARGOSY ENTERTAINMENT
Literary Representatives

LOS ANGELES   TORONTO
NEW YORK   LONDON

Don't press your luck, Gordon. Just because they bought it three times already doesn't mean you can turn it into a cottage industry.

And what do you know from interracial? Until you were eight years old you thought that black people came from employment agencies.

Gordon, please. I'm an old man. I gave you love. I gave you a home. I gave you all the support you ever needed.

FROM THE DESK OF
Gordon Duboise

Bullshit. You divorced my mother and sent me to boarding school.

ARGOSY ENTERTAINMENT
Literary Representatives

LOS ANGELES   TORONTO
NEW YORK   LONDON

To build your character. Now it's built. Give me a goddamned
love story.

FROM THE JOURNAL OF
Travis Puckett

Up until the Magic Moment, it was a day that had disaster written
all over it. First the laundry was delivered with one sock missing,
which is enough to throw me off balance for at least a month. (Do
you get rid of the other one too, or just let it lie there mocking you
every time you open the drawer?) Then came breakfast when I discovered that Gordo had not only invaded my half of the kitchen
again but broken the Paper Towel Rule on top of it. ("When we
get down to three rolls, buy more. I don't like eating into the
buffer.") Finally, there was lunch with Andrea Fox and the dean—
a last-ditch effort on our part to convince him that (a) the Alexander Hamilton book proposal was worth the $30,000 grant, and (b)
I'm really not pathological. By the time the entrees had arrived,
Andrea had almost succeeded in the former and was establishing
a beachhead on the latter when she caught me lining up the ends
of my asparagus and stabbed me in the thigh with a fork. None of
this was lost on Dean Koutrelakos, who decided instead to use the
money for fifteen new toilets in Bovard Hall. Which means I get
to finance the book myself on $941, a T-bill I'm not allowed to
touch, and two Happy Meal coupons from Denny's. Thank God
Gordo's rich.

GORDO: Kewl. I never had a kept boy before.

TRAVIS: If you're going to put it that way, just drop it. Nothing's worth a word picture like that.

So it was in my Scarlett O'Hara "As God Is My Witness I'll Never Go Hungry Again" mode that I reached into my campus mailbox and found it—squished between an American Express statement, a third payment notice for a barium enema I never had, and my May issue of the *Advocate*.

UNIVERSITY OF SOUTHERN CALIFORNIA
UNIVERSITY PARK · LOS ANGELES, CALIFORNIA 90007

Doheny Library
Faculty Research Request

DATE: <u>April 23, 1998</u>   FROM: <u>Travis Puckett</u>
DEPARTMENT: <u>History</u>   BUILDING/ROOM: <u>VKC/223</u>

MATERIALS NEEDED

Your phone number.

SPECIAL INSTRUCTIONS
You couldn't begin to guess.

Travis, this is your last warning. I'm only human—and even though you're not exactly a hunklet, on a Cute Scale of 1-to-10, you're an easy 12. So don't push me. You really don't want to go there.

~

Naturally, my next two classes were hell. I named Philadelphia as one of the thirteen colonies, I couldn't remember what the War of 1812 was about, and I referred to James Madison's wife as Dolly Levi. If I'd kept it up for another fifteen minutes, their final exams would have ended in a mistrial. But it was worth the anxiety attack when I pumped up the steps to Doheny Library two at a time and made it to the reference room three minutes before he went off duty.

I was out of breath—and he was waiting for me.

PERSONNEL OFFICE   CONFIDENTIAL

Julian Eric Brennan
d.o.b. February 14, 1970, Dubuque, Iowa
Ht. 5'10", Wt. 161; Eyes: Blue; Hair: Lt. brown
Position: Assistant Librarian
Location: Doheny Library Reference
Hours: Monday–Friday 8:30a–4:15p

(The penalty for Xeroxing confidential staff information is swift and merciless—but if they really wanted to enforce the rule, they wouldn't keep the records room unlocked.)

Evaluation
1. Dubuque is practically around the corner from Field of Dreams, and he was born on Valentine's Day. (Good.)
2. He likes Starbucks cappuccino and he wouldn't let me pay for our cookie. (*Very* good.)
3. The first book he ever read was *Valley of the Dolls.* (Not so good.)
4. He hates baseball. (Bad.)
5. He prefers "older men." (Ouch!)

Okay. This is what's called a 50-50 shot. Either we wind up spending the rest of our lives together or else it ends the way it always does:

REAL LIFE vs. THE MOVIES

Breaking Up in the Movies

Boy #1:   This isn't working out, is it?

Boy #2:   Sort of not, huh?

Boy #1:   You can't say we didn't try.

Boy #2:   We sure did. Besides, we're still best friends.

Boy #1:   Forever.

Boy #2:   This is terrific pasta.

Breaking Up for Real

Boy #1:   Are you asleep?

Boy #2:   Does it sound like it?

Boy #1:   I'm sorry about the tuna fish.

Boy #2:   It isn't the tuna fish! It's the last six months!

Boy #1:   You're an asshole.

Boy #2:   Let go of my cock.

Make that 60-40.

3

Craig

CITY OF SARATOGA SPRINGS POLICE DEPARTMENT

POLICE REPORT—MINOR CHILD

Date <u>April 24, 1998</u>   Page <u>4</u>

NAME: Noah Kessler	SEX: M	ADDRESS: Unknown	AGE: 10–11

Investigating Officer's Comments

At 2:26 A.M., we received a radio dispatch advising that the night manager of the downtown Greyhound terminal had reported a small child traveling alone after midnight.

We found the boy in the waiting room, wearing a Utica Blue Sox backpack, a Utica Blue Sox cap, and a Utica Blue Sox jacket. (After that, the bus ticket to Utica came as no surprise.) He attempted to cover his tracks by claiming that his mother was in the ladies' room; however, on checking out his story, we located only a cleaning woman and a Franciscan nun. So we brought him down to the station.

He gave us no information whatsoever, although an ID tag on his GameBoy identified him as Noah Kessler. He cried just once—when he thought we were taking away his bus ticket—and then stated he wanted to speak to his attorney. In fact a call was placed to Craig McKenna, of McKenna & Webb, at an unlisted home telephone on Loughberry Lake.

McKenna arrived at approximately 3:41 A.M., and the boy was remanded to his custody.

McKENNA & WEBB

A LAW PARTNERSHIP

118 CONGRESS PARK, SUITE 407

SARATOGA SPRINGS, NEW YORK 12866

MEMORANDUM

TO:	Craig McKenna
FROM:	Charleen Webb
DATE:	April 24, 1998
SUBJECT:	Calendar and Other Matters

Craig:

1. Judge Costanzo granted the Pioneer Scouts' motion to dismiss when he found out you were suing them (again) for lighting matches in a state park. His telephonic ruling: "Jesus H. Christ, Charleen! That's what makes them pioneers!" This is the third time, Craig. What were you expecting—a toaster?

2. Your mother called from St. Louis. She says to tell you that Alma Colson's son just opened his own practice. He's a urologist. She wants you to come home for the holidays and have dinner with him because she's convinced he'll

sweep you off your feet. What does she think you and Clayton have been up to for the last twelve years?

3. I have a 2:30 deposition in *Lindborg vs. Bluecover,* but I need to be out of here by 5:00. If it runs over (and it will—according to Martindale-Hubbell, defense counsel hasn't stopped talking since 1946), can you cover for me? Derek is taking me to a white-collar crime seminar (orchids are obviously optional) on what's destined to be both our fourth date and our last. Once he'd reenacted his allegedly hilarious moot court trial (he misplaced an interrogatory and Bunny Bixler stepped on a ping pong ball), there was nothing left to talk about. Oh, well. Ex-boyfriends are essentially useless, but at least they prove you haven't wasted your entire life.

4. No offense, but you look like shit. Have you been fighting with Clayton? Are you having an illicit affair? Did you chain yourself to another of Harvard's libraries? Were you able to make friends with the SWAT team this time? Or were you chasing Noah Kessler all over Saratoga Springs again?

5. Lunch. Sweet Shop. 12:30. Bring the *Hoskot* transcripts. Sexual harassment lawsuits are as close as I get to romance these days.

McKenna & Webb
A Law Partnership
118 Congress Park, Suite 407
Saratoga Springs, New York 12866

Memorandum

TO:	Charleen
FROM:	Craig
DATE:	April 24, 1998
SUBJECT:	Calendar and Things

Charleen:

1. I didn't chain myself to Widener Library on purpose. It started out as a simple rock concert that turned into a routine protest—the riot wasn't my fault. Did you expect me to keep my mouth shut? Harvey Milk was dead and nobody was doing a damned thing about it. And by the way, that was twenty years ago. Get over it.

2. I concede that the Pioneer Scouts loyally uphold the Constitution of the United States—that yellowed piece of parchment in the National Archives that proves beyond a reasonable doubt that this country was invented for rich, white, upper-class, Anglo-Saxon Protestant, heterosexual men. Everybody else needed an amendment. The Saratoga Springs Scout chapter contains no African Americans, no Latinos, no Jews, and no Democrats. Furthermore, when they found out that one of their 14-year-olds had a boyfriend, they bounced him out on his ass and took back all nine merit badges. But they're protected by their nonprofit "go fuck yourself" status, so the only thing I can actually prove is that they were lighting matches in a state park—which by the way violates four municipal codes and two federal statutes. If I have to drag in Bambi to nail their asses to the wall, I'll do it.

3. My mother claims she didn't raise her son to settle down with a construction foreman who operates his own hardware chain. Even with the M.B.A. from Harvard. But it's not really the blue-collar thing that crawled up her ass. She and Clayton haven't agreed on anything since she found out he makes more money than she does.

4. I'll handle the depo, but the party for your windbag ends at 6:00 P.M. on the button. Clay's got something up his sleeve tonight that I'm not supposed to know about. I think he's going to give me the wedding ring that you probably helped him pick out. Judging by the travel brochures he keeps hiding from me, he's planning a honeymoon in either Denmark or Canada or one of those other arsenals of democracy that'll allow us to register as groom and groom. (It won't mean shit to the IRS when we come home, but at least we'll be legal *somewhere*.) So how come it always makes him edgy whenever I organize a teensy little Freedom to Marry march on Washington?

5. It's Noah again. This time I found him down at the Third Precinct after they'd caught him at the bus station with a one-way ticket to Utica in his pocket. Evidently his mother and her new husband went to Germany for eight weeks to spy on the Mueller automotive plants (I didn't realize he was *that* Mueller), leaving him with a Teutonic housekeeper on loan from the Luftwaffe who's clearly more preoccupied with strafing London than keeping her eye on an 11-year-old runaway. So I brought him home with me and we called Jody in Utica, who didn't seem to mind that it was 4:00 A.M. on a game day. Once he'd gotten Noah to stop crying, I put the kid to sleep on the couch in the den. (We still have his pajamas with the Martians on them, left over from his Continental Airlines caper last month.) This morning we made him pancakes with chocolate syrup and then he challenged Clayton to an arm-wrestling tournament. Clayton lost.

Charleen, this boy belongs with his father and everybody knows it. Even Judge Costanzo. So what are the chances we can swing a custody reversal in *Kessler vs. Kessler*?

6. Today is Barbra Streisand's birthday. After you dump Derek, go home and watch *Funny Girl*.

MCKENNA & WEBB
A LAW PARTNERSHIP
118 CONGRESS PARK, SUITE 407
SARATOGA SPRINGS, NEW YORK 12866

MEMORANDUM

TO: Craig
FROM: Charleen
DATE: They Call Me Second-Hand Rose
SUBJECT: Noah

You're forgetting Mueller Electronics and Mueller Shipyards and Mueller Communications and Mueller Entertainment. Craig, you don't seem to appreciate the kind of money we're dealing with here. Did you ever see their house lit up at night? The first time I drove by, I thought it was Syracuse.

The chances of a reversal? You're joking, right? The mother wears Halston originals, drives a Bentley, owns a Da Vinci, and plays the market. The father wears a jockstrap, drives a scooter, owns a Shell station, and plays first base. Relatively speaking, Craig? Dim. So count me in—but on two conditions: (1) You're *not* to leave me alone with Jody Kessler. He makes me very nervous. And (2) Go easy on Judge Costanzo. He's not going to be thrilled about this.

Ch

P.S. Clayton turns edgy whenever he's afraid you don't need him any more. The rest of the world learned that in 1979. Where were *you?*

McKenna & Webb
A Law Partnership
118 Congress Park, Suite 407
Saratoga Springs, New York 12866

Memorandum

TO:	Charleen
FROM:	Craig
DATE:	Color Me Barbra
SUBJECT:	Noah

---

1. In addition to being a terrific father, Jody's responsible, intelligent, kind, redoubtable, loyal, cavalier, hunky, and moral. I can see why that would put you off. Especially when he pulls degenerate stunts like leaving red roses under your windshield wiper.

2. All right. If it'll keep Costanzo happy, I won't sue the Pioneer Scouts again until July. *Early* July.

3. In 1979, I was asleep in Clayton's arms.

Craig McKenna   **Attorney Notes**

Things to Do
___ Don't bite off more than you can chew.

The only up side to the kind of day where you should have blown your brains out at 8:00 in the morning is driving your Miata through the sleepy elms that ring Loughberry Lake, knowing that in about ninety seconds you'll be pulling into the driveway of the two-bedroom-with-den that you've shared for twelve years with your very own Lancelot, who at this precise moment is waiting to fold you into his heart, kiss your troubled brow, and tell you that everybody in the world is wrong except you.

But he isn't there. The lights are still off and his Bronco is gone. So you fight off the disappointment, you remember how much you love him, and you take it in stride. *Fuck you! You're an asshole! I want a divorce!*

Then you find the note on the dining room table, the champagne glass with the forget-me-not in it, and the box containing a wedding band that had to cost at least three million dollars.

CLAYTON'S HARDWARE
serving Saratoga Springs since 1988

Honey:

You might as well go ahead and open this now. I wanted to give it to you in front of a fire, but I've gotta work late.

You'd better like it. I paid retail.

C

This is what we call romance, Clayton-style. And it comes in many flavors: When he popped for my thirtieth birthday trip to France, it was only to keep me from booking us on a cruise instead. ("I'm not gonna spend fourteen days watching three hundred horny guys look at you.") When we nearly got into a fistfight in the Ikea parking lot after I'd tried to buy us a king-sized mattress and he'd insisted on a double, his reasons turned out to be deceptively simple. ("The one place I'm not gonna lose you is in bed.") And when neither of us could afford the five days in Greece but we went anyway, it didn't have anything to do with the wonders of the Ancient World. ("I always wanted to make out with you in the Acropolis.")

One thing I learned a long time ago. Nobody argues with Clayton and wins.

> "There's this new judo-kind-of-thing called tai chi. I've got a class in twenty minutes."
>
> "Clayton, tai chi has been around for four thousand years."
>
> "Bullshit. I only heard about it in October."

Clayton wouldn't admit until our first anniversary that he'd begun scoping me out a solid two weeks before I'd ever set eyes on him without his football helmet. Not that I'd have noticed him anyway, since I already had my hands full trying to convince the Harvard athletic department that the 5-foot-8 walk-on wasn't a practical joke—and once the shock had worn off, they were actually willing to let me stick around until final cut, sort of as a consolation prize (not, however, with a straight face). That lasted until our third scrimmage, when I was lying on the bench working out a kink and an interior lineman accidentally sat on my head. ("You're easy to miss," he said by way of apology.) So when I claim that my career was cut short by a football injury, I'm telling the truth. As long as wounded pride counts.

What I hadn't learned during my four years as a Beckley gridiron celebrity was that, in the real world, they have a term for a player who's at least a foot and a half shorter than the rest of his squad: "lunch." Recreationally, I was a moving target; therapeutically, I also turned out to be terrific exercise for any jock who needed to stretch his rotator cuff by tossing me across the 50. So in both practice and theory, there was no reason to expect that I wouldn't eventually be removed from Soldier's Field in a Baggie—except that nobody ever got the chance. Instead, I'd find myself tearing toward the 10 with the ball under my arm and three pairs of pounding feet closing in on me like a pack of velociraptors that hadn't eaten since the Cretaceous Era, when suddenly—coming from the right—I'd hear an unexpected CRUNCH! and a SOCK! and a POW! and a "Get lost!" in rapid succession, and seconds later I'd turn up in the end zone—free, clear, and not bleeding. Though this happened a good half-dozen times, I never actually learned the identity of the tackle who'd appointed himself my own Han Solo—because in full uniform, he was indistinguishable from the Prudential Tower.

"How come you kept them from smithereening me when we didn't even know each other yet?"

"You never saw your ass in football pants. It would have been like letting them take a jackhammer to the Mona Lisa."

Clayton played hard-to-get right from the start. So I let him. When he pretended to be aloof, I was aloofer. When he went out of his way to avoid me, I avoided him first. When he'd greet me with a blunt "Hey, McKenna," he'd get an even blunter "Hey, Bergman" in return. Nothing makes him crazier than not having the upper hand. And once I'd figured that out, he was a marked man.

"Charleen, who's the hunk with the buzz cut?"

"Sssssh!" she hissed. "That's Clayton Bergman. He's from the Bronx, his father was a longshoreman, and he's straight."

"In your dreams," I whispered back. "Not with a body like *that*." It was the second week of freshman year, and we were sitting in the fifth row of a three hundred–seat amphitheater that passed for one of Harvard's smaller classrooms. Though I didn't learn the truth for months, Clayton had deliberately plunked himself squarely into my line of vision so I could watch him ignoring me for an hour. It worked.

"*Hannibal the Carthaginian defined modern warfare blah blah blah.*" Where did he get those shoulders? "*Not to be confused with Alexander the Great blah blah blah.*" He could pass for a war hero. *Any* war. I wonder what he'd look like in a tunic? Wrestling me. "*An ingenious military tactic called the phalanx blah blah blah.*" He's *got* to know I'm staring at him. The least he could do is stare back. "*Lessons learned the hard way during the Peloponnesian War blah blah blah.*" I wish I were dead.

After class, I made Charleen tag along with me as we followed him across Harvard Square. The issue confronting us was how to run into him accidentally so it didn't look like we were doing exactly what we were doing; of secondary concern was beating the traffic light across from the Coop before we lost him in the crowd. In the process, we caused a four-car pile-up—but that was only because Charleen lost a shoe while we were running from the oil tanker just before it veered away from us and plowed into the FedEx van parked in front of BayBanks.

"That's the end," she insisted as we caught our breath on the sidewalk next to the Wursthouse. "Effectively, unequivocally the end. Craig, I will *not* allow them to scrape me up from Mass Ave just so you can get laid!"

"Look! Look!" I cried, grabbing her arm and pointing half a block to the east. "He's going into Grendel's!" Charleen relaxed immediately as though the whole matter were settled.

"Perfect," she said briskly, getting her Darien, Connecticut, voice back. "They have a salad bar. Nobody's going to suspect a chance encounter over the endive." Yes! What did Travis used to say? The journey of a million miles begins with a single step.

The restaurant was jammed, but since neither one of us was hungry anyway, we picked up a couple of very small plates and waited until Clayton had reached the chick peas. Then we snuck in line behind him.

"Hey," I said, looking up in phony surprise as our arms bumped over the scallions. "I liked the way you took him to the mat about Hannibal. You really put the old fart in his place."

Clayton gave me the once-over like he was trying to figure out where he knew me from, while I made a point of not staring at the sexy stubble on his chin or the way his nose wrinkled up when he was deep-thinking. It was the longest three seconds of my life. Then he shrugged and said, "So?" And he left.

> *"Honey, if we could get married, would you do it?"*
>
> *"I don't believe in appropriating heterosexual rituals."*
>
> *"Not even if I got you a ring?"*
>
> *"Platinum?"*

Twenty minutes later, over coffee at the Greenhouse, I was examining four different ways of bumping myself off when Charleen looked up from a nonfat decaf double chocolate mocha and blurted, "Oh, shut up. Didn't you notice the way he was stringing you along until you looked away first? You couldn't have played into his hands any better if you'd called him Captain Butler and swooned into the dill. Men are so transparent." For just a second, all thoughts of lynching myself were put on hold while I leaned in to her urgently.

"Wait a minute," I demanded, "and think before you answer. You mean I have a *chance?*"

"I mean the ever-dwindling supply of heterosexual males just shrunk some more," she sighed.

"No, no," I assured her empathetically. "It shrunk a long time ago. You're just finding *out* about it now. What should I do?"

"Dish it right back to him," she ordered. "He's got it coming and *you* need a hobby. Besides, you haven't mentioned Travis in four hours."

Charleen and I had first met in the Freshman Union shortly after I'd unpacked my jockstraps and decided I hated my roommate, I hated my life, and I *despised* Boston. Truth to tell—and except for the roomie, who really *was* an asshole—I'd been moping around campus for three days, daring a broken heart to heal. (Nothing feels better than knowing you're the only guy since Romeo who figured out true love after he lost it.) His name was Travis and I'd met him in high school. At first I thought we were just buddies—until the third or fourth time I woke up naked and found him sleeping in my arms like a fucking angel. Duh. You don't have to hit *me* over the head.

"I just can't figure this out," I said, kissing him yet again.

"It's easy," he replied, kissing back. "You love me."

"Oh. Right." From there on it was the Craig and Travis Show—or vice versa depending on who wanted top billing. We got through final exams together, we invaded Manhattan together, we took summer jobs at Colony Records together, and we rented a one-room sublet on West 92nd Street together—with a tiny bed that was still way too big for just us. (That's where we figured out Chin-in-the-Neck and Falling-Asleep-Kissing, two separate routines that took a lot of practice.) It was only for eight weeks and I guess I should have seen the handwriting on the wall—but when you're 18, you always think it's going to last forever. It doesn't. Putting him on the plane to USC in September was the hardest thing I've ever had to do, especially with both of us pretending it was only temporary but deep down knowing otherwise. It felt like my whole life had ended before it had even geared up to start.

We sent each other goofy letters for a couple of weeks, but then he stopped writing to me. And Harvard didn't make it any better. Our freshman orientation advisor looked like Travis, the guy in the Coop walked like Travis, the guy in the cafeteria smiled like Travis, the guy in the library talked like Travis, and the guy on Mt. Auburn Street had a butt like Travis—except nobody in the world has a cuter one. It didn't make any sense. Fenway Park was around the corner. Carlton Fisk and my Red Sox were practically neighbors. But who cared? The boy who'd taken a piece of me with him was 2,988.2 miles away. Zip code to zip code.

Charleen was a different story. Tall and honey blonde, she'd escaped gleefully to Cambridge after a lifetime of recreational asphyxiation in Upson Downs, where she'd never quite managed to introduce her Connecticut half to her liberal half. (She showed up at her coming-out party dressed in 501s and a tank top. Darien is still reeling.) But when she plopped down next to me in the Union lounge, she wasn't in much better shape than I was.

"Look," she snapped, without preamble. "You're the seventh cute guy I've met since I got here. The other six had boyfriends. If you tell me the same thing, I'm going right out a window." Without glancing up, I sighed miserably—a soulful tremor that had "Montague" written all over it—and told her exactly what she didn't want to hear.

"I have an ex. Need a push?" So for the next two hours she got my Master's thesis on Travis; after that, we introduced ourselves.

Which is why Charleen was the perfect partner in crime. We were both single, we were both pre-law, and we both liked men. Nobody else could have piloted Project Clayton the way she did:

1. **Don't ever look at him again.**
   Right. This is the same as telling an 8-year-old kid not to think about a hippopotamus—particularly when the hippo in question is built like Knute Rockne, with 52-inch pecs and 17-inch arms and a raw masculine intensity that could power the entire eastern half of Massachusetts every time he sneezed. But I tried. It nearly killed me, but I tried.

2. **Wait until he's eating alone in the cafeteria, then don't sit with him.**
   An opportunity that presented itself at least once a day and four times on weekends. I'd make sure he saw me standing at the register with my tray, scoping out the room to see if I could find a buddy to join. At first he'd

turn his head away in advance, until he realized that I'd passed right by him and hadn't even noticed he was there. (By now my peripheral vision had become a sixth sense: I could walk a straight line and still tell you exactly what was happening behind me, provided I didn't collide with a wall while I was doing it.) This went on for less than a week before it really started to burn his ass. I could tell. Even peripherally.

3. Get yourself a study group and don't include him.
This was far more effective. Two weeks of extra-credit reports, theoretical analyses pulled out of my ass as I went along, and other more traditional brown-nosing tactics all paid off when the Psych 101 professor named me the head of group 3. In addition to Charleen, I chose four other students—the one sitting in front of Clayton, the one sitting to the left of Clayton, the one sitting to the right of Clayton, and the one sitting behind Clayton. Now he was getting pissed.

4. Create an event not to invite him to.
That one fell right into my lap when the Boathouse sponsored a dollar-a-brew talent night for any Harvard kid who thought he had an act. Even though I'd never actually performed in front of live people before (except for the boy who still owned my heart), I pulled out the acoustic guitar anyway, along with a set that—if not exactly calculated to give his testosterone a run for its money—would at least force him to pay attention (I hoped). Charleen and I ran off fifteen hundred fliers and handed them out to every professor and every freshman on campus. Except Clayton. He noticed.

5. Whatever you wear onstage, make it tight.
Try a sprayed-on T-shirt, sprayed-on jeans, Reeboks without socks, and no underpants.

"You think it's too much?" I asked Charleen apprehensively, just before I went on. She glanced down for a long moment.

"That depends," she finally replied. "What are you selling—circumcisions?"

6. *Let him have it.*

I'd figured on warming them up with a little Laura Nyro until I saw Clayton's silhouette leaning against the packed bar. There were maybe two hundred people crammed into the joint, but when I kicked in to "Light My Fire" instead, I was playing to an audience of one. And he knew it.

7. *Start reeling him in.*

Half an hour later, covered with sweat and holding my trophy, I ran into him staked out by the front door. We were face-to-face. Together at last. Neither of us said anything, but I swore I wasn't going to be the one to cave. So he didn't have much of a choice.

"Not bad," he grunted. I gave him the once-over like I was trying to figure out where I knew him from. Then I shrugged and said, "Thanks." And I left.

"How come you stopped trying to get into my pants?"

"Because it was easier getting into Harvard. *And my mom said you deserved to squirm."*

"Your mother hates me."

"Come on, Clay! What did she ever do to make you think that?"

"She told me so. There wasn't any guesswork involved."

I knew I was making progress a few days later when he bumped into me in the Co-op and mentioned this tai chi class he was taking. He didn't actually invite me to it, but it was the *way* he didn't invite me that got me to go along with him—and to suspect that maybe he'd arranged the whole encounter. (I was right.) And within a week we were sitting together in the cafeteria and seeing *Casablanca* at the Brattle Theater and having brief but meaningful conversations over fries and cream sodas at the Tasty.

"You ever been whitewater rafting?" he asked hesitantly (managing to avoid my eyes while he was doing it—which I loved).

"No."

"Oh."

But it was the riot that clinched things.

"Remember our first time?"

"Like I wouldn't? December 7, 1978. Harvard Yard. You were singing 'Blowin' in the Wind' and I had a hard-on."

"I didn't even know you were there."

"The hell you didn't."

Right around Thanksgiving, San Francisco supervisor Harvey Milk and Mayor George Moscone were shot and killed by a twinked-out homophobe named Dan White. By the time we'd gotten back to Cambridge after the holiday (Charleen and I had done the turkey thing in Aryan Darien), White's attorneys were already planning an involuntary manslaughter defense by implying that Milk was just a queer who didn't rate a murder rap for their client. Now, if it hadn't been for Travis, I might have slept through news like that the same way I'd slept through most of my life before I'd met him. But he was the one who'd taught me about getting mad and getting even—all you had to say to him was "Anita Bryant" and his ears stayed red for three days. Now it was *my* turn.

"This is bullshit," I blurted in the middle of Philosophy 108. "What's this got to do with what's happening in San Francisco?" The prof, an old guy in his forties who was used to this kind of thing, stopped dead in his tracks halfway through one of Plato's tired old dialogues and tried to keep it light.

"As it pertains to Ovid?" he asked with his constipated grin and the usual stick up his ass. I could hear a couple of snickers in the amphitheater, but so what? Let 'em laugh. Right, Trav?

"No, goddammit! Those guys have been dead for two thousand years. Who have we had since then except Eleanor Roosevelt and John Lennon? Okay, look—" By now I was really getting up a good head of steam. "There's straight people and there's the rest of us. I'm not asking for a new Bill of Rights, but I want some answers. This is Philosophy, isn't it?" From the back of the room, a kid wearing an Indiana T-shirt began to clap slowly, and then a guy on the rowing team stood up.

"He's right," he said. "Me and my boyfriend got the shit kicked out of us in Marblehead and all we were doing was linking pinkies on the beach. What's *that* all about?"

"Yeah," said another. "The same thing happened to us in Gloucester."

"Shut the fuck up and sit down," said a third. "If you don't like it, go back to Provincetown where you belong." And that pretty much did it for Plato and Ovid and the remainder of the toga club. By the end of the class I had a B+ in Philosophy and twenty-three freshmen of every orientation imaginable crowded in a circle around me as though Ann Landers had grown a dick. *Nice going, McKenna.* Now *what?* So rather than own up to the fact that I was an ordinary fraud with a big mouth, I just pretended to be Travis and said the first thing that popped into my head: Harvey Milk had believed in dignity for everyone, so we were going to honor him with the same kind of respect. We'd celebrate his life with a rock concert in his memory, and we wouldn't stop singing until Dan White found his sorry ass behind bars for the next 120 years. *Craig, dude—where is this* coming *from?* As I watched them tumble out of the room with an energy that hadn't been there before, I turned to Charleen, mystified.

"Uh—what just happened here?" I asked mildly.

"You're a troublemaker," she replied with a smirk. "I *knew* it!"

(P.S. I'd been doing the peripheral thing from force of habit and noticed that Clayton hadn't taken his eyes off of me for forty-five minutes. But for once I didn't give a shit. Much.)

Charleen squared everything with Harvard, though it wasn't easy. After they found out what the concert was about, they didn't want to give us the Yard between Memorial Church and Widener Library—until Charleen began shooting off her mouth about civil liberties violations and de facto discrimination and wouldn't it be unfortunate if the *Boston Globe* got their hands on a story like that? (When Charleen puts her mind to it, she can be a bigger pain in the ass than I can.) Within an hour and a half, she had a permit, a stage, eighteen speakers, four electricians, and the phone number of a hunky little math major she'd met in the elevator.

The night of the concert was practically tropical by Boston standards: 41 degrees and dropping. (Of course, had I known I was going to wind up stripped down to my underpants, I might have been more cautious. But I didn't, so I wasn't.) Thanks to Charleen, who'd blabbed to the *Globe* anyway, we'd lined up eight solid acts from the student body and two real ones: a first-ever reunion of Buffalo Springfield and the eternally subversive prodding of Crosby, Stills, Nash & Young. (Let's face it. How much consciousness were we really going to raise on Craig McKenna and his magic guitar?) I thought it was kind of fitting that our Harvey Milk tribute was taking place in front of a church—an irony that wasn't lost on the Archdiocese of Boston either. So in response to their hate mail, we gave them a free ad in our program.

The corps of forty-five hundred cheering Harvard kids sardined into the cozy confines of the Yard represented nearly twice the turnout we'd expected (the prospect of free rock and roll inspires temporary idealism in many)—and by the time Buffalo Springfield had brought down the house with "For What It's Worth," word had spread to Kenmore Square, where two thousand future alumni from B.U. were jamming the "T" and heading for Cambridge as well. While Grid Tarbell and His Dunster Funsters were blasting John Mayall's "Room to Move" into flinders, we were joined by another eight hundred from MIT. And the Boston College contingent showed up at the tail-end of my Dylan set—just in time to see me curl my lip into a sneer, twitch my ass, and direct "I Want You" to a well-muscled Travolta lookalike in the front row. (Subtlety, as ever, has rarely been a compulsory part of my act.)

And that's when it happened.

I was in the middle of my third bow—the glare of the arc lights silhouetting thousands of my screaming public against the stately old ruins called Harvard—when some hothead from the Student Freedom League chose that moment to take the stage and announce that we needed a human symbol to show that we weren't going to tolerate the violence any more. The only question was who. Then an obviously horny Travolta shouted it out from down front.

"Dylan! Strip Dylan!"

"Yeah! What about Dylan! This whole thing was his idea anyway." If I hadn't been preoccupied with a popped E string, I might have had time to react before it was too late. *Sure, sure, Dylan. Jesus, it's getting cold. If I could—DYLAN?!* Horrified, I looked up wildly just in time to see Grid and the Funsters pounce gleefully on top of me—and the next thing I knew, my clothes had been yanked off, I'd been doused with ersatz blood (disguised as Hunt's ketchup), and some schmuck from Accounting 108 had chained me to a pillar in front of Widener Library as the living emblem that we'd had our fill of blind justice. Naturally, I was outraged—the least they could have done was ask first. But I also recognized an easy audience when I saw one, so I added a touch of my own.

"Fuck you, Dan White!" I shrieked, to no one in particular. They went nuts. (What the hell. I hadn't canonized Joan Baez and Woody Guthrie for nothing.) The effect was electrifying. Nine thousand people holding lit candles for Harvey Milk crowded around us while Graham Nash sang "Teach Your Children" to my tattered body. If I hadn't been freezing to death, my hair would have been standing straight on end.

However, by that time word had also reached Jamaica Plain, where five hundred rednecks had piled into their vehicles, carrying bottles and sticks and anything else they could throw. And it only took them nineteen minutes to reach the Square.

The first Molotov cocktail exploded just as we were chanting "Carry On" with David Crosby and Stephen Stills. Thinking it was probably a practical joke, nobody paid much attention until the fire began spreading across the Yard. Then a brick hit someone in the chest and the real panic started. Stills and Nash grabbed their mikes and begged the crowd to stay calm, but by then it was way too late—kids were bleeding, rocks were flying, and Harvard Yard had turned into Okinawa, Part II. Meanwhile, I was still chained to a fucking pillar in my blue-and-white striped Jockeys and I couldn't break free. If it hadn't been for an uncharacteristically ruffled Charleen muscling her way past two truck drivers and a stevedore, I might still be hanging there.

"Good Lord, what have you gotten yourself into *now?*" she demanded impatiently, attacking the chains. With my body temperature down to 16 degrees, I was in no mood to be ragged on.

"Get me out of here," I snapped.

"Where's the key?"

"*What* key?"

"To the padlock."

"There's a *padlock?!?*"

Once she'd worked my hands loose enough to slip me out of the damned thing, I grabbed her wrist and dragged her through the mob toward the Mass Ave gate, just as the first SWAT team showed up. There was only one impediment standing between me and my goal: a large individual with a beer belly and a bullet head who was occupying most of the real estate in the Yard.

"Excuse me," I said.

"Fucking faggot," he replied, smashing his fist into my face. I cocked my right arm back to return the favor—but since he was at least twice my size, what resulted was a significantly unimpressive jab to his left tit which he probably didn't even feel when he again attempted to eject my lower jaw onto Holyoke Street. I'd barely had time to topple over backward under the boots of eleven different assailants before I dimly heard an unexpected CRUNCH! and a SOCK! and a POW! and a "Get lost!" in rapid succession. And just as I was losing consciousness, I was pulled to my feet by the strongest pair of arms I'd ever felt in my life. Even without peripheral vision, I knew they had to be Clayton's and that nothing was going to hurt me now—so I grinned groggily to myself and then I blacked out.

> "I said no. If you start one more riot, we're finished."
>
> "Clayton, three hundred people are dead, and Reagan's head is still up his ass!"
>
> "You're gonna have to make a choice."
>
> "I hope you don't mean this."

"Ouch."

When I opened my eyes again, I was lying on his bed in Lionel Hall, wrapped in a blanket and trying to figure out which part of me hurt the least. He'd already checked my arms and legs to make sure nothing was broken, and now he was wiping the blood off my forehead with a rolled-up Purdue T-shirt. *Let's see. The last thing I remember is—*

"Charleen," I croaked in a panic, beginning to rise. But Clayton pushed me back down onto a pillow that smelled just like he did.

"Recovering with a double chocolate mocha at the Greenhouse."

"Nonfat?" I asked weakly.

"And decaf." By now his little finger was somehow stroking my chin too. God only knows why. I must have looked like shit and stunk like ketchup.

"Schmuck," he said, in the quietest voice I ever heard him use. "See what happens when you shoot off your mouth?"

"*Somebody* has to do it," I replied, feeling for broken teeth and inexplicably tasting pineapple.

"Then leave it to the other guys. You're too short to make waves." I pushed his hand away and struggled to sit up.

"You know what?" I shot back, letting him have it with both barrels. "In case nobody clued you in, there's a war going on and we're *all* soldiers. Anita Bryant kicked us out of Dade County and John Briggs tried to pull the same crap in California and if we don't start covering each other's asses—"

So Clayton did the only thing he could think of to shut me up. He kissed me.

"Hey."

"Hey."

"You look great."

"So you do."

"Have coffee with me?"

"Are you going to ask me to move back in?"

"Only if you don't ask first."

After that, it all happened pretty quickly. By Christmas it was so unlikely that you'd see either one of us without the other, we were known all over campus, at various times, as the big one and the little one, the agitator and the bruiser, and (my own personal favorite) the prince and the pea. Fortunately, we'd gotten the falling in love part out of the way during the eight weeks we'd been ignoring each other, so we were able to save a little time and cut to the chase: (a) who buys more Rice Krispies when we run out; (b) who turns off the alarm clock when it rings; and (c) who says I'm sorry first. It was usually (c) that gave us the most trouble, because you just don't put two hard-headed guys together and expect the Cleavers to happen. Charleen was the only one who could spot the primary warning sign: If I wasn't wearing Clayton's Cornell sweatshirt, it meant there were typhoons in Paradise.

"*Princeton?!*" she'd shriek in mock horror. "What are you fighting about *now*?" But nobody needed to be loved more than my boyfriend did. When the father he'd idolized had found out his kid liked men, he'd thrown him out of the house bodily. ("You make me sick," he'd said, slamming the door on his only son.) Clayton never sufficiently recovered, especially after the old man died. Instead, he inherited a legacy that became his trademark: *If it looks like they're going to dump you, beat them to it. It saves a lot of wear and tear on the heart.* So I never allowed our skirmishes to get in the way for long. Bundled up against the cold, we'd walk along the Charles River at 1:00 in the morning holding hands. (Bashers tended to stay away from Clayton. One "faggot" and they'd be hunting for their teeth in the dark.) After moving into our microscopic two-room apartment on Concord Street, we'd spend hours at a time painting the walls and each other—initially by accident and then deliberately. (It was a *great* excuse for taking a shower together at 1:30 in the afternoon. And 2:15. And 3:05.) And even on Princeton nights, I'd always fall asleep curled up in his arms.

Our routine was established pretty quickly: he'd make the

coffee and I'd watch. I'd drop off the laundry and he'd pick it up. He'd insist on HBO and I'd switch to the Red Sox. I'd put on "Subterranean Homesick Blues" and he'd groan. He'd go to class and I'd write a brief. (Once in a while, he'd call me at lunch time if he couldn't decide between a shrimp salad sandwich or a turkey on rye, but mostly he just felt like hearing my voice.) At night, after we'd made dinner together, I'd read him what I'd written and he'd tell me what needed work. Then I'd stop speaking to him for two days until he dragged me to Pogo's for a burger. (Note: Pogo's is where we always made up, 33 Dunster is where we celebrated his birthday, the Union Oyster House is where we consecrated mine, and Grendel's is where we had dessert on our anniversary. These establishments were off-limits at all other times.) Once I'd gotten him to apologize for hurting my feelings, I'd wait a week and then make every change he'd suggested, hoping that by then he'd have forgotten it was all his idea. He hadn't.

So except for a three-and-a-half-year misunderstanding that we got out of the way early, we haven't had to look back since 1986. When Charleen and I decided to go into practice together the same week that Clay found a bankrupt hardware store and 125 available acres in Saratoga Springs, it was a done deal. And for some reason, I couldn't help thinking of Travis—because whenever he was really happy, he'd always quote Ethel Merman:

"Who could ask for anything more?"

> *"I don't want you marching on Washington. What if something happens to you?"*
>
> *"Clay, nothing's going to happen to me if you come too. We'll stay at the Shoreham in Room 626, and we'll have dinner at Pierre's and you'll hate the Cajun shrimp so I'll eat it instead, and then we'll go for a walk by the Tidal Basin so I can sing something dopey from 'Bye Bye Birdie' and you can tell me to shut up."*
>
> *"I'm trying to pick a fight here. You're not making it easy."*
>
> *"That's my job."*

It *was* platinum. And he paid retail.
(Grin.)

4

Travis

UNIVERSITY OF SOUTHERN CALIFORNIA

UNIVERSITY PARK · LOS ANGELES, CALIFORNIA 90007

Doheny Library
Faculty Research Request

DATE: <u>May 4, 1998</u>   FROM: <u>Travis Puckett</u>

DEPARTMENT: <u>History</u>   BUILDING/ROOM: <u>VKC/223</u>

MATERIALS NEEDED

SPECIAL INSTRUCTIONS

Julian: I'm sorry. Please please please please *please* try dinner with me again. I promise that no matter what happens we'll at least make it to the restaurant. See, it's an old Toyota and the manual says a 50,000-mile tune-up and if we hadn't been lucky enough to find a garage that stayed open late, the timing belt could have gone out at 50,001. Actually, it's pretty amusing when you think about it.

No, Travis. Bette Midler is amusing. Lea DeLaria is hysterical. Handling a grease gun in a $129 Armani shirt doesn't even come close.

By the way—a kiss might have been a good idea. Even narcissists have feelings. (I can't believe I'm leading you on. . . .)

FROM THE JOURNAL OF
Travis Puckett

Our first real date—after the preliminary Starbucks let's-pretend-we're-not-thinking-about-each-other-naked summit—was a casual lunch that only took me three days to get ready for. He chose an open-air café on Santa Monica Boulevard that specialized in avocado-and-cilantro sandwiches, two ingredients that, even individually, render the concept of induced vomiting obsolete. But Julian was so dazzling in his snug white T-shirt and one-dimple grin, I ate a pair of them and actually managed to stay away from a bathroom for almost an hour.

"Are you okay?"

"I'll be out in a minute."

Two days later we went to Our First Movie, where we held hands and let our feet play with each other and I bought him more popcorn when he tried to eat mine before the previews started. (Incidentally, the three-fifths-of-the-way-back-on-the-aisle rule suffered its first veto in twenty-three years: Julian won't sit anywhere except the middle row, smack in the center—but I could learn to love that if I had to.)

On our third date, I took him to Dodger Stadium during a home stand with the Mets. By the top of the ninth, New York was leading 2–0, Benitez was pitching a no-hitter, and we'd both decided we'd rather have sex with Eric Karros than Todd Hundley.

Date Number 4 was an unmitigated disaster, and by mutual consent we agreed that we'd never mention it again.

But the fifth date was the charm. We were on our way to Dan Tana's for seafood risotto and another two hours of shameless flirting, when he suddenly leaned over the hand brake and kissed me. Happily, there were no pedestrians on the sidewalk when I jumped the curb and rammed a gas pump—and after I'd paid $300 for the cracked hose with my Shell credit card, Julian put his hand on my ass and asked me to turn the car around. That's when I learned that it's really not a good idea to drive a stick shift while you're hyperventilating.

"Move the car, you fucking asshole!"

Oh, yeah. The seafood risotto never happened. We had bigger fish to fry.

~

Hours later, his head was resting blissfully on my shoulder as we bathed in the scarlet glow of a red lava lamp manufactured a good year before he was born and at least nine years after I was.

"Travis?"

"Mmmmm?"

"We aren't really going to fall asleep like this, are we?"

"Don't you want to wake up in my arms?"

"Do I have to?" Not that it matters, but Julian hates being held. Instead, he turns away and curls himself up into a little ball, just like a cuddly hamster without the cuddling.

I could learn to love that, too.

TRAVIS PUCKETT'S BOYFRIEND CHECKLIST

Name: Julian Brennan   **Duration:** 2 weeks so far
Occupation: USC Librarian   **Where we met:** Over microfiche

Beginner Level

___ Can say "I love you"
✓ Isn't hiding another boyfriend
✓ Thinks kissing is sexy
✓ Has a glowy smile
✓ Is at least marginally sensitive
✓ Will probably remember my name the next morning

Intermediate Level

___ Can say "I love you" without my saying it first
___ Likes me enough to tell me I'm special
✓ Trusts me enough to tell me I'm wrong
___ Always lets me pick the first fortune cookie
✓ Teases me when I need it but knows when to stop
___ Pursues making me laugh as a hobby
___ Pretends to like the same things I do even when he doesn't
✓ Misses me when we're apart
✓ Isn't afraid to fight with me
✓ Allows me to drive him crazy
___ Would rather do nothing with me than something by himself
___ Can fall asleep in my lap while I work—and still call it a date

Top-of-the-Line Level

___ Can say "I love you" with his eyes
___ Never lies (except to spare my feelings)
___ Doesn't worry about losing me because he knows he can't
___ Forgets there was a time when we didn't know each other
___ Kisses me for no good reason
✓ Celebrates my faults
___ Sighs when I hold him
___ Knows all the lyrics to *Flora, The Red Menace* (optional)

Strong Points: Looks like a puppy when he pouts.

Shortcomings: Pouts too much.

Comments: We're getting there.

Vidiots

Santa Monica's Favorite Video Store

CUSTOMER: Travis Puckett **ACCOUNT NO.:** 7643757
DATE OUT: May 6, 1998 **DATE DUE:** May 7, 1998

....

TITLES

I WANNA HOLD YOUR HAND   2.99

TOTAL   2.99

....

THANK YOU FOR RENTING FROM VIDIOTS

Tell Gordo we said Hi. And how come he doesn't
come in anymore? Cherie.

FROM THE DESK OF
Gordon Duboise

T:

Suppose you liked girls. Suppose you found yourself being chased by a 19-year-old knockout who was also brainy and funny—and who wasn't (a) psychotic, (b) chemically dependent, (c) on the lam, or (d) a studio executive. Would you stop to remember that you were twice as old as she was, or would you ignore the whole problem and elope to Tahoe?

I need an answer quick. Once our clothes come off, it's out of my hands.

G

P.S. Leave your verdict on my desk. Mona and I won't be out of the bedroom until at least Thursday. (She's the *other* one I might marry. How am I supposed to know for sure unless I try them both out first?)

FROM THE JOURNAL OF
Travis Puckett

G:

You might as well. The last time you corked somebody half your age, we were 32. At least we won't have to worry about the Child Welfare Department this time.

You're hopeless. How do these people *find* you?

T

BEWARE!

You have just entered

GordoStud.com

home page of

GORDON DUBOISE
screenwriter/lover/bon vivant

[ ] Click here to find out more about me

[ ] Click here for a list of my credits

[ ] Click here to find out if I'm available for work

[ ] Click here to find out if I'm available for play

[ ] Click here for pictures of me in my Speedos

[ ] Click here for information on my next party
(romantic women only)

[ ] Click here to send me e-mail

[ ] Click here to post a message on my bulletin board
(keep it sensitive––I have a poetic heart)

BULLETIN BOARD

Dear Gordo,
Thanks for the pictures. Is all of that *you*? If so, send more.
—Sue in Milwaukee

Dear Gordo,
I'm 23, I have big tits, I'm working on my master's, and I could suck the filament out of a lightbulb without breaking the glass. Let me know if you're ever going to be in Georgia and I'll show you.

—Rae Ellen in Atlanta

Dear Pig,
You're disgusting. If you ever got out of the 1970s, you might learn that they made this really incredible discovery: women actually have something more to offer than a dust rag and a hole. Assuming you have any brains, you might consider taking them out of your dick.

—Liz in Chicago

Dude.
I know it says Girls Only, but I've got a really creative mouth and I'm in L.A. too. Think about it.

—Blowbuddy

Gordon:
This is your father. I've been trying to reach you for three days, but the goddamned line is always busy. Universal should only know why.

If I don't have a finished script in two weeks, you'd better see if Blowbuddy is willing to pay you, because nobody else will.

FROM THE DESK OF
Gordon Duboise

Pop:

Take your pick:

1. Two sportswriters, boy and girl. Hate each other on sight but fall in love anyway.
2. Bad boy meets bad girl. When they fall in love, they turn good. (Somebody dies in this one.)
3. Boy and girl meet in college, sleep together, it doesn't work. So they marry other people but wind up together anyway.
4. Secret agent falls in love with pretty woman who convinces him he's fighting for the wrong side.

ARGOSY ENTERTAINMENT
Literary Representatives

LOS ANGELES   TORONTO
NEW YORK   LONDON

Gordon:

1. *Woman of the Year*
2. *Rebel Without a Cause*
3. *When Harry Met Sally*
4. *Casablanca,* for Christ's sake

Gordon, how difficult could it be? People are falling in love all the time! Listen to Liz in Chicago and get your brains out of your dick. Remember that old TV show? Seven million tales in the Naked City, and one of them could be happening right under your nose.

UNIVERSITY OF SOUTHERN CALIFORNIA
UNIVERSITY PARK · LOS ANGELES, CALIFORNIA 90007

Doheny Library
Faculty Research Request

DATE: <u>May 8, 1998</u>   FROM: <u>Travis Puckett</u>
DEPARTMENT: <u>History</u>   BUILDING/ROOM: <u>VKC/223</u>

MATERIALS NEEDED

SPECIAL INSTRUCTIONS
Julian: The beach in Santa Barbara would be a lot less lonesome if we were holding hands on it. What do you think?

You're not listening to me. Do you know what my idea of romance is? A blowjob between the salad and the entree. You need a real boyfriend. I'm not him.

P.S. And stop staring at my ass while I'm working. Don't you have a class to teach?

<u>American History 206</u>
Professor Puckett
May 8, 1998

Final Exam Review Questions

Guys: If you can pull this one off, you shouldn't have any problems with the real thing.

1. Alexander Hamilton was about as popular as a piranha at a skinny dip. Yet without him we wouldn't be here. Whom

does he most resemble and why? (Note: I'll accept a wrong answer if you can persuade me.)

    (a) Branch Rickey

    (b) Curt Flood

    (c) Jim Bouton

    (d) Bob Gibson

2. Benedict Arnold and the 1919 White Sox had a lot in common. They were both called traitors, yet they both did what they believed was right, given the gross inequities of the system. How would the Series have ended if the Black Sox had been managed by Arnold instead of by Kid Gleason?

3. Two of the most significantly related landmarks in U.S. history are Independence Hall and Fenway Park. Choose another pair and state your reasons:

    (a) Saratoga and Shea Stadium

    (b) Valley Forge and Ebbets Field

    (c) Fort McHenry and the Polo Grounds

4. Pick a Revolutionary War All-Star team that includes General Dan Morgan behind the plate and spitball pitcher Benjamin Franklin on the mound. Then pit them against the 1911 New York Giants. Box scores, please.

5. I've been dating this guy for almost three weeks and I really like him. (I could be wrong, but I think he feels the same way.) How long should I wait before I ask him to wear my ring?

Final Exam Review Answers
Tony Norris

5. Nobody asks people to wear their ring anymore. Who have you been talking to? When I started getting serious about Maggie she knew it because I did things like fix her tires

and not notice the zit on her chin and stop fucking other girls. I'm guessing it works the same way with guys.

Chuck Navarro

5. You know what your problem is? You're too much of a tightass. Go back to Question 1 about Alexander Hamilton. "Whom does he most resemble and why?" Travis, people say "who" not "whom" and nobody gives a shit whether it's right or not. If you like this guy, pop him. What the hell are you waiting for?

Gary Petrie

5. Don't take this the wrong way, but this is the first time in my life I ever used the word cornball. Trav, it's 1998. If you really want to score points, give him some stock options instead.

Ray Sorren

5. What do we look like—Dear Fucking Abby? I'll make a deal with you. If I tell you how to get laid, I get an A. No questions asked. And the same goes for all the other guys too, except for Hatten, who never should have been put in at the end of the fourth quarter with only nineteen seconds left on the clock.

Doug Hatten

5. You want to know how to sweep this guy off his feet? Take everything Sorren says and do exactly the opposite. He wouldn't know a lateral pass from a Coke machine if he got hit in the head by both of them. P.S. You're not acting dopey enough to be in love. Trust me on this.

Corey Gambel

5. Never ever ever ever ever give them a ring when you're horny, because you'll only wind up trying to get it back later when it's way too late. (I made that mistake soph year

with an economics major named Sandy and she's still stalking me.) Do you really love him? If the answer is yes, then go for it.

UNIVERSITY OF SOUTHERN CALIFORNIA
UNIVERSITY PARK • LOS ANGELES, CALIFORNIA 90007

TO: Travis Puckett
FROM: Andrea Fox
DATE: May 11, 1998
RE: Good News

Travis:

Marsha Holmes of the Poli-Sci department overheard two football players in the hallway arguing about *The Federalist Papers* and agreed to push Dean Koutrelakos for the grant. ("My God, Andrea—jocks who think! Imagine the possibilities!") And the only time Koutrelakos ever ignored Marsha's advice was when he lost $2,000 betting against Michigan in the Rose Bowl. So we may have another shot at this after all.

I tried calling your office to let you know, but they said you were at the library again. Travis, don't work yourself too hard.

Andrea

UNIVERSITY OF SOUTHERN CALIFORNIA
UNIVERSITY PARK · LOS ANGELES, CALIFORNIA 90007

Doheny Library
Faculty Research Request

DATE: <u>May 11, 1998</u>   FROM: <u>Travis Puckett</u>
DEPARTMENT: <u>History</u>   BUILDING/ROOM: <u>VKC/223</u>

MATERIALS NEEDED

SPECIAL INSTRUCTIONS
Julian: I have something a little scary to ask you, but it can only be done over dinner with French wine. Tomorrow?

Oh, no. This has "marriage" written all over it. Travis, read my lips: remember that Fellini film with the prostitute who says that every new sunrise makes her a virgin? It doesn't work that way with me. Even the sun thinks I'm a slut.

FROM THE JOURNAL OF
Travis Puckett

THE PUCKETT/DUBOISE DEBATES

GORDO: I just don't get it. He's skinny, he never smiles, and he doesn't have a sense of humor. Who introduced you guys—Dracula?

TRAVIS: Hand me the oregano.

GORDO: Are you listening to me?

TRAVIS: No. I wanted to pop the question at Le Petit Chalet, but at those prices I'd have to take out a loan against my T-bill—

GORDO: Wear the pink shirt with the red and blue tie. You look good in that.

TRAVIS: If I can just get him to move in with me—

GORDO: Travis, never bring up living together until the tenth date. It doesn't work.

TRAVIS: How would *you* know?

GORDO: Tried it once on a flight attendant. She went running out of my bedroom like a fan jet blew up.

Cardinal Rule Number 2—Nothing's worse for your equilibrium than a best friend who tells you the truth.

Okay, so Julian isn't perfect. I'm not either. I line up my peas. I rotate my socks. I have rules about toilet paper. Who could fall in love with that?! Besides, nobody ever said it was easy, and I've got the proof: I'm 37 years old and I've had four root canals I didn't need. Along with twenty-six broken hearts and another dozen near-misses.

But this time I'm going to make it work. What the hell am I waiting for?

Le Petit Chalet

Les Spécialités de la Maison

Pâté Maison   65.00
Your choice of our special homemade pâtés

Feuillete de Poulet et Champignons   25.00
Succulent chicken in a special mushroom sauce with puff pastry shell

Feuillete d'Oeufs, Jambon et Fromage   22.00
Piquant marriage of egg, ham, and cheese in puff pastry shell

Salade Niçoise   25.00
Mediterranean salad of tuna, potatoes, tomatoes, olives, and anchovies

Pasta Provençale   28.00
Tangy tomatoes, onions, tarragon, and fresh basil

Onglet à l'échalote   36.00
Savory skirt steak with shallot sauce and fried potatoes

Saumon Provençal   38.00
Zesty and grilled with broccoli

Our Orchestra Is Pleased to Welcome
Those Couples in Love

Cheek to Cheek

It Only Takes a Moment

I Get a Kick Out of You

Chances Are

They Say It's Wonderful

Embraceable You

Almost Like Being in Love

FROM THE JOURNAL OF
Travis Puckett

$38 FOR FISH?! Are these people out of their fucking minds?! What do they put in the cream sauce—plutonium? And get this: $9 for verre d'eau. Know what that means in English? Glass of water! "Our orchestra is pleased to welcome those couples in love." Yeah? For $38, you'd better *blow* me.

I can't believe they played that song. Out of eighteen million songs they could have picked, they had to play *that* one. This was an ambush. I'd barely had time to finish a $14 dinner roll and take Julian's hand to keep him from cruising Apollo at the next table when the ass-kissing orchestra chose that moment to ruin my life with "Almost Like Being in Love." Twenty years I've gotten away without hearing it. Twenty! And now I know why. It was like the prince kissing Snow White—when I woke up, Julian had evaporated, the ring was still on my finger, and I couldn't even taste the $25 bowl of soup.

Craig.

Craig with the crinkly eyes and Craig who invented the single dimple and Craig who called me Smerko and Craig who taught me about cookie fights and Craig who never laughed at my popcorn and Craig who found a thousand other ways to say "I love you" without using any words. And we let it slip away from us. Just like that. *Why do they entrust youth to kids?!*

Somebody ought to kick my ass. How bright do you have to be?

TRAVIS PUCKETT'S BOYFRIEND CHECKLIST

Name: Craig McKenna   **Duration:** 20 years
Occupation: I don't know   **Where we met:** Brigadoon

BEGINNER LEVEL

- ✓ Can say "I love you"
- ✓ Isn't hiding another boyfriend
- ✓ Thinks kissing is sexy
- ✓ Has a glowy smile
- ✓ Is at least marginally sensitive
- ✓ Will probably remember my name the next morning

INTERMEDIATE LEVEL

- ✓ Can say "I love you" without my saying it first
- ✓ Likes me enough to tell me I'm special
- ✓ Trusts me enough to tell me I'm wrong
- ✓ Always lets me pick the first fortune cookie
- ✓ Teases me when I need it but knows when to stop
- ✓ Pursues making me laugh as a hobby
- ✓ Pretends to like the same things I do even when he doesn't
- ✓ Misses me when we're apart
- ✓ Isn't afraid to fight with me
- ✓ Allows me to drive him crazy
- ✓ Would rather do nothing with me than something by himself
- ✓ Can fall asleep in my lap while I work—and still call it a date

TOP-OF-THE-LINE LEVEL

- ✓ Can say "I love you" with his eyes
- ✓ Never lies (except to spare my feelings)
- ✓ Doesn't worry about losing me because he knows he can't
- ✓ Forgets there was a time when we didn't know each other
- ✓ Kisses me for no good reason
- ✓ Celebrates my faults
- ✓ Sighs when I hold him
- ___ Knows all the lyrics to *Flora, The Red Menace* (optional)

Strong Points: All of them.

Shortcomings: Nothing I can't handle.

Comments: He was the real thing. Find him.

5

Craig

Noah Kessler
6026 Foxhound Run
Saratoga Springs, New York 12866

May 12, 1998

ATTORNEY-CLIENT COMMUNICATION

Craig McKenna, Esq.
McKenna & Webb
118 Congress Park, Suite 407
Saratoga Springs, New York 12866

Dear Craig,

I think my stepfather is a Nazi. I even had to learn projectile
vomiting in case he starts goose-stepping. Mostly I wait until
he puts on Wagner and then I let it fly. And he wants me to call
him Pop-Pop. Gag me.

Also Frau Schneller is one too. At night when she thinks I'm asleep she calls Berlin and talks in code. She's a bad influence. She sings "Liebowitz" in the shower. I don't think I should be left alone with her while my mother and the Brown Shirt are in Hamburg.

If we tell these things to a judge, will they let me live with my father?

Noah

P.S. What if they take me to Germany with them next time? Maybe they'll turn me into a Storm Trooper.

McKenna & Webb

A Law Partnership

118 Congress Park, Suite 407

Saratoga Springs, New York 12866

May 14, 1998

ATTORNEY-CLIENT COMMUNICATION

Mr. Noah Kessler
6026 Foxhound Run
Saratoga Springs, New York 12866

Dear Noah:

First of all, it's "Lieberstrum." Second of all, Frau Schneller isn't talking in code and you know it—that's German. Third of all, I agree that "Pop-Pop" is pretty barfy, but do the best you can. Fourth of all, your stepfather's crazy about you. But fifth of all, we're going back to court anyway to see if we can kick some butt this time. I can't promise you anything, but if your dad can hit one out of the park with a pulled hamstring, we ought to be able to do the same thing without one.

So stop puking on the walls.

Guess who loves you? (a) Your father. (b) Me. (c) Clayton. (d) Charleen. (e) All of the above.

Craig

Craig McKenna   **Attorney Notes**

Interview with Jody Kessler
5/18/98

- Met with client at his Shell station in Utica.

- Helped client change a universal joint.

- Fought with client about the Bill Buckner error in the 1986 Series. Client maintains it was Buckner's fault that the winning run crossed the plate. Attorney argued that if somebody with half a brain had pulled Schiraldi off the mound before he'd given up the nine thousand singles, there wouldn't have been anybody on base to score in the first place.

- Client threatened to kick attorney's ass.

- Facts of case were discussed. Client claims he lost the custody battle in 1997 because he washed the socks he'd gone 4-for-4 in. Attorney argued that the stench wouldn't have been a viable alternative either.

- Meeting was interrupted when client received a telephone call from his son, which lasted almost an hour. Among the issues discussed: a second Little League trophy, Beavis and Butthead, people living on Jupiter shaped like Jello, cupcakes, Rollerblading raptors, building a time capsule, and Darth Vader farting.

- Attorney requested permission to file a second custody petition. Client replied, "Hell, Craigy. You don't stop swinging just because you're in a slump." Attorney interpreted this to mean "yes."

- The usual fee arrangements were made and a check was exchanged for a fully executed retainer agreement. Client is still under the impression that a superior court action can be prepped, deposed, litigated, tried, and adjudged for $300. If client ever finds out the truth, client will break attorney's neck.

- Client invited attorney, attorney's sig oth, and attorney's law partner to Utica for a home stand with the Troy Bandits next weekend. ("I get Noah for three days, so we can make it a family thing.") Attorney accepted on behalf of all parties.

- Attorney filled his tank with Shell Premium and hit the road. Before he did, client re-emphasized that the weekend invitation included attorney's elusive law partner as well. ("Doesn't she know I'm crazy about her?") Attorney assured client that he got the picture, even if the law partner didn't.

Total Time:	6.5 hours @ $200/hr.	$1,300.00
Travel:	178 miles @ 30¢/mile	53.40
Total Billable:		00.00

Special Handling: Write it off to office supplies.

Jody Kessler was our Golden Boy. Tall and blond with a grin wide enough to light up most of Saratoga County, he was the kid down the street who'd slept in a Red Sox jersey for most of his adolescence, who'd married his high school sweetheart in the on-deck circle between halves of a semi-pro doubleheader (her parents were furious), who'd fed his family and bought more baseballs by overhauling entire transmissions in forty-five minutes flat, and who'd routinely broken plate glass windows up and down Union Avenue with one implausible home run after another. (In a unanimous vote, the City Council agreed to push the diamond five hundred feet farther away from downtown in order to prevent any more damage. It worked—but barely.)

By the time we'd moved to Saratoga Springs, Jody was already something of a sandlot legend. Before we'd even met our neighbors we knew what kind of toothpaste he used (Aim), where he bought his Reeboks (The Foot Emporium on Nelson), what he ate for breakfast (sausage and eggs up, rye toast, and grapefruit juice), and which Red Sox hero he most resembled (fistfights sometimes broke out over this one—it was usually Carl Yastrzemski or Rico Petrocelli, but for my money, he was a dead-ringer for an unsurly Tony Conigliaro). Together, he and his wife were the Jack and Jackie of Carriage House Lane—Jody with his .373 average and Annette with her B.A. in literature from Cornell—and when Noah was born in 1987, all that was missing to complete the snapshot was a minor league contract. It wasn't long in coming.

FINAL # The Saratoga Courant 25¢

JODY HEADS FOR UTICA!

"Jesus, look at him fly!" whistled Clayton on Opening Day. We were sitting over the Blue Sox dugout in Utica, having driven six hours through a near-hurricane just to see if Jody could pull off his mythical hocus-pocus in front of the Big Guys. And once the sun had come out, it was a day made for baseball: the sky was so blue and the grass was so green, you kind of got the feeling that if there had been an eleventh commandment, it would have been "Thou shalt cover third."

Over by first base, bouncing on the balls of his feet and chewing one stick of Doublemint after another, Jody Kessler actually looked nervous for the first and only time in his professional career. That lasted until Sammy Tucker came to the plate for the Syracuse Sparks and hit a sizzling line drive at least three thousand feet over Jody's head. Some say that when he made the catch, he didn't seem to realize what a spectacular play it really was. Actually, it was a lot simpler than that: nobody had told him a rookie wasn't *supposed* to put one over on Sammy Tucker. Then later in the game, he sent Billy Glavin's lead-off pitch into the deepest part of the Mohawk River and didn't even bother to blush when he crossed the plate. Nobody'd told him he wasn't supposed to do that, either.

FINAL ### The Saratoga Courant 25¢

IT'S FENWAY PARK FOR JODY!

When the Red Sox inevitably called him up in 1993, their ticket people weren't exactly anticipating an order for eight hundred seats from Saratoga Springs—but they didn't really have much of a choice. You just don't fuck with a local hero. Jody wound up with his own cheering section ten feet east of the Green Monster, and when he made his first appearance during batting practice (with 6-year-old Noah on his shoulders), you'd have thought that Ted Williams had shed forty years and come back for one more dose of magic. Even the usually cynical sportscasters didn't know what had hit them.

Neither did Jody when a 2-and-1 fastball shattered his jaw.

FINAL ### The Saratoga Courant 25¢

JODY CHANGES HIS SOX AGAIN

It took him nearly a year to recover—and when he returned to uniform as a pinch hitter for Utica, even long-suffering Red Sox fans refused to believe that one at-bat at Fenway Park was the only big-league chance he was ever going to get. We were wrong. He struck out on three consecutive pitches that day—but five thousand people in the ballpark gave him a standing ovation anyway.

Over the next few seasons, we learned to ignore the rumors. And there were plenty: Jody was on his way down to single-A, Jody and Annette were splitting up, Pawtucket wouldn't renew Jody's contract, Jody and Annette were getting back together, Camelot was teetering on the brink again—but nobody wanted to hear it. So I was thoroughly unprepared for the envelope I received on March 14, 1997, that looked for all the world as though it had been addressed by a kid.

Dear Mr. McKenna,

I am 9 years old. I saw a picture of you on TV about childrens rights when the little girl got teased in school and nobody did anything about it.

My father is the world famous baseball player Jody Kessler but they won't let me live with him because he's not rich like my mother's boy friend who she just married.

Am I allowed to get childrens rights too? If I am then how come nobody listens to me?

Noah Kessler

POST-IT NOTE

Charleen:

We're taking this case sight unseen. Remember when I let you represent the Women's Defense League for free and you said you owed me one? This is the one you owe me. And if he can't afford to pay us, we'll settle for a pair of autographs.

Craig

POST-IT NOTE

Craig:

When did you get to be such a pushover?!

What the hell. The kid's adorable and the father's no slouch either.

Charleen

A week after I'd gotten the letter, we met with Jody and Noah in our large conference room (we call our small one "the kitchen"). It was a Saturday and Jody had a full afternoon of visitation rights mapped out, but they managed to squeeze us in between the batting cage and the ice cream cones. Kevin had gotten there early to set up—bagels and French roast decaf for the grownups; Oreos, hot chocolate, and half a dozen computer games for the kid. (We used to have two secretaries and a receptionist until we found Kevin—our blue-eyed boy toy who handles the mail, takes care of our filing, screens our calls, corrects our pleadings, rewrites our letters, makes us coffee, deposits our checks, keeps our accounts, sets our depositions, and gets us out of hot water before it starts to boil. On one memorable occasion, we were a day late filing a motion for summary judgment: the battery in my watch had croaked, so I was twenty-four hours off. This is what's known in the trade as "mistake, inadvertence, or excusable neglect," but no amount of cajoling, bartering, threatening, or imploring was sufficient to persuade an unusually obstinate court clerk to get with the program—until Kevin said, "Craig? Go into your office, shut the door, and don't come out until I tell you to." Then he invited the clerk to lunch. One hour later, I had a hearing date and Kevin had a boyfriend. If he ever quits, we go Chapter 11.)

"Sorry I'm late," said Charleen briskly, sweeping into our tiny wood-paneled waiting room as though she were being filmed. Kevin didn't even bother to look up from his monitor.

"Save the entrance, Tallulah," he shot back. "They're not here yet."

"I'm sure I don't know *what* you're talking about," she retorted, clearly disappointed but tossing her jacket carelessly onto a rattan chair as though she weren't. That's when I knew something was definitely up. In addition to a well-rehearsed air of indifference, she was wearing an eye-popping summer dress splashed with sunbursts of color that was supposed to look like it had just come off the rack at Target when in fact it had "Dolce e Gabbana—$900" written all over it. Whenever Charleen smells unattached testosterone, she goes shopping.

"Why didn't you tell me we were aiming for the Rodeo Drive look on a weekend?" I chided her. "I'd have worn the jeans with smaller holes."

"What, *this* old thing?" she asked incredulously, plucking at the fabric. "Surely you've been smoking the drapes again."

"Then how come the price tag's still on the zipper?"

"*Where?!*"

"Gotcha," I fired back smugly. We stopped just short of "nyah, nyah, nyah" only because our clients chose that moment to arrive, and it was clearly in the best interests of all concerned to pretend we were adults. Noah took care of the preliminary introductions, which consisted of a nimble "Hiya" before he made a beeline for Kevin's computer to see if Doom was on it. The rest of us remained facing a winningly awkward Jody in a baby-blue T-shirt stretched across his torso, a pair of baseball pants, and a tousled haircut that made him look like the world's biggest little boy. Though we realized that swooning was definitely out of the question, that didn't stop Charleen from checking out his eyes, me from scoping out his chest, or Kevin from staring at his crotch. Guess which one of them I kicked?

"I've heard a great deal about you," said Charleen warmly.

"Why don't we all go inside?" I offered.

"Ow," said Kevin.

The first twenty minutes of the meeting were notably unremarkable if you could overlook the subtext, which was about as delicate as a heart attack. Noah and I got into a fight about Tom Seaver, Jody stared at Charleen, and Charleen took notes. Noah showed me snapshots of him and his mom at Lake Tonawanda, Jody stared at Charleen, and Charleen poured coffee. Noah recited every one of the state capitals by heart, Jody stared at Charleen, and Charleen buttered a bagel. Then, by prearranged signal, Kevin took the kid into my office for ten rounds of Chip's Challenge (nine of which Noah won). This left Jody staring at Charleen, Charleen polishing the spoons, and Craig with no one to talk to. That we ever got as far as a courtroom is a legal accomplishment worthy of Professor Witkin.

With a representation letter signed and our $300 fee paid in advance, we scheduled a meeting with Annette—an energetic 5-foot-2 bundle of dynamite who turned out to be funny, articulate, and a good sport. Though she loved her kid way too much to consider giving him up, she wouldn't allow Jody to pay child support and she still called him Big Guy. Clearly, a messy divorce hadn't stopped them from remaining partially crazy about each other.

"If I kick your ass in court," she challenged her ex, "you have to buy me lunch." Jody leaned across the conference table with make-believe fire in his eyes.

"But you leave the tip," he growled. "*I'm* not the one who married three billion dollars." Annette grimaced in mock pain.

"Below the belt, but it's a deal." Halfway through the conference, Charleen excused herself to take a phone call, and Jody was immediately on his feet, helping her out of her chair. None of this got by Annette, who turned to me quizzically. I shrugged. Then she grinned. So I grinned back. It's tough playing hardball when you like the other team.

Later that evening, Jody took Charleen to dinner alone. (The Pergola was out of his price range, so he chose a Sizzler with dim lighting.) He was under the impression that it was a date; she, however, brought along a legal pad, two felt-tipped pens, and a hand-held voice recorder. Duh. Give Charleen a deadbeat who's emotionally unstable, marginally psychopathic, or generically unemployable, and she lights up like a five-dollar slot machine with four jackpots across the center line. Deal her a hunky and chivalrous first baseman who's absolutely crazy about her, and her cursor freezes. But Jody didn't get to be Rookie of the Year by tossing in the towel whenever he went 0-for-4. The next morning he had two dozen daisies delivered to the office. *And Charleen couldn't figure out why!*

"Are you sure they're for *me?*" she asked dubiously.

"No," retorted Kevin. "Actually they're for me. Didn't I tell you about our interludes in the men's room? It was splashed all over the *Enquirer*."

𝔖uperior 𝔠ourt of the 𝔖tate of 𝔑ew 𝔜ork in and for the 𝔠ounty of 𝔖aratoga

In the Matter of: <u>Kessler vs. Kessler</u>
Case No.: Fam. 81699
The Hon. John J. Costanzo, Judge Presiding

It is the opinion of this Court that the minor child's interests would be best served were he to remain in the custody of his mother, Annette Kessler Mueller.

PETITION DENIED.

That was a year ago. Jody made it to first base with Utica but not with Charleen, I continue to walk a very thin line with Judge Costanzo, and Noah's Martian pajamas wound up in my den. Oh, yeah. The Red Sox landed in fourth place. When life decides to suck, it really bites the big one.

But none of it was Bill Buckner's fault.

CLAYTON'S HARDWARE
serving Saratoga Springs since 1988

Hey, Sleepyhead.

In case you were wondering, I turned off the alarm clock on purpose. When I kissed your ear, you didn't even wiggle—which is a sure tip-off that you need at least two more hours of sack time. I already called the office and told them you'd be late. Charleen and Kevin can cover for you.

Honey, you can't keep working yourself like this. Noah's an unhappy little boy who ought to be with his father, but you're not going to score any points with Costanzo if you're walking into walls. Remember what you promised me at Harvard? No more saving the world single-handedly.

I'll take care of dinner tonight. Then we're going to bed early. We may even get some sleep.

I love you.

The Boyfriend

P.S. Forget Denmark. They'll let us get married, sure. But then we have to *live* there! Is Denmark where they have the tulips, or is that Anne Frank? I always forget.

MCKENNA & WEBB
A LAW PARTNERSHIP
118 CONGRESS PARK, SUITE 407
SARATOGA SPRINGS, NEW YORK 12866

MEMORANDUM

TO: Charleen
FROM: Craig
DATE: May 20, 1998
SUBJECT: *Kessler vs. Kessler*

---

1.   (a)   <u>Jody's Annual Income</u>

         Blue Sox   9,500
         Shell Station   41,000

  (b)   <u>Jody's Liabilities</u>

         Mortgage   10,250
         Insurance   2,200
         Legal Fees   300

  (c)   <u>Jody's Asset</u>

         A hot butt. (Did he always have one or is this a new development?)

2. We're going to hit Costanzo with a petition for split custody—six months apiece. How can he argue with *that?*
"Beard the lion in his lair, none but the brave deserve the
fair." (Gilbert and Sullivan, *Iolanthe.*)

3. Jody's invited us to Utica next weekend. Especially you.
But don't take it the wrong way just because he said
"Charleen" nineteen times. He probably needs somebody
there who knows how to fold laundry.

4. Clayton and I can only get married in Denmark if we learn
how to speak Flemish or Dutch or whatever the hell they
talk over there, so we're looking into Sweden. Question:
how close is Vermont to making us legal? And what about
other liberal states like West Virginia? Think it over and
tell me at lunch. Sweet Shop, 12:30.

McKenna & Webb
A Law Partnership
118 Congress Park, Suite 407
Saratoga Springs, New York 12866

Memorandum

TO:	Craig
FROM:	Charleen
DATE:	May 20, 1998
SUBJECT:	*Kessler vs. Kessler*

1. I'm unavailable to spend two nights in the same house
where Jody Kessler takes showers naked. Furthermore, I've
already booked a previous anxiety attack for next weekend,
so perhaps you'd better invite Iolanthe instead.

2. Of course Costanzo can argue with split custody! "Jesus H.
Christ, Craig! You expect me to bounce that kid from

school to school twice a year like a goddamned tennis ball? Beat it." We need to talk Jody into moving back to Saratoga Springs. And whatever you're thinking, don't go there. I assure you I have no personal stake in this whatsoever.

3. No need to deliberate—West Virginia would never allow same-sex marriage. It prevents inbreeding.

4. Kindly keep Jody's ass out of this. He's one of the only three straight men left in New York.

MCKENNA & WEBB
A LAW PARTNERSHIP
118 CONGRESS PARK, SUITE 407
SARATOGA SPRINGS, NEW YORK 12866

MEMORANDUM

TO: Charleen
FROM: Craig
DATE: May 20, 1998
SUBJECT: Jody's Ass

Wouldn't it be funny if Anita Bryant was right and we really *could* recruit them?

MCKENNA & WEBB
A LAW PARTNERSHIP
118 CONGRESS PARK, SUITE 407
SARATOGA SPRINGS, NEW YORK 12866

MEMORANDUM

TO: Craig
FROM: Charleen
DATE: May 20, 1998
SUBJECT: Jody's Ass

Yes, Craig. That would be a riot.

LOUISE McKENNA, M.D.   Jefferson Medical Plaza, Suite 100
OBSTETRICS/GYNECOLOGY   903 Saint Charles Street
                                      St. Louis, Missouri 63101

May 22, 1998

Darling:

I'm enclosing another snapshot of Douglas Colson, M.D. Isn't he something? By the way, those muscles are real.

Sweetheart, I have nothing against Clayton, per se, but you owe it to yourself to marry into the medical profession. It's in our blood. And we've always had good luck with doctors. Face it—if you hadn't been born, I wouldn't have had an affair with your pediatrician and your father wouldn't have found out about it and God forbid I'd still be stuck with him.

I got your pictures from Cape Vincent. Lovely. But please don't send any more with Clayton in them. The temptation to cut off his head is far too great.

Call if you need anything.

Love,
Mom

Craig McKenna   **Attorney Notes**

<u>Anatomy of a Fight</u>
Craig McKenna vs. Clayton Bergman
(Available on Pay-Per-View in Some Areas)

LOCATION: A kitchen on Loughberry Lake, dinnertime.

CHARACTERS: You and your sig oth.

SETUP: He's stirring the hollandaise sauce, you're checking up on the lamb chops, and for some reason—probably a metaphoric one—you wait until the asparagus begins to boil before you bring up the Freedom to Marry March on Washington.

"That's the weekend we're going to Rehobeth Beach," he says brusquely, turning off the burner. "Here, taste this." Then he sticks a hollandaise-covered finger in your mouth, hoping it makes you (a) hungry or (b) horny—anything to shut you up. It doesn't work.

"Not enough butter," you tell him. "Clay, Delaware's going to be around for a while, and—"

"So's Washington," he cuts in. "Hand me a bowl, would you?" At that moment, the potato timer rings.

ROUND ONE
The Dinner Table

You're both eating very slowly. It's difficult to chew through a couple of clenched jaws.

Who	What's Said	What *Isn't* Said
You	Could I have the pepper?	Don't you have a political conscience?
Him	Here.	Don't you have a *life?!* What comes next— Buffalo Springfield and your usual police action?
You	Thank you.	I hate your hollandaise.
Him	How are your lamb chops?	Know what you need? You need to be spanked and sent to your room.
You	Good. They're good.	I have nothing more to say to you. Ever.
Him	Want some wine?	Pout at your own risk. You're only going to make me pop my cork. And you really don't want to see that happen.
You	No.	How's your blood pressure, asshole?

ROUND TWO
The Den

The dishes are done and you're watching a movie—but from opposite couches.

Who	What's Said	What *Isn't* Said
Him	What did you rent?	Nice meal. It was like eating granite. Can't we fight during the day instead?
You	*I Wanna Hold Your Hand.*	Don't even *think* about calling a truce. You have at least three more hours of suffering left.
Him	Never heard of it.	You're not gonna budge an inch, are you?
You	Trust me.	(Smirk.)
Him	Don't I always?	Honey, work with me on this. Rehobeth was supposed to be about you and me and a beach and a bed, and four days that belonged to just the two of us.
You	I guess.	Clayton, I know that—and I'm not trying to change the world. I just want to clean up our corner of it.
Him	Who's that?	Am I actually scoring points here?
You	Bobby Di Cicco. I met him once.	Okay. Maybe only *two* hours of suffering.
Him	Yeah?	You're gonna lose this one.

ROUND THREE
The Bathroom

According to the Geneva Convention, you're still required to take a shower together, even if you aren't speaking. However, you're not allowed to soap each other up without written consent first.

Who	What's Said	What *Isn't* Said
Him	You missed a spot on your back.	I could do that for you.
You	Ooops.	All right—only twenty minutes of suffering. But that's as low as I go!
Him	Shit. Shampoo in my eyes.	Honey, help me understand you. Please?
You	Hold still, I'll get it off.	Clay, I need you to rewrite the rules with me. Don't you see? Why are we running halfway around the world to get married when we ought to be able to do it right here? We wouldn't even need carry-on luggage.
Him	Thanks.	I love you.
You	Dope.	I'm going to lose this one.

ROUND FOUR
The Sink

You're taking turns brushing your teeth and trying not to look at each other in the mirror.

Who	What's Said	What *Isn't* Said
Him	Okay. What if I trade you Rehobeth Beach for a whole week to be named later? *Just us.*	I'll make a deal with you. If we both give in at the same time, everybody wins.
You	Sure. We can make it Miami in November. There's this referendum on the ballot that I want—	You mean I got away with a pout?!
Him	Hey!	I'm saying yes.
You	I'm *kidding!*	I love you too.

ROUND FIVE
The Double Bed (from Ikea)

You're lying against his chest and doing something nonsexual with one of his nipples. He doesn't like Chin-in-the-Neck *or* Falling-Asleep-Kissing, but he's invented the Playing-with-Your-Hair thing, which works almost as well. Both of you are a little worn-out—it's been a long night.

What's Said / What *Isn't* Said

"Honey?" he murmurs gently.

"Mmmmm?"

"Didn't two guys go to Bolivia once to tie the knot?"

"That was Butch Cassidy and the Sundance Kid."

"In your dreams."

Then he kisses the top of your head and you fall asleep.

FINAL SCORE: DOUBLE TKO

Would it have killed them to make being in love a little easier?

6

Travis

T:

1. Here's what I found on the Internet: there's 118
   McKennas in St. Louis, but no Craig. There's 74 Craig
   McKennas in the U.S. white pages, but none in St.
   Louis. I'm printing out all 192 phone numbers because
   you're going to ask me for them anyway. Are you sure
   you want to do this?
2. The Missouri State Bar doesn't have any record of a
   Craig McKenna, so I checked Massachusetts too in case
   he liked their boys when he was in college and decided to
   stick around Boston. But he ain't there either. T, you
   don't know for sure that he went to law school. And if he
   did, maybe he changed his mind when he found out
   what kind of an asshole they were turning him into.
3. I talked to a hot little babe in the Harvard alumni
   office who wound up e-mailing me one of her year-

book photos. Yikes! She's not allowed to give out any info over the phone, but she says if I'm ever in Cambridge she'll have dinner with me to discuss it. Don't say I wouldn't go to the mat for you.

4. We're all out of paper towels, you left the refrigerator door open again, the Häagen-Dazs melted all over my spareribs, and your room's beginning to smell worse than mine does. You're really scaring me, man.

G

UNIVERSITY OF SOUTHERN CALIFORNIA
UNIVERSITY PARK · LOS ANGELES, CALIFORNIA 90007

Doheny Library
Faculty Research Request

DATE: May 25, 1998   FROM: Travis Puckett
DEPARTMENT: History   BUILDING/ROOM: VKC/223

MATERIALS NEEDED

SPECIAL INSTRUCTIONS
Any information on an attorney named Craig McKenna. I don't know where he practices, I don't know where he lives, and I'm not even sure he's a lawyer. Spare no expense. I'll pay whatever it costs.

Julian, I'm sorry. You were right. The man I belong with is the boy I first kissed twenty years ago. Now all I've got to do is find him again.

What are you sorry for? Didn't I say you were a Prince Charming?

I need everything you've got on this guy: birth date, physical description, distinguishing characteristics, dick size (for my own catalog only). Don't worry. If Sleeping Beauty's out there, we'll find him.

UNIVERSITY OF SOUTHERN CALIFORNIA
MESSAGE CENTER

TO:	Prof. Travis Puckett
FROM:	Andrea Fox
DATE:	May 25, 1998
STATUS:	URGENT

THERE'S A GRANT MEETING SCHEDULED FOR
10:00 A.M. ON WEDNESDAY. MARSHA HOLMES RAL-
LIED THE ENTIRE HISTORY DEPARTMENT BEHIND
YOU, AS WELL AS TWO PROFESSORS FROM THE
SCHOOL OF PALEONTOLOGY (!).

SO IF YOU DON'T RESPOND TO AT LEAST ONE
OF MY LAST EIGHT MESSAGES, I'M GOING TO
BREAK ALL TEN OF YOUR OBSESSIVE-COMPULSIVE
FINGERS.

ANDREA

FROM THE JOURNAL OF
Travis Puckett

1. ~~Craig McKenna: Clear Lake, Iowa~~ *Retired Marine Corps colonel*
2. ~~Craig McKenna: Lake Forest, Illinois~~ *14 years old*
3. ~~Craig McKenna: Shreveport, Louisiana~~ *Out on parole*
4. ~~Craig McKenna: Hagerstown, Maryland~~ *Has seven grandchildren*
5. ~~Craig McKenna: Canton, Georgia~~ *Tried to sell me mail-order shoes*

I'm disintegrating in front of my eyes. I haven't shaved in three days. They'll bury me in a dirty T-shirt and unmatched socks. How's that for irony? But it's my own fault. I had him and I let him go. We

*could have been the luckiest people in the world. Oh, Christ. I'm
quoting Barbra Streisand at 4:00 in the morning. That's one step
away from turning into Norma Desmond. I don't even know what
I'm talking about any more. HOW MANY CRAIG McKENNAS
COULD THERE BE?! Sleep, Travis. Go to sleep. But don't dream
about Craig again. Please?*

~

June 1978. It was the longest two weeks of our lives. Once we'd
realized that Cupid had shot us both in the ass at the same
time, we were doomed. If we weren't making plans for our next
twenty years together, we were checking each other out in the
showers. If we weren't sneaking off into the woods to fool
around, we were reapplying to colleges so we'd be closer
together in the fall. And by the time we'd clocked our first
four-minute kiss, our hormones had grown fissionable: all we
had to do was lock eyes in the middle of English and it was like
firing a U-235 bullet into a uranium core. *Radiation alert!
Radiation alert!* But prep schools in 1978 weren't exactly bas-
tions of large-mindedness, and if they'd actually found two
boys in bed together, the statue of Mrs. Beckley would have
taken a copper crap right in the middle of the Quad.

"What was King Lear's tragic flaw?"

"He had a boyfriend named Travis with a cute butt who he
wanted to get naked with in private but couldn't."

"Craig! You're not making this easier!"

"Sorry."

Actually, there was no real point to cramming, because our
final exams were going to be based on whatever we'd learned
before we'd tumbled headfirst into each other's lives. After that,
if it wasn't about Craig's Arms 101 or Intermediate Travis, it
wasn't worth knowing. That included the collected works of
William Shakespeare, three thousand years of world history, all
four sides of a parallelogram, and 218 genuses of ferns. As for

the ten million French verbs we were supposed to have mastered, there was only one that we really wanted to conjugate.

"J'ai le béguin pour toi."

"'I have a crush on you.' Nous pouvons vivre d'amour et d'eau fraîche."

"'We can live on love alone.' Je te mange avec mes yeux."

"'I consume you with my eyes.'"

Clearly, we were reaching critical mass; as we'd both come to learn, nothing's more persuasive than a teenage heart that's calling all the shots—even if we hadn't figured out what to do about it yet. It was Craigy who inadvertently came up with the idea while we were passing notes back and forth during study hall.

Would you still love me if you found out I once stole a box of York Peppermint Patties?

Would you still love me if you found out I once snuck into *Gypsy* without a ticket?

Would you still love me if you found out I once fucked a bagel?

Would you still love me if you found out I once fucked one too?

Would you still love me if I kidnapped you and took you to Harvard with me in September?

Would you still love me if I knocked you unconscious and wouldn't let you go back to St. Louis this summer?

Would you love me even more if I told you I'd figured out a way for us to be together for the next three months?

Does that mean *alone* together?

Absolutely.

I'll do it.

You haven't even heard the battle plan yet!

It doesn't matter!

(Grin.) Hand me some paper.

Dear Mom,

I've been doing a lot of thinking lately, and I'm beginning to feel ashamed that I'm the only kid in my class who doesn't have a summer job. Just because I got into Harvard doesn't mean I won't have to work for a living like everybody else does, and suppose I come up short because I've never had any experience before? It's really starting to worry me.

So here's what I'm thinking. My best friend Travis (who's the smartest kid in our class) is looking for a job too. But since his father's wife won't let him stay at their house on East 65th Street, they told Travis he could find a summer sublet by himself. Which is kind of scary when you're not even 18 yet. So maybe you'd let me and Travis share an apartment so that we could keep an eye on each other and make sure neither one of us goofs off.

I'm sorry I won't be able to spend the summer with you and Aunt Emmy at the house in Lake Charles, but we can always do that next year. And I really think it's important that I learn how to earn my keep.

Love,
Craig

Dear Dad,

I've been doing a lot of thinking lately, and I'm beginning to feel ashamed that I'm the only kid in my class who doesn't have a summer job. Just because I got into USC doesn't mean I won't have to work for a living like everybody else does, and suppose I come up short because I've never had any experience before? It's really starting to worry me.

So here's what I'm thinking. My best friend Craig (who's a shortstop just like your all-time favorite Bucky Dent) is looking for a job too. But since he lives in St. Louis and wants to stay in Manhattan, his mother told him he could find a summer sublet by himself. Which is kind of scary when you're not even 18½ yet. So maybe you'd let me and Craig share an apartment so that we could keep an eye on each other and make sure neither one of us goofs off.

I'm sorry I won't be able to go on another Teen Tour, but you've sent me on six of them already and there's not much left to see. (I also have a real problem with staying at a four-star hotel in Bangladesh. It's just not right.) Besides, I really think it's important that I learn how to earn my keep.

Love,
Travis

Parents are such pushovers. My father grudgingly conceded that he was proud of me, and Craig's mom called from St. Louis in tears, claiming that her little boy had turned into a grown-up practically overnight. Meanwhile, Craig and I were both so horny we could have directed traffic with our dicks.

"They said yes," he sighed, running his hand across the front of my T-shirt longingly. "*Now* can we practice?"

"Not so fast," I warned him. "We still need to find gainful employment and a place to live." We were sitting cross-legged on his bed, staring openly at each other's primary erogenous zones and poring through the *Village Voice*.

"Dental hygienist."

"No."

"Drill press operator."

"Nope."

"Legal secretary."

"Forget it."

"Then I give up," I whined. "What am I qualified for?"

"Modeling underpants," he sighed wistfully. "As long as I get to watch."

"*Craig!*"

The apartment issue was a lot simpler—all we really needed was a bed and a door that locked. And thanks to the *Voice*, we found exactly what we were looking for in an old brownstone on West 92nd Street, just off Riverside Drive: "Cozy remodeled studio, wood floors, charming neighborhood, available immediately." Translation: "Renovated one-room rat-hole, no carpets, live-in drug dealer, nobody wants it." The tenant was an atonal singing waiter named Barry Brush who, through an extraordinary stroke of luck (a hearing-impaired casting director), had booked a summer stock engagement at the Totem Pole Playhouse in Fayetteville, Pennsylvania. (Given the fact that he was barely 5-foot-3, I assumed he was playing Og in *Finian's Rainbow*, but somehow it didn't seem polite to ask.) At first he appeared to be a little reluctant to turn over his postage-stamp-with-furniture to a couple of kids—particularly when they kept eyeing the bed as though they'd never seen one before—but a cashier's check for $286.20 changed his mind. (Craig's mom wanted us to start off on the right foot.) We left with a set of keys and a promise that we could move in the day school let out—and as Barry led us to the door, Craig covertly put his hand on my ass. My carotid artery imploded on the spot.

The jobs fell into our laps completely by accident. On our way back to Grand Central, we stopped in front of Colony

Records at 49th and Broadway because there was an Ethel Merman album display in the window, and naturally I needed to make sure they were all present and accounted for: *Gypsy. Annie Get Your Gun. Anything Goes. Summer Help Wanted. Happy Hunting. Call Me Madam. Something for the—* Summer Help Wanted?! In an Ethel Merman store?! For a brief but electric moment, I understood the whole Buddhist concept of karma.

"Oh my God," I breathed, instantly fogging up the glass in front of *Panama Hattie*. "It's Kismet. It's destiny. It's divine intervention." Craig wasn't nearly as sanguine.

"Like hell it is," he groaned. "If we have to *work* for that old bag, forget it." The truth turned out to be a shade less glamorous—they just needed a couple of stock boys until September. Of course, the pay was shit, but Craig's mom had already sent us a check for $500 just in case (the right-foot thing again). During a tour of "the plant"—as it was referred to by way-too-serious manager Douglas, a middle-aged former hoofer from Queens who'd inexplicably acquired a European accent—our responsibilities as "directors of inventory" were laid out in explicit detail: (a) hang around the basement and (b) move some boxes. Together. Alone. For eight hours. *Shit! There go the hormones again!*

"I hope you guys are friends," he chuckled almost apologetically, pointing to the narrow aisles and the cozy cardboard hiding places. "Because you're not going to have anybody else to talk to." Craigy and I agreed that we got along pretty well and didn't anticipate a problem. Then, as soon as Doug's back was turned, we kissed each other. When life decides to work, it's *perfect*.

The last four days of school passed in a blur. I remember absolutely nothing about final exams except that my octagons somehow came out with nine sides, and Craig said that Othello was too much of a moron to have a tragic flaw—unless stupidity counts.

"You didn't lose the keys to our apartment, did you?" he nudged me three times a day.

"Stop asking me that!"

Commencement was our last hurdle. As soon as we'd taken our seats in the packed auditorium dripping with streamers of black and gray—Beckley's traditionally funereal colors—we knew we were sunk. Scheduled to last between one and two hours (depending on how many creaky old alumni they'd black-mailed into saying a few words), the ceremonies were generally interminable under the best of circumstances. But when you've had the same erection for ten days, it's worse. *Much* worse.

"Ow."

"Me too," hissed Craig. "Shhh."

Across the aisle, a couple of halfbacks grinned at him dopily in that fraternal bond that people with jockstraps like to show off, waiting hopefully for a similar smirk in return. (They had a pretty good reason, too: ever since Craig and I had begun hanging out together on an average of every minute of our lives, they were no longer exactly sure which team he was play-ing for—and if they'd actually suspected what was going through his head at that particular moment, they never would have peed in a locker room urinal again.)

Happily, the headmaster gave Craig his Victory Cup before intermission, and our diplomas followed shortly thereafter. By the time Reverend Sheedy stood up to bless the departing sen-iors and introduce some handpicked fossil from the Class of 1910, there were two empty seats in the fifth row. We probably should have stuck around until the end, but when you're ninety minutes away from learning all the secrets of your best friend's body, nostalgia over four years of preparatory education tends to be reduced to as few syllables as possible: *Bye. See ya.*

Oh, yeah. We both got A's in French. *J'ai le béguin pour toi,* Craigy.

~

"You nervous?"

"Are you?"

"No."

"Then me neither." We were undressing each other slowly in the living room-bedroom-kitchen-dining room-den of our new apartment. (Barry had left us some flowers and a pair of comps to *Finian's Rainbow*, just in case we happened to be in Fayetteville over the weekend.) Though the train ride down the Hudson had been playfully erotic by Travis-Craig standards, that all changed as soon as we turned onto West 92nd Street. In fact, once we'd unlocked our front door for the first time and stepped into a room that belonged to just us, our smiles faded swiftly—along with our self-confidence, our swagger, and (impossibly) our hard-ons. There's a word for this kind of thing: panic. *Oh my God. Who are we kidding? I've never made love to anybody in my life and Craigy's only fooled around with a couple of girls. What if we don't know what to do? What if we hate it? What if this was a mistake? What if he leaves and I never see him again? Why is he kissing my shoulder? What happened to my shirt? Boy, that feels good. Maybe I should take his off too. Why are there so many buttons?!*

"Are you sure you want to do this?" he whispered nervously, holding me close. "I mean, we don't *have* to."

"How much time do I get to answer?" I mumbled back tentatively, touching his cheek and shaking like a 4.7 temblor two miles beneath Marin County. Then he pulled away and one-dimple-grinned me—the same damned smile I'd first fallen in love with—and everything exploded at once. *We have liftoff!* With a yelp, I pushed him backward onto our pocket-sized mattress, yanked off his shirt (fuck the buttons), and dove. There's a word for this too: *Banzai!*

Round One lasted sixteen hours. Then we slept for another nine and started all over again. They say that biology limits what two guys can do together, but you sure as hell couldn't prove it by us.

"Oh God," he groaned, coming up for air. "What do you call that?"

"Improvisation," I gasped in reply.

"Do I get to improvise too?"

"If you think you can measure up to—*Yikes!*" For the next three days, we never saw sunlight. There was something so right about being naked together in the dark—about eating potato chips off of each other's stomachs while we watched *Dobie Gillis* at 3:00 in the morning, about reaching for each other's bodies when we were still hungry, about exploring our different parts and learning how to make one another sigh, giggle, and especially squirm. We were a perfect fit—back-to-front, head-to-toe, top-to-bottom—and when we stumbled out into the blue-and-gold nimbus enveloping West 92nd Street on our first day of work, we discovered that the whole world had changed while we were in bed.

"This is a great peach."

"This is a great plum."

"This is a great subway."

"This is a *terrific* sidewalk." And we meant every word.

Remembering the rest of that summer is like peering through a kaleidoscope: the night games at Yankee Stadium, the hot dogs in Battery Park, pretending we were Lucy and Fred on the Staten Island Ferry, walking through Central Park in the rain just so we could watch one another get wet, chasing each other across the boys-only section of Jones Beach and falling into the sand together like a couple of horny puppies, making out at the top of the Empire State Building and educating a stupefied couple from Davenport, Iowa, while we were doing it, and discovering that our boss at the record store wasn't such a stuffed shirt after all—once he'd realized we were boyfriends.

"Dougie, can we sneak out early? It's our anniversary."

"Oh, bullshit. You just had one last week!" There's nothing quite as intoxicating as two boys throwing out all the rules and discovering freedom together for the first time. And when the same two boys happen to be head-over-toes in love with each other—well, think *Field of Dreams* squared.

One memory stands out above all the rest: June 24, 1978—
my eighteenth birthday. It wasn't so much the breakfast in bed
that Craig had insisted on (Hostess cupcakes and Swiss Miss),
or the surprise carriage ride around Central Park with his head
on my shoulder, or the unbelievably out-of-print copy of
Henry, Sweet Henry that Doug had helped him pick out and
wrap, or the candlelit dinner at Beefsteak Charlie's (we brought
our own candles), or the mezzanine seats that had cost him
most of a paycheck just so he could watch my face light up
when Liza Minnelli tore apart the Majestic in *The Act,* or even
the fact that he stayed awake though the whole thing just for
me. What I remember most is later on, in the shower, when he
sang "Almost Like Being in Love" to me while we were standing under the spray together and letting our noses play with
each other. And the way he dried me off gently, took my hand,
and led me to bed—where we spent three hours proving that
every lyric was absolutely true.

"Travis?" he murmured in a sleepy whisper, holding me
tight. "You're the only one. No matter what happens, you're the
only one. Happy birthday." Then he drifted off blissfully before
I could reply—so I smiled into his chest and squeezed his hand
instead. It was the only time he ever made me cry.

~

I hope he meant it. Because one way or another, I'm going to
find out.

7. ~~Craig McKenna: Flemingsburg, Kentucky~~ *Doesn't speak
   English*
8. ~~Craig McKenna: Weslaco, Texas~~ *White supremacist*
9. Craig McKenna: Manchester, New Hampshire
10. Craig McKenna: Sacaton, Arizona
11. Craig McKenna: Johnstown, Pennsylvania
12. Craig McKenna: Antigo, Wisconsin

FROM THE DESK OF
Gordon Duboise

T:

1. The people at Vidiots are ready to put a hit on you if you don't return *I Wanna Hold Your Hand* and *Brigadoon*. They wouldn't even let me rent *Tina Swallows the Leader* until I paid your late charges. $34!

2. If you play that fucking song one more time, all of your CDs are going into the toaster oven. And Barbra Streisand burns first.

3. Remember in high school when they gave us *Great Expectations* and there was this crazy old bat who locked herself in a bedroom for thirty years with a wedding dress and a bride-and-groom cake covered with ants? Keep it up. You're getting there.

G

UNIVERSITY OF SOUTHERN CALIFORNIA
UNIVERSITY PARK • LOS ANGELES, CALIFORNIA 90007

Doheny Library
Faculty Research Request

DATE: <u>May 27, 1998</u>   FROM: <u>Travis Puckett</u>

DEPARTMENT: <u>History</u>   BUILDING/ROOM: <u>VKC/223</u>

MATERIALS NEEDED

SPECIAL INSTRUCTIONS
I've got to break into the Harvard alumni database. This is urgent. Do we have any computer hackers on staff? I'll indemnify the university in case any federal subpoenas start showing up.

I'm on it. Odds are that their backdoor password is "FUCK-YALE." (We do the same thing here with UCLA. Nothing like airtight security.)

While I was checking out a short list of possibilities, I wound up on the phone with a Craig McKenna from San Diego. For two hours. He's a year older than I am, he's a landscape architect, and he has a 29-inch waist. Travis, if it turns out you've domesticated me, I'll kick your ass.

UNIVERSITY OF SOUTHERN CALIFORNIA
UNIVERSITY PARK • LOS ANGELES, CALIFORNIA 90007

TO:	Travis Puckett
FROM:	Andrea Fox
DATE:	May 27, 1998
RE	We got it!

The $30,000 grant is yours. You owe Marsha Holmes your life. At the last minute she pulled in a couple of Poli-Sci section heads who brought charts and graphs and parabolas to prove you had a point. Dean Koutrelakos didn't know what the hell they were talking about (and neither did anybody else), so he threw in the towel.

Congratulations. *Now* will you call me?

Andrea

FROM THE JOURNAL OF
Travis Puckett

73. ~~Craig McKenna: La Jolla, California~~ *Voted for Barry Goldwater*

74. ~~Craig McKenna: Grand Junction, Colorado~~ *Homophobic ski instructor*

There are only four possibilities:

1. He has an unlisted number.
2. He lives outside the country.
3. The phone is in his boyfriend's name.
4. Something happened to him. (Don't go there. He's alive and he's okay.)

So I lost the first round. Big deal. There's still the 118 McKennas in St. Louis plus the 1,732 McKennas in the forty-eight contiguous states and the two floating ones. If I have to call every one of them, I'll find him. Okay, maybe he doesn't need a psychopathic history professor showing up from the Twilight Zone, and maybe he won't even like me any more. But he still has my heart—and if he's not using it, I want it back. Otherwise I'm going to go on loving him for the rest of my life. And there's not a damned thing either one of us can do about it.

Somehow I never got around to telling him that.

~

September 14, 1978. The TWA terminal at JFK. No matter how hard we'd tried, we couldn't make the summer last beyond August. Labor Day showed up and Barry Brush came back from Pennsylvania, so Craig and I hailed a cab to the airport. It was the last adventure we shared together.

We sat in the terminal for three hours unable to speak, staring at each other's faces so we'd never forget the details. What could we possibly say that would fit into words?

Finally, they called my flight to Los Angeles, but neither one of us moved. This was all so obviously a bad dream we were going to wake up from any minute—the alarm clock would go off, we'd tumble into the shower together, we'd start fooling around, and Doug would give us hell for being fifteen minutes late to work. But then they announced final boarding, and it was all over. Craig reached for my hand.

"I love you, Smerko," he mumbled quietly.

"Write to me." By now the tears were streaming down all four of our cheeks, but it was way too late to do anything about it. So we kissed each other one more time—right there in the middle of the waiting room—and then I let him go.

When Flight 18 pulled back from the jetway, Craig was still framed in the window of the terminal, watching the plane and waving. That's the way I remember him.

People sometimes tell me I'm hyperbolic. "The sexiest thing that ever happened to me." "The coldest shower in North America." "The spaghetti that gave me back religion." But even after twenty years, saying goodbye to Craig was the worst moment of my life.

~

Okay. Maybe he went into another line of work that's easier to trace. They have national listings for architects and engineers and real estate agents and people like that, don't they? Or medicine. What if he became a doctor like his mother? The AMA is always putting out those membership bulletins every couple of—

Hold it.

Just a second.

Holy shit.

His mother was a doctor.

SEARCHFINDERS.COM

BUSINESS CODE

| 2213301—DOCTORS | ⇩ |

FIRST NAME

LAST NAME

McKenna

CITY

St. Louis

STATE

| MO | ⇩ | SEARCH |

SEARCH RESULTS

1 OF 1 MATCHES

Dr. Louise McKenna
Jefferson Medical Plaza, Suite 100
903 Saint Charles Street
St. Louis, Missouri 63101

WHAT YOU HOPE FOR

Dr. McKenna?

Yes?

My name is Travis Puckett and—

Oh, good heavens! Travis! My son Craig hasn't stopped talking about you for twenty years!

He hasn't?

Of course not! Ever since that summer the two of you spent together in New York. How have you been, dear?

I'm fine. Did Craig ever become a lawyer?

Oh, no. He lives in Santa Monica, California, and he writes romance novels under a pen name. I think you had a lot to do with that.

Wow. Is he still single?

What do *you* think? He's been waiting for you since 1978.

WHAT YOU'LL SETTLE FOR

Dr. McKenna?

Yes?

My name is Travis Puckett.

Yes?

I think I went to high school with your son. Craig?

Yes. I have a son named Craig.

Well, I was sort of thinking about him and I just wanted to find out how he's doing.

Isn't that thoughtful of you? He's doing quite well, actually. He's a customhouse broker in Baltimore.

Did he ever get married?

Why don't I give you his number so you can catch up with him yourself?

WHY YOU'RE A SCHMUCK

Hello?

Is this Dr. McKenna?

Yes.

Doctor, do you have a son named Craig?

Who wants to know?

Doctor, I'm an old friend of his from high school, and I was just wondering—

Do you own a hardware store?

No, ma'am.

Then, yes—I have a son named Craig.

Doctor, if you could just tell me where he lives, maybe a phone number—

What line of work are you in?

I teach American History.

Forget it. He can do better.

Doctor, wait! Please! Just give me a hint! What hemisphere?

* CLICK *

Oh my God. Pay dirt. The big score. Somewhere inside that woman's head is the address of the only man on earth who knows the way back to Brigadoon. Send her roses. Buy her a new house. Hire somebody to torture it out of her. *MAKE HER TALK!*

And what the hell does she have against history professors?!

American History 206
Professor Puckett
May 28, 1998

Final Exam

Extra Credit Question

Guys: The right answer is worth ten points. Tell me what I want to hear.

So I got off on the wrong foot with Craig's mother. These things happen. But she's still the only lead I have. What's the appropriate course of action?

    (a) Remember that there's laws against stalking, so let it go and look for love in the more usual places;
    (b) Pay a professional to start a Craig hunt;
    (c) Drop everything, drive to St. Louis, take his mother to lunch, and let her see that my heart's in the right place;
    (d) Other: _____.

Final Exam Answers

Extra Credit Question
Ray Sorren

(c) "What hemisphere"?! Why didn't you just ask her for his fucking jockstrap while you were at it? It worked for Jack the Ripper!

Go to St. Louis, you deadhead. This is what you have a
life for. And if you get arrested, we'll tell them it was our
idea.

Doug Hatten

(c) Here's what it looks like from my end of the bench: you're
about to flip off a $30,000 grant it took you two years to
get, you haven't got any money but you're blowing it on a
cross-country trip anyway, and for all you know this guy
could have changed teams, gotten married, and popped
twelve kids out of the oven. Guess what? *Now* you're acting
dopey enough to be in love. Hit the road, Jack.

Chuck Navarro

(c) I vote for St. Louis because you're ready to handle it. Know
how I know? Go back to multiple choice (a). "There's laws
against stalking." Wrong. "There *are* laws against stalking."
Welcome to the Human Fucking Race.

Tony Norris

(c) Duh.

Corey Gambel

(c) But it was a toss-up with (d): "Find a shrink." Then
Alexander Hamilton changed my mind. I mean, if he
could invent a country and then get himself shot in a duel
for something he believed in, the boyfriend thing ought to
be a no-brainer. Especially without an asshole like Aaron
Burr in the picture. Isn't this what you've been teaching us?

Gary Petrie

(c) I probably shouldn't be telling you this, but you need to
hear it. The only reason I did all those extra-credit reports
and cut football practice so we could work on them
together was because I just wanted to hang out with you. I
guess I knew that nothing was going to happen, but so

fucking what? Falling hard for somebody makes you do things you never thought you'd do before. Like pulling off an A in History or finally facing the truth about yourself.

Craig's the one, Travis. Get him back.

~

Final Grades

Ray Sorren	A
Doug Hatten	A
Chuck Navarro	A
Tony Norris	A
Corey Gambel	A
Gary Petrie	A+

FROM THE JOURNAL OF
Travis Puckett

Reasons Not to Go to St. Louis	Reasons to Go to St. Louis
I can't afford it.	*"A month ago I was just Travis Puckett without the 'Smerko.' Now I've got Bobby Di Cicco's autograph and Craig. And no matter what else happens, I'm keeping them both for the rest of my life."*
It's irresponsible.	
I have a book to write.	
The naked carpet cleaner is coming on Tuesday.	
I might get my heart broken again.	

UNIVERSITY OF SOUTHERN CALIFORNIA
UNIVERSITY PARK · LOS ANGELES, CALIFORNIA 90007

TO: Andrea Fox
FROM: Travis Puckett
DATE: May 29, 1998
RE: Slight Change in Plans

This is kind of funny when you think about it, but I don't actually have time to write the book after all. See, I'm leaving for St. Louis in about three hours and I'm not exactly sure when I'll be back, *if* I'll be back, or whether I'm going to be spending the rest of my life in prison (a dim possibility). It's a complicated story, but one not lacking a certain demented charm.

I'll try to call you from the road. I'm sure we can work this out. Meanwhile, as long as the $30,000 is just sitting there, could I borrow it?

Travis

UNIVERSITY OF SOUTHERN CALIFORNIA
UNIVERSITY PARK · LOS ANGELES, CALIFORNIA 90007

TO: Travis Puckett
FROM: Andrea Fox
DATE: May 29, 1998
RE: I Dare You

Travis:

I hope this is your idea of anal-retentive humor. Because I just convinced twelve very rational men that Tom Sawyer and Shoeless Joe Jackson rewrote the Bill of Rights. And I don't even know who Shoeless Joe Jackson *is*.

For your sake, this had better be a mild nervous break-down. Otherwise, if you're not back by July 1, I'll hunt you down myself. With weapons.

Andrea

P.S. *No, you can't borrow it!*

FROM THE JOURNAL OF
Travis Puckett

THE PUCKETT/DUBOISE DEBATES

TRAVIS: Can you lend me a couple hundred? All I've got is $837 and a Neiman-Marcus credit card.

GORDO: What happened to the T-bill?

TRAVIS: It hasn't matured yet.

GORDO: Look who's talking.

TRAVIS: Hand me those socks.

GORDO: Where do you think you're going?!

TRAVIS: St. Louis. All I have to do is convince her I'm not a nut case.

GORDO: But you *are!*

TRAVIS: That's easy for you to say. You never kissed him. I just hope it's not too late.

GORDO: Travis, write to him first. Harvard'll forward it. All I have to do is send one of my Speedo pictures to the babe in the alumni office and—

TRAVIS: And suppose he doesn't answer? You think I could survive that? G, if Lambda Legal Defense can spend six years fighting for my domestic partner benefits, the least I can do is use them.

GORDO: What about the grant?

TRAVIS: There'll be another one.

GORDO: Then take my laptop. If you call and I'm not here, leave me e-mail. This has trouble written all over it.

TRAVIS: Car keys!

GORDO: In your hand. Travis, where did the guts come from all of a sudden?

TRAVIS: Ethel Merman. "Some People." Trust me on this.

FROM THE DESK OF
Gordon Duboise

Pop:

Remember—you're the one who wanted a love story:

Boy meets boy when they're both 17. They fall for one another like a ton of bricks. Then they head for college on opposite coasts and never see each other again.

Twenty years later, one of them wakes up and smells the coffee. All he can think about is that first kiss—so he puts his whole life on hold and starts out on a coast-to-coast hunt for the boyfriend.

That's all you get for now. I don't want to give away the ending yet.

Will it work?

ARGOSY ENTERTAINMENT
Literary Representatives

LOS ANGELES   TORONTO
NEW YORK   LONDON

If it was boy-girl, it's been done to death. But this is still a novelty—unless they get Rupert Everett to play it.

I'd have to see a draft.

Gordon, if you're going to pull a Rock Hudson on me, try to drop a few hints first.

GordoStud.com

G:

I'm at a Chevron station in West L.A. at the corner of Olympic and Bundy. My timing belt went out. I *knew* this would happen. But I don't have time to get it fixed, so I'm leaving the Toyota in a red zone. Please call the Auto Club and ask them to (a) tow it to the top of Mulholland Canyon, and (b) push it off.

There's a guy here named Brandon with an orange Corvette who says he can take me as far east as Amarillo. Do we know anybody in Texas with a floor I can sleep on?

                                                                                 T

163

UNIVERSITY OF SOUTHERN CALIFORNIA
UNIVERSITY PARK • LOS ANGELES, CALIFORNIA 90007

Doheny Library

DATE: <u>May 29, 1998</u>   DEPARTMENT: <u>History</u>
TO: <u>Prof. Travis Puckett</u>   BUILDING/ROOM: <u>VKC/223</u>

Search Results

Martindale-Hubbell Online provided the following information:

Craig S. McKenna, Esq.
McKenna & Webb
A Law Partnership
118 Congress Park, Suite 407
Saratoga Springs, New York 12866

You go, girl.

—Love, Julian

7

Craig

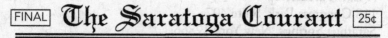

FINAL | **The Saratoga Courant** | 25¢

Vol. MCXXII, No. 118   SARATOGA SPRINGS, NEW YORK   MAY 29, 1998

CURRAN DROPS OUT OF ASSEMBLY RACE
QUITS WHEN GOP REVEALS SCANDAL

ALBANY, MAY 28—Kenneth Curran, Democratic candidate for the New York State Assembly, has withdrawn from the race as a result of Republican allegations that he engaged in sexual misconduct with a 16-year-old girl.

"The Fifth Congressional District doesn't want a man so morally lacking in character to represent its interests in the State House," thundered Republican nominee Patrick Marder in a campaign speech here yesterday.

In response, Curran admitted that the relationship took place, but stated he was 17 years old and a junior in high school at the time. Nevertheless, his approval ratings plummeted fourteen points overnight in the wake of the breaking scandal.

"Effective immediately, I am no longer a candidate for public office," he declared at a hastily improvised press conference on Thursday. "I won't have my wife and children subjected to this kind of nonsense."

Curran has served on the County Board of Supervisors for six years. He was the primary architect of the Shelter Project and the Feed-the-Kids Program.

"This is shameful," charged Saratoga Springs attorney Craig McKenna. "No one is better qualified than Ken Curran to represent the Fifth District in Albany. If these idiots can get away with something like this, what's next? Roasting a candidate because he pulled down Margo Somebody's underpants in nursery school?"

NEW YORK STATE DEMOCRATIC COMMITTEE

ALBANY HEADQUARTERS   151 STATE STREET
                              ALBANY, NEW YORK 12207

May 29, 1998

VIA FACSIMILE

Craig S. McKenna, Esq.
McKenna & Webb
118 Congress Park, Suite 407
Saratoga Springs, New York 12866

Dear Mr. McKenna:

Please contact me at your earliest convenience regarding the Kenneth Curran matter. As this is an issue of some urgency, I would greatly appreciate hearing from you as soon as possible.

Very truly yours,
Wayne Duvall

MCKENNA & WEBB
A LAW PARTNERSHIP
118 CONGRESS PARK, SUITE 407
SARATOGA SPRINGS, NEW YORK 12866

May 29, 1998

VIA FACSIMILE

Mr. Wayne Duvall
New York State Democratic Committee
151 State Street
Albany, New York 12207

Dear Mr. Duvall:

Thank you for your letter of today's date. I've known Kenny for eleven years and am both shocked and appalled at what appears to be nothing short of an inquisition.

Pursuant to the message I left on your voice mail, I am happy to provide whatever assistance you require.

Very truly yours,
McKenna & Webb
Craig S. McKenna

McKenna & Webb
A Law Partnership
118 Congress Park, Suite 407
Saratoga Springs, New York 12866

MEMORANDUM

TO:	Charleen
FROM:	Craig
DATE:	May 29, 1998
SUBJECT:	Pressing Matters

---

1. Did you see my name in the paper this morning? I'm famous! (Thank God the GOP didn't find out about the strip club we booked for Kenny's bachelor party. They'd have brought back lynching.) I'm attaching a letter I just got from the Democratic Committee—it looks like they want us to represent Curran in a defamation suit against the Republican Party. I'm already horny just thinking about it.

2. Clayton decided to get personalized plates for the Bronco. They came on Tuesday: CLAY CRG. Hello? If he loves me so much, how come I'm the one who gets abbreviated? So yesterday I went down to the DMV and ordered plates for the Miata: CRAIG CL. When he found out about it, he made me sleep on the couch.

3. Our getaway house in Cape Vincent is practically finished— and except for a couple dozen carpenters, plumbers, and electricians, we built it ourselves. Clay drove up to make sure the roofers had left, but when he came back home he said the living room was crooked. That's when I remembered the support things I was supposed to put in my half of the floor but I went to take a piss first and when I came back I got sidetracked by the ribs and baked beans he was making on the grill. He didn't accept my alibi with much grace. While he

was chasing me across Loughberry Lake, I kept trying to explain that he should have known better than to trust a job like that to a boyfriend who still looks for an on-off switch on a hammer. But he wouldn't listen.

4. He's about to buy three hundred acres next to Saratoga Lake. Given what it's going to cost him, we have three choices: (a) We can live on Cheetos and Gatorade for the next nine years; (b) he can sell two and a half million power mowers by Friday; or (c) you and I can fabricate a reason to sue U.S. Steel and win. He wants to build eighteen condominiums, a golf course, and a high-toned shopping mall— sort of like Levittown for the loaded. I told him he has a moral obligation to consider affordable housing for low-income families that haven't gotten any breaks yet, and then I called him a bloated plutocrat. So he called me a mismanaged Robin Hood—and a short one.

5. You now have all the facts. Which one of us is the dreamboat and which one's the insensitive capitalist bully? Be impartial.

6. We're driving to the Cape for the weekend. In addition to learning how to walk uphill in our living room, we talked each other into renting a sailboat that neither one of us knows how to sail. If I don't show up on Monday morning, call the Coast Guard.

McKENNA & WEBB
A LAW PARTNERSHIP
118 CONGRESS PARK, SUITE 407
SARATOGA SPRINGS, NEW YORK 12866

MEMORANDUM

TO: Craig
FROM: Charleen
DATE: May 29, 1998
SUBJECT: Pressing Matters

1. The score is 2–1, Clayton. You're lucky you weren't shut out entirely. If you'd pulled the license plate crap on *me*, I'd have run you over with the Bronco.

2. On my way back from the Ballston Spa depo, I stopped off in Utica to pick up Jody's financial statements. He was wearing an olive-green T-shirt. Did I ever tell you about my Marine Corps fantasy? If not, I'll fill you in at lunch.

3. Yes, I saw the newspaper. Who was Margo and why did you pull down her underpants?

4. Would you date an attorney named Evan if you'd met him in the mergers and acquisitions section of the law library? Decide quickly because he's taking me to dinner at T-Bird's on Monday night. You and Clayton are invited. If you think he's another rhinestone in my necklace of dead-ends, just tell me so. I'm almost 38. I no longer have the time to find these things out for myself.

McKenna & Webb
A Law Partnership
118 Congress Park, Suite 407
Saratoga Springs, New York 12866

MEMORANDUM

TO: Charleen
FROM: Craig
DATE: May 29, 1998
SUBJECT: Nice Try, Sweetheart

1. You stopped in Utica on your way back from Ballston Spa? That's an eighty-mile detour. Each way!

2. I'll reserve judgment on Evan until dinner Monday. But remember the law of inverse proportions: the bigger the bore, the bigger the dick. This is what we mean by "mitigating circumstances."

3. Margo was the first of three heterosexual impulses I was obliged to endure between birth and the day Travis fell into my arms. (Number two resulted in a social disease, which simultaneously shocked my mother and earned me a bigger allowance from my father. Aren't men gross?)

4. You'd be well advised to keep your Marine Corps fantasies to yourself over lunch. Otherwise, you're going to have to hear mine—and you don't want to go there. Neither does anyone else in the Sweet Shop.

McKENNA & WEBB
A LAW PARTNERSHIP
118 CONGRESS PARK, SUITE 407
SARATOGA SPRINGS, NEW YORK 12866

MEMORANDUM

TO: Both of You
FROM: Kevin Grobeson
DATE: May 29, 1998
SUBJECT: Hey!

Craig: Clayton is the original Prince Charming and you have a depo in twenty minutes.

> Charleen: Small word. Sounds like "motion to compel." Department C. 10:30. If you need further motivation, pretend Jody's going to be there.

> Now can we get some work done?

KG

LOUISE McKENNA, M.D.   Jefferson Medical Plaza, Suite 100
OBSTETRICS/GYNECOLOGY   903 Saint Charles Street
                                      St. Louis, Missouri 63101

Darling:

Disregard my last letter. Doug Colson met an ophthalmologist named Brad and they've already signed a two-year lease in Maplewood. You see what happens when you don't seize an opportunity? But I'll keep my eyes open—after all, we can't afford to be picky. Unless it's some crank from high school who's trying to track you down. (This one had issues, so he didn't get your phone number. But watch your back anyway.)

I appreciated Clayton's birthday card, but I wish he wouldn't. It's so difficult being pleasant to him. Especially when he writes "Happy 64th" three times in the same sentence. Don't tell me he didn't do that on purpose.

Call me. I'm always here.

Love,
Mom

1998 WEEK AT A GLANCE	MONDAY MAY 25 THRU SUNDAY MAY 31
CLAYTON BERGMAN	CRAIG McKENNA
MONDAY, MAY 25	**MONDAY, MAY 25**
Memorial Day Observed	*Memorial Day Observed*
Store opens at 8: 00	Prep Stringer trial
TUESDAY, MAY 26	**TUESDAY, MAY 26**
Loan papers re: Saratoga Lake property	Prep Stringer trial
FIGHT WITH BANK	Research re: Kessler petition
WEDNESDAY, MAY 27	**WEDNESDAY, MAY 27**
Air conditioners and barbeques due in	Prep Stringer trial
THURSDAY, MAY 28	**THURSDAY, MAY 28**
Train new cashier	9:00 A.M.—Stringer trial, Dept A
INVENTORY—Late night	Prep Halvorson depo
FRIDAY, MAY 29	**FRIDAY, MAY 29**
New window display	10:00 A.M.—Halvorson depo, here
FIGHT WITH BANK	1:30 P.M.—Lunch with Jody Kessler, here
SATURDAY, MAY 30	**SATURDAY, MAY 30**
SUNDAY, MAY 31	**SUNDAY, MAY 31**
GOLD TIME WITH CRAIG— CAPE VINCENT	ME AND CLAY AT THE CAPE

We found Cape Vincent completely by accident shortly after we'd violated the Federal Uniform Boyfriend Act, Title IV, Article 3. ("Never Ever Ever Vacation with Your Sig Oth in Provincetown.") It's a complex story that involves a routine tea-dance, a boy in tumescent Speedos with his hands on my ass, an anthropological observation to Clayton ("Boy, was he cute!"), a shoving match in the middle of Commercial Street, and a change of venue to a hotel in Sackets Harbor ("a charming bayside community populated exclusively by retired couples"). But somehow we made a wrong turn out of the Tower Records parking lot in Watertown and ended up at Cape Vincent instead.

"Honey, look at that," breathed Clayton, forgetting that we hadn't been on speaking terms since Speedo Boy seventeen hours earlier. The dirt road had dead-ended at a purple-pink sunset over a green sliver of land—wedged between a glittery Wilson's Bay on the left and an indigo Lake Ontario on the right. Instinctively, we reached for each other. How could we help it?

FEDERAL UNIFORM BOYFRIEND ACT
Title IV, Article 6
("The Cape Vincent Law")

If you build it, he will come.

Six weeks later it was ours. Now we have a deed, a house, a tilted living room, a Great Lake in our backyard, and a rented sailboat tied up to our very own pier. (I'm still not sure how Clayton worked it, but ever since escrow closed, our sky's been the color of a turquoise Crayola crayon, and we've cornered the controlling interest in the breeze cartel.) It's the kind of hideaway where two people can forget all about the ass-kicking week they've both survived in the real world and grapple with the issues that really count:

11:00 *Wearing only cutoffs, we're lying on our backs in the sailboat, my head on his chest and his fingers all tangled up in my hair. Clayton's eyebrows are bunched up, so I can tell he's got something hefty on his mind. Finally he spills it.*

"Remember the time we drove down to Baltimore to see the Sox play at Camden Yards?" he mumbles absently. Who wouldn't? We rear-ended Brady Anderson in the parking lot.

"What about it?"

"Where did we go for dinner?"

"The crabcake place. You had clams."

"Oh," he sighs, relaxing all at once. "Right." His eyebrows go back to normal. Sometimes he's so very easy to fix.

Noon *Lunch. Marc Antony is feeding Julius Caesar red grapes. He's also pouting in an entirely un-Richard-Burton-like fashion.*

"Why don't you have a nickname for me?" demands Clayton, licking grape juice off my nose.

"Huh?"

"You know what I mean!" he insists, possibly blushing for only the third time since I've known him. "I call you 'Honey', but you still call me 'Clay'. It's just not right." I prop myself up on one elbow and play with his navel. There's a fast cure for *this* crisis.

"What if I called you 'Pokey' instead?" I suggest, staring up into his big brown eyes with counterfeit sincerity. Hastily, he shoves another pair of grapes into my mouth.

"Forget I said anything," he growls.

1:00   *A passing motorboat kicks up a spray that sends us bobbing gently into one of the pilings. Clayton sits up and steadies the keel (or whatever the hell it's called). He looks a little distracted.*

"Honey?" he mutters nervously, picking up a towel and drying us off. "Should I go through with the Saratoga Lake deal?" I knew this was going to happen sooner or later. Even tough guys get scared sometimes.

"Cold feet?" I ask, as though it hadn't even occurred to me.

"Uh—yeah."

"Don't worry," I assure him, toying with his always-sexy stubble. "I'll keep them warm for you." With a relieved grin, he loops the towel around my neck and yanks my face toward his.

"I love you," he says.

"Duh," I reply.

2:00   *I flip over on my stomach so he can rub sunscreen on my back. He probably knows it's making me horny, but I'm not about to admit it—at least not directly.*

"Clay?"

"What?"

"Can we untie this thing from the dock and take it out into the bay where nobody can see us?"

"No," he retorts, slapping my ass (which only makes things worse). "Drowning's not on today's schedule of activities. I have other plans for you." Then he rolls over on his side and flexes his lats at me. He's insidious.

3:00   *Clayton reaches into the cooler for another beer, then drops an ice cube on my neck to see what happens. I yelp.*

"How come we fight so much?" I ask, sliding one down the back of his cutoffs.

"How come a dog licks his balls?" he replies, squirming.

"Because he can."

"It's the same principle."

4:00 *A pair of cumulocirrus clouds passes directly above us. From a vantage point between Clayton's clavicle and his chin, I can make out South America. Clayton sees Ho Chi Minh's face.*

"You think we'll ever adopt a kid like Noah?" I sigh, snuggling closer. Clayton frowns.

"I already *have* a kid like Noah," he retorts. "His name is Craig."

"Kiss my ass."

"Later."

5:00 *The temperature's dropping, so we put on our T-shirts. Mine smells like turpentine. His smells like Clayton. It occurs to me that I haven't tormented him in five hours. I must be slipping.*

"Pokey," I murmur innocently. "How about if I sue the Republican Party when Ken Curran asks me to?"

"It depends on whether or not you behave," he snaps.

"What does *that* mean?"

"No tear gas. *And stop calling me Pokey!*"

6:00 *Clayton's head is on my shoulder. He's sound asleep. In a minute I'll wake him up so that he won't miss our sunset, but for now there's one last issue I need to handle by myself.*

FEDERAL UNIFORM BOYFRIEND ACT
Title IV, Article 9 (enacted 5/30/98)
("The Travis Law")

Stop wondering who's trying to get in touch
with you from high school. It's probably only
Kerry Fusaro or Tom Lee.

So put your heart back in Clayton's pocket
where it's safe. Your life is complicated
enough already.

NEW YORK STATE DEMOCRATIC COMMITTEE

ALBANY HEADQUARTERS   151 STATE STREET
                                   ALBANY, NEW YORK 12207

June 1, 1998

VIA FACSIMILE

Craig S. McKenna, Esq.
McKenna & Webb
118 Congress Park, Suite 407
Saratoga Springs, New York 12866

Dear Craig:

Thank you for your prompt reply to my letter of Friday. I'd like
to schedule a meeting with you some time during the next few
days if at all possible. Please let me know if your schedule can
accommodate me.

Very truly yours,
Wayne Duvall

McKenna & Webb
A Law Partnership
118 Congress Park, Suite 407
Saratoga Springs, New York 12866

June 1, 1998

VIA FACSIMILE

Mr. Wayne Duvall
New York State Democratic Committee
151 State Street
Albany, New York 12207

Dear Wayne:

Sorry we keep missing each other. My calendar's a little jammed this week, but I can rearrange Thursday to meet with you at your convenience.

If I'm out when you call, please schedule a time with my assistant, Kevin Grobeson. He'll be expecting to hear from you.

Meanwhile, I've already begun to research Ken's suit against the Republican mudslingers and will fill you in when we get together.

Very truly yours,
McKenna & Webb
Craig S. McKenna

MCKENNA & WEBB
A LAW PARTNERSHIP
118 CONGRESS PARK, SUITE 407
SARATOGA SPRINGS, NEW YORK 12866

MEMORANDUM

TO: Kevin
FROM: Craig
DATE: June 1, 1998
SUBJECT: The Democrats

KG:

When this guy calls, get him in here as soon as you can. I need to kick some GOP ass.

CSM

P.S. If you're not doing anything for dinner, bring your boy du jour to T-Bird's. One of my college buddies is opening a sixties act he calls Johnny Angel and Venus (true names: Grid Tarbell and Rachel Schwartz), and in between sets we can all make fun of Charleen's new steady.

McKenna & Webb
A Law Partnership
118 Congress Park, Suite 407
Saratoga Springs, New York 12866

MEMORANDUM

TO:	Craig
FROM:	Charleen
DATE:	June 2, 1998
SUBJECT:	Boyfriends

Thank you for alienating my date. Had I known he was a fundamentalist, I would have done it myself. Remember when you and Clayton were considering the honeymoon in Greece? That wasn't NutraSweet he kept dropping into his tea—it was Tylenol.

Jody sent me geraniums. Why is he doing this?! Is he stimulated by rejection?

Ch

P.S. Please assure me that Grid Tarbell wasn't as erotic in college as he was at T-Bird's. My "Missed Opportunities" dance card is already at critical mass. And I can't believe it was actually Clayton who talked you and Grid into "Light My Fire" last night. Either he's forgotten what happens whenever you wander near a stage (about as likely as Bill Clinton forgetting he has genitals), or else Harvard was a lot tamer than we remember it.

Craig McKenna **Attorney Notes**

By sophomore year, I'd already earned an entirely undeserved reputation across campus as a rabble-rouser. According to a highly illegal copy of my transcript—purloined at my request by a hunky swimmer in the dean's office whom I'd once dated long enough to determine that the rumors about his cock were altogether understated—I was an instigator, a provocateur, a demagogue, and a seditionist.

"What the fuck is an agitprop?" I mumbled to myself, thumbing through the pages late one night when I should have been reading Dostoevski instead.

"It means you've got a big mouth," shouted Clayton from the shower. "I told you so."

Me?

Psychology 311

PROFESSOR: What do we call a patient with paranoid schizophrenic tendencies who still manages to assimilate himself into the social structure?

CRAIG: A Republican.

Mathematics 204

PROFESSOR: We accept that pi equals 3.14159 because theoretically it's endless and there's no sense letting it ramble.

CRAIG: Sort of like Jerry Falwell.

American History 126

PROFESSOR: Certain facts about Alexander Hamilton are still coming to light. His imperialism. His obstinance.

CRAIG: His boyfriend.

Government 210

PROFESSOR: If there's one thing we've learned since the collapse of the polis in 509 B.C. it's that change takes time.

CRAIG: Bullshit. If we had a Students for Human Rights Commission around here, it'd take about fifteen minutes.

ALETHEA: You got *that* right. Craig, I can get us the Freshman Union.

ETHAN: I can handle the fliers.

DARBY: What about a permit?

JORDAN: We don't need one. Hey, Craig. Can I chair a subcommittee?

And suddenly the sixties were back.

"It happened *again*," I moaned to Charleen over coffee at the Greenhouse. "I was only being theoretical!"

"That's what Einstein said after Hiroshima," she snapped, slicing a chicken salad sandwich into eight equal pieces and handing me two of them. (Usually I got three. She must have been *really* pissed.) "Craig, if you think I'm going to spend the next six years—including law school—unchaining your ass from a series of Corinthian columns dotting this institution of higher learning—"

"Who asked you to?" I demanded.

"Who has a choice?! Have you told Clayton yet?" The blood instantly drained out of my face.

"Oh my God," I groaned. "If he finds out about this—"

"Yes, Lucy. 'If he finds out about this.'"

"You wouldn't."

"I should."

"But you won't."

"I know."

Eventually, of course, Clayton had to discover that he was married to an unintentional subversive. If nothing else, there was the little matter of a headline in the *Crimson* that required an adroit *pas-de-deux* to 'splain away: "McKenna Welcomes Cardinal Cook with Sit-in." Not that I was completely successful with the ballet metaphor; as a matter of fact, we didn't have sex for the longest two weeks of my life—but once the Archdiocese had slapped a temporary moratorium on its queers-burn-in-hell oratory, Clayton relented. *Maybe the little shit knows what he's doing.*

"But no bottles and no bricks," he warned.

Our first SHR meeting was held in a lounge at the Freshman Union. Thirty-four people showed up. A month later, we'd clocked two hundred members and Charleen had snared us a classroom. ("I employed the 'wouldn't it be unfortunate if the *Boston Globe* got its hands on a story like this?' routine again. They fell for it. A second time. Have you ever heard of a flat learning curve before?") Maybe our agenda was a little unrealistic, but hey—we weren't even 20 yet. What the hell did *we* know?

Students for Human Rights
Meeting Minutes

1. Alethea Cathcart was refused admission to a dance club called Orion in Beacon Hill on grounds that they'd reached capacity. However, seven Caucasians were waved through the ropes while Alethea continued to wait. Craig assigned a subcommittee to draft fliers and posters warning kids to stay away from Orion. They'll be papered across Beacon Hill, Back Bay, and the Fens.

2. Jordan Halper's boyfriend, Kenji Fukuda, has been harassed repeatedly by members of the freshman soccer team. The assaults have included destruction of personal property, physical abuse, and a spray-painted warning on

the door of his room in Lowell House: "Remember Pearl Harbor." Craig organized a zap attack on the Freshman Athletic Department, to take place immediately.

3. Ethan Whaley read a statement from the Archdiocese of Boston, claiming that sexual deviates are a moral threat to Christianity. Craig requested volunteers to help him stage a sit-in during Cardinal Cook's visit to the university next month. He assured the membership that this was one of those rare occasions where we weren't required to behave. One hundred and fourteen students raised their hands.

4. Darby Burnett reported on a sports bar in the South End that has a sign over the mirror reading "No Dykes." Craig suggested that 150 lesbians show up during next Sunday's playoff game, and then he appointed an ad hoc committee to spread the word.

We kicked and we screamed, but we got the job done. And nothing was going to stand in our way.

~

The honeymoon ended on July 3, 1981. Two things happened that day that made me wish Travis had never taught me what "irony" meant. First I received an unexpected letter from a kid with shy eyes who'd once been afraid to tell anyone his name:

Dear Craig,

Living in Indiana was like hiding out from the law. All they had to do was find out certain things about you and suddenly you had broken body parts.

I didn't think Boston was going to be any different until you stood up in front of a class filled with mostly straight people and talked about your boyfriend. It was like hearing the Declaration of Independence read out loud for the first time, or get-

ting to start your life all over again. That's why I joined the
SHR.

Anyway, I just wanted to say thanks. Bet you never thought
you'd be anybody's hero before.

Ethan Whaley

Then I opened the *New York Times*. Buried on page A20
was a tiny headline that nonetheless packed the wallop of an
impending nightmare:

RARE CANCER SEEN IN 41 HOMOSEXUALS

Yeah, right, sure, I thought, beginning to sweat bullets. *Just
another excuse to scare us.*
As it turned out, Ethan was the first in our group to find
out otherwise.

~

*Petrified, I picked up the telephone and dialed our number, praying
that he'd answer. Please be home Please be home Please be home
Please be home Please—*
"Yeah."
"Clay, it's me." The words tumbled out in a rush. I was so fucking grateful to hear his voice, I swore I'd never fight with him
again. "Something's the matter with Eeth."
"Honey, stop crying," he said, hugging me with his voice. "Just
tell me what happened." Behind me, my study partner was doubled
over on his bed, retching violently.
"I don't know," I sobbed. "There's two more purple things on his
face and white stuff inside his mouth and when I tried to give him
soup, he threw up blood. Now he can't stop." In the background I
could hear Clayton picking up his car keys.
"I'm calling an ambulance. Sit tight. It'll only take me ten minutes to get there."

"Clay, I'm really scared."

"I love you."

~

AIDS pretty much ended things between me and Clayton. Once the figures began pouring in from the CDC—with a polite "No, thanks" from Nancy Reagan's husband—the message was loud and clear: We were alone in the trenches fighting for our lives, and meanwhile I had a lover who didn't want me to make waves.

"How can you ask me to keep my mouth shut!" I cried, hurling a medical dictionary at him late one night. "Ethan was killed by a *sheep* disease and nobody gives a fuck! Including you!"

"*I said leave it alone!*" he thundered, throwing it back at me and storming out of the apartment.

~

The phone rang at 2:14 in the morning. We were still pretzeled together from our earlier "I-Love-You-I-Hate-You-Shut-Up-and-Fuck-Me" tango, but I had enough of an arm free to grapple with the receiver.

"'Lo?" I mumbled, trying not to wake him up.

"I'm at Mass General," said a barely controlled Charleen, a Code-Blue page clearly audible behind her. Alarmed, I sat up in bed and dropped the whisper.

"Darby again?"

"He's got pneumonia and they can't control it." A deep breath. "Craig, have you ever known me to panic?"

"No. Why?" The minute her voice cracked, I knew that Darby was going to die.

"Because I don't think he's going to make it this time."

"I'm on my way," I blurted, hanging up instantly. I kissed Clayton, hit the dirt, grabbed my Jimi Hendrix T-shirt and a pair

of sweatpants, and ran all the way to Massachusetts General. This couldn't *be happening to Darby.*

~

In spite of Clayton's edict, I didn't exactly leave it alone—I turned into a half-pint Larry Kramer in a Red Sox cap. Die-ins, bleed-ins, memorial marches—anything to wake people up. But no matter how many peaceful protests I organized, they always seemed to attract the National Guard: according to the box scores, I was arrested nine times in eleven months. (Charleen usually bailed me out with a credit card. At an 18 percent APR. Activism converted to profit, courtesy of Citibank.) Jail didn't really bother me, though. It was the only place I got any studying done.

By then Clayton and I were barely speaking: a pair of grunts at breakfast and a who-gets-the-bathroom-first parley at night. (Did we really used to shower together?) We were way too unhappy to fight any more—kind of like Lucy and Desi at the very end. It finally came to a head when I cooked up a three-state strike in front of the White House.

"I said no," he demanded, spinning me around to face him in the middle of Harvard Yard. "If you start one more riot, we're finished."

"Clayton," I hissed through gritted teeth, "three hundred people are dead, and Reagan's head is still up his ass!"

"You're gonna have to make a choice."

"I hope you don't mean this." He glared at me for an angry moment, then let go of my shoulders and pushed past me wordlessly.

He meant it. When I got back from Washington, he was gone.

~

Charleen and I sat in matching ghastly blue plastic chairs and stared vacantly at the swinging doors with the words Emergencies

Only stenciled in red above the glass. After a moment, they opened to reveal an apologetic Chinese American intern whom, under other circumstances, I would have found blindingly cute.

"I'm sorry," he said softly, kneeling in front of us. "We couldn't stop the hemorrhaging. Jordan died at approximately 3:26." After the customarily awkward condolences, he stood up and left us alone. Charleen and I turned to each other.

"Whose turn is it to plan the memorial service?" I asked idly. Charleen shrugged.

"I picked up the last two," she replied. "You owe me one." Then she took my hand and we went back to staring at the swinging doors.

~

For the next three and a half years, I was Jack Kerouac without a Neal Cassady: I smoked pot, I watched my friends die, I hitchhiked to California, I hunted for Travis, I got drunk when I couldn't find him, I went to law school, I got laid, I felt for swollen glands, I watched my friends die, I stayed away from the Harvard Center for Business Administration so I wouldn't run into Clayton, I pretended I didn't see him when I ran into him anyway, I passed the bar exam, I got laid some more, I searched for lesions, I got my blood tested, I grew up, and I watched my friends die. It was all quite tragic and inevitably romantic.

"Don't I remind you of Lenny Bruce?" I asked Charleen. At my insistence, we'd gone to a smoky jazz club so I could wear dark glasses, drink rosé wine, and brood.

"Impersonating whom?" she retorted. "Rosalind Russell?"

But Clayton and I couldn't possibly stay apart forever, and we both knew it. Shortly after I began clerking for my first law firm (Schnitzler, Fickman, Something & Something), I stopped by Wordsworth Harvard Square on my way home. Normally, you wouldn't have caught me dead in the philosophy section, but I was just lonely enough to look toward Socrates for answers: Why was my Walkman broken and why had another friend gone off life support and why did they forget to put the mushrooms on my pizza and—

"Hey," said Clayton from somewhere behind me. I could smell his soap before I'd even heard his voice.

"Hey," I mumbled, turning to face him. We stood there staring at one another awkwardly for a good fifteen seconds. He'd put on at least ten more pounds of muscle (like he needed it) and he was wearing the Moody Blues T-shirt I'd bought him in Woodstock. We each seemed a little wearier than the other remembered.

"You look great," he sighed, eyeing me from top to bottom while I was doing the same thing to him.

"So do you." It wasn't really necessary to figure out where all this was going. After you've spent four years kissing somebody's perineum, the subtext talks louder than the words do. And I was way too tired to fight it.

"Have coffee with me?" he suggested hopefully.

"Are you going to ask me to move back in?"

"Only if you don't ask first."

I didn't, but he did. So I requested five minutes to think it over, and then I said yes. It was the Moody Blues T-shirt that did me in.

~

Charleen's right—Harvard was a long time ago. Besides, I'm not a troublemaker any more. Those days are over.

NEW YORK STATE DEMOCRATIC COMMITTEE

ALBANY HEADQUARTERS   151 STATE STREET
                                    ALBANY, NEW YORK 12207

June 2, 1998

VIA FACSIMILE

Craig S. McKenna, Esq.
McKenna & Webb
118 Congress Park, Suite 407
Saratoga Springs, New York 12866

Dear Craig:

I'm looking forward to our Thursday meeting. However, it appears as if we've gotten our signals crossed. Though we're always interested in filing suit against the Republican Party, that's not why I contacted you. We want you to run for State Assembly on behalf of the Fifth Congressional District.

Sorry for the misunderstanding. See you Thursday.

Very truly yours,
Wayne Duvall

8

Travis

THE PERILOUS JOURNEY OF TRAVIS PUCKETT

PART I
Travis and Brandon in an Orange Corvette
(Traveler's Advisory: If you're going to accept a ride from a guy in an Orange Corvette whom you meet at a Chevron station when your timing belt goes out, make sure you determine his taste in music first.)

L.A. to Needles

If I didn't already loathe ABBA, the first ninety miles would have convinced me to nuke my copy of *Muriel's Wedding*. We bonded to "Dancing Queen"—fifteen times on the way to San Bernardino. *In heavy traffic!*

Unimportant stuff: He's 28 years old, his last name is Tracey, he's a record producer, he lives in Holmby Hills, and he owns a ranch in Amarillo.

Critical stats: He has sandy blond hair, heterosexual-green eyes, biceps many men would pay to bite, and I'm guessing 8 inches by 6 inches, cut. On the McKenna scale, he's a 9.

Needles to Flagstaff
(Same CD. By now I didn't just hate ABBA, I hated Sweden too.)

In a desperate effort to drown out "Fernando," I began comparing opinions with Brandon on Super Bowls and point spreads and earned run averages and personal fouls. He seemed particularly impressed when I suggested that the Jets had made a big mistake in 1993 after they'd dumped Kenny O'Brien for Boomer Esiason.

"Why O'Brien?" he asked smugly. "Ever check out his stats?"

"Ever check out his ass?" Credentials established.

Then I told him about Craig. He handled it pretty well.

Flagstaff to Albuquerque

"You mean you haven't seen this guy in twenty years?!" he asked incredulously. "What if he looks like Jesse Helms by now?!" We fought all the way to the New Mexico border—partly because I had Craig's honor to uphold and partly because as long as we were calling each other assholes he wasn't playing ABBA.

"I know what I'm talking about," he insisted hotly. "I had one of those too. Jennifer Carson. When she moved to Chicago, it ended. So what? Life happens."

"Do you still have dreams about her?" I demanded, ignoring Gallup. He shrugged.

"Maybe."

"Do you still love her?"

"What difference does it make!" he blurted, banging the steering wheel impatiently. By then I was pretty sure I had his number (1–800-JULIET), so I began harassing him with pointed references to *Brigadoon,* the chocolate chip cookies, the first kiss in the rain, and still ordering hot-and-sour soup every June 4th because that's the anniversary of the day Craig and I discovered it together. Brandon claimed I was nuts and changed the subject. Then we pulled into Albuquerque and I mentioned that Ethel Mertz had been born there, but he didn't seem to give a shit about that either.

Albuquerque to Amarillo

We drove the next 176 miles in absolute silence (i.e., no ABBA). Then suddenly he hit the brakes, cut across four lanes of traffic, slid down the Tucumcari off-ramp, and skidded to a stop at a Phillips 66 station.

"Be right back," he said brusquely, hopping out of the Corvette and heading for a phone booth. I suspected he was calling Jennifer and I wasn't wrong. For two hours I studied his face through the windshield and watched the way he bounded across the asphalt when he was done. He was wearing the same kind of magic I'd been seeing in the mirror all week.

"Is St. Louis on the way to Chicago?" he mumbled, buckling himself in. I couldn't help grinning at the sheer breathlessness of it all. Been there, done that, got the T-shirt.

"Yep."

"Then you've got yourself a ride," he said. We took off doing about eighty.

Amarillo to St. Louis
*(With a brief stop in Commerce, Oklahoma, so we could drop
a couple of 7-Eleven flowers in front of the house that Mutt
Mantle and his son Mickey Charles had once called home.)*

By the book, it was 764 miles. But we had a lot of rehearsing to do. After all, this wasn't going to be a routine first date for either one of us:

1. *Play it cool.* If they find out we can't stop thinking about them, we're sunk.
2. *Make it romantic.* Restaurants are okay, but pick places we know they'll like. (Thai for Jennifer, Italian for Craig.)
3. *Keep the reminiscing PG-rated.* It's okay to bring up losing the glass monkey in the snow (Jen) and the mistletoe in August (Craig), but leave the naked stuff out of it. There'll be plenty of time for that later.
4. *Listen to your heart.* The first kiss is going to be one for the books, so wait until it feels right. Then go for it.
5. *Don't rush things.* Falling in love all over again takes work. Face it—you're not a kid any more. "And I don't think you'll ever be a kid again, kiddo." (Elaine Stritch, *Company*.)

By the time we'd reached the Gateway Arch and a rainy downtown St. Louis, we had our signals straight. All we needed to do was tie up a couple of panicky loose ends.

"What if Craig doesn't remember me?"

"Suppose I don't appeal to Jen any more?"

"Yeah, right," I grumbled, eyeballing his grin-and-body combo. As I struggled with both a Gap backpack and a Corvette seat belt, he reached across my lap and flipped open the glove compartment.

"Wait a second—I've got something for you," he said, fishing through it nimbly. "Sort of a good luck present." He came up with *ABBA Gold*. In two volumes. Turns out that Brandon supervises all of their American recording sessions.

"Wow," I lied, staring into his two thousand perfect white teeth. Then, on impulse, he leaned over the hand brake and hugged me.

"Thanks, Trav," he mumbled quietly. "Maybe we'll make it a double wedding." Though I was wearing a denim shirt, I could still feel his 50-inch pecs pressing against my 42s.

Jennifer's got it made. For life.

GordoStud.com

T:

Sick as it sounds, I miss the smell of Pledge. Just let me know you're alive. Please? 48 hours without a word—now I know how a parent feels when he sends his 6-year-old to first grade.

G

G:

I found 5135 Kensington Avenue, where Esther and Tootie lived in *Meet Me in St. Louis*. (It's actually a vacant lot now, but the Boy Next Door's house is still there.) While I was taking pictures, I bumped into a young man with gold teeth and a Mohawk. Guess who'd never heard of Judy Garland before?

Since Brandon didn't drop me off until 4:30, it was too late to track down Craig's mother this afternoon, so D-day's tomorrow. Meanwhile I'm staying at a Motel 6 five blocks from Busch Stadium. $89 a night! Is there such thing as a Motel 3?

By the way, I met the woman you're going to marry. (And I insist.) Her name is A.J. and she owns the restaurant next door. I couldn't figure out what made her call me Beaver Cleaver until she enumerated the seven times I used "kind of" in the same sentence. Thanks for nothing. Isn't it *your* job to spot these character kinks before they get out of hand?!

Oh, yeah—three more stats. She's our age, she wears James Dean T-shirts, and she drives a black Buick named Robert Mitchum. There didn't seem to be any point in asking why.

As soon as I get my hands on Craig's address, I'm out of here. I'll let you know where I'm headed. Fingers crossed that he doesn't live in Turkey.

T

T:
If I got rid of all your character kinks, there wouldn't be anything left but a spleen.

    Go back to the part about A.J. Who does she look like?

G

G:
Remember in twelfth grade when we saw *Grease* and you fell in love with Stockard Channing? Same ballpark.

T

T:
Sigh. Give her my Web link. I'll be your best friend.

G

G:
I already did and you already are. I need a bigger payoff than that.

T

FROM THE JOURNAL OF
Travis Puckett

When you have a meeting with the Head Beagle at 9:00 in the morning, there shouldn't have to be a night before.

—*Snoopy*

Streaker's is an eating establishment built to look just like turn-of-the-century St. Louis—gas lamps along the walls, hitching posts in the men's room, and a railed bar that's a dead ringer for the Riverboat Saloon. Even the lunch counter could have come right off the MGM back lot—a fact I aggressively pointed out to the future Mrs. Gordon Duboise without stopping to think that since she first took over the restaurant eight years ago, at least 15,612 of Dorothy's Midwestern friends have probably told her the same thing.

"Know what's missing?" I mused to A.J., color-coding my peas and carrots in even rows of eight as I eyeballed an authentic 1903 railroad track running around the perimeter of the floor. In reply, she leaned across my Salisbury steak and deliberately dropped an intrepid cherry tomato splat in the middle of my orange-and-green plate arrangement.

"Beaver, so help me God," she warned, "if you even *think* 'Clang, clang, clang, went the trolley', you're out of here on your ass." (Busted!) So I bypassed the customary Vincente Minnelli monologue, left the peas in chaos, and filled her in on my updated Craig itinerary instead. After that, dinner was on the house—despite the fact that it only took me thirty-six minutes to begin irritating the shit out of her (possibly a new gold medal record).

Streaker's

Restaurant and Bar
(around the corner from the St. Louis Cardinals)

CUSTOMER COMMENTS

A.J., I didn't mean to piss you off about the olives. I just thought the bar would look neater if all the pimentos were pointing down.

Do you need any help cleaning up? I'm a little nervous tonight.

Beaver, stop setting the fucking tables. I'm not insured for you. And the customers think you're an outpatient.

Go back to your hotel. Get into bed. Go to sleep. You're making me nuts.

Motel 6 is a terrific place for staring at the ceiling in the dark. Especially when your entire life is hanging in the balance. If you've got four quarters, the bed vibrates. Big deal. Craig used to make it do that for free.

What if his mother's on vacation? What if she won't tell me where to find him? How do I get her to trust me?!

OPTION 1: Dr. McKenna, I've just gotten over a bad case of strep throat, and I wanted to make sure I wasn't contagious any more. By the way, how's Craig?

OPTION 2: Dr. McKenna, I've been having this pain in my abdomen, and I just wanted to make sure it wasn't appendicitis or—Oh my God! That picture on your desk! I went to school with that guy! He's your *what?* You're kidding! What's his address?

OPTION 3: Dr. McKenna, I'm the history professor you spoke with on the phone and I was hoping— OW! Doctor, my fingers are still in the door!

OPTION 4: Dr. McKenna, I don't really have irritable bowel syndrome, I'm just in love with your son. How much do you want for his phone number?

OPTION 5: Where's the Rolodex, bitch?

A.J.'s right. I've lost my mind. But I'll go with appendicitis anyway.

GordoStud.com

G:

Why didn't somebody tell me she was a gynecologist?! Do you know how it looked?! Nine pregnant women in the waiting room, and I'm up at reception holding my stomach and moaning! "What trimester are you in, sir?" Fuck you, lady!

G, I couldn't have been more than 15 feet from his address. I could practically smell it. So here's the plan. Unless one of your Internet harlots lives in St. Louis and can help me out, I'm going to ask A.J. I have an idea.

T

T:

I know where this is going. Don't.

G

**FROM THE JOURNAL OF
Travis Puckett**

Streaker's

Restaurant and Bar
(around the corner from the St. Louis Cardinals)

CUSTOMER COMMENTS

A.J., please don't take this the wrong way, but would you have any strenuous objections to playing the part of my wife? It'd only take half an hour. Just long enough to have a pelvic exam. I can explain if you want me to.

Apparently, there are fixed limits to A.J.'s sense of romance. I just found them.

My life is over. When I die, they'll discover me on this bench in the middle of the same downpour, staring at a vacant lot on Kensington Avenue in St. Louis. "Roses are red, John's name is Truett, Esther's in love, and we always knew it." Kiss my ass.

These are the facts: (a) His mother is the only one who knows where he lives; (b) She thinks I'm a serial killer; (c) Unless I grow an ovary, I'll never get in to see her; and (d) It's raining on me.

Oh, no. Not another déjà vu. . . .

~

August 1978. The Mets game was rained out, so we took our hot dogs and each other to Flushing Meadow Park, where we found an empty bandshell next to the Unisphere that was custom-built for making out in the middle of an achingly romantic thunderstorm. Since we were soaked to the skin by then, we pulled off our Mets T-shirts in a single yank. (Not that we really needed the pretense. Being naked with one another—even a little bit—remained a potent narcotic. Fuck pot.) In moments, we were stretched out on the rain-spattered grass and locked together in an embrace so singular in its execution, we'd already applied for a patent.

"Craigy?" I murmured, kissing the top of his head. "How come they call snapdragons 'snapdragons'?"

"Because 'snapdragon' is Chinese for 'eternal sunshine'," he replied, not looking up. "Like you."

"It is?"

"No. But it sure sounded real, didn't it?" This was his cue to reach for my hand and nod toward the big steel globe in front of us.

"Hey, Smerko?" he asked, pointing at North America. "If I promised you all of that, would you believe me?" Suspecting he was serious and determined to find out for sure, I crinkled my forehead as though I were deliberating in front of Congress.

"I dunno," I mumbled dubiously. "That's a lot of work. It'd prob'ly mean we'd have to spend the rest of our lives together." As soon as the one-dimple thing happened, I knew I'd given him the right answer.

"When do we start?" he grinned.

~

We start right now, Craigy. Remember what Madame Rose said in *Gypsy?* "Desperate people do desperate things."

FROM THE JOURNAL OF
Travis Puckett

THE PUCKETT/DUBOISE DEBATES

GORDO: Hello?

TRAVIS: Gordo?

GORDO: Travis, where are you? Why are you whispering?

TRAVIS: I'm in Dr. McKenna's office. I had to break in.

GORDO: You *what?!*

TRAVIS: How else was I going to get my hands on her Rolodex?

GORDO: Travis, that's a felony!

TRAVIS: No. The cleaning people are here and the door was already open. It's only a misdemeanor. Now, listen to me. I found Craig. He's in Saratoga Springs, New York. If I can hitch a ride as far as—

GORDO: You're going to call him first—right?

TRAVIS: Call him? You mean *talk* to him?

GORDO: Isn't that the general idea?

TRAVIS: What if he figures out who it is? If he
            remembers me like *I* remember me, I'm
            sunk.

GORDO: Travis, you're squeaking again.

TRAVIS: I have to go.

GORDO: Don't leave any prints.

TRAVIS: I've already dusted.

FROM THE DESK OF
Gordon Duboise

Pop:

The first half of the outline. Let me know what you think.

ARGOSY ENTERTAINMENT
Literary Representatives

LOS ANGELES   TORONTO
NEW YORK   LONDON

Gordon:

There may be a problem on page 6. Are you sure you want to
have him break into her office? No one's that much of a nut
ball.

When do I get to find out what happens?

GordoStud.com

Gordo:

You don't know me, but I own a restaurant in St. Louis and Travis is in jail. He called me from the police station and asked me to remind you that the freezer needs to be defrosted next week.

It's probably my fault that he wound up in the clink. I shouldn't have kicked him out for rearranging my olives or asking me to pose as his wife. Ever had a pelvic exam? It's like driving a Ferrari through a keyhole. If this doesn't make any sense, tough shit. Pathologize him yourself.

The arraignment's at 2:00 A.M. All he needs is somebody to vouch for him (I ought to have my head examined) and $175 for the trespassing fine. That's if he doesn't tell them what he was *really* doing in a gynecologist's office at midnight. Personally, if I was a judge and he spilled the genuine beans, I'd lock him up for ten to twenty. Maximum security. Anybody who's willing to hitch three thousand miles after twenty years to find a boy who's probably forgotten him in the first place is either a public menace or an angel. And so far the evidence is pretty conclusive.

After I spring his ass, he's sleeping on my living room couch where I can keep an eye on him. Call it a time-out. He can have his motel room back when he learns how to behave.

By the way, your website is pretty unappetizing. Most women already think that men are just penises with support systems. You're not helping.

A.J. Larkin

A.J.:

Which olive routine did he pull? Taking out the pits or pointing the pimentos down?

He's only got $837 in traveler's checks on him (not count-
ing the Neiman-Marcus credit card), but he needs it to find
Craig. So I just wired $175 to the Western Union office on
Lewis and Clark Boulevard. It's in your name and they're open
all night.

I think you got the wrong impression from my website. I
am a penis with a support system. Didn't you check out my
Speedo pictures while you were there?

Call me as soon as you get Travis home. I don't care how
late it is. I have a date tonight, but since I can't remember her
name we ought to be in and out of bed pretty quick. (Actually, I
made that up—but I figure you deserve a run for your money.)

Gordo

P.S. One word of advice before you invite him over: lock up
the Pine-Sol.

ST. LOUIS POLICE DEPARTMENT

STATEMENT

*Please detail your recollection of the circumstances surround-
ing your arrest. This statement is inadmissible as evidence
until you have signed it where indicated.*

Dear Your Honor:

In the event you have issues about sexual orientation, please
global-search the name Craig and replace it with Mar or Beth
or Heather at your discretion. In any scenario, the points of law
remain the same.

Craig and I fell in love with each other when we were kids,

but for some reason it didn't sink in until last week. So I tried to track him down and ran into a brick wall instead. Then I remembered that his mother was a doctor in St. Louis—but when I called her, she didn't seem to respond well to the fact that I was sleep-deprived and incoherent. That's why I decided I needed to talk to her in person. But after I got here, I found out she was a gynecologist, so I couldn't exactly make an appointment with her. Which brings us to the night in question.

While I was pacing the streets deciding whether to jump out a window or hang myself, I passed the Jefferson Medical Center, which is approximately two blocks from my motel. It was then I noticed that the front door was open and the security guard was nowhere to be seen (presumably, he was relieving himself elsewhere). I didn't intend to enter the premises, but the opportunity was irresistible. It was kind of like when Fanny Brice stuck the pillow under her wedding dress just before the bride number so she'd look pregnant. She didn't mean to do it, but it was sitting there on the couch practically daring her.

Once inside, I discovered that the door to Dr. McKenna's suite was ajar and a cleaning cart was in the hall. Since I saw no one else present, I kind of squirmed my way past the reception desk and into the doctor's office. Which is actually kind of touching when you think about it. After all, it's not like I was stealing anything.

Having found Dr. McKenna's Rolodex sitting on her desk, it was only a matter of moments before I'd located Craig's address and telephone number. Period. That's all I did. But by then I could hear a vacuum cleaner coming down the hall, so I knew I couldn't go out the way I came in. And seeing as Suite 100 is on the first floor, I saw no harm in leaving by the window. That's when the alarm went off. They have an excellent security system, Your Honor.

If I hadn't slipped in the mud and landed in an azalea bush, I'd have been back at Motel 6 before the police even showed up. But it didn't work out that way.

That's the whole truth, Your Honor. And if you were in love, you'd have done the same thing.

Respectfully submitted,
Travis Puckett

On second thought, this is a really bad idea. Especially if they still have firing squads in Missouri. Maybe I'd better lie. Through my teeth.

1	**MUNICIPAL COURT OF THE ST. LOUIS JUDICIAL DISTRICT**
2	**COUNTY OF ST. LOUIS, STATE OF MISSOURI**
3	
4	CITY OF ST. LOUIS,) CASE NO. M98–020331
5	)
6	Plaintiff,) ARRAIGNMENT
7	)
8	vs.)
9	)
10	TRAVIS PUCKETT,)
11	)
12	Defendant.)
13	_____)
14	
15	**TRANSCRIPT OF PROCEEDINGS**
16	The Honorable Brent Carter, Judge Presiding
17	BAILIFF: THE COURT CALLS THE DEFENDANT,
18	TRAVIS PUCKETT.
19	(THE OATH IS ADMINISTERED)
20	THE COURT: WHAT WERE YOU DOING ON THE GROUNDS
21	OF THE JEFFERSON MEDICAL CENTER
22	WHILE THE ALARM WAS RINGING?

1	DEFENDANT:	YOUR HONOR, I'M FROM OUT OF TOWN
2		AND I THOUGHT IT WAS A HOTEL.
3	THE COURT:	THAT'S THE MOST IDIOTIC THING I EVER
4		HEARD.
5	DEFENDANT:	IT WOULDN'T BE IF I TOLD YOU ABOUT MY
6		BOOK PROPOSAL. IT'S CALLED "ALEXANDER
7		HAMILTON AND THE DESIGNATED
8		HITTER", AND—
9	THE COURT:	KEEP QUIET!
10	MS. LARKIN:	THAT'S THE WAY IT HAPPENED, YOUR
11		HONOR. I WAS THERE.
12	THE COURT:	WHO THE HELL ARE YOU?
13	MS. LARKIN:	A.J. LARKIN. I OWN A RESTAURANT CALLED
14		STREAKER'S.
15	THE COURT:	THAT PLACE NEAR THE BALLPARK WITH
16		THE CRAPPY CALVES' LIVER?
17	MS. LARKIN:	YES, YOUR HONOR.
18	THE COURT:	CAN YOU VOUCH FOR THIS MAN'S
19		CHARACTER?
20	MS. LARKIN:	I CAN.
21	THE COURT:	GUILTY OF TRESPASSING. PAY THE BAILIFF
22		AND DON'T LET IT HAPPEN AGAIN. NEXT
23		CASE.

FROM THE JOURNAL OF
Travis Puckett

I don't get it. First she tosses me out of Streaker's on my ass, and then she perjures herself for me. Now I've been grounded. She gave me vanilla ice cream and then she put sheets and pillows on the couch and made me go to sleep. No TV. The only thing that qualifies as entertainment while you're lying on your back is the poster gallery called her living room. "James Dean in *East of Eden*." "James Dean in *Rebel Without a Cause*." "James Dean in *Giant*." As we were making up my bed, I mentioned that James Dean is what happens when you Xerox Marlon Brando. Badly. That was a mistake.

Let's see how she handles Gordo—assuming she ever gets off the phone with him. Serves him right for turning my life into a screenplay. I warned him after the baseball cap thing that I'd rough him up if he ever did it again. Does he listen? "I miss the smell of Pledge." Translation: "I need a second act. *Do* something."

118 Congress Park, Suite 407, Saratoga Springs, New York. (12866.) I wish I was Stephen Sondheim so I could set it to music. Only two more days of hitchhiking, Craigy. I promise.

Maybe I should leave right now. Maybe I should sneak out a window and—Yeah, right. Nice learning curve. Besides, I've been awake for twenty-nine hours straight. I could barely keep my eyes open in the detention cell. And I practically fell asleep right in the middle of

GordoStud.com

Gordo:

Dump Jolene and do it now. Then take your brains out of your ass. How did you ever wind up with a degree from NYU? A relationship that starts with intestinal parasites isn't going anywhere. If that's not clear enough, Starbucks has a new blend called Moroccan roast. Buy it. Open it. Smell it.

Thanks for the Speedo pictures. I like your eyebrows. The smile works too. But you really need to get the Adobe Photo-

Shop upgrade. It won't leave any shadows the next time you expand the bulge.

I just checked on Beaver. He should have been out cold by now, but instead he's scribbling something into a note-book with the same sort of ardor one usually associates with Anne Rice when she's taken too many amphetamines. Have you actually put up with this for twenty-four years?

A.J.

A.J.:

Ouch! Busted! Caught red-handed! Please don't blow the whistle. I'll lose my endorsements from Hebrew National.

The shot of you in the black dress at the cocktail party makes a piquant screensaver. But how come you're the only one in the picture without a date? You couldn't possibly be sin-gle. Maybe that's why you left Cleveland. Maybe all the eligible men there threw themselves off a parapet when you said no.

Seriously, I'm smitten. T was right. (That's all I'm going to say.)

That's not a notebook, it's his journal. He doesn't want to forget anything, ever—especially if he's on a Quest. When we were kids, I always used to worry that he was going to get his heart bashed in from wearing it on his sleeve 24/7. Now I sometimes wish I was him instead of me. He understands passion. All *I* understand is horny.

Want to have some fun? Tell him I opened a window and two of my dustballs blew over to his side of the living room. Then watch what happens.

What does A.J. stand for?

Gordo

Gordo:

A.J. stands for Alene Jeanette. Keep it to yourself or Hebrew National gets e-mail. And take me off your damned screen-saver. I can only imagine the company I'm in.

They have no parapets in Cleveland—just malls and cemeteries. This is why Noah Webster coined the word "escape." So I took him up on it. Naturally, my mother was crestfallen. We'd always been close friends. (Except for one occasion in 1974 when she slapped most of my face off. I don't remember what I did to deserve it. I may have called her a cunt.) But she guessed that I'd fallen in love with Toby Heller—who had James Dean's face and Ben Affleck's ass—so she let me follow him to Northwestern, where (in no particular order) he gave me his frat pin, asked me to marry him, found me an abortion clinic, and discovered Sorority Row. Then my phone stopped ringing. So while he was fucking his way through the Greek alphabet and flunking out of grad school at the same time, I was nailing a B.A. in journalism just for the hell of it. That led to an offer from one of the St. Louis papers to cover the Cardinals—my big break—which lasted until our first staff meeting, when they found out that A.J. Larkin was, in fact, a Vagino-American. After they pulled the plug on me ("overqualified and no scrotum"), I took a job as assistant manager at a restaurant called Streaker's, where I was second banana to a vindictive lox named Lorraine. So I sold some stocks, bought the joint, and fired the bitch. And in between payroll and inventory, I write an advice column for women in an alternative weekly called the *St. Louis Other*. It has a readership of three, and one of them just died.

That's the résumé. Aren't you glad you asked?

Beaver's sound asleep. And he's smiling. Know what? I don't want him hitchhiking to Saratoga Springs. What if he gets picked up by a pervert like you?

Good night, Gordon.

A.J.

P.S. I just checked out your credits. Why did you write that Mel Gibson movie? Did you lose a bet or something?

A.J.:

The Mel Gibson movie started out as an animated feature about two talking squirrels during the Civil War. Then Universal got their hands on it. Remember the scene in the strip club where the bartender says, "How about a grape juice, buddy"? That's the only line they didn't cut. And it was originally said by an owl.

You'll like the new one. The hero's a nut-head who points his pimentos down and ties his shoelaces chronologically. Know what happens? He hits the highway hoping to find the guy who popped his cork in high school and winds up in a St. Louis pokey instead. But this is classified information. DO NOT TELL TRAVIS. He hates it when any of his neurotic nuances wind up in letterbox format. One summer he got it into his head that he wanted to own a baseball cap for each of the major league teams—so instead of picking them up at Scoreboard in North Hollywood, he drove to all twenty-six stadiums. (You have to understand the way he thinks. Any other option would have disrupted the order of the universe or something.) When he found out I'd used the cap story in *Honolulu Honeymoon*, my life was hell for six weeks. He even Windexed my oatmeal. While I was eating it.

But there's just been an unexpected plot twist involving Pimento Boy's best friend and a long-distance romance he hadn't counted on. Will he ever get to meet her for real? Are eyebrows and a smile enough? Stay tuned.

If I could write the ending ahead of time, Travis and Craig would live happily ever after. But somehow I think it's going to be a little more complicated than that. So when you cave in and decide to drive him to Saratoga Springs yourself, watch out for his feelings. They bruise easily.

Toby Heller was an asshole.

Good night, Alene.

Gordo

9
Craig

Noah Kessler
6026 Foxhound Run
Saratoga Springs, New York 12866

June 2, 1998

ATTORNEY-CLIENT COMMUNICATION

Craig McKenna
McKenna & Webb
118 Congress Park, Suite 407
Saratoga Springs, New York 12866

Dear Craig,

In case you still don't know if you should stop being a lawyer and get elected instead, these are my thoughts. Do it. First of all you get to make laws like taking the lights back out of Wrigley Field and inventing new holidays, and also because if you run for an office and get in it, the judge will have to do what you say and let me live with my father because you'll out-rank him. So tell the Democrat guy yes.

My Dad went 3-for-4 against Syracuse last night. He called from the clubhouse to tell me, even though I was already asleep. I think Frau Schneller put dope in my chocolate milk.

Just so you know, we're suppose to leave him alone with Charleen once in a while this weekend, so maybe you and me and Clayton can go to the batting cage or play pool. How come she still won't let him kiss her when everybody knows she wants to?

I have a question. Since Clayton is your boy friend and Charleen is your partner, if she marries my Dad does that mean we'll all be related?

Noah

MCKENNA & WEBB
A LAW PARTNERSHIP
118 CONGRESS PARK, SUITE 407
SARATOGA SPRINGS, NEW YORK 12866

June 3, 1998

ATTORNEY-CLIENT COMMUNICATION

Mr. Noah Kessler
6026 Foxhound Run
Saratoga Springs, New York 12866

Dear Noah:

Guess what? We're *already* related. In some countries—espe-cially this one—the attorney-client privilege is even more sacrosanct than marriage. ("Sacrosanct" is your word for the week. It'll be a lot easier to remember than "ubiquitous" was.)

Clayton says that playing pool with you is like trying to put one over on Minnesota Fats, and you always out-hit me at the batting cage. How about the zoo instead? It'll save us a couple of bruised egos. (Look up "ego" too.)

I'm meeting with the Democrat people in Albany tomorrow and I'll try to keep all of your instructions in mind. One thing, pal. No matter what happens, you're *still* too young to be a secretary of state. So get that idea out of your head.

Don't worry about Charleen. First she said she wouldn't go to Utica at all, then she said she might, and then she bought two new dresses. Men are usually easier to figure out than women, but not sometimes. So I'm guessing that the kissing thing is on deck.

Remember—nobody knows about the offer from the Democrats except you and me, and we need to keep it that way. At least for a while. (So no blabbing.)

See you Friday. I love you.

Craig

Craig McKenna   **Attorney Notes**

Interview with Wayne Duvall
6/4/98

- Attorney implied to his law partner that he had a last-minute deposition in Albany. Had she known the true purpose of the trip, she likely would have removed attorney's head—thereby creating an unnecessary personal injury/workers' comp situation.

- During the drive south, attorney attempted to psych himself up by playing *Mack and Mabel* at full volume. Then he began rehearsing the word no.

- Attorney met with Wayne Duvall, chairman of the New York State Democratic Committee, at his offices on State Street. Upon being served coffee and pastries, he noticed that the blueberry croissants from Au Bon Pain were still hot. This was obviously going to be a frontal assault. Attorney began practicing a negative headshake as well.

- Attorney was advised that he had been unanimously chosen by the committee as the candidate best equipped to replace Ken Curran on a civil liberties and child welfare plank. ("You can be a pain in the ass about the environment on your own time.") Attorney declined, but Wayne kept talking anyway.

- Attorney expressed grave reservations over his qualifications for office. The matter was summarily discussed and disposed of. "Do you have a valid driver's license?" "Yes." "Ever murder any relatives?" "No." "You qualify." Attorney demurred, but Wayne wasn't finished yet. This man is dangerous. He could probably talk Mamie Eisenhower's remains into running too.

- With the evident time constraints of a November election, attorney was given ten days to deliver an answer. He was also given the remaining blueberry croissants to take home to his sig oth. Attorney accepted the pastry and refused the offer. Apparently Wayne didn't hear him. "Will you think about it?" "Not a chance." "Sure, you will. See ya."

- When attorney returned to the parking lot and started his car, the Dolby speakers picked up right where they'd left off. "Jumpin' Saint Jude, look what happened to Mabel," sang Bernadette Peters. Oh, shut up.

I can't believe I'm even considering this. I barely know how to coach a Little League game—how the hell am I supposed to run a state? Assets: a big mouth. Period. Suppose they ask me questions about budgets and stuff? Sooner or later they're bound to notice the thumb up my ass.

"The floor calls upon the representative from the Fifth District. How much do you feel the County of Saratoga should allocate for the Waterford landfill?"

"Uh—a couple thousand?"

This isn't going to work in a million years. And I can prove it. (1) I have no charisma; (2) Clayton would kill me; (3) I'm not all that cute any more, so forget about "Oprah"; (4) Clayton would kill me. (5) If I leave Charleen with a caseload that includes the Pioneer Scouts, she'll never speak to me again; (6) Clayton would kill me; (7) My gym card's not valid in Albany. And (8) Clayton would kill me.

By the time the Miata and I had lost the I-787 on-ramp and made a U-turn out of an unexpected forest (having inexplicably wound up at a 7-Eleven in New England twenty minutes earlier), I'd sufficiently recovered from toxic shock syndrome to keep from rolling down the window and vomiting on Vermont again. *Get a grip. This could actually work. After all, these are the same people who elected Dan Quayle, and he was no Bobby Kennedy either. How tough could it be? Think about it—if anybody's dumb enough to vote for me, maybe I'm just dumb enough to pull it off. Besides, who knows where it could lead? "Congressman Craig McKenna." Wow.*

Okay. I'll kick it around for ten days. But no promises!

NEW YORK STATE DEMOCRATIC COMMITTEE

ALBANY HEADQUARTERS   151 STATE STREET
ALBANY, NEW YORK 12207

TO: Albany Office
FROM: Wayne Duvall
DATE: June 4, 1998
SUBJECT: Craig McKenna

He's going to do it. I could tell by the way he kept turning me down.

I gave him a week and a half to get back to me. In the meantime, I'm attaching his off-the-record curriculum vitae.

Let's get moving.

WD

Craig Steven McKenna
Born January 18, 1960—St. Louis, Mo.
Father: Alan C. McKenna, U.S. Attorney
Mother: Louise Pearl McKenna, OB/GYN

- Graduated Harvard summa cum laude, 1982; placed third in his law school class, 1985.

- Began singing in coffeehouses when he was 18. Bob Dylan and Woody Guthrie. (Good sign.)

- Chained himself to Widener Library in 1978 to protest Harvey Milk's murder and inadvertently incited the first riot of the semester.

- Spearheaded the Students for Human Rights Commission and succeeded in closing down seven Boston establishments that discriminated against minorities.

- Locked Vice President Bush in a toilet in 1984.

- Launched Harvard's first AIDS hotline—manned it himself.

- Organized a half-dozen zap attacks on the White House to protest the Reagan administration's silence on AIDS. Came to know most of the D.C. police force—particularly his arresting officers—on a first-name basis.

- Wrote Pat Buchanan's obituary for the *Harvard Crimson,* which was picked up by all the wire services. It took Buchanan three days to convince anyone he was still alive.

- Fell for Clayton Bergman—a construction and hardware entrepeneur—in 1978. Been living with him for twelve years. (Liberals'll love that, and we may even have a shot at the conservatives once they begin calculating the two disposable incomes.)

- Admitted to the New York State Bar in 1986 and founded the firm of McKenna & Webb in Saratoga Springs. Has since obtained verdicts in eighteen out of twenty-one cases—civil liberties, family practice, and environmental preservation. Your bluebook Republican nightmare.

- Believes in kids, the Red Sox, and equal rights across the board.

- Doesn't understand the word "don't."

- He's our man.

McKenna & Webb
A Law Partnership
118 Congress Park, Suite 407
Saratoga Springs, New York 12866

Memorandum

TO: Craig
FROM: Charleen
DATE: June 4, 1998
SUBJECT: "Men are usually easier to figure out than women, but
           not sometimes."

I'm attaching a copy of the letter you sent to Noah. You left it
by the Xerox machine. Always destroy the evidence, Craig.
Remember the Rosenbergs.

How was the "depo" in Albany? You'll note that I employ
quotation marks to signify skepticism. Is there anything you
want to tell me? Something that rhymes with "campaign"?
What about "Charleen, you may need to hire a temp for a couple of years"? I could see this coming in 1981 when you sent
the Ku Klux Klan application to Anita Bryant.

Your face is ash-gray. Just like my mother's after her hys-
terectomy.

McKenna & Webb
A Law Partnership
118 Congress Park, Suite 407
Saratoga Springs, New York 12866

Memorandum

TO: Charleen
FROM: Craig
DATE: June 4, 1998
SUBJECT: "My fellow Americans"

___

I told him no three times. It was like talking to a mailbox.

This is nuts! I have a life! Am I supposed to give it up just so Kitty Kelley can write scummy things about my relatives? And why did they pick *me?* How come they didn't ask Jenny Pizer at Lambda Legal? She's more qualified than *I* am. And she kicks ass a lot harder too.

They want me to give them an answer by June 15. Right now it's a probable "nope." Kind of. I'm not sure. Is there any way I could get elected to office without Clayton hearing about it? Maybe if you kept him distracted for two years.

Which reminds me—the First Lady and I are doing hot-and-sour soup and spareribs tonight. Want to join us?

Cr

P.S. Actually, I'm handling this pretty well. I can almost keep food down again.

P.S.2. As you've undoubtedly gleaned from the Pumpkin Papers Alger Hiss apparently left by our Xerox machine, my front man in Utica advises me that Jody intends to kiss you this weekend. You'd better call the witness protection program. I think he's at the end of his rope.

P.S.3. I changed my mind. It's a definite no.

MCKENNA & WEBB
A LAW PARTNERSHIP
118 CONGRESS PARK, SUITE 407
SARATOGA SPRINGS, NEW YORK 12866

MEMORANDUM

TO:	Mr. President
FROM:	Charleen
DATE:	June 4, 1998
SUBJECT:	Kitty Kelley

There's nothing I savor more than hot-and-sour soup—unless it's swallowing mercury. Really, Craig. Between Jody's kiss and your nomination, that'll make two of us throwing up on the table. Clayton's bound to suspect something. I can always claim PMS—what's *your* excuse?

Before you tell Clayton you're running for office, try to give me enough lead time to seek safe harbor outside the radiation zone. Iowa, perhaps. You might also consider spilling the beans *after* you've accepted your candidacy. Fewer moving parts are involved that way. (See *Ricardo vs. Ricardo*, when Lucy bought the turquoise tea hat with pearls on it before she promised Ricky she wouldn't.) Besides, assassination is a federal offense.

Assuming, *arguendo*, that I earn my scarlet A with Jody, who's to say he won't lose interest once the mystery's worn off? Remember Clark? He looked like the real McCoy too—until breakfast. And I'm not hunting for a casual relationship. My biological clock is running on fumes.

Ch

P.S. I'm sure the Democrats already considered Jenny Pizer. But they probably wanted to start small.

McKenna & Webb
A Law Partnership
118 Congress Park, Suite 407
Saratoga Springs, New York 12866

Memorandum

TO: Charleen
FROM: Craig
DATE: June 4, 1998
SUBJECT: Starting small

Thanks for the vote of confidence. And Clark was an exorcist. You get what you pay for.

By the way, Jody's been pursuing you for a year and a half. The statute of limitations on "casual" expired eight months ago. And who ever said you were mysterious?

You might want to stick around when I tell Clayton. If this shapes up to be the fight of the century, I'll need somebody to handle the popcorn concession.

Charleen, could our lives get any *more* tangled?

LOUISE McKENNA, M.D.   Jefferson Medical Plaza, Suite 100
Obstetrics/Gynecology   903 Saint Charles Street
                                 St. Louis, Missouri 63101

Darling:

I just met the loveliest woman on the leg press at the gym. Her name is Sylvia and she has an available nephew. How do you feel about gastroenterology? And don't be a snob.

Somebody got into my office last night and pillaged my Rolodex. Meanwhile, the $300 from the basketball pool was practically under his elbow and he didn't touch it. Instead, he rearranged my Post-its by color. I'd have gone to the police, but with a story like that, they'd have locked me up.

Give my best to Clayton. No need to pretend I mean it.

Love,
Mom

CLAYTON'S HARDWARE
serving Saratoga Springs since 1988

Honey—

I figure we'll leave for Utica around 6:00. I've got to wait for a shipment of threepenny nails, so why don't you pick up Charleen and the kid in the Bronco and then meet me at the store?

Love you.
C

Craig McKenna   **Attorney Notes**

Never try packing a suitcase when you've got something burly on your mind. Otherwise, you and your sig oth are going to be stuck wearing ski pants in June.

He rearranged my Post-its by color.

First she gets a phone call from an unidentified crackpot who all but bribes her for my address. Four days later, somebody breaks into her Rolodex—but before he leaves, he cleans her office.

Circumstantial evidence is generally inadmissible, but a verdict is still a verdict.

Travis.

It had to happen sooner or later. And he was always a lot

braver than I was. *(Who hitchhikes to Scranton for a record album?!)* Let's see—he probably kicked off the mission by hunting down every Craig McKenna on the Internet. (Grin.) When he figured out my number was unlisted, he raked his irrepressibly methodical brain for a clue he'd overlooked. *Did he become a lawyer after all? Should I check with Harvard? How about the Massachusetts State Bar? Air raid alert! His mom was a doctor in St. Louis!* That's when he called her. But chances are good that his capillaries were already popping by then—just like when Liza Minnelli came into the record store searching for one of her mother's old albums. *("Oh my God she looks exactly like Sally Bowles I forgot how to breathe should I talk to her?" "Travis, I can't understand a word you're saying.")* Poor Mom. No wonder she hung up on him. So after that, he booked the first available flight to Missouri—which makes perfect sense as long as you're Travis. He probably figured he'd be an easier sell if Mom could meet him face-to-face. I hope he didn't try to schedule an appointment with her. I think I forgot to tell him she was a gynecologist.

Yo! Craig! It's 96 degrees in Utica! Unpack the thermal underwear!

I haven't stopped smiling in three hours.

Uh-oh.

The Utica Post Tribune

Vol. MCLVI, No. 98	UTICA, NEW YORK	JUNE 5, 1998

BLUE SOX TAKE ON TROY IN GRUDGE MATCH
WEEKEND SERIES WITH BANDITS BEGINS TODAY AT 1:00

Jody and His Boys Primed for a 3-Game Sweep at Schuyler Park

Craig McKenna   **Attorney Notes**

The Road to Utica
starring Noah and Charleen and Clayton and Craig

Noah was the one who drew up the seating chart for the Bronco: me and Clayton in the front, Charleen and our Munchkin in the back. He also had a mile-by-mile itinerary charted out—from Foxhound Run in Saratoga Springs to Oswego Street in Utica.

"Ready, dude?" he asked Clayton as we nosed our way out of the hardware store's parking lot.

"Dude me again and watch what happens," warned my other half. Then he reached back with his free arm and mussed up the kid's hair. Affection insurance.

"100 Bottles of Beer on the Wall"

Always a perennial favorite whenever we take him places, the object is to see who can go the longest without getting bored. (I usually clock out at sixty-something, and Clayton's never made it past eighty-four.) But on this particular occasion, Charleen—decked out in a Jody-motivated yellow-and-white $800 Prada—decided to put up a road block of her own just as we were passing Saratoga Lake.

"You're eleven years old and you're *not* singing that song," she informed Noah briskly in her "cross-the-line-and-you-lose-the-toes" voice. "It promotes alcoholism." *I'll be damned,* I thought with misplaced pride. *She's beginning to sound like* me. But Noah wasn't taking it with nearly as much equanimity.

"Does not!" he glowered.

"Does too!" she glowered back. As soon as it became apparent that the Lincoln-Douglas debates were about to break out in the middle of Route 67, Charleen reached into

Noah's backpack for the pocket Webster's (her Auntie Mame present to him on his tenth birthday) and made him look up "promotes" and "alcoholism."

"Go ahead," she ordered, crossing her arms the way grown-ups always do when they know they've already won. Guessing he was trapped but convinced he could find a way out anyway, Noah flipped through the onionskin pages slowly.

"A-L-C-H—," he mumbled, stalling for time.

"A-L-C-*O* and you know it," she cut in sharply. Noah grimaced. *Caught in the act.* When he found what he was looking for, there was a long silence as his forehead got all crinkly under the brunet bangs. Finally he closed the book and handed it back to Charleen.

"Definitely uncool," he decided.

So for the next twelve miles, we all sang "100 Bottles of Sprite on the Wall."

Questions You've Always Wanted Answers To

Another Noah concoction. According to the junior Kessler rule book, "You pick a thing that even scientists can't figure out and then you ask the person on your clockwise. But nothing that has formulas in it."

Charleen to Clayton: Since there's no air on the moon, would bubblewrap still pop there? *Answer:* Yeah, but you'd have to catch it first. Don't forget the gravity thing.

Clayton to Craig: If a brontosaurus couldn't run, how did it protect itself against a T. rex? *Answer:* With its tail. Sort of like a prehistoric inside-the-park homer.

Craig to Noah: When the Wicked Witch of the West was hanging around her castle in the middle of the night without anybody to scare, how did she spend her time? *Answer:* She wore a black nightgown and she ate bowls of Cap'n Crunch, but without milk so her mouth wouldn't melt.

Noah to Charleen: Do wet dreams hurt? *Answer:* That's none of my business. Pick another question.

Noah to Charleen (Take Two): Are you going to kiss my dad? *Answer:* Wet dreams don't hurt. So I'm told.

Geography

Noah already had dibs on Xenia, Ohio, and Xanithi, Greece, and Xigaze, China—so this one never lasted very long.

Chip's Challenge

This is where Noah usually turned on my laptop and competed with Charleen for Monopoly money. (He still wouldn't tell her the secret to level 105, even when she offered to buy him off with a Dairy Queen. "The taste of defeat is bitter, *isn't* it?" he smirked, quoting Lex Luthor. "Oh, knock it off," snapped Charleen.) But the often combustible contest at least permitted the adults in the front seat to take a breather.

"Mamas and the Papas okay with you?" asked Clayton absently, turning up the volume on WCKM. I nodded. It was just as well that he was still thinking about threepenny nails, because I had a few issues of my own to deal with. So we held hands and chased down our separate thoughts while Cass Elliott sang "Dream a Little Dream of Me" all the way up the Mohawk River.

Nobody listens to his heart the way Travis does. Which means only one thing: if he's got my address, he's on his way. He wouldn't call first in a million years. That's not his style. It'd spoil the whole odyssey.

I wonder if he still has the three laughs. I wonder if the same places on his body stayed ticklish. I wonder if he remembers everything I remember.

This is crazy. I have a lover who can read me like a blueprint.

We've shared the best and worst parts of our lives with each other. Besides, I'm going to be in enough hot water with him when he finds out I may be running for office. Which I'm probably not, but it's still out there anyway.

Travis, I could never stop loving you. Please stay away.

~

Utica's first baseman was waiting for us on the porch, but the hugs had to be quiet ones because Noah was already sound asleep. So Jody and his biceps reached into the backseat and gently lifted his son out of Charleen's arms.

"Hey," he whispered, almost shyly.

"Hi," she whispered in return. Instinctively, their fingers brushed and her eyes met his—but for once they stayed that way. (Given what she'd paid for the dress, it wasn't courage as much as economic necessity.) Neither of them seemed to be in much of a hurry to break the mood, and if you didn't know any better, you'd swear they were falling in love.

There was a song about that once.

The Ballgame
featuring Jody

Saturday. Mustard-and-relish time. And this was the place for it.

Schulyer Park sits on the banks of the Mohawk River underneath a sky that couldn't possibly be any bluer unless it were hanging over Wrigley Field. Built eight months before Pearl Harbor, it seats only five thousand people—a study in intimacy that allows the fan an up-close opportunity to examine the sweat, the grit, and the players' asses.

"Give me the goddamned binoculars," I snapped at Charleen, yanking them back and nearly strangling her in the process. "You've had them long enough." There was a brief but savage tug-of-war before she relented.

"Why is it that you get them for three minutes and I'm barely permitted a fleeting instant?" she demanded, searching her neck for rope burns.

"Because I'm a boy and you're not," I taunted. "Learn to live with it." To my left, Noah leaned in to us from a comfortable perch on Clayton's lap and gave us one last chance to behave ourselves.

"Craig," he warned, "if you don't let Charleen have a turn, you're getting a time-out." The sneer died on my lips. There's nothing worse than rebuke-by-11-year-old. So I scrunched down in my seat and returned the binoculars meekly. Who needed a time-out?

Not that it really mattered. My sonar could pick up a hunky guy in a snug jockstrap even if I had no retinas at all. By the end of the second inning, my law partner and I had already tallied the final score: the Blue Sox may have owned the more impressive stats, but the Bandits were infinitely more fuckable.

"Love the uniform numbers on their pants," I muttered quietly.

"Yes," she whispered back. "Too bad they're not in Braille." I couldn't help marveling at her aesthetic integrity. We really were two halves of the same nickel.

"Oh, Charleen," I breathed with mock sincerity. "If only you were a guy."

"Oh, Craig," she shot back, scrutinizing a particularly tasty left-fielder through the lenses, "if only you were one too." Then Jody stepped into the batter's box, and the binocs were off-limits to everybody but Noah. And Charleen.

Nobody knew for certain exactly what had transpired the night before, but after we'd put the kid to bed and settled into our rooms, she and Jody had disappeared for what was supposed to have been a twenty-minute walk to Pixley Park and back. They didn't get home until 2:15 in the morning. On a game day! By then, Clayton was out like a light, Noah was lost to Dreamland, and I was pacing the floor in an Eleanor Roosevelt T-shirt and blue gym shorts.

"Do you know what time it is?" I hissed, corralling her in the darkened hallway after Jody had gone to bed. "I was *worried.*" Presumably on her way to the bathroom but heading into a linen closet instead, Charleen was wearing a $350 Gucci negligee and a distracted half-smile that was either (a) bewitched, (b) bothered, (c) bewildered, or (d) stoned.

"What?" she mumbled, somewhat dazed and comprehending absolutely nothing.

"Did he kiss you?"

"*Who?*" she asked blankly. Recognizing a dead end when I saw one, I opted for a more fundamental approach.

"The quick brown fox jumped over the lazy dog," I advised her, playing a hunch. Charleen leaned against the door frame and nodded wistfully.

"I know," she sighed.

Yep. He'd kissed her.

~

"Kessler, you suck!" cried an outraged fan directly behind us. In seconds, Noah's dukes were up and he'd already begun scrambling over Clayton's shoulders, tendrils of smoke shooting out of his nostrils.

"Easy, sport," said my boyfriend, restraining him. "If your dad can roll with the punches, you can too." Down on the field, even the Blue Sox couldn't believe what they'd just seen. With a 2-and-2 count, Jody had slugged a long fly ball to deep right that had bounced off the wall and should have been a routine double. Instead, Troy's improbably miniature 5-foot-2 shortstop had corkscrewed himself three feet into the air to catch the relay from the center fielder single-handedly. *Holy shit! What just happened here?* Trapped between the bags, Jody had engaged in a back-and-forth battle of wits with the Troy leprechaun for almost half a minute—until he miscalculated by sliding headfirst into second base, a hair too late. *Tagged on the ass. Sorry, Charlie. No runs, no hits, inning over.* And as I watched the other Bandits pounce on their diminutive hero back in the dugout, I was nailed by one of the most illogical metaphors I'd ever owned up to: "We hold these truths to be self-evident that all men are created equal."

It was a Travis moment.

My whole life I've tried to remember the things he taught me. Not just about Ethel Merman and the Japanese American internment, but about finding the truth in everything you touch. Being Travis was a full-time job, yet that never kept him from teaching me how to be Craig.

Romance isn't just about roses or killing dragons or sailing a kayak around the world. It's also about chocolate chip cookies and sharing The Grateful Dead and James Taylor with me in the middle of the night, and believing me when I say that you could be bigger than both of them put together, and not making fun of me for straightening out my french fries or pointing my shoelaces in the same direction, and letting me pout when I don't get my own way, and pretending that if I play "Flower Drum Song" one more time you won't throw me and the record out the window.

Maybe he just wants to catch up on the old days. Maybe he's in a jam and he needs my help. Maybe I'm full of shit and know it. There can only be one reason he's tracking me down after twenty years: he wants to find Brigadoon again. But this time for keeps.

I'm in big trouble.

The Barbecue at Jody's
starring all of us
(roles assigned by Noah)

1. **Dad and Craig get to buy the ribs and chicken and Tater Tots and corn and Fritos and Milky Ways but no salad or anything that has green in it, especially any kind of sprouts.**

Ever watch two men standing in front of a poultry case trying to figure out the difference between Best of Fryer and Tender Slivers? It's scary. At least Jody has an excuse. He's straight.

We cheated a little on Noah's list—somehow broccoli made its way into our shopping cart. But first we hid it in an empty Gummi Bears box so we could sneak it past the kid. (It didn't work.)

2. Charleen gets to be in charge of tablecloths and napkins and plates and forks and spoons.

"Did you ever hear of gender stereotyping?" she groaned, searching through the kitchen drawers for silverware.

"Nope," rebutted Noah, tailing her closely to make sure she was following orders. "Should I look it up?"

"Would you?"

3. Clayton gets to light the grill and cook everything.

Starting the fire took six seconds. This left half an hour free before Jody and I got back with what we hoped would turn into a meal. But Noah had Clayton's downtime figured out too. "You have to throw a football with me while we're waiting," insisted our little Mussolini. "It's hidden in the rules."

4. I get to fill up the glasses with Snapple, so tell me what flavor you want.

Once the ribs were on the grill, Noah circled the patio with a small pad and a ballpoint pen, taking our orders quite professionally. I chose lemonade, Charleen picked Orange Crush, Jody went for iced tea, and Clayton decided on grape. At least, we *thought* we did.

"This tastes like strawberry kiwi," I observed suspiciously, lowering my glass.

"So does mine," concurred Charleen. And Jody. And Clay.

"It is," replied Noah with a shrug. "That's all we had. But wasn't it fun pretending I was a waiter?"

Dinner reminded me of a kid's game we used to play called Telephone: I told Charleen that one of her less savory ex-boyfriends was Clayton's loan officer at the bank, Charleen told Jody that Clayton had just bought three hundred acres of land by Saratoga Lake, Jody told Clayton that he'd once spent two summers building houses in Schenectady, Clayton told Noah that there's more kinds of concrete than Charm Pops, and Noah told Charleen that Yoda didn't have a penis.

family \ 'fam-(ə)-lē\ *n, pl* -**lies** [ME *familie*, fr. L *familia*] **1 a** : a group of people united by love.

"We make families of our own," Travis whispered in my arms on the last night we spent together. "It starts with you and me and then it spreads. And whatever happens, there'll always be a part of me that's part of you. No matter what."
Clayton. Jody. Noah. Charleen. Travis gave them to me.

The Swings
starring Noah and Craig

Jody's got a backyard built for kids: jungle gyms, a log cabin, two treehouses, and a fort. Grown-ups are permitted by invitation only, but Noah had issued me an open-ended visa with the following stipulations: he gets to sit on the swing and I get to push.

"What kind of a wimp *are* you?" he asked irritably, sailing up toward the trees. "Why didn't you just tell the Democrat people yes?" As my double-0 operative, he claims his middle name is Omerta ("It means 'code of silence,' Craig," he'd explained patiently), but you could practically read "What happened in Albany?" scribbled across his forehead all through dinner—and if I didn't fill him in pronto, it would only be a matter of time before he blurted it out in front of an audience.

"Because midlife decisions don't happen that fast," I retorted, trying to keep my voice down. Over by the patio, Jody had ensnared my boyfriend's undivided attention by mapping out Clayton's entire housing development on the back of a takeout menu from the Shanghai Palace (which, like everything else Jody touched, only took him ten minutes to complete). So both of them were unaware that the future of the United States Constitution was being resolved on a $199 swing set from Toys "R" Us.

"*I* made a midlife decision once," Noah informed me confidently.

"No, you didn't. Trust me."

"Did too," he insisted. "And it's simple. Do you *want* to get elected?" I should have known he was going to pull a stunt like that. I *despise* cross-examination—especially by someone less than forty-six inches tall.

"Yes," I finally conceded, complying with the terms of the ambush.

"Then you're a lowlife for not telling them you'll do it."

With his opinion on my candidacy now entered into the record, we moved along to the campaign issues. To my immense relief, he approved of my position on practically all of them—AIDS funding, housing discrimination, school subsidies, and free ice cream for kids. (Okay, so I made that one up. But a vote is a vote. Lyndon Johnson would have done the same thing.) The only matter that troubled him was the Freedom to Marry initiative. I knew we were in for a filibuster because he jammed his feet into the ground, skidded to a halt, and glanced up at me with his father's eyes.

"They won't let you and Clayton get married, right?" he asked pensively, collecting the pertinent facts.

"Right."

"And a long time ago, they wouldn't let Rosa Parks sit in a bus either—right?" I could see where this was going and I loved him for it.

"Right."

"And now everybody thinks the people who arrested her were skanks, right?"

"Right."

Noah shrugged and swung himself into the sky again. As far as he was concerned, it was an open-and-shut case.

"So how come they don't know that in a hundred years we'll think the same things about the skanky guys who won't let you get married?" Since there was no practical answer, I stopped looking for one and hugged him instead. He had it coming.

Then we hit the jungle gym.

~

That's what made Travis so special. While the rest of us were learning the conventional crap that comes with growing up, he never forgot that we all start out like Noah. Equations are a lot simpler that way.

"What happens when we go to college?" I asked him nervously. "Is that the end of us?" He glanced up from my chest and frowned as only Travis could frown.

"Do you love me?" he countered.

"Down to my toes."

"Then shut up."

Our Bedroom in Utica
costarring Craig and Clayton

Three-thirty in the morning. The breeze from the Mohawk fluttered past the flimsy curtains and brushed over our still bodies. Tonight we were sleeping back-to-front; Clayton had an arm wrapped around my chest and a cheek in the hollow of my neck, while his steady breathing syncopated our heartbeats into a single cadence. Ever since we met, our bed's been a place where we can find each other again whenever we lose our way—but now I was wide awake and on my own.

Clayton	Travis
Makes me feel safe.	Walked me through the scary parts.
Pulls me up short if I need it.	Allowed me to make my own mistakes.
Loves the things I am.	Loved the things I'm not.
Doesn't want to lose me.	Wasn't afraid to let me go.

I'm almost 39. I've won eighteen out of twenty-one cases. I have a best friend who trades all her secrets with me, I've found an 11-year-old boy who knows how to keep me on the straight-and-narrow, and I've loved two men who've both loved me back.

It'll all work out. I must be doing something right.

NEW YORK STATE DEMOCRATIC COMMITTEE

ALBANY HEADQUARTERS   151 STATE STREET
                                       ALBANY, NEW YORK 12207

June 8, 1998

VIA MESSENGER

Craig S. McKenna, Esq.
McKenna & Webb
118 Congress Park, Suite 407
Saratoga Springs, New York 12866

Dear Craig:

I went ahead and had the enclosed bumper stickers made up for your approval. If it appears that I'm attempting to bribe you, I am.

Looking forward to your decision.

Best,
Wayne Duvall

McKENNA
STATE ASSEMBLY

Craig McKenna   **Attorney Notes**

Mother Machree, look what happened to Mabel.

10

Travis

PART II
Travis and A.J. in a Black Buick Named
Robert Mitchum

Parnell Street to I-70

I'd made up my mind in the courtroom when she hadn't slugged the judge for calling her calves' liver crappy: I wanted A.J. to come to Saratoga Springs with me. Partly because there was a distinct possibility I might need a shoulder to cry on, and partly because I already missed her. Okay, so maybe we'd only known each other for forty-eight hours and maybe they'd been weird ones—but in a memory-book kind of way. "Baby's First Tooth." "Baby's First Haircut." "Baby's First Bail Bond." Besides, where was I going to find anybody else to call me Beaver?

"Pancakes or Rice Krispies, Beav?" she asked, dumping me out of bed. "Supplies are limited. Who knew there'd be a fugitive on my couch?"

I had no idea she was on the verge of cracking at breakfast

when I did fifteen minutes on kissing Craig in the rain. Had I known, I'd have pulled a finale out of my ass by reenacting *Brigadoon* too.

"Oh God," she sighed, biting into an onion bagel dreamily. "Just like Julie Harris and James Dean in the bean field." But she wasn't quite ready to crumble yet. First she whipped up six chicken-and-egg sandwiches ("That should last you through Ohio"), and then she insisted I count out my traveler's checks and put them in a safe place. ("Anywhere but your crotch. Why hand them a jackpot for feeling you up?") *That's* it? *What about "Hey, Beaver, why don't I go* with *you?" Okay. This may require some heavier artillery.* So I slipped on my backpack, hugged her bravely, and stepped out onto Parnell Street like Little Boy Lost.

"Call me if you get into any trouble," she insisted. "I mean it. And don't climb out of any windows." *This isn't working,* I thought to myself. *Try waving timidly.* That didn't do the trick either—but once I'd determined that she was watching me from a window, I adjusted my posture so that my shoulders were slightly stooped and forlorn. Few are resilient enough to resist the pathos. Regrettably, A.J. was among them.

The freeway was only ten blocks to the west, but my thumb and I hadn't been at the on-ramp for more than five minutes before the Buick came screeching around the corner with a suitcase in the backseat.

"Don't say a fucking word," she snapped, throwing open the door while the engine idled. "Just get in." And I would have followed her orders gleefully—had Jiminy Cricket not chosen that moment to crawl out of my pocket and sing the conscience song.

"You knew this was a setup, right?" I confessed hesitantly.

"Duh," she said. "But the shoulder thing was an artful touch."

St. Louis to Indianapolis

It was only 246 miles, but we still managed to get into four fights covering the following issues: broken red lines on a road map ("It means surface streets." "It means highway under construction—

schmuck."), who got the window seat at Denny's ("I said, 'Touch black, no back' first." "And you actually consider that *binding?*"); the two little brats on *Family Affair* ("Buffy was less obnoxious." "According to what authority? They both should have been on Ritalin."); and which state is underneath Cincinnati ("It's one of the Virginias. They'd never tolerate anything like Kentucky." "This isn't a judgment call!"). In between rounds, Gordo paged us three times, so we called him back on A.J.'s cell phone.

"How badly do you need Beaver's half of the rent?" she inquired grimly of the mouthpiece. "Because he may not be alive much longer."

"*Give* me that," I barked, grabbing the receiver as Terre Haute whizzed past the windshield. "Gordo, go into my room, get my atlas, and tell her where Wyoming is. She thinks I'm trying to fake her out with Colorado."

"Slow down," he replied (on unlimited roaming air time). "I'm still missing a couple of pieces. How did you get her to say yes? Was it the droopy head or the shoulder thing?" In the background, I could hear him typing. How much of a dumbbell did he think I was?

"What are you doing?" I demanded.

"Estimated taxes," he lied deftly. "Let me talk to A.J."

For the next three counties, they were inseparable. She told him about the gossip she'd engendered when she'd bought her first brassiere, and he countered with a similar story involving a jockstrap labeled "Boys XL." (Bullshit, Gordo. It was a medium. I remember the box.) Finally, I began to feel like a third wheel with big ears.

"Should I go outside and play?" I whispered.

"Please," she retorted, covering the mouthpiece and pointing to the fast lane.

Indianapolis to Fairmount

I learned the following information for which I have absolutely no use whatsoever: James Dean's middle name was Byron, his mother died when he was 8, he went to school in Santa Monica right around the corner from me and Gordo, and on suitable occasions he took it up the ass. Somehow the mystique eluded me, but for A.J.'s sake, I tried to be tactful.

"Can't you just imagine making love to him?" she sighed.

"I'd rather blow a goat."

"Get out of my car."

We stopped by a convenience store in Fairmount so she could pick up a pack of Chesterfields to put on his grave. (Offhand, I could count at least fifteen hundred things wrong with this scenario, but since she was holding hostage a similar list about people who get erections from root canals, I kept my mouth shut.) On our way to the cemetery, she let me pop my *Sweet Charity* tape into the cassette deck—a circumstance not normally associated with central Indiana. However, as neither of us owned the soundtrack to *Deliverance*, we made do with what we had.

"What are you thinking about?" I asked as she stared quietly at the pale red tombstone. JAMES B. DEAN: 1931–1955.

"Toby," she mumbled, in a voice that was barely audible. "Beav, do you think there's something wrong with carrying a torch for eleven years?" Obviously, she needed an arm around her shoulder just then, so she got one.

"No," I assured her. "But before you take my word for it, consider the source."

Then we hopped back into Robert Mitchum and talked about Gordo for ninety-four miles.

Fairmount to Columbus

I knew something was brewing when she began picking on my clothes. First the chinos were "antediluvian," then the loafers were "aboriginal," and finally the denim shirt was dismissed as "rat shit."

"You dress like Cybill Shepherd," she informed me without even a whiff of diplomacy. "What the hell is Craig going to think—that you've schlepped three thousand miles to clean his house?" So I reminded her of my recently deceased Wells Fargo bank balance, the T-bill I'm not allowed to touch, and the rest of my Cannery Row credentials. After that, I assumed the conversation was concluded. I was wrong. *How did she find out about the Neiman-Marcus credit card?!*

"Hand it over," she commanded crisply, like Patton before Sicily. "We're stopping in Columbus."

The damage: Three form-fitting tank tops, five Versace shirts ("Save the blue-and-white striped one for Craig. Even *I'd* fuck you in that."), eight pairs of Calvin Klein bikini briefs that would have resulted in federal prosecution had they been sent through the mails thirty years earlier, cowboy boots and a wrangler belt (this has *got* to be a fetish talking), two pairs of Reeboks with racing stripes on them, Armani sunglasses, a tiny gold earring and a pierced left lobe ("Over my dead body." "That can be arranged."), and three pairs of 501s with the button fly. ("Judging by all available evidence, you've got an ass that's worth showcasing. So why don't you?") My waist is a 30. The jeans are a 28. When I fart, the Reeboks blow off.

Columbus to Pittsburgh

The last purchase made was a digital calculator marked down to $89 that I utilized solely to figure out the bounty on my head once Neiman-Marcus turned me over to Jabba the Hutt.

"There's a comma in this!" I shrieked as we crossed the Pennsylvania border. "$1,737.49! Are you out of your mind?! How am I supposed to *pay* these people?!"

"I'll show you," she said evenly, holding out a palm. "Let me see it." So I gave it to her and she threw it out the window.

"*That's* how. Now if you're going to play *Mame,* shut up and do it. You've got fifteen minutes before she gets her tits bumped for Chuck Berry."

Robert Mitchum didn't find Pittsburgh until 3:30 in the

morning, and it was another hour before I stepped out of the Holiday Inn shower that I'd been daydreaming about since Muncie. But our itinerary wasn't quite finished yet. With a towel over my head and still humming "We Need a Little Christmas," I suddenly heard what sounded like gargling coming from the general vicinity of the sink. Alarmed, I pivoted abruptly and discovered A.J. in shorts and an *East of Eden* T-shirt, brushing her teeth and flossing—like it was the most natural thing in the world to do in front of a naked history professor.

"Don't you believe in *knocking?*" I demanded, wrapping the shower curtain around myself.

"For what?" she retorted. "I already know you're in here."

"I have a great idea: beat it."

"Not until we do something about your chest hair," she mused, eyeing my pectorals in the mirror. "It's way too light to be sexy. You want to impress Craig, don't you?" So she pulled something-by-Clairol out of her bag of tricks and spent twenty minutes applying it to my sternum, while I sat on the edge of the bathtub convinced I was intruding on somebody else's nightmare.

"There!" she announced proudly, rinsing it off and pointing to my reflection. "What do you think?" Actually, it *was* kind of hot—but I wasn't about to admit as much to A.J.

"I look like Chewbacca."

"Then why are you flexing?"

Twenty minutes later, we were tucked into a pair of 1950s-sitcom twin beds and settling snugly into the Pennsylvania dawn. And while I was yawning myself into unconsciousness, I realized dimly that for the first time in my life, I didn't know what the hell was going to happen to me next. Last night I was behind bars in St. Louis. Now I'm seventeen hundred dollars in debt and I have ash-brown chest hair.

Actually, I could get used to this.

GordoStud.com

Dear Gordo:

We're leaving Pittsburgh as soon as Beaver wakes up, but it's another five hundred miles to Saratoga Springs, so we'll probably be getting in too late to call. If you feel like it, page us in the car. All you'll be interrupting is another argument. (We still haven't fought about Arkansas yet.)

I read the first half of your Harlem script. Your father's right. Can't you hear what he's trying to tell you? You're so much better than you give yourself credit for—even with the split infinitives—I'm surprised you haven't figured that out by now. You have a *Field of Dreams* heart—stop trying to write *Die Hard*. Personally, I'd like to see what you could do with a novel. *I'd* take it to bed with me.

A.J.

P.S. Neiman-Marcus rebuilt Beaver from top to bottom. You ought to see him in the burgundy tank top, the size 28 jeans, the maroon-and-white Reeboks with the shoelaces pointing in eighteen different directions, and the french fries scattered all over his plate in no special order. I thought I was having an acid flashback.

Dear A.J.:

How did you manage to pry the Neiman-Marcus credit card out of his fingers?! The only other time he used it was when I made him buy a new tie for $76. And I thought we were going to have to hospitalize him.

A novel? With paragraphs? *Me?* That's like pitching in the minors for eight years and all of a sudden somebody tells you that you're ready to start for the Yankees. If you were just being generous, thanks. If you really meant it, *Yikes!*

I've been thinking about who should play A.J. in the Travis movie, but nobody comes close to the real thing. Could you live with Helen Hunt in a brunette wig? Or is she still too WASPy? And who do we get to direct?

Want to hear the nuttiest thing? This afternoon I had a lunch date with a bank teller named Stacy. I met her online. Silky blonde hair, .38 caliber dum-dums, and a 3-inch waist. Halfway through the Chinese chicken salad, she started rubbing her shoe on the inside of my thigh, so I paid the check and dropped her off at work. That's it. Nothing else. Normally I would have fucked her in the car—but then I'd have been cheating on you. You've ruined my life.

Is it too soon to ask you to have dinner with me? Maybe Saturday night? I realize that the three time zones pose something of an obstacle, but we could plan the menu ahead of time and do it over the phone. I don't mind eating early if you don't mind eating late.

Eyebrows and a smile *and a Field of Dreams* heart. I like the way I'm shaping up.

Love,
Gordo

P.S. They were supposed to presumably teach us grammar in eighth grade, but I was already too busy reading *Penthouse* to really pay much attention. So try to not take the split infinitives personally.

Dear Gordo:

Was ever a maid so fairly wooed? "Normally I would have fucked her in the car—but then I'd have been cheating on you." I've got to fall in love with you now. There's a razor-thin line between "appalling" and "irresistible." You just crossed it.

Keep Helen Hunt at home. I'm not that glamorous. You need to find somebody real. See if Janeane Garofalo is free that week. Otherwise, put in a call to Lili Taylor. And nobody directs me except Ben Affleck. Bareass.

Love,
A.J.

THE PERILOUS JOURNEY OF TRAVIS PUCKETT

PART III
Travis and A.J.—the Final Push
Pittsburgh to Saratoga Springs

Since our time was relatively limited, we stuck to the following agenda: From Pittsburgh to Buffalo, we analyzed Gordo's hair, Gordo's shoulders, Gordo's ass, Gordo's baby blues, Gordo's laugh, Gordo's style (sic), and Gordo's chances of ever learning that a fly can also zip *up*. From Buffalo to Syracuse, I got to map out similar longitudinal landmarks across Craig, including the squirmy spot above his butt, getting lost for hours inside his dimple, and the way he'd always giggle whenever I kissed his belly button for its own sake (and not merely as a way station on a road trip south). Syracuse to Saratoga Springs belonged to me as well, seeing as I'd already anticipated the 141-mile anxiety attack that appeared at sunset, right on schedule, and immediately promised to devour the rest of my life.

What if he's changed? What if he's forgotten all of our secrets? What if he stopped loving me along the way? Pull over! Turn around! I've reconsidered my options!

As we passed a twinkling green-and-white Thruway sign that read "Saratoga Springs, Next Exit," A.J. and I glanced at each other spontaneously. She couldn't help noticing that my face was the color of rayon.

"This is it," I gulped apprehensively.

"Oh, don't be such a drama queen," she retorted, reaching for my damp left hand. "Once he finds out what you've put yourself through, he's yours again." I didn't believe a word she was saying, but at least lunch stayed down.

Get a grip, Trav. She's right. This is gonna be worth it.

ARGOSY ENTERTAINMENT
Literary Representatives

LOS ANGELES   TORONTO
NEW YORK   LONDON

Gordon:

A day and a half without any pages? Why are you doing this to me?

I don't know what you've got up your sleeve for Travis and Craig, but I want the boys to wind up together. If you put me through all this without a happy ending, I'll see to it that you never work in this town again.

Your Father

GordoStud.com

G:
How's this for an answering machine message?

Hey, it's Clayton. Craig and I are in Utica this week-end. If you're calling for an estimate you can try me at the hardware store on Monday. Otherwise, leave a message.

What kind of a name is Clayton?! "Clayton and Craig"?! Where's the flow? Where's the magic?!

This is the worst thing that ever happened to me. It's even worse than the time you fixed me up with the casting director who made me wear a dog collar. My life is over. Finished. Washed up without purpose. There's a bridge here with a nice long drop, so sell everything I own because I'm not coming back. And after you've paid off Neiman-Marcus, buy the worldwide rights to *Brigadoon* and eat them.

Who names a baby Clayton?! *Uncles* are named Clayton!

T

Dear Gordo:

Scarlett just went across the street for a pack of Carlton menthols. He's decided it's time to start smoking. Can you spell "brat"?

This is my own fault. By the time we'd found a Best Western with an available room (there's a Legionnaires convention in town this weekend—nice omen), he claimed he'd developed a spastic stomach, a bleeding ulcer, colitis, and hives. Since Schenectady. I thought I was going to have to drain him out of Robert Mitchum with a siphon. So I decided—falling victim to one of my rare lapses in judgment—that he'd sleep better if he could hear Craig's voice. That's why we called his machine. If he'd answered, we would have hung up—but what were the chances of that on a Friday night? Assuming he's half as cute as Beaver thinks he is, he probably slides in and out of his underpants with greater facility than *you* do.

Okay, so there's a new wrinkle called Clayton. I'll admit it doesn't look good, but there could be a whole medley of reasonable explanations. Maybe they're related.

ALMOST LIKE BEING IN LOVE

Ask her what pumpkin truck ran over her. I'm sure she got the plate number.

He's back. With a cigar. Freud wins.

Names that work well with "Clayton": Rick, Doug, Roy, Alex, Eduardo, Hank, Seth, Kevin, Aaron, Jay. Names that work well with "Craig": Travis, Sean (kind of).

Gordo, in the unlikely event I ever misplace enough of my marbles to marry you, Beaver's only allowed out of his room on Thanksgiving and Christmas. No *wonder* that guy put a dog collar on him. *I'd* have sent him to a kennel.

Oh, wait—now you're getting married? Hello? This was supposed to be *my* crusade.

Would you please tell him it still is, for Christ's sake? We know that Clayton works at a hardware store. We'll start there.

Swell. Out of all the hardware stores in Saratoga Springs, how are we supposed to figure out which one is Clayton's?!

128   Hardware—Hardwoods

NYNEX YELLOW PAGES
SARATOGA SPRINGS

Hardware Stores

Busy Bee Hardware   454 Schuyler
Clayton's   1127 Putnam
Quality Hardware   110 Excelsior
Saratoga Home Mart   2124 McGee

FROM THE JOURNAL OF
Travis Puckett

WELCOME TO
CLAYTON'S HARDWARE
serving Saratoga Springs since 1988

---

1. The storefront takes up half a block. *He thinks he's hot shit.*
2. They have two full rows of drill bits. *He's an ostentatious pig.*
3. Home Furnishings is decorated in a tacky brown wall-paper that's supposed to look like fake walnut. *He wears plaid Bermuda shorts.*
4. He sells seven different types of power mowers. *Over-compensation for a two-inch penis.*
5. He's the foreman of his own construction company. *He beats Craig daily.*

Over all fourteen of my objections, lunchtime found us in the middle of aisle 3 ("Tools and Building Supplies"). Person-ally, I'd have preferred bladder surgery.

"Shut up and smile or so help me God I'll crush your feet," mumbled A.J., eyeing a sledgehammer convincingly. "We need to find out what we're up against."

"I'll glower if I feel like it," I fired back through gritted teeth, glowering because I felt like it. "Coming here wasn't *my* idea. Especially dressed like *this*." Per her instructions, I was wearing a modest pink Versace—opened to the third button—and the least offensive pair of 501s I owned (i.e., my balls only stuck out as far as Stamford); A.J., meanwhile, had chosen her blue cocktail getup along with a matching 1920s hat that she'd seen in a thrift shop window further up Putnam Street. ("Who's going to argue with a *veil?*") The effect kind of backfired: In our bid for respectability, we looked like Madame Godiva and Her Male Strumpet.

"May I help you?" inquired a perky redhead, coming upon us nervously. Understandably, she probably thought we were there to procure as many teenage boys as we could cram into a Falk & Padgett wheelbarrow ("30% Off, Saturday Only"). But A.J.'s transformation into a Southern belle was so sudden and so complete, it left me speechless. In seconds, she'd developed an inexplicably breathless falsetto, and the hands that were otherwise capable of snapping a human neck had begun to flutter helplessly.

"Oh, I *hope* so," she whispered, sounding for all the world like Butterfly McQueen on crack. "Is Clayton here?" *What the hell is she pulling?* The saleslady relaxed immediately, obviously relieved that the store wasn't going to be shut down on a morals charge during her watch.

"I'm afraid not," she replied ruefully as I tried to hide my crotch behind a snow shovel. "He's away for the weekend." A.J.'s face fell in a perfect imitation of disappointment.

"Oh, drat the luck!" she cursed daintily. *Who* is *this woman?! And whatever happened to "Oh, fuck"?!*

"Is there something *I* could assist you with?" offered our pink-smocked helpmate timidly, doubtless contemplating the least offensive way of getting us out the back door before we encountered any small children.

"Actually," mused A.J., "maybe you could. You see, we went to high school with Clayton's other half. Class of, uh—" She elbowed me severely enough to puncture a lung.

"Seventy-eight," I muttered sourly. *Don't turn to* me *for clues. What do I look like—Annie Sullivan spelling "water" into your palm?!*

"Seventy-eight," she repeated with a forced simper. "And I'm organizing a reunion that I'm *sure* they wouldn't want to miss." At which point our unwitting adversary nodded appreciatively and uttered the four ugliest words I'd ever heard in my life.

"Oh. You mean Craig." My insides collapsed on the spot. So much for the medley of reasonable explanations.

"Do you sell rat poison here?" I blurted.

FROM THE DESK OF
Gordon Duboise

Pop:

I'm running into a little snag. I thought it'd be more realistic if Craig had a boyfriend—but I think I've written myself into a corner. How do I keep Travis from giving up?

Also, if A.J. were to say to Gordo, "In the unlikely event I ever misplace enough of my marbles to marry you," does it sound like she's just yanking my chain or like she's really hooked on him?

Read the pages and let me know. I'm at home.

Your Kid

ARGOSY ENTERTAINMENT
Literary Representatives

LOS ANGELES   TORONTO
NEW YORK   LONDON

Gordon:

1. Don't worry about realistic. It's only a movie. Besides, if these people were actually alive, they'd have been institutionalized by now.
2. Gordo and A.J. fell in love on page 7 of the outline when she called him an unappetizing pervert. Isn't that what you intended? Even a studio nitwit ought to be able to spot it. She's too bright to be single and he's too extraordinary. They were made for each other.
3. Before Travis throws in the towel (which doesn't sound too likely, given how you've developed him), he and A.J. need to do a little investigating first. She could tail Craig to find out what his story is, and Travis could drop in on

Clayton. Maybe they talk hardware. Or Travis pretends he's building a house and needs a hammer. How the hell should *I* know? That's *your* department.

This is the first time you've asked for my advice since 1967. If you made it a habit, it wouldn't be the end of the world.

Pop

P.S. "Does it sound like she's just yanking *my* chain?" Gordon, how much of this *aren't* you inventing?

FROM THE DESK OF
Gordon Duboise

Pop:

Ooops.

Did you figure it out before you called Gordo "extraordinary" or after?

ARGOSY ENTERTAINMENT
Literary Representatives

LOS ANGELES   TORONTO
NEW YORK   LONDON

You'll never know.

FROM THE JOURNAL OF
Travis Puckett

THE PUCKETT/DUBOISE DEBATES

TRAVIS: Me building a house?! There's a laugh. Remember the time I tried to fix the toaster? California Edison blamed me for a three-state blackout!

GORDO: You've got until Monday to learn the terminology. Now shut up and go over it one more time. Split-level.

TRAVIS: Steps and an attic.

GORDO: A-frame.

TRAVIS: Point at the top.

GORDO: Ranch.

TRAVIS: Naked cowboys. What if he asks me about nails and wood?!

GORDO: T, it's not like you're really going to go through with it! Get him to talk about Craig. Find out how serious it is.

TRAVIS: This is the worst idea you ever had.

GORDO: No, it isn't. Having sex with a witch doctor was.

FROM THE JOURNAL OF
Travis Puckett

I had to get out of that hotel room pronto, and it wasn't just because of the icky aqua-and-mauve bedspreads. In less than twenty-four hours, A.J. and Gordo had hopscotched from cat and mouse to "he's-in-love-with-Kim, Kim's-in-love-with-him" without even landing on cute and nauseating first. *Who ever heard of having dinner together in different area codes?!* Worse, when I tried to pry the receiver out of A.J.'s ear by alerting her that *Giant* was on channel 8, all she did was mumble, "I've already seen it," before returning to AT&T and my roommate's idiosyncratic résumé—which included a fable about a blind date who'd allegedly requested permission to chuck oranges at his ass. (Her name was Cindy and they were actually tangerines. Typically, Gordo was distorting the facts again.)

Once out on the sidewalk, I grimly accepted the fact that my world had come to a premature finish, leaving me behind like so much flotsam. But I could handle it. Just because I'd been abandoned and discarded by those I'd trusted, just because I was wounded, bleeding, and lost without hope, just because my lover had found somebody else and I'd never get to tickle his belly button again, and just because my ex-best friend wasn't able to come up with anything more erudite than suggesting I learn the finer points of barn raising, I could still watch out for myself. After all, Saratoga Springs sits smack in the middle of the most significant part of American history, and there were plenty of distractions at hand tailor-made for taking my mind off the futility of a twice-broken heart.

1. *Craig's office building.* There's a newsstand on the ground floor that sells chocolate chip cookies. This is probably where he buys them on his way back from lunch.
2. *Craig's grocery store.* The old lady who owns it told me that Craig loves McIntosh apples. Bullshit. Craig *hates*

McIntosh apples. They must be for the Abusive Shit-ball who sleeps on the other side of his bed.

3. *Craig's pharmacy.* The condoms were on a rack right by the front door, so I didn't go inside. Who needed the torment of speculation?

4. *Craig's gas station.* There was a hunky little pump jockey whose eyes never left my 501s. If I ever find out he looks at Craig that way, I'll kick his ass.

5. *Craig's house.* It has two decks, a Jacuzzi, and a double-tiered patio, doubtless built by the Snarling Douchebag while he had Craig rope-tied in a closet. The bedroom takes up the whole second floor. What bitter crops are harvested there?

6. *Craig's lake.* Directly across the street from their front yard, it's ringed by maples and elms and picnic-green grass. He and The Lump probably sit by the shore on summer nights, ruminating—assuming that Craig is allowed to speak at all.

7. *Craig's car.* He drives a blue Miata with rainbow plate holders. And on the front seat there's a CD. *Damn Yankees.* ("Smerko, play the 'Miles and Miles and Miles of Heart' song again. Pleeeeeeeeease.") The Nut-Log probably owns a Bronco.

8. *Saratoga Museum/Benedict Arnold's boot.* It's a moldy old shoe. Big fucking deal. What does that have to do with Craig?!

If Alexander Hamilton could invent a country and then get himself shot in a duel for something he believed in, the boyfriend thing ought to be a no-brainer. Especially without an asshole like Aaron Burr in the picture. Isn't this what you've been teaching us?

NOW you're acting dopey enough to be in love.

This is what you have a life for.

Falling hard for somebody makes you do things you

never thought you'd do before. Like pulling off an A in History or finally facing the truth about yourself. Craig's the one, Travis. Get him back.

Split level: steps and an attic. A-frame: point at the top. Ranch house: remember the Ponderosa. . . .

GordoStud.com

Dear A.J.,

Whenever he threatens to call it quits, expect him to come through. It always happens—as long as you don't argue with him. Example of what *not* to do:

TRAVIS: My world just ended.

YOU: Like hell it did.

Example of the best way to get him off his ass:

TRAVIS: My life is over. Think I'll go hang myself.

YOU: There's a rope in the closet.

It's like lighting a fuse. And if he starts using words like "futile" and "flotsam," watch out. He's about to launch the counterattack.

The next time we plan dinner, hang up on me if I suggest Chinese again. The cordless phone–chopsticks combo just doesn't work. (By the way, I still have eight spareribs left. Want me to FedEx them?) And maybe you want to think about picking candles that are more romantic than votives. I used the ones in those bell-shaped glasses, and all we were missing on this end was Johnny Mathis singing to us. I got the feeling you were holding out for the pope.

Four things: (1) The rattle under the hood is because the latch dried out. Shpritz it with a little WD-40 and it'll go away. I promise. (2) You were right about the temperature on Saturn. (3) Your mother doesn't have Alzheimer's—it's just the after-effects of the stroke. When she says "I have a hurricane in my purse," it may not make sense, but it means she's healing. Remember when she could hardly talk at all? How much would you have paid for one of those hurricanes *then*? (4) The kid on the Good & Plenty commercial was named Choo-Choo Charlie.

My father called me extraordinary. And you were the one who convinced him.

Love you,
Gordo

P.S. When I gave you a hard time about the Pop-Tarts, you knew I was only joking, right?

Dear Gordo,

I didn't convince your father—your father convinced *you*.

Beaver's still out sightseeing. Ask him to send you his list of hot spots. If Craig McKenna ever becomes a national icon, guess who's got the first Greyline franchise all sewn up? By tonight we can probably expect snapshots of the Toilet Craig Pees In.

Up until three days ago, I'd have closed the books on this one. Craig has a significant other and I don't believe in miracles. Right? Then what the hell am I doing in Saratoga Springs with a certifiable (though appealing) fruitcake and a long-distance boyfriend I haven't even met yet? Beats the shit out of *me*. So on Monday while Beaver's getting his ass into hot water with Clayton, I'll stake out the law firm and see what happens. Why not? If it works, I'll buy a trenchcoat and marry Lauren Bacall. Then we can all go picket that Dr. Laura idiot.

Four things: (1) Your aspersions on my blueberry Pop-Tarts scarred me for life. Can't you tell? (2) Are you sure about the Saturn thing? Because I made it up on the spot. (3) If you hadn't waited until the last minute to suggest candles, I'd have had time to shop. Ever browse 7-Eleven for mood lighting? It was either votives or a road flare. (4) You were never really an unappetizing pervert. You were a beguiling one.

This afternoon I checked in with my mother expecting more hurricanes and other natural disasters, only to have her begin the conversation with "How's Gordo?" You're the first new thing she's remembered since the stroke.

Keep your fingers crossed that Craig's not a lost cause after all. Because if there's a way out of this, Beaver'll find it. Maybe we should take lessons from him.

Love you too,
A.J.

FROM THE JOURNAL OF
Travis Puckett

Hating Clayton was going to require a lot more work than I thought. Even if I'd been blind to the pecs and the arms and the chest and the ass—which I wasn't—there were still a couple of other small matters that couldn't be overlooked: the coffee and the donuts ("You do business with a Jew from the Bronx, you don't go away hungry."), the instructions to his secretary ("I got somebody very important here—no calls."), and the gold mezuzeh around his neck ("Grandma Ida gave it to me when I was 14. It never comes off."). For two days I'd been rehearsing "sullen" and "hostile," but after five minutes in his office I knew I was going to flunk my finals before I'd even gotten to the essay part.

"Talk to me, Travis," he insisted, leaning against the corner of his desk with his legs spread, like Apollo posing for the cover of *Advocate Men.* "What kind of house are you looking to put up?" Since all of my available synapses were being utilized to keep from staring at his massive thighs, I couldn't remember a single thing Gordo had taught me.

"Uh—point at the top?" I mumbled, blushing shamelessly. But Clayton merely shrugged it off and played the good sport. (Why not? I probably wouldn't have been the first male to faint on his Adidas.) Reaching behind him, he grabbed a 3-by-5 snapshot tucked into the blotter.

"Something like this?" he asked, handing it over. Against my better judgment, I stared down at it dumbly—barely registering the black Bronco or the waterfront A-frame or a glimmering Lake Ontario in the background, which might just as well have been made out of Silly Putty. All I saw was the lithe body seated on the top step, with the snug white T-shirt and the chestnut hair and the thermonuclear one-dimple grin that had been tattooed on my heart since 1978. *Jesus Christ! How could he have gotten cuter?! It's not biologically possible!*

"Who's the guy?" I inquired casually, hoping I hadn't urinated on the floor. Clayton stared at his feet for a long moment before he replied—and when he did, it was almost a challenge.

"My boyfriend," he said carefully. "You got a problem with that?" For the first time all morning, my eyebrows unclenched. I even managed a grin of my own.

"I'm wearing an earring and size 28 jeans," I retorted. "Does it *look* like I have a problem with that?"

So he took me out to lunch. Somehow, we never got around to discussing my house.

GordoStud.com

Dear Gordo,

This is going to be a lot easier than we thought. It turns out that Craig and his law partner Charleen eat at the same noxious greasy spoon every afternoon at 12:30. (Paradoxically, somebody decided to christen it the Sweet Shop and build it right around the corner from the municipal courts building. In a pinch, it's possible to order a sandwich, come down with ptomaine, and file a lawsuit—all in the same lunch hour. You should see what passes for chicken salad in this joint.) Fortunately, they don't charge for eavesdropping, so a cup of coffee that was indistinguishable from liquid nitrogen bought me the booth next to Craig's for ninety minutes.

Here's what we know so far:

1. They have a chunky piece of eye candy named Kevin who sits behind the reception desk and pretends he's not sexually flammable. (Men only, of course. So what else is new? Vaginas and rotary telephones—relics of the twentieth century.) At first he thought I was a process server, but after we'd exchanged our respective theories on Matt Damon's genitalia, he surrendered the enigma code and pointed me toward the Sweet Shop.

2. Craig and Charleen represent a first baseman who plays with (a) the Utica Blue Sox, and (b) Charleen. Apparently, he can't afford custody of his son, so they're trying to find him a job in Saratoga Springs. God only knows why. From the sound of it, if he'd take off his pants and hop onto a calendar, he'd clean up.

3. The Democrats have just asked Craig to run for office, but he hasn't made up his mind. How come? Get this. Clayton doesn't know about it yet. And when he finds out, they're liable to be finding pieces of New York State

as far south as Ecuador. So maybe we have a shot after all. Clayton sounds like a real pip.

Beaver's right. Craig was worth waiting twenty years for. At first glance, he's merely follow-the-dots cute—but when he smiles, it's like a sunburst hitting you right in the face. And I'd kill for his eyes.

We need to arrange for them to run into each other ASAP. Whatever's going to happen is anybody's guess—but we've got nature and Beaver's moxie on our side. Who knows? After this, I might even be able to stomach *It's a Wonderful Life*.

Love,
A.J.

G:
This is going to be a lot tougher than we thought. Remember when I called Clayton an Arrogant Asswipe? Maybe I should have waited until I'd met him first.

The Bad News

1. They've been living together for twelve years.
2. Clayton calls him "Honey."
3. They built a summer house with their own four hands in a place called Cape Vincent.
4. Craig's name is on Clayton's license plate. Sort of. CLAY CRG. Craig must have hit the ceiling and I don't blame him. According to the unwritten rules, Clayton should have plates that say CRAIG 78 (the year they met), and Craig's should say CLAY 78. Duh.

The Encouraging News

1. They started seeing each other right after a Harvey Milk vigil that Craig organized. (I may have had something to do with that.)

2. They broke up for three and a half years around the time that Craig forged Anita Bryant's signature and got her elected to the American Nazi Party. (I *definitely* had something to do with that.)

3. Clayton gave him a wedding ring a couple of weeks ago, but as of 4:32 this afternoon Craig hadn't given him one back yet. (And he won't. You always have to let Craig make the first move, even if the idea's yours.)

4. They got into their first fight in 1979 and it hasn't ended yet—mostly because Craig can't say no to a human rights issue and Clayton can. (Never ever ever *ever* tell Craig not to do something. Two reasons: (a) He's got a sweet heart and he's usually right; and (b) if he's making a mistake, he'll figure that out for himself. You just have to be sure you're holding his hand in case things backfire on him.)

We wound up spending most of the afternoon together. First he took me on a field trip of the hardware store (bet you don't know what an adze looks like), then he bought me lunch, then he showed me the bowling alley, then he gave me a Tic Tac, and then we drove out to Saratoga Lake because that's where he wants to build my house. Know what he told me? I only have to pay for materials and costs. Nothing else. "That way I can prove I was your first best friend in the Springs."

G, I don't know if I can go through with this. I like him.

T

ARGOSY ENTERTAINMENT
Literary Representatives

LOS ANGELES   TORONTO
NEW YORK   LONDON

He *likes* him?

Gordon, either get yourself some new friends or talk some
sense into this one. Just remember—you've got thirty million
people rooting for Travis. Don't fuck it up.

If you're not doing anything for dinner, I'm eating out tonight.
Your stepmother's in another one of her moods. She called here
twenty minutes ago to issue the following bulletin: "If I'd had
good feet, I could have ruled the world." God only knows what
that meant.

Canter's Deli, 7:30. Maybe you can explain women to me.

                                                              Pop

11

Craig

McKenna & Webb
A Law Partnership
118 Congress Park, Suite 407
Saratoga Springs, New York 12866

Memorandum

TO: Kevin
FROM: Craig
DATE: June 8, 1998
SUBJECT: Couple of Things

1. I just got a message from Costanzo's clerk. They're going to be in trial next week for at least a month, so they've asked if we could move up the *Kessler* petition to this Friday. That's only four days from now. If we say yes, it might mean a couple of late nights. Can you swing it? Don't feel obligated. Just because you'd be leaving us adrift without an anchor while a small child's welfare hangs in the balance doesn't mean you'd be missed. Much.

2. I may be getting a call from somebody named Travis Puckett. It's a personal matter. If I'm not here, page me. I don't care where I am or what I'm doing. This is a Code 3: highest priority.

3. I'm sneaking away early tonight because Clayton and I are camping out at Saratoga Lake. (Don't ask.)

4. Where the hell is Charleen?

McKenna & Webb
A Law Partnership
118 Congress Park, Suite 407
Saratoga Springs, New York 12866

MEMORANDUM

TO:	Craig
FROM:	Kevin
DATE:	June 8, 1998
SUBJECT:	Your Couple of Things

1. Actually, I've already put the next three nights on hold in case I meet a dazzling Frenchman who (a) looks exactly like Alain Delon, (b) whisks me off to Paris for dinner, (c) feeds me wine and cheese in a barge chugging up the Seine, and (d) rapes me senseless. But if that doesn't happen, I'll be here. When have I ever left you in the lurch, you schmuck?

2. Charleen is getting her hair done again. It seems that Jody's calling her tonight and she doesn't want him to see what color her roots are over the phone. You guys must have had one hell of a weekend. At breakfast this morning, she poured coffee on her scrambled eggs. (I promised I wouldn't reveal what she did with the Lea & Perrin's. Especially to you.)

3. I assume I'm not supposed to know that the Democrats want you to run for office. Tough. What do you expect me to do—*not* read your faxes?

4. Who's Travis Puckett? And how personal is "personal"? I need to know immediately. You can't just give me an instruction like that and keep the details to yourself, especially when it sounds like the page-one lead in a trashy tabloid. Don't forget that we're protected by the employer-employee confidentiality statute, so whatever you tell me stays sealed (unless Oprah offers cash).

MCKENNA & WEBB

A LAW PARTNERSHIP

118 CONGRESS PARK, SUITE 407

SARATOGA SPRINGS, NEW YORK 12866

MEMORANDUM

TO:	Kevin
FROM:	Craig
DATE:	June 8, 1998
SUBJECT:	Omerta: Code of Silence

Travis was the love of my life. It happened when we were in high school, it ended when college separated us, and I can still taste our first kiss in the rain (Saturday, May 27, 1978, 3:21 P.M. EDT).

We haven't spoken to each other in twenty years, but certain recent discovery responses indicate that he's trying to find me.

I know I probably shouldn't, but nobody ever fit into my arms the way he did. The least I can do is have lunch with him.

McKenna & Webb
A Law Partnership
118 Congress Park, Suite 407
Saratoga Springs, New York 12866

Memorandum

TO: Craig
FROM: Kevin
DATE: June 8, 1998
SUBJECT: Dish

1. This is way too good for Oprah. It belongs on *Frontline*. Hey, if Clayton and Travis get into a Bette Davis–Joan Crawford catfight over you, can I watch?

2. Just a reminder: You already share the deepest part of your soul with a man who, among other things, might have been the by-product of a clandestine midnight union between Adonis and Dionysus. On top of that, he's sensitive, he's real, and he loves you. Haven't you learned what "rock the boat" means yet?

3. Actually, something just occurred to me. If Travis succeeds in turning your head, Clayton's going to need somebody to pick up his shattered little pieces and put them back together again. Does hitting on the boss's boyfriend constitute a dischargeable offense?

MCKENNA & WEBB
A LAW PARTNERSHIP
118 CONGRESS PARK, SUITE 407
SARATOGA SPRINGS, NEW YORK 12866

MEMORANDUM

TO: Kevin
FROM: Craig
DATE: June 8, 1998
SUBJECT: Your Interrogatories

1. No.

2. No.

3. Yes.

Craig McKenna   **Attorney Notes**

Clay, wouldn't it be funny if the Democrats asked me to run for office? No.

Clay, here's a thought. How about if I run for office? How about if you don't?

Clay, remember when Lucy tried to tell Ricky she was pregnant and couldn't figure out how? Yeah. You're not running for office.

Clay, wouldn't it be great if we had somebody in Albany who could push through a Freedom to Marry bill? Yep. As long as it isn't you.

Clay, I'm running for office. Wanna bet?

Whenever my sig oth buys a new chunk of land, we always pitch a tent and spend the first night there ourselves. Kind of like cocker spaniels leaving a scent. The routine is generally the same: we build a campfire, grill a couple of hot dogs, and tackle the thorny questions head-on.

"Honey, who was the one with the cute ass—Snap, Crackle, or Pop?"

"Crackle."

"That's what I thought." Afterward, we unroll our sleeping bags, fight about The Issue of the Day, lock eyes, forget about The Issue of the Day, and make love under the eighteen million stars that jointly decided to call Saratoga Springs home. And when we're finished, I can usually get him to say yes to anything, provided I remember that I only have a four-and-a-half-minute window of opportunity before the glow wears off.

"Clay?" I began nervously, with my arms wrapped around his perpetually astonishing chest. "There's something we need to talk about." Except for the crickets chirping, I heard only silence in return. "Clay?" Unexpectedly, he lowered his mouth gently to mine and kissed me for a good minute and a half before he finally pulled away.

"I was just thinking," he sighed finally, staring up at the Big Dipper with a dopey smile on his face. "The only two things I could never handle are the Jets winning the Super Bowl and losing you." Then he nuzzled my neck and kissed me again. "Now what's on your mind?" he murmured, running a sexy finger up and down my back. His whisper was so amorous, and the caresses so genuine, I just couldn't bring myself to do it. *Mayday! Mayday! Abort the program! He's just crashed my hard drive!* Which left me with one remaining problem: he was still waiting for me to say something.

"Why—why don't we go skinny-dipping?" I asked weakly, improvising on the spot. Before I'd even finished the question, Clayton was already reaching for our towels.

"You bet," he grinned wickedly. "But you go in first. I want to watch."

I'm in *really* deep shit.

NEW YORK STATE DEMOCRATIC COMMITTEE

ALBANY HEADQUARTERS   151 STATE STREET
ALBANY, NEW YORK 12207

June 9, 1998

VIA FACSIMILE

Craig S. McKenna, Esq.
McKenna & Webb
118 Congress Park, Suite 407
Saratoga Springs, New York 12866

Dear Craig:

Per our telephone conference, I'm enclosing a generic campaign schedule for your review. Regarding your responsibilities as state assemblyman, they essentially break down as follows: Drive to Albany, write a bill, kill a bill, go home. If I were you, I wouldn't quit my day job.

Please don't feel pressured to make a quick decision. As I said, we don't need your answer until Monday, so take your time. As long as you say yes.

Best,
Wayne Duvall

PARTIAL CAMPAIGN SCHEDULE—CRAIG McKENNA
Summer/Fall 1998

July 19. Junior League All-Star game at Ballston Spa—Craig McKenna, plate umpire. (Wear a cup.)

July 28. Hadassah Luncheon, Glens Falls. (Don't eat for two days prior. When these women feed you, they don't fuck around.) Speech should stress health care reform for seniors, with emphasis on your victory in *Brunswick vs. County*.

August 5. Lambda Legal Defense Dinner, Waterford. This'll be a Q and A about the rocky road leading to a marriage bill. Show them it can happen: bring Clayton.

August 19. Black Tie Ball for PFLAG, Albany. They've asked you to be the keynote speaker, so you'll hit them with your verdict in *LaFontaine vs. Clifton Park Unified School District* and outline a five-point program to keep the classroom safe for kids. (Note: You're expected to lead the first dance with one of the mothers, so if you don't know how to waltz, learn.)

August 30. AIDS Telethon, Saratoga Springs. You'll staff the phones and look cute.

September 11–13. Rainbow Coalition Liberty Weekend, Round Lake. You have an arsenal here, and they're all in your corner. (Why not? At one time or another, you've represented at least half of them.) You're chairing three civil rights seminars based on your verdicts in *Eller vs. State of New York, Hack vs. Richmond,* and *Senet vs. Nixon,* so pace yourself. Popularity's a bitch.

September 26. Autumn Carnival, Mechanicsville. This one's a two-parter. During the day you'll hand out goodie bags to the kids and read Winnie the Pooh stories dressed as Eeyore. In the evening, you'll meet with the Saratoga County Children's Rights Commission and use your victory in *Wilcox vs. Roe* as a foundation for another of your well-known five-point programs.

October 9. Sixth-Grade Debate, Galway Middle School. You'll be pitted against their most ferocious 11-year-olds, so watch your ass. If you can hold your own with these brats, Trent Lott should be a cakewalk.

October 31. Halloween Fright Night, Corinth Junior High. (Before I tell you about your costume, I'll need to prep you first.)

Noah Kessler
6026 Foxhound Run
Saratoga Springs, New York 12866

June 9, 1998

ATTORNEY-CLIENT COMMUNICATION

Craig McKenna
McKenna & Webb
118 Congress Park, Suite 407
Saratoga Springs, New York 12866

Dear Craig,

Eeyore? They want you to dress up like <u>Eeyore</u>? You better say no. Because if you don't, I'll go there myself with a camera and take pictures and then you'll have to give me money for the rest of my life so I won't show them to anybody. I mean it.

Craig this is bullshit. The AIDS part works and the Rainbow part and the marrying Clayton part and the old lady part, but what about kids? Just because you get to debate a couple of sixth graders with dorky hair? Big deal. You need to get in classrooms and <u>talk</u> to us so you can find out the important things for real. How come they won't let you? Just because we can't vote yet? How skanky is that?

I'm not happy about this. Tell Wayne Duvall to have better ideas and then get back to me.

Noah

P.S. Dad says the hearing is this Friday but I can't come. But I know where the court is and I have a bike. So watch out. Did anybody think about just yelling at the judge? Because if you're afraid to, <u>I</u> can do it. Even if it means the biggest time-out in my life.

McKenna & Webb
A Law Partnership
118 Congress Park, Suite 407
Saratoga Springs, New York 12866

MEMORANDUM

TO: Craig
FROM: Charleen
DATE: June 9, 1998
SUBJECT: Camelot—the Sequel

Just read through Wayne's campaign schedule. Nice "generic" plan. What happens when they get specific?

We'll need to take on another partner to cover your caseload. Kevin recommended the alliterative David DeDios, an up-and-coming civil liberties advocate at Matz & Phillips, whose qualifications include "dreamy Filipino eyes, iron quads, and glutes for days." They met at the gym. In the steamroom. Already this is way too much information.

We might as well give Costanzo what he wants and calendar the *Kessler* hearing for Friday. (It's not like we have a prayer anyway.) I finished my half of the petition while I was under the hair dryer, so stop playing Joan of Arc left to burn alone on the pyre. I can't help it if I'm old-fashioned. Jody doesn't get to second base until I've been tinted. I'm not taking any chances.

Incidentally, this isn't for general release yet, but he's quitting the Blue Sox in September and moving back to the Springs. That way he gets to see Noah every day, whether he has custody or not. So there's half of Costanzo's argument shot to shit. As to the other portion, it's not exactly as if Jody's a pauper. He may only net $32,000 this year, but he still wants to take me to Bermuda. Sigh.

Guenevere

P.S. Not to put too fine a point on it, but when exactly were you planning to share the news of your candidacy with that naked man who lives with you? Any time soon? Or do you intend that he find out about it in the voting booth?

P.S.2. While I was retrieving the *Kessler* pleading clip from your office, I couldn't help noticing the large orange Post-it on your desk—the one that had "TravisTravisTravisTravisTravis TravisTravisTravisTravisTravisTravis" scribbled all over it. It reminded me of your freshman notebook at Harvard. But you'll notice I'm not asking any questions.

McKenna & Webb
A Law Partnership
118 Congress Park, Suite 407
Saratoga Springs, New York 12866

MEMORANDUM

TO:	Guenevere
FROM:	Craig
DATE:	June 9, 1998
SUBJECT:	Trying to Keep a Secret Around This Place

You and our boy toy really need to order up a couple of 1912 hen hats so you can cluck to your hearts' content. Pickalittle, talkalittle, cheep, cheep, cheep.

Yes, Virginia. In an effort to twist-tie my life even more convincingly, I may find myself with a mild Travis crisis on my hands. Aunt Sheba at the front desk has all the dirt. I was afraid to tell you because I knew you'd kill me.

I'm attaching a letter from Noah, which I just faxed to the Democrats. They'd better do as he says—I've just made him my campaign advisor. Go ahead and double-dare me. Does it sound like I'm kidding? By the way, you'll note that he intends to crash the courtroom on a six-speed Schwinn. One of us needs to remind him that he's not too old to spank. (Come to think of it, neither am I. But that's a whole other arena that involves Clayton and a leather jockstrap, and we don't need to go there.)

I finished my half of the petition before you did (smirk smirk), and K's cite-checking it as we speak—unless, of course, he's on the phone with "hunky Tim" at the travel agency, in which case we may end up with plane tickets to Brazil again. Therefore, if the East 68th Street Busybodies can spare me for a couple of hours, I have an errand I need to run.

Love,
Carolyn Appleby

P.S. I tried to tell Clayton last night. We were lying in a sleeping bag stripped to our butts, and he was licking my entire pectoral group. Somehow the opportunity never presented itself. This isn't something you discuss with a woody.

P.S.2. Dave DeDios is one of the most honorable and hardworking civil rights attorneys in the state. He's also a lot cuter than I am. Thanks for the memory. I'm not even cold yet.

P.S.3. By the way, don't even *think* about playing Dainty June with me. Jody only has two guest bedrooms and yours was empty all Saturday night. I know. I peeked. Where did you sleep? On the porch? In the hammock? Sorry, panel. Time's up.

Craig McKenna   **Attorney Notes**

- Attorney recognized that he had less than forty-eight hours to devise a fail-safe plan for convincing an obstinate judge to let a little boy live with the father he idolizes, when in fact the obstinate judge in question is far more likely to appear at bench in a lavender tutu and perform a medley of pirouettes from *West Side Story* than grant attorney's petition.

- Attorney recognized that he had less than six days to decide whether or not to run for public office, which would entail—among other things—getting a haircut, ordering new stationery, and reinventing his entire life.

- Attorney recognized that the beaches of Normandy on D-plus-3 couldn't hold a candle to what his living room was going to look like after his sig oth found out about Eeyore and other related events.

- Attorney recognized that he might shortly be staring into the eyes of the only boy who'd ever made him smile in his sleep—and that the butterflies in his stomach were about something other than fear.

- Attorney recognized that, without Prozac, he was about to turn into the China Syndrome.

- Attorney fled.

I changed into my *Chorus Line* T-shirt and jeans in the men's room, bought some chocolate chip cookies at the newsstand downstairs, then popped the top on the Miata and headed south. It was the only journey I'd taken by myself in twelve years and one of the few things I've ever done without running it by Clayton first.

By the time I hit the Taconic Parkway, I'd already figured out where I was going, but I wasn't quite ready to admit it to myself yet. Instead, I flipped on the radio (permanently programmed to WEEI) and winced for fifteen minutes while my Red Sox gave up six runs to the Cleveland Fucking Indians. (Groan.) It reminded me of the time that Clayton and Jody and Noah and I had driven to Iowa so we could all play ball at Field of Dreams, and I'd blurted out one of my traditionally pious invocations to Fenway Park in front of our little pipsqueak. I should have known better. It always exasperates him when I do that.

"*Craig, you need to get a life,*" he insisted from the backseat. "*They haven't won anything since 1918!*"

"*You gotta believe,*" I cautioned him wisely.

"*Says who?*" he shrieked.

Chatham came and went and so did a brief Sox rally in the second, which ended on a triple play (the ugly kind that only happens to the Red Sox). During the inning break, I learned that the Dodgers had just paid $24 million for a utility infielder who was still on the disabled list, that the doubleheader at 3-Com Stadium (formerly Candlestick Park) had been rained out, and that the National League was considering adopting the designated hitter rule. *Travis would have had a field day with this. We'd have been sitting on my bed listening to the radio and his ears would have gotten redder and redder. Then all of a sudden they'd have blown off altogether.*

"*What idiot dreamed up '3-Com Stadium'?*" *he'd have yelped. "Know what comes next? 'IBM's Disposa-Dome'—the world's first disposable ballpark! When the game's over, just toss it! And why not a designated pitcher too? That way even dead guys like Cy Young could win their next eight starts! Craigy, who are these people?" Meanwhile, I'd have been rolling across the floor with tears streaming down my face—partly because he could always figure out how to make me laugh and partly because I'd know that this entire performance was for my benefit.*

Travis, why haven't you called me yet?

~

The Saw Mill River Parkway hadn't changed much in twenty years and neither had the Beckley Quad. Risking at least two demerits, I parked the Miata in a red zone directly in front of the granite-and-sandstone portico I'd once known as Wellwood Hall, then glanced up reflexively at the pair of gargoyles I'd last mocked in 1978. *Yep. They still look like Helen Hayes.* For that matter, so much of the Dickensian campus had remained untouched, I half-expected Mr. Naylor to come charging out of the ivy-clogged gateway to the English department, grab me by the collar, and begin cramming *Ivanhoe* up my ass again. The single indication that time had indeed managed to advance at least a day and a half was the lone junior with sandy hair and a calculus text, head down and lost in cosine hell as he absently ambled across the grass toward the dorms. Though he barely took notice of me, I could tell exactly what he was thinking: *"Sheesh. More alumni. I hope I never get that old."* But it didn't matter. I had an agenda to keep—and Travis was with me every step of the way.

My Room

With the light streaming in through the tiny window and hitting the same faded patch of gray linoleum, I could have sworn I'd just won back my adolescence: the bed was exactly where it had always been and the radiator *still* hadn't been painted. All that was missing was Travis, the chocolate chip cookies, Travis, *King Lear*, Travis, "ubiquitous," Travis, the Grateful Dead, and Travis. (This is where he said "I love you" for the first time.)

The Swimming Pool

Almost deserted under the canvas dome, its only occupants were two squealing boys who'd obviously crawled in through the same window I'd used myself years earlier, and who appeared ready to commit the rest of their lives to dunking each other in the water. This was one of the only two places in Westchester County where Travis and I could be naked together without anybody suspecting.

The Oak Tree Ninety-three Paces into the Woods

Where we'd go when we didn't think we could survive another ten minutes without at least one kiss—which was usually multiplied by a more substantial integer before we were through.

"Have we hit a baker's dozen yet?"
"How many's that?"

"Fifty."
"No."

A new carpet of leaves now covered the ground where we'd once cuddled, and our tree was a little bit more scarred than it had been in 1978. Running my hand up and down the trunk, I wondered illogically if it still remembered us.

The Library

The only thing that had changed was the animated young woman sitting behind the checkout desk, who was practically indistinguishable from her equally perky predecessor (leading me to wonder whether or not there isn't a mail-order catalog somewhere that specializes in cheerful high school librarians). Encouraged by her benevolent—if exhausting—smile, I made my way to the back room ("Poetry and Drama") and found the two overstuffed leather chairs I'd been looking for. On rainy days Travis and I would sit here side-by-side, reading together—*Auntie Mame* (his choice) or *In Cold Blood* (mine). This is where *I* said "I love you" for the first time.

The Dorm Showers

Either in the interests of modesty or as a result of finally figuring out what horny adolescent boys are capable of, the eight nozzles—to my unbridled dismay—had been partitioned off into separate stalls. (It's like revisiting Fenway Park after a protracted absence and discovering that they'd repainted the Green Monster Day-Glo orange.) This was the *other* place in Westchester County where we could be naked together without anybody suspecting. All we had to do was get really dirty. Three times a day.

"How long have we been in here?"
"Two hours. Why?"
"The water pressure's gone."

Study Hall

Since it was packed with kids cramming for finals, I didn't go inside. Instead, I squinted through the window until I'd spotted the pockmarked corner table where we'd pass notes back and forth disguised as English essays. As a rule, I generally don't blush retroactively, but sometimes it's unavoidable.

The Lear Perplex

King Lear was an old fart. Travis isn't. And he'd better let me touch him before fifth period.

Mourning Becomes Electra

This is supposed to be a contemporary tragedy, but the *real* tragedy is not being able to play with Craig's belly button whenever I want to.

The Chapel Rectory

No details will be revealed—now or ever. We're already going to hell for this one.

The Tarrytown Railroad Station

Underneath the tacky green-and-red mansard roof, the two cobblestoned platforms were as seedy and piss-smelling as I'd remembered. This was where all of our adventures started—and where Travis always believed we could make them last forever.

"Why don't we take the 5:10 to Poughkeepsie and never come back?"
"What's in Poughkeepsie?"
"Us. Once we get there."

Somehow, we never did.

~

Before I hit the on-ramp heading home, I stopped by Tappan Hill Park for one last kick in the ass. There was a Little League championship taking place on the diamond (with a far more reasonable score than the Red Sox had managed to maintain against the Indians) and the sky threatened rain—just as it had done once before. But the gazebo was empty and waiting. As I followed the curving footpath toward Ground Zero, I tried to count the number of times Travis and I had come back here when nobody else was around, just so we could replay our first kiss. He'd pretend our being there was an accident of Fate— *"Hey, look! The park! Let's go reminisce!"*—but I'd later find out that he'd blocked our entire route well in advance. (Smerk was the one who invented the concept of premeditated spontaneity.)

Except for another seventeen layers of rust, the seasons had stood still between the metal archways. I found the place where he'd leaned his head on my shoulder while he told me how his stepmother had thrown him out of the house; I pinpointed the spot where I'd run my fingers through his hair and confessed that I always suspected I liked boys better than girls; and I stood where we'd stood when I first took his hand and gave him my heart in exchange. Finally, after I'd gotten up enough nerve, I crouched down to sneak a peek under one of the concrete benches—and discovered at once that two decades hadn't eroded the covenant that had been so dauntlessly etched there a generation earlier: Craig Loves Travis, 6/9/78. So I pulled a blue rolling writer out of my denim jacket and added "6/9/98" underneath it.

Nobody needed to know but me.

McKenna & Webb
A Law Partnership
118 Congress Park, Suite 407
Saratoga Springs, New York 12866

Memorandum

TO: Craig
FROM: Charleen
DATE: June 9, 1998
SUBJECT: Fasten Your Seat Belt, Margo

Clayton found out about the offer from the Democrats. I'm still not sure how. The foam around his mouth was garbling his ability to articulate.

I attempted to throw him off the scent by assuring him that you've been far too busy to consider such nonsense seriously—at which point my nose extended eleven feet and precluded my riding in any elevators.

On a scale of 1 to 10, this looks like a 24. Call me if you need moral support or bandages.

Ch

CLAYTON'S HARDWARE
serving Saratoga Springs since 1988

Craig—

I can't fucking believe you'd keep something like this from me. What ever happened to "love, honor, and cherish"? Is that why you haven't given me a wedding ring back yet? Is that why you always dodge the bullet when I bring up places for us to get married? "Don't tell Clayton—he'll hit the ceiling." Thanks for trusting that I love you.

By the way (since it doesn't seem to have sunk in yet), Harvard was never about riots or civil rights or freedom marches. Harvard was about wondering every morning whether you'd be in bed with me that night or in jail or in the ICU or dead. If that doesn't prove how much you mean to me, then tough shit.

And don't tell me this is different. You already blew off Rehobeth Beach before they even asked you to run. Now we get to wait in line behind a whole fucking state. Know how many couples survive this? I'll give you a hint. Harry and Bess Truman. Period.

I'll be bunking at the store until further notice. Too many things I already regret saying—and I haven't even said them yet.

Clayton

Craig McKenna   **Attorney Notes**

He found the bumper sticker. It was hidden at the bottom of my sock drawer. Even the CIA would have missed it.

The only other time I've spent a night by myself in this house was when he went to the hospital to have his appendix taken out. I hated it then and I hate it now. It's like being single all over again—and who can remember how *that* works? Dinner, for instance. I stood at the kitchen counter for fifteen minutes trying to convert the lasagne formula from two people to one. (It was kind of like going from Fahrenheit to Centigrade—and I can't do that either.) So I gave up altogether, made it the way we always do, and then threw his half away.

The rest of the evening was just as rocky. Defiantly breaking one of our most inflexible rules, I watched *Valley of the Dolls* by myself (though I only ate half the Raisinets and I didn't say any of his Neely O'Hara lines out loud). I picked a fight with him in the suddenly cavernous shower even though he wasn't there to shout back ("Who told you to go sneaking around in my sock drawer?" *Silence.*), and I slept facing away from his side of the barely occupied bed so it'd be easier to pretend he wasn't gone. That didn't work either. Every time I woke up reaching for him, I'd poke my eye on a ten-dollar pillow sham from Bloomingdale's. But if 2:53 in the morning is generally only utilized for earthquakes of a magnitude 6.0 or greater, it also provides a handy opportunity to rewind twelve years of your life in the dark.

How did this happen? One minute I was Craig McKenna, Superhero, and the next thing I knew I had a brand burned into my ass that said, "If lost, return to Clayton." When was the last time I was allowed to make a decision? February 14, 1996, that's when. Valentine's Day. I got to pick regular unleaded instead of Techron Supreme. Major fucking wow. He even gives me a hard time about staging a teensy protest on my birthday. "Clay, twelve hundred people are being massacred on our front lawn. Can I call the police?" "No. You'll only make waves." Who asked you, you big bully? And by the way—I hate lasagne!

It's time for some affirmative action. No more backing down. From now on, I call my own shots. This is the old Craig McKenna again. The all-star quarterback with a sterling silver Victory Cup. The unbeatable shortstop who wouldn't be struck out. The summa cum laude Harvard attorney who doesn't take shit from anybody.

The Boy from Brigadoon.

~

I shouldn't have watched *Valley of the Dolls* without him.

12

Travis

CLAYTON'S HARDWARE
serving Saratoga Springs since 1988

Trav—

Stopped by the hotel on the off chance you'd be in.
There's a couple of houses out by Loughberry Lake
that I wanted you to see. Once we figure out what
we're going to build you, I can get started on the specs.

If you're not doing anything later, meet me for a beer
after I get off work. The boyfriend and I aren't speaking again. This time it really *is* his fault. And I think I
need somebody to talk to.

Clay

FROM THE JOURNAL OF
Travis Puckett

Things It's Okay to Discuss

1. Hardwood floors.
2. Lawn fertilizer.
3. The Revolutionary War.
4. "The course of true love never did run smooth." Mention Romeo and Juliet, Rick Blaine and Ilse Lund, Fanny Brice and Nicky Arnstein, and any other couples who either died or broke up.
5. The advantages of separation and divorce.
6. Ann Landers: "Toss him back and fish for another one."

General Notes

Point out the many freedoms that come with being on your own again. (Quote the Bill of Rights and most of the lyrics from *Company*.)

Remind him that an amicable breakup requires moving out as soon as possible.

Suggest that remaining friends doesn't usually work in the long run. If he asks for proof, make something up. Just don't let him go there.

Also come up with a lot of pejorative adjectives for Craig, such as selfish, inconsiderate, insensitive, tactless, greedy, parsimonious, avaricious, cold-hearted, obdurate, pitiless, venal, and callous. (But wait for Clayton to start. You might look like you have an agenda.)

I feel like I'm walking across Omaha Beach without a minesweeper.

GordoStud.com

Dear Gordo,

Beaver's in the bathroom examining blueprints. As of lunch, he'd pretty much decided on a ranch house with a split-rail fence out front. ("Doesn't it kind of look like Spin and Marty?") I think we need to remind him that this is supposed to be a ruse. Because he's about six minutes away from a lasso and chaps.

He and Clayton haven't left each other alone for two days. If they're not This-Bud's-for-You-ing, they're either reliving their favorite box scores or gamboling through lakefront lots like a couple of Scottish pipers tramping across the moors. Thursday is their bowling night. By next week, they'll have taken a condo by the sea together.

According to the frontline bulletin from the Sweet Shop this afternoon, Craig and Clayton haven't spoken to each other since yesterday. Of course it's none of my business, but from my customary radar station in the next booth (where, like the Black Dahlia in dark glasses and veil, I've become something of a local mystery), Clayton gets an automatic zero for being a stubborn and possessive slug. So what if Craig runs for office? How many interns could you possibly molest in a state assembly, for Christ's sake? On the other hand, Craig doesn't exactly score points for being a pillar of fire either. "I hate it when he's mad at me. What can I say to bring him around?" Try "Fuck off," you crybaby. It works like a charm.

(*Note:* When Craig went to the bathroom, Charleen called Jody from her cell phone and arranged a covert rendezvous at a place called Stone Ridge, which is halfway between the Springs—as we here like to call it—and Utica. Two-thirds of the restaurant overheard her. Mata Hari she ain't.)

By the way, Mom got the Andy Hardy videos you FedExed. You dope. I *knew* you were going to pull something like that. She always said that she'd have married Mickey Rooney in a heartbeat—which only means that you and I could have anticipated particularly short children.

You're sweet, you shouldn't have, and if you ever do anything that extravagant again, I'll crack your head open.

Love you,
A.J.

Dear A.J.,

I don't know how to break this to you, but your mom just called to thank me for the tapes—and she thinks I *am* Mickey Rooney. "This is Joanne Larkin in Cleveland. What a thoughtful gift! How's Judy?" It's a good thing Travis made me watch all those shitty MGM musicals, or I'd have been stuck in left field without a jockstrap.

I can't figure out why you're so worried about her memory—she sure as hell had all of her marbles with *me*. For instance, I know what happened at the kindergarten May Day pageant (say it ain't so, Joe), and I know who you kissed in fourth grade (does the name Atticus Gannaway pluck any heartstrings?). There's more, but it hasn't been released under the Freedom of Information Act yet, so you'll just have to keep wondering how much ammo I have on you. Your mother wouldn't have lasted five minutes with the OSS.

When T gets home, lock him in the hotel safe and do *not* let him anywhere near Clayton again. This is getting a little weird even for Travis.

Love you too,
Gordo

FROM THE JOURNAL OF
Travis Puckett

We closed T-Bird's at 11:00 P.M. and we closed Starbucks at 1:00 and we didn't get out of Denny's until 4:15 this morning. He bought me steak and eggs, so I picked up the tab for his nut-crunch sundae. (Clayton has weird metabolism. Even cream cheese turns into muscle. While you watch.)

So far, I hadn't had a chance to bring up Fanny and Nicky or Scarlett and Rhett or Tony and Maria or Arthur and Lancelot or any of the other mismatched misfits I'd concocted in order to make him see the wisdom in being single again. I knew I was supposed to be hinting at ways to insinuate Craig out of his life and back into mine, but somehow the itinerary changed when I wasn't looking.

"Hold it," he interrupted, dropping his spoon for the third time since I'd begun my Zack-the-Dentist confession. "You never played Hide-the-Wiener with this guy?"

"No."

"You never went bare-butt together?"

"No."

"Not even in underpants?"

"No."

"And it's a cinch you never grabbed his dick because he's into girls—which dings any chance he's gonna throw you a boner in the first place."

"Right."

"You never told him about it—"

"No."

"But you killed a *tooth?!*"

"Several," I admitted, turning my usual blend of crimson and ruby. Clayton finished his ice cream in contemplative silence, which was entirely out of step with his routine procedure. His opinions tend to be prompt, defiant, and wrong. *"Hamilton was an ignorant shitkicker. Big deal—he invented the*

Treasury Department, which by the way gave us the IRS. Thanks for nothing." In fact, he didn't say another word until we were back in the Bronco. (Macho guys always think better when they're doing something studly like flipping on the ignition.) Then suddenly he turned to me in the darkness and delivered his verdict.

"If you'd pulled something like that on *me*," he blurted, "I'd have married you on the spot."

No wonder Craig fell in love with him.

~

We sat by Saratoga Lake for another two hours, but we barely noticed the sunrise.

"Ever been in love, Trav?" he inquired idly, tossing a chunk of slate into the water. I was in the middle of retying my shoelaces when my fingers froze. Paralysis comes in many forms. I'd just discovered nine of them.

"Once," I gulped, praying that my face didn't betray the sudden disintegration of my entire nervous system. *Change the subject! Change the subject! Change the subject!* "Twelfth grade," I continued evenly, ignoring the tsunami of sweat that had consumed my entire face. "I was seventeen." *Quick! Make up a boyfriend in case he asks more questions! Name him Scotty!*

"Yeah? Who was he?"

"Crotty." *Travis, you asshole!* But Clayton didn't seem to notice the slip. Instead, he hesitated for a long moment and then began spilling the beans about a lot of things he'd never in a million years considered revealing to anyone before: The abusive father who, in random moments of paternal bonding, knocked out two of his teeth, pushed him through a storm door, broke his arm, "and played basketball with my head"; the gripping fear that began to stalk him in junior high when he first realized that locker rooms made him horny ("I'd take a shower with the other guys and try to picture things like dog shit or Hitler or vomit with corn in it—anything to keep from getting hard"); the football buddy he'd wanted to touch all the way through high school—who'd fallen into bed with him on a drunken Saturday night, only to change his mind on Sunday morning ("You're a sick fuck—stay away from me"); and the boyfriend he's guarded with his life for the past twelve years ("Sooner or later, everybody splits if you let them. Suppose he gets elected to office? You really think I'm gonna be enough for him any more?"). All of this was delivered in a tone of voice so indistinguishable from the one he used when we were discussing Ryne Sandberg's ass or the benefits of gravel driveways over asphalt, I kind of got the feeling that there weren't enough hugs in the world to make a difference. *Why hasn't he told Craig any of these things?!* But he wasn't quite finished yet.

"Say, Trav?" he mumbled, turning to me awkwardly. "I never had a best friend I could count on before. The job's open if you want it."

Benedict Arnold isn't the only traitor with his boots in Saratoga Springs tonight.

FROM THE JOURNAL OF
Travis Puckett

Clay—

I've been doing a lot of thinking since Denny's and the lake, and these are some of the reasons you need to get your ass kicked.

1. When a father with a son like you doesn't exercise his bragging rights 24/7, there's something seriously wrong with him. Your dad's the one who lost out—not you. *And it wasn't your fault!* How could it have been? You were the blue ribbon of kids.
2. Football players who need to get drunk with their best

buddies every Saturday night live in a place called "Denial Land." You had the balls to be yourself and follow your heart. He didn't.

3. Take another look at the photo you showed me—the one with Craig sitting on the front steps of the house in Cape Vincent. You see the grin with the dimple? The one that packs enough heat to melt a Nikon lens? Guess what, Clay? He wasn't smiling at the camera, he was smiling at *you*. His boyfriend. His significant other. His lifetime partner. The one who needs him too much, knows him too well, pulls him up short, and puts him through hell. That's what it's all about, isn't it? Clayton, any halfwit can see that he's already yours—right down to his toes. So don't fuck it up. Send him two dozen snapdragons, tell him you're sorry, take him to France for a week, and don't give him a hard time about running for office. Stop being such a schmuck.

4. You owe most of the Constitutional Convention an apology. Alexander Hamilton's been called many things, but "ignorant shitkicker" is out of line.

Travis

CLAYTON'S HARDWARE
serving Saratoga Springs since 1988

Trav—

- I can't say I'm sorry if I'm right and he's wrong.

- I never noticed his dimple before. Thanks for pointing it out.

- Fuck France. Maybe if they learned how to drive.

- The snapdragons I can do. (How did you know he likes them?)

- Assuming I took your screwy game plan seriously (which I don't), Hamilton's the reason we have interleague play, linoleum infields, and lights at Wrigley Field. So don't yank my chain. They're *your* rules.

- Since I've already figured out that you don't know your ass from your belly button about construction, I'm building you an A-frame. Take it or leave it. We'll go over the specs tomorrow night at bowling.

- Who are you calling a schmuck?

- Thanks for being there. I mean it.

Clay

P.S. I wasn't really a blue-ribbon kid. I used to drop Fizzies into the goldfish bowl just to see what would happen.

GordoStud.com

Dear Gordo,

If you should happen to hear on CNN that A.J. Larkin is wanted in six states for the premeditated decapitation of a history teacher, I won't be offended if you pretend we've never communicated before.

Do you know what he's doing? He's pacing the lobby with my cell phone glued to his ear, trying to talk Clayton into a He Loves Me trip to Paris. With Craig! As of fifteen minutes ago, he'd picked the hotel for them (The Crillon—at $650 a night), planned the dinner reservations (Maxim's—why not?), and orchestrated the midnight handholding along the Left Bank (they didn't even do that in *Gigi!*). But when he brought up the tiramisu-flavored condoms, I kicked him out of the room.

Hello? Am I missing a few pieces, or is the wrong groom going on the honeymoon? Meanwhile, I have a restaurant in St. Louis that's presently under the supervision of an assistant manager whose probation officer doesn't think he ought to be handling cash. What did I *come* here for?

With Clayton and Craig still not speaking to each another (Snap out of it, guys!), we had one window of opportunity that's about to slam shut on Beaver's fingers. And he's the one who's closing it! So after I bury him, I'll mail his personal effects to you in a cardboard box. Fourth class. Book rate.

Love,
A.J.

P.S. He just materialized long enough to grab his jacket and tie his shoelaces again. Says he won't be back until late because he needs to find a quiet place to sort out the flotsam the world's dumped in his lap. (I was about to suggest Bellevue, but he'd already disappeared.) There was a weird far-away look on his face that he might want to reconsider. It worked for Jackie Kennedy. It doesn't work for Beaver.

Dear A.J.,
I was afraid this would happen. When T falls in love, he does it with the whole world at once. Compared to him, Jane Austen was romantically challenged.

Get a rope, tie it to his feet, and drag him up to Craig's office. Once they're face-to-face again, he'll turn back into Normal Travis (whatever *that* is). I hope.

Your mom is watching *Babes on Broadway* as we speak. She figured out that I'm not really Mickey Rooney after all, only Gordo—but it was a nice run while it lasted. In the meantime, she's making me Karamel Krispies for Christmas but sending them out tomorrow. (When do you guys do Thanksgiving—Memorial Day?) Which reminds me—her heater's on the blink again. She says she's not going to worry about it until the fall, but you really ought to think about getting her out of Cleveland and moving her to a place that's warmer. Like Santa Monica. (Hint. Hint. Hint.)

Love,
Gordo

P.S. I'd have to know more specifically which of T's faraway looks he was wearing. There's three of them.

FROM THE JOURNAL OF
Travis Puckett

The whole idea was to get off the train at Poughkeepsie and take a cab to the estate in Hyde Park. After all, if FDR could figure out the Guadalcanal invasion reposing on the veranda with a cocktail, I could solve the Clayton-Craig conundrum doing the same thing with a Diet Coke. But it didn't quite work out that way. There's something almost hypnotic about a cobalt-blue Hudson River streaking past your right elbow at seventy-five miles an hour—it takes you places you don't want to go. *"I think I need somebody to talk to." "If you'd pulled something like that on me, I'd have married you on the spot." "I never had a best friend I could count on before. The job's open if you want it." "Thanks for being there. I mean it."* Years ago, I made a deal with my conscience: as long as I didn't give it a reason to bite me in the ass, it would stay where it belonged. But now that I'd broken the rules, it was retaliating in overdrive.

I ring the bell of the house on Loughberry Lake. Kismet has brought my two feet this far. The rest is up to me. After an interminable wait of almost fourteen seconds, the front door is flung open. My Craig is wearing little jeans, a white T-shirt, no shoes or socks, and chestnut hair that's falling into his face—just like it always did.

"Hi," he grins, one-dimply. "Is there something I can do for—" The words die on his lips when he recognizes me.

"Travis!" he sobs, falling into my arms.

"Craigy!" I sob back, falling into his.

"Hey!" calls Clayton from the living room. "What about me?"

Craig pivots contemptuously, his upper lip curled in a rictus of disgust.

"Get out," he hisses with awful finality. "You've served your purpose." Clayton begins to weep silently as he trudges up the stairs to pack his few pitiful things into a tiny suitcase. When he returns ten minutes later, shoulders hunched and pain creasing his brow, he finds us naked in the Jacuzzi, making love for the first time in twenty years.

"Do I at least get a goodbye?" he asks Craig haltingly, his voice fracturing into a dozen slivers. Craig continues licking my neck and doesn't even bother to look up.

"No," he snaps. "And leave the Bronco. I paid for it."

Poughkeepsie came and went, along with every shred of self-respect I'd ever owned. *When did I turn into such a callous shitball?* So when the conductor bellowed "Tarrytown!" I bolted out of there like a Krupp 88 mortar aimed at Tunis. Anything to get off that train.

Beckley hadn't changed much since Craig and I had last kissed there, except for the brand-new shower stalls that were now only big enough for one boy apiece (as though there were hormone-neutralizing properties in tile) and the chapel rectory, where we'd once stripped off our shirts and made out behind a

life-size canvas of Jesus and the Madonna. (Within five minutes, we'd sent Leviticus the way of the *Hindenburg*.) Everything else was just where I'd expected it to be: our joined-at-
the-hip leather chairs in the library, our belly button table in
study hall, our naked swimming pool at the gym, and the bed
in his room—where we were never afraid to spill our hearts to
each other. There was also our oak tree ninety-three paces into
the woods, which appeared to have been anticipating our
return since 1978. So for close to an hour, I sat beneath its
branches, hoping to recapture what had once been ours. But
my scruples had other ideas.

> *Christmas Eve. Two years from now. The snow falls gently
> along Fifth Avenue and Vic Damone sings "Winter Won-
> derland" while Craig and I hold hands and scope out the
> window displays at Saks. We pass St. Patrick's Cathedral
> just as midnight mass is ending—and amid the devout
> Christians descending the endless steps, we spot a familiar
> figure clad in black and sporting an inverted collar. It's
> Clayton. Unable to overcome his grief, he's converted to
> Catholicism, sworn an eternal vow of celibacy, and become
> a priest. Father Bergman.*

My last stop was the gazebo. By then I was feeling so
guilty, I couldn't even bring myself to stick my head under the
concrete bench, where my boyfriend had immortalized our
synthesis years earlier: Craig Loves Travis, 6/9/78. Instead, I
watched game three of a Little League championship and tried
to shut off my brain. I didn't have much luck.

> *Twenty years from now. Our anniversary. During a mid-
> night stroll across Lincoln Center Plaza, we pass a grizzled
> old fart who's leaning against the fountain, selling pencils.
> It's Clayton. Though he pretends he hasn't seen us, his bot-
> tom lip still quivers with yearning when he recognizes
> Craig. Moments later, he clutches his heart and keels over.*

By the time I stood up to leave, two things had happened: (a) the Hastings Hornets had taken a three-run lead in the eighth when Dobbs Ferry lost its starting lefty to a bar mitzvah lesson; and (b) the tears were streaming down my face. Poor Clayton. Broken. Splintered. A shell of the man we all once loved.

Why do I do this to myself?!

GordoStud.com

G:

There's a modem on the train, but it's $7 a minute. No time for a spell-check. Sorry.

I just went back to Beckley. Remember the bag of oranges you left in our closet? There's still a black spot where they grew into the floor.

G, I'm going to tell Clayton why I'm really here. Otherwise, he'll end up selling matches in the snow without legs— and I can't live with that. I'll explain later.

T

ARGOSY ENTERTAINMENT
Literary Representatives

LOS ANGELES   TORONTO
NEW YORK   LONDON

Gordon:

For God's sake, don't let him tell the truth! What if Clayton kills him? What if Craig finds out? This is no way to end a picture!

I want you to fly to Saratoga Springs yourself. Do whatever you have to. If you need cash, stop by my office on your way to the airport.

I'm serious, Gordon. With a finish like this, we won't even get foreign.

Pop

FROM THE DESK OF
Gordon Duboise

Pop:

Don't worry. I trust Travis. Even when he doesn't know what he's doing.

By the way—this is still a little premature, but would you be ready to handle a daughter-in-law if you should happen to get one?

Your Kid

ARGOSY ENTERTAINMENT
Literary Representatives

LOS ANGELES	TORONTO
NEW YORK	LONDON

Gordon:

I'm 67 years old. A fax like that could have killed me.

I'm reserving a table at Le Dome for 7:30. Bring a designated driver. We'll need one.

Pop

P.S. Yes. I've been ready to handle it for the past ten years.

FROM THE JOURNAL OF
Travis Puckett

Clay—

Meet me at T-Bird's when you get off work. I need to talk to you before the tournament because I don't think you should be holding a bowling ball when I say what I have to say.

Your Buddy

Beer No. 1: We were sitting at an otherwise romantic table in a corner of the bar, with an assortment of pretzels and nuts that all tasted like drywall. Since there was nobody there at 5:30 except for us—and since it's a lot easier to commit a homicide when there aren't any witnesses—I stalled for time. That's how we wound up discussing the cartoon characters who'd given us boners when we were eight.

"I had the hots for Aquaman," admitted Clayton conspiratorially.

"Big deal," I countered with a dismissive shrug, confident that I held the trump card. "I got a stiffy from Elroy Jetson." Clayton was horrified.

"Lower your voice," he growled. "That's perverse."

"I know," I nodded. "Keep it to yourself."

Beer No. 2: By now I was feeling a lot better (Clayton was still sober), so we moved on to Mouseketeer asses.

"Bobby's was the one that was asking for it," he insisted.

"Tim's was," I frowned in reply.

"Bobby's!"

"Tim's! You couldn't even see Bobby's crack!"

"No? Where the fuck were *you* looking?"

Beer No. 3: Halfway through our second pitcher, we were so knee-deep in the Hardy Boys, I didn't even notice that the room had slanted 36 degrees.

"Tell me something," whispered Clayton confidentially, checking over his shoulder to make sure nobody could hear us. "You ever wonder if Frank and Joe got it on with each other? I mean, the way F. W. Dixon was always cramming it up our butts about how good-looking they were and how many muscles they had, what the hell were we *supposed* to think?"

"Duh," I shot back, steadying the table with both hands so it wouldn't slide across the floor. "Remember *The Mystery of Cabin Island?* They were snowed in for three days. Just them and Tony and Phil and Biff and Chet. Trust me, the underpants came off after twenty minutes. I've given this a lot of thought."

Beer No. 4: Clayton was still clear-headed, but all of my consonants were gone. I didn't even realize he was talking about Craig until it was too late.

"Wanna hear a secret?" he sighed.

"Shoot."

"I still have dreams about him." Daring myself to do it, I raised my head from the table and gaped at him through varnished pupils.

"Wanna hear a bigger one?"

"What's that?"

"So do I."

Holy shit! I said it! With only vowels. Though I'd more or less prepared my body for the rain of ruin that was to follow, what ensued was the loudest silence I'd ever heard in my life. Then Clayton merely nodded thoughtfully as though he'd known it all along.

"I had a feeling something was up when I showed you his picture," he mumbled. "You looked like I'd just stuck a rake up your ass, wide-end first. Was Craig the kid from high school?"

I nodded dumbly. *When is he going to hit me?! What's he waiting for? I don't do suspense well!*

"Yes," I replied carefully. *Stop staring at me like that! Take your shot! I've got it coming!*

"Is that why you showed up here? The rest was bullshit?"

"Yes." *Hurt me! Please! Don't make me turn you into a priest!*

Clayton leaned across the table until our noses were practically touching. "Travis, level with me," he said earnestly, his forehead creasing with genuine concern. "Do you think I'm a putz?" The question was so unexpected, I didn't have time to sanitize the answer.

"Only if you leave him," I blurted. *Travis, shut up! What are you saying? Stop drinking!* "Clay, there's nobody else like Craig in the world. I know. I've looked. So he runs for State Assembly and maybe you only see each other on weekends for a while. Big wow. The rest of the world deserves him too—and if you just want to keep him locked up for yourself, then fuck you anyway." *Nice touch, Puckett. Have fun in the woodchipper.*

"Would *you* let him do it?" he challenged, snapping a pretzel as though it were my spine.

"In a heartbeat."

"Why?"

"Because he wants to, you schmuck!"

"Yeah? And what if you lost him?" That's when I finally slammed on the brakes and owned up to the truth I'd been avoiding ever since Robert Mitchum had found Saratoga Springs.

"I already did," I confessed, tossing in the towel once and for all. "You're the one he loves, Clay. Hold on to it. Because I don't want to have to go through this again in another twenty years. And I'm warning you—if you fuck this up, you're not getting him back. I'll make sure of that myself."

Our eyes stayed locked together for another couple of seconds, and suddenly I wasn't afraid of him any more. Instead, I was so damned grateful that Craig had found somebody like Clayton, I could afford to play Susan Hayward for the evening. ("I'll cry tomorrow, baby.") He must have sensed it, because all of a sudden he reached for my head, mussed up my hair, and grinned.

"Know what?" he said simply. "I trust you. Now, come on. We got a game to bowl. A-frame or no A-frame."

Right after that, I passed out.

GordoStud.com

G:
I told him the truth and he still thinks I'm his best friend. Except for Craig, nobody ever liked me that fast before. (Don't challenge me on this one. It took you eight months. I counted.)

Clayton wins. I'm not even in the running. They've shared twelve years with each other—almost a third of their lives. Conservatively, that works out to 8,760 kisses (based on a median of two a day), 1,248 fights (two a week), and 4,380 nights they've fallen asleep together (not counting the last three, which he's spent on a couch in his office). And what do *I* pop for? A two-week road trip and a trespassing fine—which, by the way, you fronted. Somebody ought to drop a cement truck on me.

We're leaving in the morning without seeing Craig. I just couldn't handle it. And neither could anybody else.

Sorry for putting you through all this.

T

FROM THE JOURNAL OF
Travis Puckett

THE PUCKETT/DUBOISE DEBATES

GORDO: T, please tell me this is a joke.

TRAVIS: Why? Doesn't the screenplay have an ending yet?

GORDO: Fuck the screenplay! Do you know who just left you a voicemail? Brandon Tracey. That guy with the Corvette who took you to St. Louis. He's marrying Jennifer in October and he says it's all because of you.

TRAVIS: Bullshit. What did *I* do?

GORDO: Travis, everybody you touch falls in love! Can't you *see* that?! The only one who's coming out of this whole deal empty-handed is you! It's just not fair. At least call Craig before you leave. You never know.

TRAVIS: And tell him what? Gordo, A.J. was right. It's been twenty years! What kind of a dope hitchhikes three thousand miles after twenty years to chase after someone who's probably forgotten him in the first place?

GORDO: *Your* kind, Travis. And remember how I kept telling you to change?

TRAVIS: So?

GORDO: Don't ever listen to me again.

GordoStud.com

Dear A.J.,

You've got to do something. This time he means it. And my bag of tricks is empty.

Here's a guy who never gives up. I could tell you lots of stories, but the one I remember most is when we were 16 and he decided he wanted to meet Steve Lawrence and Eydie Gormé. I guess most kids would have settled for autographs, but not Trav. Somehow he wound up having dinner with them, and nobody could figure out how that happened—including Steve and Eydie.

His whole life has been a rehearsal for this. We can't let him down.

I . . . love you.

Gordo

P.S. I've been a little afraid to ask, but what happens when this is over and you're back in St. Louis? Will it turn out that we were just a summer romance? Was it only T's leftover stardust? Will we forget about the sparkles in our hearts? If the answers are yes, yes, or yes, bypass the questions. I don't need the answers *that* badly.

Dear Gordo:
This is the first time I've ever seen a broken heart up close. He's gone into the bathroom three times to brush his teeth— but when he comes out, his eyes are red and his breath still smells like Cheetos. Until today, I always thought that Toby Heller was the real thing, but I was wrong. Toby Heller didn't even qualify for the preliminaries.

I *do* have a plan. But I'm not looking forward to it. In about an hour, I'm going to begin throwing a little attitude his way. (I'll probably use phrases like "pain in the ass," "spine-less quitter," and other spontaneous extracts from the Dictionary of Disparaging Invective.) That ought to create a frosty chill until morning. Then I'll stop speaking to him entirely. By the time we check out of this dump at noon, the tension should be thick enough to strangle a medium-sized house pet with. But the lid won't blow off until we turn left onto Congress Street, which is where I intend to pick the paterfamilias of all fights. At 12:35 on the nose. Right in front of the Sweet Shop. Once I've tossed him out of the car and suggested that he reacquaint himself with his thumb, he'll probably go looking for a phone so he can call you. And the closest receiver is directly behind the booth in which Craig and Charleen will undoubtedly be ordering whatever virus passes for the Friday Special.

It's the best I can do on short notice. And I hate myself for it already.

I . . . love you too.

A.J.

P.S. In spite of my venomous performance, I'll be parked around the corner waiting to see what happens. (I might as well confess that I'm a closet pushover. You're bound to find it out sooner or later anyway.)

P.S.2. After we leave here, we're stopping in St. Louis long enough to determine that my assistant manager hasn't, in fact, turned my establishment into a crack house. Then I'm pumping twelve gallons of supreme unleaded into Robert Mitchum and he's heading west. With me, with Beaver, and with Sweet Charity singing something called "I'm the Bravest Individual." Hell, if it works for Beav, it can work for me.

Just remember one thing: Be careful what you wish for. You may get it.

FROM THE JOURNAL OF
Travis Puckett

What a sordid place for the glory that was once my life to have come to an end—a fetid booth in a squalid hashery with only a toxic baloney sandwich standing between me and eternal darkness. What a dismal epitaph to so much sparkling hope. Cast rootless to the winds by a faithless kindred spirit who withdrew her troth ("Here's a quarter. Call Gordo. Have *him* bail you out.") and the errant boonfellow who won't get off the fucking phone ("That line is busy. For 75 cents, AT&T can leave a message for you."). Oh, the perfidy.

This has been a day right out of *David Copperfield*. First the hangover, now this. If I weren't so depressed, I'd kill myself. And what did I do to piss her off?! One minute she's drying my tears, and the next thing I know my ass is on the street with a torn backpack hanging from my scapula. I look like a bag lady who owes seventeen hundred dollars to Neiman-Marcus.

Big deal. So I'll hit the road. I'll hit the road and head home where I belong. If I'm lucky, maybe a trucker'll let me ride in his van long enough to die of carbon monoxide poisoning. Otherwise, I'll have to crawl over broken glass and beg Andrea to give me back my grant—assuming she isn't pointing a loaded .45 at my crotch. And if she is, let her shoot. Who needs a dick? I wouldn't fall in love again if you ladled me Ethel Merman out of a Stoke-on-Trent soup tureen. How's *that* for irony? Oh, what a desolate way to finish off what could have been a—

Holy shit.

Oh, no.

Look who's on his way back from the salad bar.

This was a setup! Duh! Now what do I do? Keep your head down—that's what. Maybe he won't notice. Who's that with him? Probably Charleen. She fits A.J.'s blotter profile. Oh God, they're coming this way. Don't sit in the next booth don't sit in the next booth don't sit in the next booth don't sit in the next booth don't sit in the—Shit! They're sitting in the next booth! Craigy, please don't look up. I couldn't bear saying goodbye to you again. Just let me sneak out of here without rocking the boat and I promise I'll never ever ever forget what we once—

He looked up.

Our eyes met.

His jaw dropped.

And for the first time in twenty years, the one-dimple grin wasn't just a memory any more.

13

Craig

McKenna & Webb
A Law Partnership
118 Congress Park, Suite 407
Saratoga Springs, New York 12866

Memorandum

TO:	Craig
FROM:	Charleen
DATE:	June 11, 1998
SUBJECT:	Wrapping Up

The *Kessler* petition's been bluebacked and filed. Not that we need any more gratuitous karma, but it turns out that Larry Dysart is representing Noah's mother. Remember Larry? The lush with the nose hairs who took me to a Swedish smorgasbord and attempted to order the server's breasts?

Craig, stop brooding and go home. You're behaving like one of those awful women in *Valley of the Dolls*.

McKenna & Webb
A Law Partnership
118 Congress Park, Suite 407
Saratoga Springs, New York 12866

Memorandum

TO: Charleen
FROM: Craig
DATE: June 11, 1998
SUBJECT: *Valley of the Dolls*

I've watched it four times this week. "Ted Casablanca is no fag—and I'm the dame who can prove it." Sigh. How could we survive without such heavenly dreck? I'm almost ready for *Mommie Dearest* again.

Home? What's that? Oh! You mean that half-empty house on Loughberry Lake where you can roll around on the living room floor shrieking "I'm Neely O'Hara!" all you want, and nobody's there to tell you to shut the hell up or take a shower with you or fuck your toes off?

I tried calling him at the hardware store to arrange a peaceful surrender at the Appomattox courthouse, but he'd already left to have drinks with a client and then go bowling with him. How did *I* get elected to do all the suffering? Is this a trade-off for not knowing how to cook?

Tell me the truth. Do I really have a reason to think that Travis is going to show up in Saratoga Springs? Or am I inventing another mirage because I need one?

Take care of my Ashley, Scarlett.

Love,
Melanie

P.S. How could I possibly remember which one Larry Dysart was? Let's get real, sweetheart. If we had to limit our caseload to those attorneys who haven't cross-complained against us just so they could sniff your nylons, we'd be practicing in another state by now.

P.S.2. By the way, aren't you proud of me? You've been sleeping with Jody for three days and I haven't even asked you how big it is yet.

McKenna & Webb
A Law Partnership
118 Congress Park, Suite 407
Saratoga Springs, New York 12866

Memorandum

TO: Melanie
FROM: Charleen
DATE: June 11, 1998
SUBJECT: How Big Is It?

Craig,

I realize that during the past two decades, I haven't exactly been the soul of discretion—that my often-inexcusable lapses in tact and good taste have found me revealing intimate secrets about men who deserve a good deal better from me. But that's over. I've reformed. You might as well get used to the idea.

However, in deference to the confidential chumminess we nurtured for lo, those many years, I'll admit this much. When Ethel Mertz said, "I have sufficient," she'd obviously never fucked Jody.

Since you asked, Travis is *not* on his way to Saratoga Springs. An enigmatic phone call to a gynecologist in St. Louis doesn't necessarily point a finger at Colonel Mustard with a candlestick in the library. There could be a number of other rational explanations—though, offhand, I can't think of any either.

Don't be too hard on yourself. First love is always the perfect one—but it never lasts. That's what makes it perfect. If boyfriends actually bounced back after twenty years just because we still ached for them, we'd have to rewrite the book on romance. And even Elizabeth Barrett Browning wouldn't believe it.

Try to get some sleep. We have an irascible judge we need to tame at 10:00 A.M. I'll bring the whips.

By the way—I love you.

Ch

McKenna & Webb
A Law Partnership
118 Congress Park, Suite 407
Saratoga Springs, New York 12866

Memorandum

TO:	Charleen
FROM:	Craig
DATE:	June 11, 1998
SUBJECT:	Rewriting the Book on Romance

Rent *Brigadoon*, then talk to me about miracles in the morning. Better yet, talk to Travis. He invented them.

By the way, I love you too.

Cr

Craig McKenna   **Attorney Notes**

The nearest jazz club is way down in Albany, but they serve rosé wine and the air is thick with lazy curls of cigarette smoke. So after a desolate dinner of lima beans and a Shake 'n Bake chicken breast that left the kitchen looking like Mrs. O'Leary's cow had just paid a house call, I put on my dark glasses and hit the road. Lenny Bruce was back.

If this were 1942, I could have syncopated my anguish to Charlie Parker on alto sax, Dizzy Gillespie on trumpet, Kenny Clark on drums, and Ray Brown on bass. Instead, I got stuck with the Goldschmidt Brothers, whose idea of dangerous is "Chattanooga Choo-Choo" played in A-minor. But it didn't matter. After two hours, my options were clear:

1. *Run for office, lose Clayton.*
   And what good is changing the world if you have to fall asleep by yourself? Remember Fanny Brice? "Flo, I love hearing an audience applaud—but you can't take an audience home with you!"

2. *Keep Clayton, lose Craig.*
   Maybe in ten more years he'll let me pick the movie on Saturday night. Meanwhile, I can sign all of my credit card receipts "Mrs. Norman Maine."

3. *Knock off the rosé wine unless you want to lose* **Kessler vs. Kessler** *to a hangover.*
   How am I going to tell Noah that the court said no again? How can I look into those eyes and admit that I let him down? Even the Miles and Miles and Miles of Heart song won't work this time.

4. *Grow up and admit that Travis doesn't even remember you any more.*

But what if Charleen is wrong? That happens occasionally. Suppose he's heading north on I-87 right now, deliberately breaking every statute in the Vehicle Code for me? What would he say when he got here? Would he let me borrow a page from his playbook?

redoubtable

Formidable, fearsome; Carlton Fisk in 1975; you in a couple of years, after you've won your first hundred cases.

cavalier

Chivalrous, noble; remember when the guy in the Pacer called you an asshole? That wasn't cavalier. Remember when you pretended to lose the coin toss so I could be Smerko? That was.

ubiquitous

Craig.

5. *Remember what he taught you and go for broke.*

KESSLER'S SHELL

351 Kemble Street   Utica, New York 13501

Dear Craig,

No matter what happens in court this morning, I just wanted to say thanks for kicking ass the way you have, even all those times we came up short. Also for keeping an eye on my kid when I couldn't be there to do it myself. And for trying to make me think that $300 was enough to even the score. (Come on, Craig. I may not know law but I know that I can't replace wheel bearings for less than $271 in labor. And that only takes me two hours.)

If Charleen says she'll marry me (and she will, you think?) I'm going to ask you to be my best man. But come to think of it, you already are.

Thanks for making us family.

Jody

Noah Kessler

6026 Foxhound Run

Saratoga Springs, New York 12866

June 12, 1998

ATTORNEY-CLIENT COMMUNICATION

VIA FACSIMILE

Craig McKenna, Esq.
McKenna & Webb
118 Congress Park, Suite 407
Saratoga Springs, New York 12866

Dear Craig,

Good news. Frau Schneller tried to sabotage us by putting my rabbit's foot in the washing machine, but the joke is on her because none of the blue came off. So it still works.

I have to go get my haircut at Kiddy Corner (give me a break), but I'm keeping my pager on. So as soon as court is over, call and tell me what happened. If we lose, I'll probly be depressed and mope and kick rocks because I'm sad and flunk out of sixth grade and not get into college and turn into a burglar. But guess what? The circus is coming to Albany and if you take me there three times, maybe none of those things will happen.

Noah

Craig McKenna   **Attorney Notes**

If Charleen and I were Ally McBeal, we'd each have six thousand very white teeth, yuppie hair, perfect bodies, witty friends who didn't know what the far side of 30 looked like, a salty judge who nonetheless owned a heart of gold and whose acerbic ripostes gave the impression that he'd earned his law degree at the Improv, and a caseload so teeming with freckled faces, lovable grandmas, and other testaments to the richness of our souls, not even Rosemary's Baby could have ruled against us. But Charleen and I aren't Ally McBeal.

"This is what it feels like the first game of the season," whispered Jody apprehensively. "I wish I was wearing my cup." Beside him at the mile-long petitioner's table, Charleen squeezed his hand and winced.

"Jody?" she implored. "Would you do me a huge favor?"

"Anything."

"*Don't* tell that to Judge Costanzo."

The cavernous courtroom, with its Doric columns and ornate inscription over the bench ("Built to Intimidate" in Latin), was beginning to fill up with the usual collection of plaintiffs, defendants, and salivating onlookers who apparently couldn't wait to dine on human suffering until Jenny Jones and Oprah dished out their daily doses later in the afternoon. *Either Costanzo has a heavy docket this morning, or some people really need to get lives.*

Jody was dressed in a form-fitting charcoal gray pinstriped suit that Charleen had helped him pick out, a powder blue Armani shirt, and a navy-and-crimson tie that—taken as a package—was unable to mute the broad shoulders, the tousled hair, or the little-boy twinkle that he wore like a signet. I had no idea whether or not he was going to impress His Honor, but one thing was certain: if he walked through the West Village looking like that, there wouldn't be anything left of him at the other end.

"Good morning, Charleen," oozed an oily voice to our right, interrupting our group excursion into muffled panic. We all glanced up at the same time. There was Larry Dysart, attired in sharkskin, with all nineteen nose hairs intact.

"Good morning, Lawrence," she replied evenly.

"Best of luck," he offered, leering at my partner's breasts.

"You too," she countered, in a voice colored with every shade but sincerity. Clearly disappointed that she hadn't offered to blow him on the spot, he took a seat at the respondent's table and glowered at us.

"Who was that?" asked Jody suspiciously.

"Larry Dysart," replied Charleen, interlacing her fingers with his. "He's the reason we need lawyer jokes."

I was about to say something tacky, crude, embarrassing, and unnecessary, but at that moment I spotted Clayton. He'd just taken a seat in the third row—and even if he hadn't been on the lam since Monday, I'd have had trouble recognizing him. His shirt was rumpled, his usually erotic stubble had begun to evoke unsavory images of Fidel Castro after the Bay of Pigs, and he had "sleepless in Saratoga" branded across his forehead. His eyes met mine only briefly—but long enough to assure me that we were still on the same team.

"Clayton's here," I sighed happily, feeling both human and catty again for the first time all week. "Who looks worse? Him or me?" My confederates both turned to wave at him, with Jody adding a thumbs-up to the bargain.

"You do," said Charleen finally.

"It's a draw," said Jody.

"Court will come to order," said the bailiff.

Show time.

Superior Court of the State of New York
in and for the County of Saratoga

JODY B. KESSLER,	)	CASE NO. Fam. 81699
	)	
Petitioner,	)	FRIDAY, JUNE 12, 1998
	)	10:00 A.M.
vs.	)	
	)	
ANNETTE KESSLER MUELLER,	)	
	)	
Respondent.	)	
_____	)	

HEARING ON PETITION FOR JOINT CUSTODY

The Honorable John J. Costanzo, Judge Presiding

TRANSCRIPT OF PROCEEDINGS

Attorneys for Petitioner, Jody B. Kessler:

Craig S. McKenna, Esq., Charleen Webb, Esq.

Attorney for Respondent, Annette Mueller: Lawrence F. Dysart, Esq.

1	BAILIFF:	Superior Court of the State of New York for the County
2		of Saratoga, the Honorable John J. Costanzo presiding.
3		All rise.
4	THE COURT:	Be seated.
5	BAILIFF:	In the matter of *Kessler vs. Kessler*, docket number
6		81699, Hearing on Petition for Joint Custody.
7	THE COURT:	Are counsel and parties present?
8	MR. McKENNA:	Craig McKenna and Petitioner, Your Honor.
9	MR. DYSART:	Lawrence Dysart, Your Honor. Mrs. Mueller is in

1		Europe with her husband, but I have notarized copies of
2		all financial statements and affidavits should the Court
3		require them.
4	THE COURT:	Thank you, counsel. That won't be necessary.
5	MR. McKENNA:	Shit. He's not even going to consider it.
6	THE COURT:	What was that, Mr. McKenna?
7	MR. McKENNA:	Excuse me, Your Honor. I thought I was mumbling.
8	THE COURT:	You weren't.
9	MR. McKENNA:	It won't happen again.
10	THE COURT:	Mr. Kessler, may I ask you a personal question?
11	MR. KESSLER:	Yes, sir.
12	THE COURT:	Exactly how many times are you going to petition this
13		Court for custody of your son?
14	MR. KESSLER:	As many as it takes, Your Honor. Sooner or later you're
15		bound to throw me a fastball.
16	MR. DYSART:	Objection, Your Honor.
17	THE COURT:	Overruled, counsel. Sit down and shut up.
18	MR. KESSLER:	Was that the wrong answer?
19	THE COURT:	No. Unfortunately for the taxpayer, it was the right one.
20	MR. KESSLER:	Then can I have him? I wanted to take him to Nan-
21		tucket next weekend, and they have this deal where if
22		you buy your tickets early, you can get them at half—
23	THE COURT:	Mr. Kessler—
24	MR. KESSLER:	—we're going fishing so I can show him how to hook an
25		angler—
26	THE COURT:	Mr. Kessler, I understand how you feel—
27	MR. KESSLER:	Then why won't you give him to me!
28	THE COURT:	Because you can't afford him! Do you think he won't need
29		braces just because you love him? You think Princeton'll
30		let him in for free because he says you're his best friend?
31		Mr. Kessler, there's a great deal more to it than that. There
32		shouldn't be, but there is. And if you can't—
33	(Mr. Bergman rises.)	

1	MR. BERGMAN:	Excuse me, Your Honor.
2	THE COURT:	Are you a party to this action?
3	MR. BERGMAN:	I am now, Your Honor. Clayton Bergman. I've got a
4		hardware store on Putnam Street, three hundred acres
5		by Saratoga Lake, and a new partner who's sitting at the
6		petitioner's table.
7	THE COURT:	I presume you're referring to Mr. Kessler?
8	MR. BERGMAN:	Look, Your Honor—I have eighteen condos and a dozen
9		houses to put up in the next five years, and I can't do it
10		by myself. So Jody's going to be running construction
11		while I handle the store, and he'll probably wind up
12		making more than you and me put together.
13	THE COURT:	Mr. Kessler, is this true?
14	MR. KESSLER:	Uh—yes, sir.
15	THE COURT:	I see.
16	*(His Honor confers with the bailiff.)*	
17	THE COURT:	Court will recess for five minutes.
18	BAILIFF:	All rise.

Craig McKenna   **Attorney Notes**

Larry Dysart looked as though he'd been stabbed through the heart with a pitchfork, Charleen hadn't quite rebounded from the shock either, and Jody was bewildered beyond the point of comprehension—usually he'd be out on the sidewalk by now, attempting to explain to his little boy why we'd failed again.

"What does a recess mean?" he asked tentatively, not daring to believe the obvious.

"It means extra innings," murmured a white-knuckled Charleen, gripping his arm tightly. "Hold your breath." Recognizing a tender moment when I saw one—and having a few of my own on deck—I made myself scarce. *What did Celeste Holm say to Gary Merrill while he was cradling Bette Davis? "I guess at this point I'm what the French call* de trop." So I mumbled my excuses and tore up the aisle.

Clayton was waiting for me in the marble foyer outside of Department A, but before I could say anything, he put a finger to my lips and pointed to a burnished oak door across the hall.

"What's in there?" he asked furtively.

"Empty jury chambers," I replied, mystified.

"Come on," he said, grabbing my hand. As usual, he led and I followed—but for once it didn't yank my chain the wrong way. Especially after he'd flipped on the lights in the musty old room and wrapped me up in those big arms of his.

"First things first," he sighed, stroking my cheek. "Craig, I'm so sorry." Though I was absolutely determined to make him crawl through lit kerosene before I even *considered* relenting, my resistance wilted as soon as he kissed me—and by the time we'd come up for air, we'd already lost a full minute of the four we had left before recess ended.

"Sir Galahad," I chided him, toying with his chest. "Rescuing Jody in the nick of time. What a hot dog."

"Well, *somebody* had to bail your ass out," he grumbled. "That's part of my job, isn't it?"

"How long have you been planning this?"

"Ever since Utica when he mapped out the whole Saratoga Lake project between dessert and coffee on two napkins and a menu," he confessed, practicing the fingers-through-my-hair thing even though he already had three gold medals and a bronze in that particular event. "I'd have clued you in sooner, but it would have meant calling a cease fire." By then I was ready to forgive him just about anything—and he knew it.

"Clay, why don't we just forget—"

"Honey, wait," he insisted, pushing away from me as he stumbled for the right words. "There's something I need to say and it isn't easy." Inwardly, I panicked. If it was "goodbye," I didn't want to hear it—now or ever. But that's not what he had on his mind.

"I—I want you to run for office," he stammered finally.

What? Hello? Who are *you and what have you done with Clayton?* It was perhaps the first time in twenty years that he'd stunned me speechless. In fact, I couldn't have been more surprised if he'd told me he was really Lady Bird Johnson.

"No, you don't," I blurted.

"No, I don't," he blurted back. "But if it gets this thing out of your system—"

"Clay, it's not a thing, and I may *never* get it out of my system," I protested. *"Then* what happens?"

In reply, he reined me in so tightly that my chin was grafted to the hollow of his neck. Uh-oh. Bad sign. This was a maneuver usually reserved for birthdays and crises—and I wasn't going to be 39 for another seven months.

"Honey," he whispered gently, "the only reason I own a store is because I like knowing where things are. And marrying you just so I can keep you in one place isn't a good enough excuse." There was the briefest of pauses as he took my hand in his. "Look, we'll probably work this out the way we always do. But we may have to make some choices this time." Without any further prompting, my eyes began to well with tears.

"Don't say that," I mumbled, burying my face in his shoulder. Either he hadn't heard me or he didn't want to, because all he did was kiss me again—and after we'd pulled apart, he stared at my mouth and grinned.

"I'll be damned," he marveled. "You *do* have a dimple."

"What was *that* supposed to mean?"

"Trade secret," he retorted cryptically. Then we turned off the lights and raced each other back to the courtroom before anybody had a chance to disbar me.

Someone's been talking to him.

Superior Court of the State of New York in and for the County of Saratoga

JODY B. KESSLER,	)	CASE NO. Fam. 81699
	)	
Petitioner,	)	FRIDAY, JUNE 12, 1998
	)	10:00 A.M.
vs.	)	
	)	
ANNETTE KESSLER MUELLER,	)	
	)	
Respondent.	)	
	)	

HEARING ON PETITION FOR JOINT CUSTODY

The Honorable John J. Costanzo, Judge Presiding

TRANSCRIPT OF PROCEEDINGS

Attorneys for Petitioner, Jody B. Kessler:
Craig S. McKenna, Esq., Charleen Webb, Esq.
Attorney for Respondent, Annette Mueller: Lawrence F. Dysart, Esq.

1	BAILIFF:	Superior Court of the State of New York for the County
2		of Saratoga, the Honorable John J. Costanzo presiding.
3		All rise.
4	THE COURT:	Be seated.
5	BAILIFF:	In the matter of *Kessler vs. Kessler,* docket number
6		81699, Hearing on Petition for Joint Custody.
7	THE COURT:	The Court would like to make two preliminary remarks.
8		First, it's difficult to argue against such unanimity of
9		opinion. Second, if I deny this petition, Mr. McKenna
10		will only file another one. Is that correct, counsel?

1	MR. McKENNA:	It is, Your Honor. But not until after I nail the Pioneer
2		Scouts to the—
3	THE COURT:	That's enough, counsel.
4		Pending Mr. Kessler's relocation to Saratoga Springs
5		and the commencement of his employment, joint cus-
6		tody is awarded to the father for a six-month trial
7		period, at which time the Court will review the matter
8		again.

Petition granted.

McKENNA & WEBB
A LAW PARTNERSHIP
118 CONGRESS PARK, SUITE 407
SARATOGA SPRINGS, NEW YORK 12866

MEMORANDUM

TO: Charleen
FROM: Craig
DATE: June 12, 1998
SUBJECT: Peace in Our Time

I appreciate the fact that you and Jody have moved from attorney-client privilege to fornicating on the kitchen floor, and further that he intends to pop the question momentarily (which is supposed to be a state secret, but if I didn't spill the beans I wouldn't be Craig any more—and I know you wouldn't want that). But did he have to kiss *me* too? In front of the bailiff? What if somebody thinks I'm queer?

Clayton and I have made up. Sort of. Stay tuned. He didn't exactly say he'll dump me if I run for office, but the implication was left sitting there just the same. Now I know how Vicki Lester felt when she sang "The Man That Got Away."

I'm still a little forlorn. Can you tell?

McKenna & Webb
A Law Partnership
118 Congress Park, Suite 407
Saratoga Springs, New York 12866

Memorandum

TO: Vicki Lester
FROM: Charleen
DATE: June 12, 1998
SUBJECT: Men Who Get Away

Of course I can tell. Nobody does forlorn better than you do. That's why I hit on you in college. Before I found out you were irredeemable.

Craig, at last count there were only sixteen constants left in this otherwise witless world, and—together—you and Clayton are one of them. Even when you stop speaking for three and a half years, you're still inseparable. So if you're worried about losing him, it's way too late for that. You belong to each other in ways that no one else can touch. Learn to live with it.

Lunch is on me. We need to celebrate. You can practice dolorous on your own time.

Ch

P.S. Thanks for alerting me to my impending proposal. Please let me know when I'm pregnant too.

CLAYTON'S HARDWARE
serving Saratoga Springs since 1988

Honey—

I was reminded recently that you like snapdragons.
Three dozen may be over the top, but when I say I'm
sorry, I mean it.

I'll be home in time for dinner, but we have a lot to
talk about. One thing you need to know: whatever
happens, I'll back you all the way. You're not the only
one who's grown up since Harvard.

I love you. Always.

C

Craig McKenna   **Attorney Notes**

When they write the history of the twentieth century, they're
going to have to title a whole chapter "What If?" What if
Kennedy hadn't gone to Dallas? What if Hitler had been stopped
at Munich? What if the *Titanic* had hit the berg head-on? What
if Bucky Fucking Dent had had diarrhea on October 2, 1978?
What if Barbra Streisand's parents had had a boy? What if
Margo Channing had figured out that Eve was a louse right off
the bat? What if Craig and Charleen hadn't eaten lunch at the
Sweet Shop on June 12, 1998, at exactly 12:43 P.M.? What if
Craig hadn't looked up from his chopped Italian salad exactly
when he did?

"Oh, Craig," snapped an exasperated Charleen, relieving
me of two olives and an anchovy. "The man sent you three
dozen snapdragons. Does it *look* like he wants to leave you?"

"Try telling that to my inner child," I retorted grimly,
going for my traditional Tony nomination ("Best Dramatic

Performance Over Lunch"). "He's a tougher sell than I am. He's practically . . . he's . . . he's—" And that was when I spotted them. Right over Charleen's left shoulder. The sparkly eyes I could never hide from—gazing directly into mine for the first time since we said goodbye to each other a life and a half ago. And even though I'd been expecting him to turn up any minute, it still seemed to take another pair of decades before we both stopped staring at each other long enough to stand.

Okay, Craig. One foot in front of the other. That's the way it usually works. Do we talk first or hug first? Hug first. Who the hell needs words?

"How did you find me here?" I mumbled into his ear.

"*Peabody's Contemporary Criticism,*" he mumbled back.

~

After he'd squeezed into our booth with us and turned Charleen's pimentos upside down, we got a Reader's Digest version of an odyssey that could only have been concocted by Smerko. Charleen, of course, was still a novitiate, so she couldn't afford to miss a word—but having earned my Ph.D. in Travis twenty years earlier, I was able to patch it all together without even working up a sweat.

"But the Craig McKenna in Murfreesboro was an ichthyologist, so I knew *that* couldn't be you . . . then I had an atomic anxiety attack when your mother answered the phone . . . but I didn't think I really had the nerve to head for St. Louis until Alexander Hamilton convinced me . . . so I broke into her office by pretending I was a maid . . . and I found out that in Missouri they arraign people in the middle of the night . . . because she named her Buick Robert Mitchum . . . but I knew I'd need to assume a new identity after Neiman-Marcus put a hit on me . . . so when we got your answering machine and heard Clayton's voice, my life ended for the third time that week . . . and the only thing I could think of was to ask him if he'd build me a house . . . A.J. spied on you and found out stuff like you and Jody falling in love—by the way, congratulations . . . but when Clayton gave me a Tic Tac and told me about kissing you at Harvard, I knew I could never take you away from him . . . I mean, what if he became a priest and it was all my fault? . . . and that's how I got here."

By then Charleen and I were both punchy with laughter—not just because it isn't something you hear every day, but because he was so *serious* about it. Only Travis could have gotten away with a story like that and still managed to keep his eyebrows furrowed.

"You were right," mused Charleen reflectively as I led her to the door. "All this time, I've thought that the Craig McKenna I first met was just another lovesick brat who positively adored feeling sorry for himself."

"Oh, I *do*," I assured her eagerly.

"But Travis really was worth the broken heart," she conceded, throwing down the gauntlet once and for all. Then she glanced back at Smerko (still organizing olives) and took the same kind of pause she generally draws just before delivering her closing argument to a jury. "Craig, pay attention," she insisted, reaching for my hand. "You've got a lot of decisions to make and some of them are going to hurt—but for the first time in your life, there aren't any wrong choices. Only right ones. *God*, you're brave."

It's tough to say who hugged who first, but I think I beat her by a hair. And it wasn't merely for what she'd just said, but for the past twenty years as well.

~

Travis and I found a run-down old gazebo in Saratoga Park and settled into a wrought-iron love seat so we could compare notes on the two or three things that had happened to us since that awful day at the airport. ("I started college, made trouble, met Clayton, turned into a lawyer, got this offer from the Democrats, and missed you. Your turn." "I started college, found the sacrifice fly rule in *The Federalist Papers,* earned my teaching degree, broke up with twenty-seven boyfriends who all looked like you, got a $30,000 grant that I put on hold when I heard 'Almost Like Being in Love' again, and missed you back.") Once that was out of the way, we spent the rest of the afternoon reliving what neither one of us had ever forgotten.

"Smerk, if you hadn't fallen off that ladder and into my arms, we wouldn't even *be* here now."

"You really think that was an accident?"

"You mean it *wasn't?*"

"Duh."

"Remember when you nearly got us fired from the record store for grabbing my ass?"

"Look who's talking. What about my birthday? We did it four times that night."

"Three. That thing by the refrigerator didn't count."

"Like hell it didn't."

I also discovered that the absolutes upon which I'd constructed my entire life hadn't changed a bit since our summer on West 92nd Street: he still straightens out his french fries, his shoelaces still point in the same direction, he still doesn't eat his popcorn until the movie starts, and he still loves me with his whole heart.

"But you and Clayton belong together," he said gently, doing his damndest to make me believe him. "It'll work out because it's meant to."

"What about *us?*" I asked glumly, staring down at the four feet that used to play with each other so frivolously. "Didn't you once tell me that it was you and me always?" I knew I was beginning to piss him off, because his forehead instantly went into overdrive.

"Craig, listen to me," he blurted, taking my hands the way he last had on September 14, 1978. "For 2,829.9 miles, all I thought about was kissing your nose and chin-in-the-neck and tickling your belly button every two and a half minutes for the next eighteen months. But guess what? That's the part we *don't* need. Remember when I promised you that we'd share our lives with each other until the end?"

"So?" I replied, glancing up hopefully.

"So we're back in a gazebo saying 'I love you' just like we used to. And we don't even have to be naked to do it! See? Who could ask for anything more?"

Then he nailed me with his baby blues and won the round on the spot. *Home free. When he quotes Ethel Merman, he means every word.*

"Travis, I'm so mixed up," I sighed miserably, squeezing his fingers so he couldn't let go. "What do I do?"

"Look at me," he said, grinning.

So I looked at him. And for the first time since I was 18, I found in his eyes the Craig I'd started out to be.

McKENNA & WEBB
A LAW PARTNERSHIP
118 CONGRESS PARK, SUITE 407
SARATOGA SPRINGS, NEW YORK 12866

June 12, 1998

VIA FACSIMILE

Mr. Wayne Duvall
New York State Democratic Committee
151 State Street
Albany, New York 12207

Dear Wayne:

Sorry I've made you wait until the eleventh hour, but there were some personal matters that required resolving before I came to a decision.

I'm honored to accept the Committee's nomination to run for State Assembly. Though I'm something of a rookie in this regard and may need a little help learning the ropes, I don't intend to disappoint anybody who believes in me. I trust you already know that you're getting a pain in the ass—and what I can promise you is more of the same.

Looking forward to an exciting campaign.

Best regards,
McKenna & Webb
Craig S. McKenna

cc: Noah Kessler

Six Years Later

14

Craig AND Travis

Congressional Record

NOTES

Rep. Craig McKenna (D-NY) is expected to introduce a sweeping federal hate crimes bill that would outlaw all acts of violence based on race, religion, ethnicity, age, nationality, gender, and sexual orientation. Last Tuesday, McKenna stood behind his proposed legislation in an informal debate with Sen. Trent Lott (R-MS), televised nationally on CNN.

LITERARY DIGEST

Book Corner

Travis Puckett, author of last season's surprise bestseller *The Late, Great Game*, has just completed his second nonfiction title for Random House. *Here She Is, Boys! Here She Is, World! Here's Rose!* links the evolution of alternative sexuality in twentieth-century America with the career of musical comedy legend Ethel Merman, and is scheduled for release on January 16—Merman's birthday.

FROM THE JOURNAL OF
Travis Puckett

A.J. and Robert Mitchum hadn't given up on me after all. We made it back to L.A. in four and a half days, with only a few unscheduled stops along the way. ("What happened to the freeway? Where are we?" "Granada, Colorado. There was a Japanese American internment camp here that I thought we should—" "*Another* one?! Beaver, switch places with me. I'm driving.") She and Gordo were married a year later and—pursuant to my instructions—began providing me with godchildren at the rate of one every twenty-seven months. Katie's only 2, but she can already sing "Bushel and a Peck" all the way through without cheating, and Jessica—age 4—knows the entire score to *How Now, Dow Jones*. Uncle T takes no prisoners.

Andrea decided in the end not to assassinate me, so I got my grant back, paid off Neiman-Marcus, and finished the book. Before it was even Xeroxed, I'd already lucked into my agent, Gail—a centrifugal force with voice mail who lives in Brooklyn and talks faster than I do. (Our first lunch meeting at an Italian restaurant on West 44th Street exhausted every waiter within earshot.)

Craigy called me every night. Sometimes the issues were complicated—

> "Smerko, my campaign is teetering on the verge of collapse. Are you busy?"
>
> "Not for the next six hours. Is that going to be long enough?"
>
> "Maybe."

—and sometimes they were cakewalks.

> "Trav, what was the most embarrassing thing that ever happened to me?"

"Getting your cock stuck in the vacuum cleaner hose."
"Was that worse than the M&M thing?"
"Yes."
"Okay. Bye."

Naturally, he won the election in a landslide (who *wouldn't* vote for him?), and by the time he'd convinced most of New York State that it needed hate crimes legislation on the floor, he already had his own cable modem on Capitol Hill. Washington hasn't even begun to recover.

> TO: Smerko1978@earthworks.com
> FROM: Craigy1978@earthworks.com
>
> Smerk, help me out here. This Matthew Shepard bill is already two days late, and what I'm trying to say is that I'll push it through even if I have to stump all fifty states myself. What's a good word for that?

> TO: Craigy1978@earthworks.com
> FROM: Smerko1978@earthworks.com
>
> U-B-I-Q-U-I-T-O-U-S. Duh.

> TO: Smerko1978@earthworks.com
> FROM: Craigy1978@earthworks.com
>
> Oh. Is *that* what it means? Why didn't you say so in high school?

> TO: Craigy1978@earthworks.com
> FROM: Smerko1978@earthworks.com
>
> I did. But we were throwing raisins at each other. See what happens when you don't listen?

TO: Smerko1978@earthworks.com
FROM: Craigy1978@earthworks.com

That's because I knew that some day you were going to be a world-famous author who'd remember these things for me. Go ahead. Argue with *that*.

FROM THE JOURNAL OF
Travis Puckett

THE PUCKETT/DUBOISE DEBATES

TRAVIS: Hello?

GORDO: I have an Oscar-winning idea for a movie.

TRAVIS: No. Forget it. I'm hanging up. I've been here before.

GORDO: Just give me a chance! It's called *Me and Mickey*, and it's about these two kids who decide they're going to bring Mickey Mantle home for their dad's fortieth birthday.

TRAVIS: Does this have anything to do with the time you made me sneak into the Yankee clubhouse with you by pretending my leg was broken?

GORDO: Um—in a vague way.

TRAVIS: That's what you said about *Almost Like Being in Love*. And it's been six years!

GORDO: These things take time. Universal wants to preserve the integrity of the story.

TRAVIS: Then why did they cast Brad Pitt and Julia Roberts as me and Craig?

GORDO: To give it broader appeal.

TRAVIS: By making us *detectives?* Let me talk to
A.J.

GORDO: She's in Toronto.

TRAVIS: I don't blame her.

FROM THE DESK OF
Gordon Duboise

Pop:

Any word on *Almost Like Being in Love?* I've got an antsy collaborator on the East Coast who's ready to slit my throat long distance.

G

ARGOSY ENTERTAINMENT
Literary Representatives

LOS ANGELES   TORONTO
NEW YORK   LONDON

Gordon:

Good news. They're not cops any more. Now they're dueling reporters assigned to the 1962 Mets. (Somebody's nephew is doing the rewrite. He thinks it needs a shark.)

On an unrelated front, Bruce Willis wants to play a musketeer, but he doesn't like swords or long hair or fluffy collars. So I sent Universal another copy of *Code Name Shapiro* with a new title page that says *Die Hard IX.* Just got a call from Business Affairs. They want to buy it. Again.

By the way—I'm kidnaping my granddaughters on Saturday. There's a puppet show at Chucky Cheese. You can come if you like, but your lap stays empty. I outrank you.

Grandpop

BEWARE!

You have just entered

GordoDad.com

home page of

GORDON DUBOISE
screenwriter/father/former heartthrob

Click here to find out more about us

Click here for a list of my credits

Click here for pictures of Katie and Jessica

Click here for pictures of Jessica and Katie

Click here for A.J.'s L.A. Times column

Click here for Katie's first painting
(of Mommy and Daddy)

Click here for Jessica's first poem
(about Elmer the Patchwork Elephant)

Click here for pictures of me in my Speedos
(edited by my wife for home viewing)

Click here to send me e-mail

Click here to post a message on my bulletin board
(Keep it clean. The kids can work a Web browser.)

Dear A.J.,

1. Dinner was a disaster. Jessica ate her broccoli and chicken, but Katie ate crayons. A blue one and a red one. Now her diaper looks weird.

2. Jessie wanted to stick the *Zip-A-Dee-Doo-Dah* singalong tape into the VCR herself, so I let her. Do head cleaners work on grape jelly? Because Uncle Remus is glued on Pause.

3. Before I could catch her and plunk her in the tub, Katie ran out into the front yard and began shrieking "I'm naked! I'm naked!" to most of Santa Monica. We can probably expect a visit from Social Services any minute.

4. We survived a major crisis when Jessie dropped Dipsy and Po into the toilet to see if they'd flush. The plumbers left twenty minutes ago, but while they were down there they also found Elmo and $18 in change.

5. What does "Daddy no chockit" mean? Katie started chanting it right after Travis called and the kids were fighting over who got to talk to Uncle T next.

My dad's preempting them on Saturday and your mother's taking them to the zoo on Sunday to see the raffes and the effants. Would I be considered a lousy father if I moved while they were gone?

Incidentally, had I known four years ago that "dusting off" your journalism degree meant losing you to Canada for ten days, I'd have set fire to it first—so in case you've forgotten how to take a hint, the Toronto Film Festival doesn't need you nearly as much as your children do (not to mention your other half).

I love you. I miss you. I'm lost without you.

G

Dear Mr. Mom:

This morning they screened your Richard Gere movie. To quote the man I married, "Yikes!" Wait until you see my review in the *Times*. (Don't worry—you're the only one who doesn't get the blame. "Despite a taut script by Gordon Duboise. . . .")

Loosely translated, "Daddy no chockit" means "Uncle T gives me Hershey Kisses and toys and pony rides and anything else I want, but Daddy is a cranky old doodyhead who says things like 'No' and 'Stop it'." Don't take it personally—I get the same routine after they've spent an afternoon with Grandy: "Mommy no ice pops."

I'll be home in three days. Lock up the Crayolas until then. (Especially the green ones. That's her favorite flavor.)

I love you back. So do Dipsy and Po.

Mrs. Mom

P.S. I've thrown up three times since breakfast, and not because of Richard Gere. This one's going to be a boy—he's already too much of a pain in the ass to be anything but. All things considered, I've pretty much settled on naming him Travis Craig Duboise, but you get a vote too. We can always call him T.C. or Beav.

TO: Craigy1978@earthworks.com
FROM: Smerko1978@earthworks.com

Are you still there?

TO: Smerko1978@earthworks.com
FROM: Craigy1978@earthworks.com

Who wants to know?

TO: Craigy1978@earthworks.com
FROM: Smerko1978@earthworks.com

I've got to write my bio for *Who's Who*. Would it be fair to say that I look like Tom Cruise?

TO: Smerko1978@earthworks.com
FROM: Craigy1978@earthworks.com

Yes. Except for your eyes, your nose, your mouth, and your hair. Besides, he's a lot younger than you are.

TO: Craigy1978@earthworks.com
FROM: Smerko1978@earthworks.com

Did anybody ever tell you that you're heartless?

TO: Smerko1978@earthworks.com
FROM: Craigy1978@earthworks.com

Only Heathcliff, Catherine, and the Pioneer Scouts. But they didn't mean it.

Superior Court of the State of New York
in and for the County of Saratoga

CITY OF SARATOGA ,)   CASE NO. CIV. 100455
SPRINGS,)
        Plaintiff,)
)
vs.)
)
THE PIONEER SCOUTS,)
a nonprofit corporation,)
        Defendant.)
_____)

HEARING ON DEFENDANT'S MOTION TO DISMISS
The Honorable John J. Costanzo, Judge Presiding

TRANSCRIPT OF PROCEEDINGS

Attorneys for Plaintiff, City of Saratoga Springs: Charleen W. Kessler, Esq.
Attorney for Defendant,
The Pioneer Scouts: Derek Hershman, Esq.

1	THE COURT:	Are all counsel present?
2	MS. KESSLER:	Plaintiff, Your Honor.
3	MR. HERSHMAN:	Defense, Your Honor. Requesting dismissal on
4		behalf of the Pioneer Scouts.
5	THE COURT:	Again? *Now* what did they do?
6	MS. KESSLER:	It seems they removed a troop leader for having a
7		boyfriend—
8	MR. HERSHMAN:	Objection, Your Honor. Counsel attempts to cite
9		the New Jersey appellate decision in *Aronson vs.*
10		*Boy Scouts*, which has no jurisdiction in this Court.

1	MS. KESSLER:	It does now, Your Honor. House Bill No. 7972.
2		Enacted into law at midnight. "No organization
3		qualifying for nonprofit status shall promote any type
4		of discrimination based upon sexual orientation."
5	THE COURT:	Who pushed *that* one through?
6	MS. KESSLER:	Craig McKenna.
7	THE COURT:	Why did I ask? Did he really tell Trent Lott to—
8	MS. KESSLER:	Yes, Your Honor. And may I remind the Court
9		that he's still admitted to the bar of this state? So
10		if, for some unlikely reason, defendant's motion is
11		sustained, I'll have to ask the Congressman to try
12		this case himself.
13	THE COURT:	Just what I need. Motion denied. The complaint
14		stands.
15	MS. KESSLER:	Thank you, Your Honor.
16	MR. HERSHMAN:	Objection!
17	THE COURT:	Next case.

LOUISE McKENNA, M.D.   Jefferson Medical Plaza, Suite 100
OBSTETRICS/GYNECOLOGY   903 Saint Charles Street
                                              St. Louis, Missouri 63101

Darling:

You made all the papers here. "St. Louis Boy Kicks Trent Lott's Butt." Alma Colson is livid. The only thing *her* son did last week was remove a kidney stone.

Clayton has a birthday coming up. He never did accept gifts graciously. This year he's attempting to put me off by claiming he wants a boa constrictor. I may just send him one.

Call me.

Love,
Mom

CLAYTON'S HARDWARE
serving Saratoga Springs since 1988

Craig—

We finally fixed the living room tilt at the house in Cape Vincent, but then Brian went and left a pile of varnish rags on the floor. While we were at dinner, they spontaneously combusted, so now we need a new wall too. Since you're the one who hired Kevin, and since Kevin's the one who set up the blind date with Bri, this is all your fault. So if I end up on the losing end of a spousal abuse suit, I expect you to represent me.

I'm enclosing an article that was in the *Courant*. They bleeped out what you said, but they kept the photo of Trent Lott with his mouth hanging open. According to page 3, your approval rating just went up another six points. Can't you just imagine what would have happened if you'd pulled a stunt like that when we were still living together? You'd have been sleeping on the couch through basketball season. Without sheets.

This isn't for publication, but they're angling to bring a Double-A franchise to Flatbush, and Jody and I may have a shot at the contract for the ballpark. (Travis is going to break my neck if we don't make it look like a little Ebbets Field, so what choice do we have?) I'll be down in the city from the 14th to the 18th—save me two lunches, a dinner, and a Mets game to be named later.

I love you.

C

Noah Kessler
1255 Carriage House Lane
Saratoga Springs, New York 10266

Dear Craig,

Okay. Maybe we need to redefine our terms. When I said you should tell Trent Lott to kiss your ass, I was being facetious. Mocking. Comical. Without significant purpose. I didn't mean you should actually do it—and *definitely* not in front of CNN.

You once told me that the only thing I needed to know about being a man was that one less sock always comes out of the dryer. You were full of shit. This is just a random sampling of the minefield I live in—*and I'm not even 18 yet!*

1. There's this girl. Her name is Soupy. (Not really, but we have three Susans in our class so we identify them by their last initials. Sue B., Sue L. and Sue P. Soupy's got sort of amalgamated.) She ignored me for most of two semesters and then she cornered me in a coat room and asked me if I wanted to kiss her. So I told her yes and proved it. Now she says she'll go to the junior prom with me but it doesn't mean anything serious because kissing her before I found out about stuff like her favorite bands and movie stars, etc., means that I'm not emotionally available yet. What's *that* all about?

2. They had Mother's Night at school. Mom and Charleen both came. I tried to keep them away from Mr. Landey and his Comp Lit classroom, but they found it anyway. So he showed them my last book report. ("*Canterbury Tales.* There was a cook and he had a venereal disease and he got it in the food. Do I really need to *know* this?") The other kids only have one mother to kick their ass. *I* get yelled at in Dolby.

3. Dad thinks that because I'm 17 he needs to walk me through The Talk again. Get this: "You're okay with mas-

turbation, right?" Okay with it? Craig, I *invented* it. Five years ago! Remember when we all went to the Hall of Fame for my birthday weekend? And remember at dinner when we had that really pretty waitress with the big you-know-whats and all of a sudden I got sick in the middle of the salad and asked if I could go up to my room and lie down? Hello? Did I *look* sick?

4. My best bud Glen is having boyfriend troubles, so in between prepping for my SATs and practicing my emotional availability, it's part of my job to help him plot strategies for running into Doogie by accident—which is supposed to remind them about how much they love each other. (Doogie, incidentally, would be a major league asshole if he tried a little harder, but he's not motivated enough to move past minor league dipshit.) Meanwhile, there's this terrific kid named Ricky who plays football and sits two rows in front of us in Trig, and he hasn't been able to take his eyes off Glen all semester. Everybody knows it except Glen. Is it a guy thing, or are men just morons?

5. Since I already know that I'm going to major in either politics or television, there's only two colleges I want to apply to: Syracuse and Columbia. But Syracuse means that Mom and Dad and Charleen and Clayton and Brian and whoever else feels like it can sneak over there to check up on me when I'm not looking, and Columbia means that you'll do the same thing and don't try to tell me you won't. I need Travis to help me write a Declaration of Independence so the adults in my life can get a hint that I'm not a kid anymore.

But you were right about the socks.

I love you.

Noah

P.S. Can Soupy and I come and stay with you this summer? Maybe you can convince her that I have sensitivity.

TO: Craigy1978@earthworks.com
FROM: Smerko1978@earthworks.com

You're working too hard. Want to play hooky and go to a movie with me?

TO: Smerko1978@earthworks.com
FROM: Craigy1978@earthworks.com

You have too much time on your hands. Why don't you write another book?

TO: Craigy1978@earthworks.com
FROM: Smerko1978@earthworks.com

About what?

TO: Smerko1978@earthworks.com
FROM: Craigy1978@earthworks.com

How about the parallels between Bobby Di Cicco, the Cold War, and the time Lucy and Ethel stole John Wayne's footprints?

TO: Craigy1978@earthworks.com
FROM: Smerko1978@earthworks.com

I hate you.

TO: Smerko1978@earthworks.com
FROM: Craigy1978@earthworks.com

Why do you hate me?

TO: Craigy1978@earthworks.com
FROM: Smerko1978@earthworks.com

Because that actually gave me an idea. Now I won't be
able to harass you any more.

TO: Smerko1978@earthworks.com
FROM: Craigy1978@earthworks.com

(Grin.)

Craig McKenna   **House of Representatives**
                                    Washington, D.C.

In 1965, Liza Minnelli starred in this Broadway show where
she played a gullible kid named Flora Meszaros. By the end of
the first act, she'd stumbled headfirst into everything she'd ever
wanted, so she sang about it (duh) in a song called "A Quiet
Thing."

I won the election by six thousand votes, but Eeyore wasn't
the only cartoon I wound up portraying. True to his word,
Noah took candid snapshots of Craig-as-Barney, Craig-as-
Tinky Winky, and Craig-as-Gepetto, then hid the negatives at
the bottom of his toy chest. They've since been scanned onto a
30-gigabyte hard drive along with the e-mail addresses of every
tabloid in the Western Hemisphere. If I ever consider legislation that doesn't meet with his approval, my career is over.

Clayton and I managed to struggle through another half-
year before we decided to quit while we were ahead. ("Honey,
why don't we try it solo for a little while and see if the urge to
kill goes away?") But even after he moved out, we'd find ourselves at the movies together on Sundays, on the telephone at
2:00 in the morning, and routinely in conference with one

another on the daily crises that always seemed to be threatening our lives. And since I hadn't yet bothered to learn the difference between a garlic press and an ignition cap, he'd still come over three nights a week to make us dinner. ("Ma," he'd bark at my mother over the phone, "would you please tell him he's got to eat?") It was an unusual way to split up—but when four months had passed without so much as a scowl from either one of us, we knew we'd made the right call. Besides, Charleen had already nailed it: Clayton and I are a lifelong team, period. End of discussion.

"Oh, shit," I groaned, flipping off the AM station that had just quoted my How Many Republicans Does It Take to Screw in a Lightbulb speech. "What was I *thinking?* Clay, couldn't you just kick me in the ass for old time's sake?"

"Not a chance," he retorted, grinning maliciously. "When you're sitting in the cheap seats for a change, it's fun to watch." This particular conversation took place in the Bronco on our way to Jody's wedding. A last-minute switch in the lineup had found Clayton and Noah splitting the best man spot two ways instead of three, only because Charleen had asked me to be her maid of honor. ("But in a tux," I reminded her ominously. "Let's not give the Moral Majority any more ammo than they think they already have.") The minister didn't bother to protest. He merely assumed we were all from California and left it at that.

I couldn't have survived the year without Travis. Sometimes he called just to yank my chain and sometimes he called for real—but he always managed to remind me that he was in my corner, no matter what.

"Hello?"

"*Craig, if you had to be stuck on an island with either Brady Anderson or Ryne Sandberg, who would you pick?*"

"*You mean naked?*"

"*Absolutely.*"

"*Troy Aikman.*"

"That's what I thought. Me too. Talk to you tomorrow."

We learned how to take turns leaning on each other again. When he was seven paragraphs away from finishing his first book, he found himself face-to-face with a bad case of flop sweat. ("Craigy, what if they hate it?") So for two hours I convinced him that as long as he was still the only boy in the world who could wake up a whole village with his heart, what difference did seven paragraphs make? (P.S. He polished them off while we were on the phone.) On the flip side, he was the one I called when I found out that Clayton and Brian had fallen for each other faster than a collapsing dam that had just been hit with a SCUD missile.

"If I'm so fucking happy for them, why am I crying?" I sobbed.

"Because when you love somebody, you do it down to your toes," he reminded me gently. "That's what makes you Craig." And he wouldn't hang up until I'd fallen asleep.

So after we'd spent close to $3,000 on airfare, hopping from coast to coast on one phony pretext after another ("I was thinking about checking out the Auto Show in L.A. on Saturday." "I'm coming to New York on Tuesday for *Kiss Me, Kate*."), we allowed the rest to happen all by itself. *Kiss Me, Kate* led to a carriage ride through Central Park, then a trip to Colony Records, then a couple of Italian ices on the stoop of our old brownstone, and finally a brief stop by the fast food joint that was once known as Beefsteak Charlie's. Fodor's would have called it the Travis-Craig Walking Tour of Manhattan, with a single conspicuous addition: according to Smerk, every one of the hundred thousand restaurants in the greater New York metropolitan area was mysteriously booked for dinner (on a *Wednesday?*), so we'd have to make alternate arrangements—which, by sheer coincidence, Travis had taken care of from California three weeks earlier.

"*That* was convenient," I mused, as we headed down the ramp into Grand Central Station.

"Wasn't it?"

History was rewritten on that warm spring evening in May—exactly twenty-one years after he'd toppled off a ladder and into my life—when we found ourselves standing beneath the green-and-white awning of the elegant Tappan Hill in Tarrytown, a mere eight blocks from our gazebo. So we had two choices: we could either keep our 7:00 P.M. reservations in the glamorous Hudson Room or we could lock hands and return to Brigadoon instead. Not exactly a tough call.

"Hey, look! The park! Let's go reminisce!"

That's where I discovered, for the second time in my life, that he really *can* wake a village with his heart.

TO: Craigy1978@earthworks.com
FROM: Smerko1978@earthworks.com

Did you finish the Matthew Shepard bill yet?

TO: Smerko1978@earthworks.com
FROM: Craigy1978@earthworks.com

Since your last e-mail five minutes ago? Or in a larger cosmic sense?

TO: Craigy1978@earthworks.com
FROM: Smerko1978@earthworks.com

I can't help it. I miss you.

TO: Smerko1978@earthworks.com
FROM: Craigy1978@earthworks.com

I'm only in the *den*!

We celebrated our two-and-a-half-year anniversary the day we decided I should run for Congress. (Actually, Smerk had the idea first, but I don't plan on admitting as much until we're at least a hundred and ten.) It was Christmas Eve in the West Village, "light flurries" had given way to a Rudolph-requiring snowstorm right outside our bay windows, Vic Damone was crooning "Winter Wonderland" over our sound system, and we were curled up together in front of our fireplace. Even Norman Rockwell would have approved.

"Hey, Trav?" I murmured, chin-in-the-necking him while I played with his hair. "What do you call it when there's a smile in your stomach that starts when you wake up in the morning and doesn't go away until you're asleep?" Travis sighed audibly in my arms before glancing up from my chest in wonder.

"You mean you have one of those too?"

Flora was right. It's a quiet thing.

FROM THE JOURNAL OF
Travis Puckett

✓   Knows all the lyrics to *Flora, The Red Menace* (optional)

It was bound to happen sooner or later.

▄ Perennial

Books by Steve Kluger:

LAST DAYS OF SUMMER
A Novel
ISBN 0-380-79763-1 (paperback)

Joey Margolis—a young, wisecracking, Jewish baseball enthusiast growing up in Brooklyn in the 1940s—is in desperate need of a hero. He fixates on Giants rookie sensation Charlie Banks. Through a series of letters, postcards, newspaper clippings, and the like, the story of their improbable friendship unfolds.

"Funny . . . sentimental and moving." —*Parade*

ALMOST LIKE BEING IN LOVE
A Novel
ISBN 0-06-059583-3 (paperback)

In their senior year of high school, a jock and nerd fall in love. After an amazing summer of discovery, the two head off to their respective colleges—keeping in touch at first, then slowly drifting apart. Flash forward twenty years. Travis and Craig both have great lives, careers, and loves . . . but something is missing. Travis is the first to figure it out. He's still in love with Craig, and come what may, he's going to go after the boy who captured his heart, even if it means forsaking his job, making a fool of himself, and entering the great unknown.